By J. M. Dragon

ISBN   0-9716812-3-6
Second Printing February 2003, First Printing 2002
Cover photo by **Limitless**
Photographer: Deb McLain
Cover design by Anne Clarkson

Published by:
Dare 2 Dream Publishing,
Lexington, South Carolina 29073

Find us on the World Wide Web
http://www.limitlessd2d.net

Printed in the United States of America by
Axess Purchasing Solutions
PO Box 500835
Atlanta, GA 31150

Dedication

When a friend is in need, I have a friend Linda to challenge me. Without her constant faith and encouragement this story would still be on my laptop, never to see the light of day. This is simply a story for her!

Special Notation

Please note that our authors are international. You may see spellings and some words that are unfamiliar to you. These words are not spelled incorrectly but, rather, represent the national spelling of the writer. We at **D2D** encourage international authors to submit their manuscripts to us and have elected to leave them in their original format so that you may enjoy the international flavor as much as we do.

Acknowledgements

As with most things although one person appears to gain the acclaim there are many people in the background who have equal share in the pride one feels at getting to this point in their life. Sam & Anne didn't indicated how long this piece could be, and they are aware I ramble; they edited the story and are publishing it as well, God bless them.

Thank you to my original beta readers on the net, Elizabeth who started the ball rolling with the first five parts, and Betty who completed the mission and urged me to continue.

To the ladies of fantasies granted, what an interesting bunch you are! Such wonderful and diverse personalities, thank you for coming into my life and offering your friendship and support when I needed it the most.

Alice what can I say…little did you know that reading this story on the net and emailing me, it would embroil you in every other story I've written since, and I hope in the future, thank you.

This story was a springboard to many friendships I am honoured to be part of, Linda who had hassled me for dare I say it two years to at least have someone look at the story with a view to publishing. Kay who chats with me online Sundays, occasionally we put the world to rights or not as the case may be. T and Ro for being good sports when I have a 'novel' evening set up for them in chat. Vi and Carmen for constant constructive feedback and a wonderful friendship.

There are people who come into your life because of a special event, for me putting DD on the net was that event, Mel, what do I say? You bring a smile everyday into everything from our chat's, to the website and the stories. Thank you for your generous unwavering support, the kick when I need it, my website and most of all being a good friend.

I said I rambled but I'm near the end, in my wildest dreams I would never have thought DD would be where it is now!

Gordon my husband bless him he lets me sit for hours, hours and more hours writing and chatting, I certainly can't do this without him. You now owe me a Mont Blanc pen!

Finally, to everyone who reads net fiction and their continuous support, we 'bards'… and we all know where that came from… I think it starts with an X, thank you. We make a rather wonderful team!

Chapter One

Catherine Warriorson looked over the lush green fields of her ranch, Destiny; which was situated on the South Island in New Zealand, and smiled. Her expression was invariably fierce without the softening of the odd smile she gave now and again. Although, that only occurred in her own home to her only friends: her housekeeper and the ranch foreman. She wasn't a native New Zealander. Being English by birth, with an English father and a Greek mother, she was quite the cosmopolitan. Her reserve, to the locals in particular, often proved to many that all the English had a natural affinity for being aloof and stoic. This, they felt, just came naturally to the English and to this woman in particular.

Anyone looking at the woman would see a beauty, without a doubt. She had a lean, well-trimmed six-foot body with long, shining ebony hair that was customarily pulled back into a ponytail. The most distinctive feature however, were the ice blue eyes, which often looked at people with bored tolerance or outright impatience. All who knew her held her in the highest esteem for her unfailing abilities as an astute ranch businesswoman. Never would they dare approach her in a friendly manner. She just never let anyone inside her kingdom and Destiny was definitely the Warriorson kingdom!

Catherine once again looked over her domain and smiled briefly, giving her eyes a glowing effect, had there been anyone else around to see it! A hand loosely held the reins to a powerful grey mare, which looked equally as regal and aloof as her mistress. Catherine shifted her gaze to the movement on the next ridge. Unable to obtain a clear picture of the activities on one part of her property, she reached into the saddlebag.

"Well, well, well Tralargon, I wonder what we have here my friend? Nothing to the good if I haven't heard about it, that's for sure!"

Catherine had a smirk on her face that told its own story. She would be having a word with the person or persons involved that was certain. Pulling out small, powerful binoculars, she proceeded to view the activities and a sneer came over her face as she evaluated what she saw. Pushing the binoculars back into the saddlebag, she mounted the mare with graceful and athletic ease and pulled the reins towards the adjoining ridge.

Jace Bardley looked harassed! Well, she knew that filming a short documentary about the old and new landowners was never going to be easy; not when one of the most powerful of them refused to even talk about it.

Zeus knows there will always be one fly in the ointment and my fly just happens to be the largest landowner in this part of New Zealand, C X Warriorson! Why did Hudson add this particular country to the schedule? It makes very little sense really, but she is the boss.

Jace pushed back a lock of her blonde hair and smiled with compassion towards her young film crew. They had carried all the camera equipment up the ridge because their contact person, who provided them with the information about the comings and goings of a certain recluse landowner, just happened to have another appointment unexpectedly as they arrived. Unpredictably, he hastily departed with the all-terrain vehicle they used to transport the equipment. Now, to make matters worse, it had started to rain! The predominantly Californian film crew looked on, with open disgust, at the gathering dark clouds.

Peter Adamson, the director, moved closer to Jace and looked directly into her sparkling green eyes. Her eyes never ceased to amaze him in their open appreciation of the world around them; not even after five years around the Hollywood sets where she was Personal Assistant in charge of Publicity for Producer Clarissa Hudson, the head of the film company.

"So Jace, what wonderful stunt do you think our little go between will spring on us now, heh?" He smiled at the small blonde, who stood little more than to his shoulders.

"Oh, come on Pete! Salamon was trying to make money out of our recluse here! We went with it! In those circumstances, his going belly up on us is all part of the story, don't you think?"

Her eyes sparkled with laughter at the picture of the rotund Salamon who seemed scared of his own shadow. He appeared so vulnerable and her compassionate heart responded to this as it had in other situations, in the past.

"Maybe.... But what's the boss going to say?" Pete asked and smiled as he recalled the numerous times he tried to date the bubbly woman who stood only inches from him. He was always amazed with her total lack of depravation from the society with which she was affiliated. Although he'd tried, she'd rebuffed him on more than one occasion, never giving him more than her usual bright smile as she let him down gently with every offer.

"Hopefully nothing! I'm hoping you're going to get your footage and then we're out of here. To Hades with the 'Warriorson Kingdom Recluse'! I'm not sure I want to meet him anyway. He sounds a bit archaic to me. Anyone would think he was still running a ranch in the 1800's!" She spoke bravely and with a measure of conviction her size didn't always belie.

"Hate to say this Jace...!" Peter almost stuttered over the words as he saw a cloud of dust appear within a mile of them.

"What! What do you hate to say?" She looked at the rest of the crew and focused on what everyone had apparently seen: a large cloud of dust, gathering ever closer.

"I guess you're going to get to meet the Warriorson recluse after all." Peter shook his head and his tousled brown hair dropped over his angular boyish face.

It was definitely all up to Jace now. She needed to come up with the words and actions to get this story, or all hell would break lose with Hudson. She was a mean producer; that's for sure.

"Oh! Hades balls, am I ever in trouble here!" Jace looked at the approaching horseman, made even more intimidating by the powerful grey he was riding.

All eyes moved from the approaching rider to Jace and then back to the ever-closer, oncoming rider. It was a very amusing sight to all the onlookers when the rider vaulted off the horse in front of Peter and Jace with supreme command over their body movements.

Catherine Warriorson paced slowly around the two people who looked as if they were in charge of the film crew. Her stance communicated the impression of barely suppressed anger. She gradually stopped her stalking of the two people in front of her and, with a low growl, asked them what they were doing on "this property".

Peter Adamson looked at the beautiful woman in front of him and released a sigh of relief. *'Thank God, it's only a lackey, but a hell of a beautiful one, and she looks breathtaking when she's angry.'* He couldn't keep the admiring smirk from his face, as he looked directly at her.

'Oh! Gods, whoever is up in the heavens, thank you! Thank you for not sending Warriorson.' Jace looked discreetly at the woman who was visibly bristling with anger. *'Maybe this was who Salamon was afraid of, not Warriorson, but one of his employees. This*

particular employee looks like she could scare the Hades out of anyone.'

"I'm sorry, but who are you? And what gives you the right to ask?" Peter was the first to break the silence; he smiled his most beguiling smile.

"If I were you Mr....? I would rephrase your answer!" Catherine wasn't used to being questioned, especially by someone who was trespassing on her property! Her anger, now fuelled, levelled him with a piecing gaze from icy blue eyes that looked ready to freeze the Arctic.

Jace watched the interchange between her friend and colleague and the very irritated woman in front of her, marvelling at the stature and confident ease with every move she made. This definitely is a woman you never, ever, misjudged or wanted to cross either if it came to that! Her eyes speak volumes on their own.

'What must it feel like to have those eyes reflect back at you with warmth? Did I really think that? Zeus I'm going crazy here. The woman wouldn't even notice me if she were staring me in the face because she had to.' Still, something in Jace's subconscious was telling her that wouldn't be true, for some unknown reason.

"I'm sorry, perhaps we can start again? My name is Jace Bardley and this is Peter Adamson. We represent Union City Pictures. I guess you've heard about us?" Jace looked up at the cold demeanour in front of her and tried another tactic.

"Then again, maybe you might not have! But, we've tried to get an interview with, I assume, your boss: C X Warriorson? Unfortunately, he's unavailable for comment, and we heard from a contact that it would be okay to film from here." She smiled one of her most outgoing smiles and noticed the woman raise her left eyebrow virtually to the top of her forehead. If it hadn't been a serious conversation, Jace would have laughed.

'It's a start... at least she listened to my plea.'

"Oh you did, did you? I hope you don't mind my reminding you of My Boss's intolerance of trespassers on any of the properties?" Catherine snorted and glanced at the heavy clouds building in the sky; she wanted to be home before this storm fully raised its head. She had guests arriving for dinner and hated being late, or anyone being late for any appointment with which she were involved. Although, she had been quite impressed by the way the young woman in front of her tried to wriggle out of the situation.

'Those green eyes look so innocent I wonder just how innocent Jace Bardley is?'

"Well, actually we kind of hoped that just this once, maybe we could get a couple of shots of the ranch area and get out of your hair. So to speak, that is?" Jace looked closely at the woman as she turned her head to the heavens and saw the darkening clouds, the rain already falling in a persistent drizzle.

Catherine looked directly at the woman, ignoring the man entirely, and noted her strength of purpose and the friendliness in the green eyes that looked so beseechingly at her.

"Ms. Bardley, the weather is closing in, and you're on an exposed ridge with no protection. Hopefully your guile and fortitude are strong because you sure as hell are going to need it. When you get your shots, by all means come and see the Boss at the ranch house. I'm sure 'he', will have something to say to you, too!" She turned around and strode towards her horse.

"Thanks, but hey, can't you help us get this equipment out of here...?" Jace didn't have time to finish the comment, never mind get an answer. The woman had vaulted onto her horse and was heading back in the direction she came without so much as a backward glance.

Pete looked at Jace, who was looking at the very wet film crew and holding her hands up in a gesture of triumph? Acceptance? Or was it just, what the Hades was that all about?

"Okay people, let's move our asses or this small concession we seem to have gained will be ruined." He moved away from Jace and went to talk to the crew.

Jace continued to look at the retreating figures of the woman and her horse and sighed, not really knowing why. Something about the woman triggered elements deep within her. She dreamed weird events from time to time but they never became tangible in her mind after she woke up. Well, almost never.

'I guess we are going to meet the recluse after all!'

She watched the film crew set up and considered her options...getting soaked to the skin was about the best one offered as far as she could see. Shrugging her slight shoulders, she moved to a large boulder and sat down to contemplate the recent events.

With that, a loud crack overhead brought down heavier rains and lightning.

Chapter Two

Catherine Warriorson led her beloved mare to the stables to be cosseted by one of the stable workers, as she needed to leave and prepare for her guests.

'The audacity of that film crew to assume I am a man! For god's sake didn't they ever do any decent research? Obviously not! Mind you, coming from that Production Company it was foolish to expect anyone to be professional. The guy was a waste of space, that's for sure. The woman has something about her at least. She wasn't intimidated and that is always a good sign. Lord-a-Mighty she has the most wonderful and intriguing green eyes! Christ, I wonder where that thought came from? I wonder what she will think when she actually meets C X Warriorson?'

With that last thought came a fleeting smile as she walked towards the large house; which was waiting with welcoming lights blazing and was definitely drier than out in the open, especially up on Cutter's Ridge.

Walking into the kitchen storage area at the back of the house, Catherine removed her boots and the leather jacket that had kept some of the driving rain from her inner clothes, but not much. She smirked as she thought of the outsiders up on the ridge getting totally drenched with each passing minute.

'No protection up there, that's for certain.' She thought.

Grace Thornton saw the approaching figure of her boss and friend, noticing her rain drenched clothes and the water literally dripping from her face. She was a striking woman to behold and, had circumstances been different in her life, maybe she would look happier too! Although, Catherine kept her private life very, very private!

Waiting until she heard the door of the kitchen area open and the thud of boots being removed, Grace snatched up the large, fluffy towel warming on the radiator.

"I didn't think you would have stayed out quite so long, knowing the storm was brewing Catherine." Grace commented, pointedly handing her the towel.

Catherine looked up and briefly smiled at the woman in front of her. Taking the proffered towel and releasing her hair, she started to brusquely towel it dry.

"Thanks Grace."

Grace Thornton was in her late twenties and joined Catherine's staff in the early days. Due to a car accident the year before she arrived on Destiny she was unable to pursue the profession she had trained hard for, that of a policewoman. Her legs were severely damaged and she now walked with a decided limp. She decided to get away from it all for a while and took the job as housekeeper for the newly arrived Englishwoman, Catherine Warriorson. Sometimes it felt like yesterday as she recalled the initial interview.

"Sit please, Ms. Thornton." The taller woman in the room spoke quietly but intensely. Grace wondered now if it had been a good call on her part to answer the ad in the Christchurch newspaper, having seen it by chance and needing a total break from her current situation. The woman might be beautiful to look at but she had a closed in look about her, reminding Grace of a statue - without feelings.

"Thanks, it's a beautiful day don't you think?"

Ice blue eyes starred at her intently, making Grace shiver inwardly, cold...no not cold, glacial would be a more apt description.

"You have a resume, I take it?" Tapering fingers from a large slim hand moved towards her, taking the document Grace held securely in her hand.

"Well, sure I do but maybe it's not quite what you were looking for."

"I'll be the judge of that Ms. Thornton." The cultured voice rose a fraction as she walked to the window overlooking the drive to the house. They were in, she assumed, the study; which had a magnificent bookcase one side of the room.

Grace felt comfortable in the house but less so with the owner. Struggling to decipher the accent - was she English, Canadian or American? Certainly, she wasn't a New Zealander or Australian. She didn't think so anyway.

Looking at the slim figure in front of her, she thought the woman with the raven hair was perhaps thirty; her skin was flawless and had a natural olive skin tone that enhanced the beauty of the bone structure.

"Have you seen enough to make up your mind about me?" That voice again but this time it held amusement, as did the eyes, which twinkled for a few fleeting moments. It was only a few moments but it was there, Grace was sure. More than that, it quite changed the woman, making her appear younger and with none of the pain that was clear if you looked carefully at the face.

"Have you?" Grace shut her eyes, knowing that wasn't exactly a remark you make to a potential employer.

Flicking the papers in her hands Catherine Warriorson gave Grace Thornton her full and undivided attention. Moving back to her desk, she sat down opposite the younger woman.

"It was an enlightening experience reading your resume Ms. Thornton. I see you have no experience at being a housekeeper; a peace keeper perhaps but I'm afraid those type of skills shouldn't be necessary here on the ranch."

"How do you know that for sure?" Grace knew it was a long shot when she'd applied for the post but she doubted many would want a post like this, she hoped anyway.

"Do I look the dangerous type to you Ms. Thornton?" Blue eyes became remote as if recalling a memory of something that was painful to her.

"No. Then again, danger comes in many forms and maybe you might need a keeper of the peace for your family from time to time."

"I have no family Ms. Thornton and trust me when I say this, I never will have!"

The finality touched Grace's heart. She knew, then and there that this was the place for her and this woman had come into her life for a reason. Maybe it was meant to be, the cosmic tumblers, fate! Whatever it was, she was going to convince Mrs. Warriorson that she was right for the post; whatever it took to do so.

"I'm kind of at a loose end myself at the moment as you saw from my resume. How about taking a chance on me?"

Catherine Warriorson mused over that comment for a moment or two and then shook her head. It wouldn't work out. The woman was far too sassy; she didn't need that right now. Solitude was her goal and solitude she would have. Except, according to her lawyer, this was the only candidate so far, what a choice!

"I don't think it would work out somehow."

Grace stood up and limped over to the door. "I guess that's the end of that then. Can I ask one question?"

"Sure, go ahead." Catherine waited for the question and felt sorry that the woman looked quite stricken that she hadn't been given the post.

"Have you ever run a ranch before?"

Choking slightly at the audacity of the woman, she had to give Grace her due. It was a rather enterprising question. "No actually, I haven't."

"Okay. I thought so." The place did kind of look run down.

"Is that all you wanted to say?"

"Yes, somehow I thought it wouldn't work out." Grace opened the door and smiled slightly; at least she didn't feel so bad at leaving now.

Catherine couldn't believe it. Here was someone who was answering her back with a similar demeanor, someone who wasn't afraid of her, maybe just maybe....

"Ms. Thornton, please wait."

Grace turned to look at the woman and grinned like a kid as she heard the next word. "Touché."

"Anytime Mrs. Warriorson." Smiling, she turned again to leave but was stopped by the taller woman.

"I've reconsidered my position Ms. Thornton. If you want the position, it's yours."

Grace wanted to give herself a high five, however it was rather difficult, and not quite the time.

"In that case Mrs. Warriorson, the name's Grace and when do I start?"

"Start? Why, you start immediately."

"Great. I packed the car on the off chance."

"Really? How very...astute of you Ms. Th...Grace." This time Catherine grinned back at her and those blue eyes that were glacial and ... lonely. Yes, lonely; that was the word. The eyes changed. Perhaps one day, if she had anything to do with it, they would stay happy for good.

"That's me: ready for anything Thornton, Mrs. Warriorson."

"I'd prefer Catherine, Grace. Welcome to Destiny."

That had been five years ago and here she stayed, not only because of her own tragedy but also for the lonely, ice blue eyes that needed a friend. ....

"So, what makes you smile, if you can call that a smile?"

"Actually it's more a smirk, I think. If you think I stayed out so long you should see the others who are still out there." Catherine smiled wickedly back at the woman.

Grace looked her over and heard the hidden cruelty in the tone. "Who? Who did you leave out in this weather? Must be a foreigner or they would have been prepared," she asked, knowing that pushing for information from Catherine Warriorson wasn't always a wise decision.

Catherine looked at the brown haired, brown-eyed woman who was six years younger than she and lifted an eyebrow in censure. Not expecting an answer after that expression, Grace turned away and headed back into the main kitchen area.

"Grace!" The voice spoke with authority, expecting the woman to turn around and face her again.

"Yes." Grace dutifully turned and looked at the beautiful, but at times exceptionally intolerant, woman.

"I told you some film people wanted to film footage here on the ranch and with me?" Not waiting for an answer, but seeing the faint nod of the head, she continued. "I declined. They arrived without permission, so now they're getting wet. End of story!" To Catherine, that was explanation enough.

Grace, on the other hand, thought that was typical of her boss's attitude toward people.

Not sure if she should proceed, Catherine came up behind her as they moved into the spacious, brightly lit kitchen.

'What the hell? She can only ignore me and I'm used to that!'

"Catherine, how many did you leave behind and where?" she tried to ask indifferently, but Catherine raised an eyebrow acknowledging her friend's concern.

"Oh, come on Grace, surely you can't be worried? Hell, they're only Californians and they deserve a touch of reality, especially those from LA!" Glancing at the concern in the woman's face, Catherine conceded the point, just this once!

"About a dozen of them, up on Cutter's Ridge." Then she walked out of the kitchen to her room, never glancing back to gauge the reaction from the other woman.

Grace let out a heavy sigh as she contemplated the scene on the ridge. Of all the places to be caught in a heavy storm, Cutter's Ridge was potentially the worst - in this area, at least.

Looking out at the worsening weather, she made a decision and picked up the mobile to dial a familiar number. I wonder why she hates Californians and, in particular, those from Los Angeles.

Jace was freezing and soaked to the skin, her clothes quite literally dripped as she stood and watched an equally drenched camera crew film in torrential rain and windy conditions.

Peter Adamson looked decidedly grim as he motioned the final scenes he wanted to capture.

Got to hand it to that woman, she certainly wasn't kidding when she said we would need some fortitude. Hades! It's a good potential for pneumonia here! Looking at the track they had taken to arrive at the ridge, she noticed it looked like a mudslide now. What on earth will they do about the equipment? Hudson will have both Peter's and my hide if something happens to that expensive kit.

Then her thoughts drifted to the woman who had left them defenseless on the ridge.

'I bet she's now home, warm and dry. Laughing at our predicament while she explains our presence to her boss. Please, please, please someone out there take pity on us and send decent weather!'

Suddenly, she heard a roaring sound that seemed far into the distance.

'Could it be a vehicle? Maybe it could be two vehicles? Or is it just my over active, positive imagination?'

Looking over at Peter she noticed he too heard the noises and that they were getting closer!

"Hey Jace, think we could be getting the cavalry?"

"Zeus knows, but if it's anything that can get us out of here, I'm first in line."

One of the crew pointed towards a peak to Jace's left and grinned. Smiles radiated from everyone as they saw what they hoped wouldn't turn out to be an apparition. On the horizon was a large olive green all-terrain vehicle looking like a cross between a tank and a bus, followed by an olive green Land Rover.

"Hey Jace! It looks like I was right, the cavalry is here." He waved to the crew to get the equipment ready, as no one wanted to be last in this god-awful weather.

"I wonder who sent the cavalry is more to the point?" Jace spoke softly… seemingly to herself, as Peter wandered off to marshal the people and the kit together.

Finally, the vehicles arrived and two men came towards them. Both looked weather worn and obviously worked the land. They certainly had the physique to go with it, tanned and lithe, with the token duster hat, jeans and denim shirts. They smiled as they approached the crew, seeming not to notice the ravages of the weather or feeling it either, for that matter.

"You folks lost?"

Actually no, we're filming a short documentary. Seems we didn't predict the weather though." Jace smiled and held out her hand to the first man who spoke and then to his partner.

"Ah, well Miss, you have to watch the weather carefully this time of year, especially with winter approaching. Does anyone care for a ride out of here?" He smiled as he saw the relief on the faces of everyone.

Jace suddenly remembered what the woman rider had said. Never a better time, she thought. "Can they all get in that giant?" Jace asked, pointing to the larger vehicle.

Colin Montgomery the ranch foreman smiled as he replied. "Sure, Why?" He asked in interest.

"I need to pay a visit to your b☐ss, I assume. He must have sent you?" Jace looked directly at him for any reaction.

Colin looked a little pensive. He'd done what Grace wanted by picking up the strangers, expecting them to want to go back to their hotel. But, this was something else again! Jesus, the boss had dinner guests. Not only that, she didn't know about this rescue and would be ticked off when she found out, if she ever did. The odds had just tipped in her favor with the comment from the pretty blonde.

"I think the boss would appreciate it if you got yourself some dry clothes before you walked in there. Besides, the boss has guests for dinner."

"Ah, what better way to see him; especially since the woman said once we had finished, we must go and see him!" Jace secretly wanted nothing more than a hot bath, a glass of good wine and some dry clothes.

"Now which woman would that be, Miss?"

"Why, the woman on the grey mare. She's tall, ebony hair and the most fascinating blue eyes I've ever seen. You know who I mean?" Jace blushed as she realised what she'd said about the woman.

"Oh yeah, I know exactly whom you mean. Well in that case, I guess I have no choice." He motioned for the ranch hand to get the passengers on board the large vehicle.

Peter looked at Jace and smiled a weak smile. "Do you want me to go with you?"

" No, go ahead and get the film developed Peter. I'll take care of this."

"Guess I'm with you Mr....?"

"Colin Montgomery, and you?"

"Jace, Jace Bardley. Thanks for coming, I guess she must have sent you?"

"Oh, well, let's just say you would be surprised." He smiled and engaged the gear of the Rover as they pulled towards the path leading out of the ridge. Jace glanced at him but didn't comment any further.

Chapter Three

Catherine reclined in her chair as she listened politely to the Reverend extolling the virtues of the sanctity of friendship and love. Tonight was the only evening of the year she invited the local dignitaries to her home. They included the Mayor, the Doctor, the Chief of Police, the Vicar and small holders who held some of her land on lease.

Don't know why I ever let Grace talk me into this all those years ago. Now, it's such a pain in the arse. Does this guy even know what he's talking about? Looking around the room, it was the same old faces; and to be honest, she didn't so much hate them as she found them boring and uninteresting. Then her thoughts travelled to a blonde with green eyes, who at this moment was probably drenched from the torrential rain and cursing her very name.

'Well, if she knew my name of course, that will really be a slap in the face for her when she finds out.' Smiling at the thought, she turned to the Reverend who was looking directly at her and obviously waiting for an answer to some ridiculous question!

"Yes, okay, no problem," was all she could think of to say. Her mind was not on tonight's dinner but on the people on the ridge, one person in particular.

The Reverend suddenly shouted to the rest of the room. "Ms. Warriorson has agreed in principle to join our battle to bring more love into the world!" Clairence Stott fairly beamed at his new recruit.

'Oh, God! This is something out of a Jane Austin novel. Jesus what the hell did he say? Grace! Grace! Where the hell is she? Surely she will know?'

Looking around at the interested and frankly astounded faces, Catherine spied Grace lounging at the far end of the room, talking to the local doctor.

"Grace, could you spare me a few minutes alone please?" Catherine barely forced the polite words from her mouth.

Grace looked over at her and winked, knowing Catherine would hate that, but what the hell! "Sure no problem, I need to check on something in the kitchen anyway. Excuse me Doctor Simpson, I will be back later."

"For god's sake Grace, what the hell have I just accepted in there?" The force behind the words clearly underlined the woman's frustration.

Grace knew that, for maybe the first time since she met this woman, she might just have the upper hand. Although, it would be interesting to find out why she hadn't been paying attention; that, in itself, was unheard of.

"Well, you know the vicar and his pet projects? It appears he wants people to take on kids that have little or no chance, due to circumstances in their life. You, my friend, appear to have said yes to helping out." Grace looked at her boss and friend and couldn't halt the grin as a look of comprehension came across Catherine's face.

Thinking about the problem, Catherine suddenly smiled. "Oh, that's no problem then; only money. I can do that!"

Grace didn't chuckle, but she so wanted too. After four years of these dinners, Catherine still didn't know how some of these people ticked. "Well, actually it's time, not money that's most important about this project. You get the kid and it is a question of faith, love and friendship that gets the result! According to the good Reverend, that is." Grace added hastily, seeing the expression on Catherine's face.

"For god's sake, why do these people even bother? The kids are probably way past any help, if I know anything about this sort of project!" Catherine was trying her damnedest to think of a way out of this one.

"How would you know? It's not as if you've ever had to suffer any hardship!" Grace quickly regretted her words, noting the changing pallor of her boss. "I'm sorry Catherine, that was uncalled for."

"What exactly did you mean?" Catherine spoke quietly, but with a tone bordering on savage as she pinned Grace with an icy stare from her cold blue eyes.

"I just meant... Well...I... For god's sake, Catherine! It's a child were talking about, not an adult! Maybe it will help you get over your own personal tragedy!" Grace knew she had over-stepped the line and waited for the venom to pour from the angry woman.

Catherine swung round and came very, very close to Grace. "Never, ever mention my family in any context do you hear me!" Catherine spoke in a tone the housekeeper had never heard before and it frightened Grace.

"Yes." Was all she could muster, shocked at the vicious tone with which Catherine delivered her message.

"Tell whomever you have too, that we will participate. But my dear Grace, you are the loving influence in this household; it's all yours. I'm going to my study, say goodnight for me!" She walked off towards the study, leaving a very demoralised and upset housekeeper in her wake.

A knocking on the door a few minutes later brought Grace out of her reverie. She opened the door to see Colin and an obviously weather-worn, petite woman.

"Sorry to disturb you Grace, but the lady here says that the boss is expecting her." He looked at the woman in front of him and saw the tears that she tried to hide. "You okay Grace?" He asked, wanting to kick the hell out of whoever had made her cry.

"Yes, yes I'm fine Colin. So, who do we have here?"

"My name is Jace Bardley and I'm from Union City Productions, I would like to see C X Warriorson." Jace answered confidently. Although, she realized it must be difficult to take her seriously when she looked like a drowned rat.

Has Catherine made an appointment with one of them? Impossible! Especially when she was entertaining. Tonight is certainly turning out to be a trial, in more ways than one. "Hmm, I'm not sure it's a good time. There are guests here at the moment. I find it difficult to believe that tonight was a firm appointment." Grace looked at the woman with concern due to her appearance and because she was starting to shiver.

"Look, I know it's strange turning up like this, out of the blue; but his employee did say once we had finished on the ridge we were to come and see him!" Jace answered desperately. Perhaps it hadn't been a good idea after all.

"How about you dry off a little and tell me about the employee who set up the meeting?" Grace suggested gently as she handed Jace a thick towel. "Tell you what, I'll get you something to change into, just in case you do happen to see the boss." She smiled and went into the laundry room where she found a white shirt belonging to Catherine and a pair of her own shorts. Giving the items to Jace, she motioned her to change in the storage room and turned to Colin as she closed the door behind her.

"What the hell is she talking about Colin? Catherine never mentioned anyone else coming tonight!"

Colin looked at the toe of his boot and shrugged then shared what Jace said in the car. So, Catherine is playing games is she? Wonder if she knows that some games backfire.

Jace returned as Colin was leaving and looked sheepishly at the other woman. Grace nodded approvingly at the dry condition of her unexpected guest. "Colin told me about the woman who said it was okay to come here to see the boss; seems she forgot to advise us here in the house."

"Thanks for the change of clothes, guess I needed it. When can I meet the recluse?" She made the question appear like a joke, her green eyes alight with laughter.

"Oh, well I'd better check for you. Give me a few minutes okay?" Grace left the room and went towards the study.

Jace looked around the well used but modern kitchen area obviously designed for convenience. The smell of food was causing her to feel sick from lack of it. God I hope you're in a good mood Mr. Recluse, because I don't think I can take much more today, it sure has been a long one.

Grace walked back into the kitchen and motioned for the woman to follow her.

Grace cautiously knocked on the door knowing Catherine would be none to happy to be disturbed, especially by her! Once she explained why she was there Catherine suddenly backed off and gave her an odd look. An expression of interest passed over her stoic features, almost as if she couldn't believe it.

"Better send her in Grace since she obviously wants to see me."

"She thinks you're a man!"

"Oh, I know that already. Is she alone or with others?"

"She's alone, or at least that's how it appears." Grace replied as she went out the door.

Catherine smiled. "Alone. Well, well, things are looking up." She softly said to the closing door.

Grace led the woman to the study door and knocked, waiting for instructions to enter. Upon hearing 'enter' from inside, Grace opened the heavy oak door and motioned for Jace to go inside.

"You're not coming in too?" For the first time feeling her bravado displaced by a feeling of trepidation.

"Sorry. It's your appointment. I have other guests that need attention, please excuse me." Grace smiled in encouragement and left the woman hovering at the door.

Jace managed a deep breath and walked through the doorway into a dimly lit room.

The surroundings reminded her of her father's study, yet it had a distinctly un-masculine feel about it. Though it smelled of polished wood and leather, very much like her father's, there was a definite fresh cologne smell, which seemed vaguely familiar. A large desk dominated the room; along one wall was a bookcase, which covered the full length and every available space was filled with books. Forgetting for a moment where she was, Jace stared in wonder and wanted nothing more than to look through every shelf.

Movement from a large leather swing chair being pivoted in her direction brought her out of her wayward thoughts. Turning quickly, her face immediately paled as she recognised the person sitting, watching her with interest.

Catherine Warriorson had watched the small blonde slowly enter the study. Unlike most, she didn't immediately look for the occupier; instead, she looked the room over and seemed to take in its very essence…particularly the bookcase. This woman was a reader; that was for sure. Her face glowed and Catherine could see the hand moving towards the books, itching to touch them. Catherine had seen that look before, the expression of someone who loved books, all books. Unwanted memories, bringing their own pain, invaded her thoughts. That's when she moved the chair to announce her presence in the room.

"So Miss Bardley, you managed to get your shots, and managed to get off the ridge without too much hassle, I see." Catherine spoke in a low, soft voice.

"I'm, I'm...not sure what's going on, but you said I would see C X Warriorson!"

A deep throaty laugh came from Catherine. *'The audacity of this young woman! Doesn't she have any idea about what is happening? Surely she isn't that dense?'* "Oh Miss Bardley, didn't anyone ever tell you assumptions can be very dangerous?" Maybe this woman doesn't have the spark I thought I saw earlier.

Jace looked at the confident woman and realised exactly what she meant.

'Oh, no! I can't believe we didn't get that information! What the hell must she think of us, of me particularly?' Unable to articulate exactly what she felt, Jace looked down at her feet, realizing they were bare having taken off her sodden boots when she changed clothes.

Catherine glanced over to the spot the girl was nervously looking at and noticed the bare feet and what was overtly a much larger shirt on the woman, and shorts too. *'Oh, I see Grace has been doing her compassionate bit again!'* Looking at the blush and the obvious embarrassment of the young woman, she took pity on her state of undress and obvious discomfort.

"I suggest you take a seat before you fall down and we will discuss the matter of trespassing on MY property as the opening gambit!"

Jace looked up with a start, sat down heavily opposite the woman, and thought now might be a good time to curl up and die. *'Wonder if the fates would be with me on that one.'* Already her head was beginning to pound and she was hungry... she generally did not allow herself to forget her meals!

Chapter Four

After some skirting of the main issues, it came down to the name of the person who had the audacity to let the film crew on Warriorson property.

"You must have had inside help on this little escapade of yours. Did they do it for money, or just to get back at me? Not that it matters; if you don't tell me, I will find out soon enough. That sort of exploit you can't keep quiet for long in these smaller communities, a little like the States I should think." Catherine had been talking at the girl for nearly an hour and really hadn't resolved anything, since the girl refused to reveal the contact's name. Yet, she couldn't get angry with her. The young woman reminded her so much of Lucas....

Jace was tired. She was shivering from the combined cold of the day and the chill in the study. Coupled with that, she was hungry and her stomach was growling impatiently at her. It was a wonder the other woman hadn't heard it over her softly spoken but harsh words.

Suddenly, Catherine moved around the desk and walked over to the young woman seated in the low-slung chair. She noticed the pallor of her visitor and how the coolness of the room made her shiver. It was now after ten in the evening and surely the woman hadn't eaten; yet, she never complained!

"It seems to me that we will not resolve the matter today! You look like death Ms. Bardley. Why didn't you say you were cold? Are you hungry?" Catherine spoke in a clipped voice as she looked down at Jace with little warmth in her eyes.

Jace couldn't believe the change in the conversation. Within minutes it had gone from a confrontation situation, neither giving an inch, to one with a little compassion. Maybe not with any real feeling, but at least Ms. Warriorson had noticed her deteriorating condition! Trying to get up, she stumbled forward out of the chair and the tall woman quickly leaned forward and held her to stop the fall.

Catherine looked at the woman in her arms and felt a strange emotion that she couldn't quite fathom. For some reason Jace Bardley made her want to understand the younger woman to a greater extent. Looking into green eyes that held warmth, even for her, she was reminded once again of someone she had lost. *'Perhaps that is the connection. Whatever it is, I want to get to know this woman better. Only how can I do that when the only conversations we've had*

*are adversarial? Christ, with my current record, I would be lucky to
ever see the woman again after today.'*

"Thanks," came the tentative overture from Jace. Green eyes
looked deep into crystal blue as Jace attempted a smile, unsure if it
would be returned. Suddenly, she was given a smile, however brief,
that went straight to the eyes. Knowing she was responsible for that
smile made her feel enough to forget she was cold and hungry, well
the cold at any rate.

"You're welcome. Let's go and get you some food and warmer
clothes." Catherine led the way towards the kitchen, noting the
silence in the rest of the house.

*'Great, Grace managed to get rid of the locals. Hell, I hate the
entertainment responsibilities. Good thing Grace only makes me act
sociable once a year. I can live with that!'*

Walking into the kitchen, Jace saw Grace watching them
approach. Grace smiled at Jace while giving Catherine a curious look
for any instructions.

"Grace, I see you managed the guests with your usual charm and
tact?"

Never having seen a total stranger bring Catherine out of her
shell before, Grace was surprised at her obvious good mood. "Well
one of us around here has to be. After you hit them with the offer to
help, I think it was all hands to the project to see who they can give
us."

Jace could feel the tension between the two women. She
tentatively smiled at Grace while they watched Catherine's antics.

Catherine was looking around the kitchen and going through
cupboards, muttering, obviously trying to concentrate on a task so
alien to her. Suddenly, Grace placed a hand on her shoulder and
smiled softly. Looking up perplexed, Catherine raised an eyebrow in
question.

"How about I look for the food. It is food for Ms. Bardley that
you want, I presume?" Grace couldn't help the grin that crossed her
lips.

Catherine was about to rebuke her for the smirk but the sight of a
gently smiling Jace Bardley made nothing else important. "Yes, you
presumed right Grace; guess I'm not much good in my own kitchen,
huh?" She allowed a small smile to play around her lips and then

looked towards the laundry room. "Give me a minute." She left the room, not waiting for a reply.

Jace shook her head in astonishment as the woman left the room. Is this the same woman who hours earlier berated us on a cold, wet ridge then left us to fend for ourselves? Yet now she is suddenly caring and dare I say the word... friendly.

"Uuh, I hate to ask this, but is she always like this?"

"Actually, no!" Grace supplied, her astonishment clearly imprinted on her face.

"It's something new? Do you think it's catching?" Jace couldn't help but chuckle at the thought.

Grace laughed along with this small, green-eyed, pretty young woman who in the space of an hour cracked open the shell of one Catherine Warriorson. *'Whatever is next?'*

"Oh, let's hope if it is, she keeps catching it and we don't lose it overnight. That would be fine with me."

Suddenly the door opened quickly and Catherine came blustering into the kitchen with some clothes.

"I think these will do...that is, if it's okay?" Catherine raised questioning eyes towards her young visitor tentatively.

Jace couldn't help the tender smile that came to her lips as she observed the woman before her. "Thanks, I need to get warm before I go back to the hotel."

"You could stay here tonight if you want. It's still very wild out there!" Catherine responded quickly, unable to stop the flow of words from her lips.

'This can't be Catherine, no way! What the hell happened in that study? They were only in there an hour, right?' Grace thought and then quickly offered. "I can make up one of the spare rooms, no problem."

Jace was tired and the thought of going back out in the rain did not appeal to her. She could ring Peter so he wouldn't worry and this would be the ideal opportunity to work on C X Warriorson for an interview. "I guess I'm tired. Sure, thanks for the hospitality. Can I make a phone call?"

Catherine, who didn't realize she was holding her breath for the answer, gave a sigh of relief. "Great! Has Grace found you something to eat?" A smile was clearly evident on her face.

Within an hour Jace was fed, the phone call made and a bed waiting for her at the ranch of the recluse, C X Warriorson. *'Hudson is going to be so impressed with me! Nothing has changed; yet, in a subtle sort of way, it appears she likes me. I don't know why, but I want to find out. What involvement does she mean, does it have to do with me? And why did it make this tall, dark and quite simply beautiful woman change her total personality? Lots of questions and it's much too late tonight to find out any answers, except maybe to one!'*

"Hope you don't mind me asking, but what do the C X represent?"

Grace had gone to bed a few minutes before, leaving the two women alone in the kitchen.

"Catherine." Was the only reply she received.

"That lets me in on the C, but what about the X?"

"If you ever get my complete trust, you get to know what the X means."

Jace smiled, shaking her head in disbelief. "It must be on one of the public records, surely I could just go look it up?"

"You could try! Then again, maybe you can't get hold of it that easily. Tell me, are you afraid that you won't ever earn my complete trust?" Clear blue eyes bored into green.

Green eyes vying with blue suddenly dropped to a spot on the far wall. "Oh, I think it could be enlightening to gain your trust."

"Perhaps in more ways than you think, Jace Bardley." Catherine responded enigmatically.

Jace looked at the recluse closely. *'Exactly what did she mean by that response?'* Then complete exhaustion set in as Jace yawned and realized she was totally worn-out.

"Time for bed I think."

Catherine glanced at the drooping eyes of the woman opposite her and smiled. "Yes, I think it's time for you to turn in. Goodnight, Jace Bardley. I'll see you in the morning." With that she motioned the young woman in the direction of the room Grace had prepared, then turned in the direction of the study.

"Goodnight Catherine Warriorson." Jace spoke softly to the retreating back.

Chapter Five

Catherine had too many questions buzzing in her head to contemplate, and sleep was the furthest thing from her mind at this moment.

Here she was: thirty-five years old, independently wealthy, passably good looking to the eye and single, well, widowed at any rate. Living in an adopted country, but missing her own roots from time to time, with few friends, and a whole lot of emotional baggage that didn't ever go away entirely. It just disappeared for a while and then came out to smack her between the eyes at the most inopportune moments.

Now, here she was thinking a green-eyed stranger could somehow alleviate the pain she went through from time to time.

"Hell, what am I thinking, she's just a girl!" She said aloud to herself.

Catherine wiped her brow with her left hand and looked out of the large window overlooking the ranch yard. It was dark and therefore little could be distinguished, but she knew what was out there. There was the large hanging tree, as she called it because of it's shape; the small herb garden to the right of the house, where Grace would spend the odd hour or two. Of course there was also the large drive, housing her Land Rover and the Jeep that belonged to Grace. Beyond the drive were the ranch foreman's house and then the bunkhouse for the single men that worked on the property. It was very much an old fashioned styled ranch, but with all the modern conveniences; and the pay was good, or so she was told.

People didn't mind working for the Warriorson holdings, mainly because the woman who owned them left the day to day running of the ranch to Colin Montgomery and that kept everyone happy. He was a very capable man, was well liked by the men and also respected by his boss. Somehow, she had gotten lucky with Colin.

Then there was Grace! At times Grace would get on her nerves, almost to the point where she wanted to fire her, but always at the last minute, she stopped herself. Grace seemed to be all the things she wasn't: compassionate, happy and contented with her lot in life. At least that's how Catherine viewed it, from her standpoint. *'Is that really the case? Grace, are you happy here with me?'* Sudden thoughts came to her and she didn't have the answer, hadn't really considered how Grace felt. She knew that there had been times when the woman surely should have packed up and left.

'Maybe it's time I found out! But what will I do if she isn't happy here? Would I really care? YES!'

'Why now? What is it about the young woman that has me thinking on these lines? I haven't been particularly nice to anyone in years! Is it because Jace Bardley had the look on her face when she saw the books in the study, the look that reminded me of Adam? Is that the only reason? Or is it her gentle smile that radiates in a room and fills it with sunshine, even though it's dark and raining outside...just like Lucas, my brother?'

Shaking her head, she tried to clear the thoughts of her family. It still didn't make sense to her. Why had she been left behind while the good part of her family had been tragically taken away? Every morning she woke up, she asked herself the same question.

'Why them, shouldn't it have been me?'

The day always mocked her and somewhere in her head a voice answered her. *'Your time will come. When it does, don't expect to meet them on the other side; they have gone to a better place. You need to find redemption before you can follow that path.'*

Always the same answer and didn't she know it? Yet, what had she done in the last five years about that redemption? *'NOTHING! Hell, if anything I have made things worse!'*

As her fingers touched a leather-bound novel that looked like it had been read on numerous occasions, she thought of her family and how everything had begun.

Her mother had been a descendant of a Greek gypsy line. She believed in the after life and fortunes and the fates. Her mother believed even down to premonitions, which often amused her and her younger brother Lucas. Although there were times when it appeared their mother had been right!

Elena Xianthos had been a singer in a nightclub in London when she met Catherine's father, Stewart Devonshire. He was a young publisher and had recently acquired the rights to a book by an upcoming author, Adam Warriorson. Several months later Elena and Stewart married and Adam had been their best man. Two years later, the book **There Can Only Be One Soulmate**, was a best seller and making both men a lot of money.

Catherine had been born earlier that year and five years later, Lucas came along.

For the first ten years of her life Catherine had the love of both of her parents, but the time of only her mother, as their father was just so busy making the family fortune, or so he said!

Unexpectedly her mother contracted cancer and died within six months. It wouldn't have been quite so hard except their father wouldn't or couldn't release his emotions over his wife's death. Instead, he moved the publishing house to America and left the children in the care of his wife's sister Constantia, in London.

For the next ten years Catherine went to all the best schools and received the finest education that the private system in England could offer. She was a very intelligent girl, but apt to be wayward and disruptive for no apparent reason. Unable to gather any true friends, she went through the University because she had to or her father would dispense with her allowance - and that, she wouldn't forego. It gave her the freedom to take drugs, alcohol and whatever else she could lay her hands on. She also moved around Europe, in a daze most of the time, not caring much about anything except her brother, who had just started his final year at school before going to the University.

Lucas was a happy young man. He loved life, even if it hadn't been entirely easy in terms of parental love for him or his sister. He made the most of all the opportunities his father's money could offer him. He wanted to become a doctor and had the intelligence and compassion to make it happen.

When Catherine turned twenty-two, she ended up in jail. Not only had she been taking drugs, but she had been pushing them too. For a year Catherine was held in a medium term prison and alienated herself with not only the inmates but also the prison staff as well. It was a very long year, and one she wouldn't forget. She had the scars, both emotional and physical, to prove it.

A month after she was released from prison in Germany, she was called home.

A drunk driver had killed Lucas in a car accident. He was only eighteen, on the brink of life. The driver had been to an all night party and was only twenty. He'd died two days later from injuries sustained in the accident.

Catherine was devastated and didn't know where to turn. Her Aunt had disowned her and her father wanted nothing to do with her either.

Adam Warriorson came into her life. He was twenty-five years older than she was, a contemporary of her father, and also his close friend as well. Adam helped her kick the drugs and alcohol and made her look inside herself for a reason to live, beyond the rage she felt. They drifted into marriage. He loved the beautiful young woman, who had a heart ready to give so much love, if only she could find it within herself to let it out. She wanted stability and security in her life. Adam offered her both. Love was never an option.

A year later Lucas was born. This event allowed Catherine to remove barriers she had set up within her heart to stop the anguish of loved ones leaving suddenly. The marriage was relatively happy. Catherine loved Adam and while she knew deep down she wasn't in love with him, Adam was as in love with her as any man could be. He watched her give a part of her heart to their son, but never to him. It broke his heart.

When Lucas was two, Stewart Devonshire died of a massive heart attack. Catherine knew she was his only living child, but had long since surrendered any thought of her father leaving the business to her. She hadn't exactly been his favorite child, after her prison term anyway.

However surprised, Catherine Warriorson became the new heir to the Xianthos Publishing Corporation and all that entailed. It became the ultimate challenge that her life as a wife and mother was not.

Within six months she had left her London home, her husband and son, and headed for New York and the lure of power!

Catherine became ruthless, devious and a down-right bitch in the company she had inherited. It was obvious she derived great pleasure from seeing others fail and loved to bait them and, whenever possible, defeat her corporate enemies in bitter boardroom battles and takeovers.

Adam Warriorson waited for his wife to come to her senses--she never did. He had decided to buy a ranch in New Zealand, where his parents had been reared. He wanted to raise their son away from the stories of his mother and her zealous dealings. He had everything ready, the house, furniture and his numerous books. All he needed was Catherine's permission to leave the country with Lucas.

Catherine had made noises about coming home more often, but it never happened. Now she wanted to see the new family home merely as a gesture. In Adam's eyes, Catherine was still the most beautiful woman he had ever met, and he loved her; but lately she had a cold and calculated look. He never wanted his son to ever come into contact with that element of his mother's personality. She relented and gave her permission. As she left the ranch house, Adam passed her a book.

"Catherine, when you have time, please read this and let me know if our relationship ever felt this way to you?" He passed her a leather bound copy of his first novel, **There Can Only Be One Soulmate**.

"Fine Adam. I will, when I get time!" She told him curtly and left with him looking at her back as she strode off to the waiting car.

A week later she flew back. Her husband and son had been killed in a light aircraft accident on their way to the ranch from Christchurch.

Whatever pieces remained of Catherine Warriorson's heart died that day. She buried them on the ranch, overlooking a beautiful mountain pass with a steady stream winding along its path.

Adam had named the ranch Destiny. For Catherine, it was a most fitting possession for her to have. Love and happiness weren't part of her deal in this life. She was destined to be denied the pleasures and feel only the pain that life had to offer. But hadn't she deserved it for her excesses?

"I'm sorry Adam, but how could you ever have been my soulmate? I never even loved you! Then again, I'm not even sure that I believe in the existence of one." Catherine closed her eyes and let a single tear roll slowly down her cheek.

She hadn't wanted to think about the past, but it had come to her - waking this time, not in sleep, as it usually did. Her finger stopped its spiralling movement over the leather bound book and she placed it on the desk. *'Wonder if Jace Bardley has bad dreams? No, how could she? She's only a kid and a happy looking one at that!'*

Catherine turned off the light and left the study.

Moonlight streamed into the window of the study and bounced on the carved out title of the book resting on the desk, illuminating it as if in answer to a question crying out to be answered.

Chapter Six

Catherine was up at her usual 5.30 a.m. and walked into the kitchen area, showing none of the traits of only having two hours sleep; but she had slept and that was unusual.

Grace glanced up from her preparation of breakfast for Catherine, Colin and herself and, this morning, for a certain young guest also! Although she doubted Ms. Bardley would see the light of 6 a.m. Smiling, she motioned Catherine to her seat at the head of the large oak dining table that was central to the room.

Approaching Catherine with a fresh mug of tea for the strangely serene looking woman, "Our guest hasn't stirred I see." Grace said more as a statement than a question to her employer.

Catherine quirked her eyebrows and frowned. "Actually, I never told her our breakfast hour. Sorry."

Grace once again glanced back at her friend who had never apologised before for not doing something. "No problem, I'll feed her when she does get up. She kind of looked all worn out to me last night. Did you two stay up long after I left?" Not really expecting an answer from the other woman, she carried on with the breakfast preparations.

Catherine gathered her thoughts and softly said. "No, she went to bed a few minutes after you did. She was very tired."

Grace was astounded. This was the most communicative Catherine had been in the five years they had lived under the same roof and shared this daily routine. Wonder what else she's going to surprise us with today?

"What about you, did you sleep well?" Both women knew that she didn't sleep well; they just had never discussed it after Catherine had nearly bounced her off the ranch for asking once in the early days.

Catherine wanted to snap at Grace for what she considered prying, but instead something overrode her usual privacy mode and she answered. "I had a lot on my mind, didn't go to bed until 3 a.m. But when I did, I slept."

Grace turned round to face her friend. "I'm glad," was all she said as she put the eggs on the griddle. Colin would be here soon.

Over breakfast Catherine would discuss the ranch and its small holdings with Colin and Grace. If ever Catherine were away, Grace would help Colin with any decisions. It had been a very good solution to running the ranch.

Although Catherine no longer lived in the city, she still held the reins of the Xianthos Publishing Corp. from afar, via her computer; linked up several hours of the day to certain strategic world locations. Today she wanted to discuss a certain Union City Productions with her New York Vice President, Paul Strong. He had taken over her figurehead role in the Corporation with ease and professionalism and he was doing a very fine job. Few people knew that she had the final decision on all the major policies. They had assumed she had just run away from it all after her personal tragedies. No one had cared if she was dead or alive; they were just glad that they didn't ever have to be confronted with her again! Ms. Devonshire had made an impression on people, but not a happy one.

Twice a year she would have a meeting in Sydney to discuss with the Vice Presidents of each of her global operations problems and tactics for the coming months. Paul Strong was by far the most senior VP and he would be the ear for all the other VP's in the event of a crisis in their operations as Catherine wasn't available. Catherine was due at just such a meeting in three days; by then Paul would have all the information she needed.

"So Colin, how do you see the ranch progressing now that we have the livestock and the employees?"

Colin blushed a little. Although he was sure of his abilities, the beautiful woman in front of him always made him self-conscious, so he looked at Grace for support. She smiled at him to continue. "I...I guess, it's just up to us now to get the profits you need to buy up more land and make this the biggest ranch in New Zealand," he stuttered.

Catherine smiled at him. She had a great respect for the man and his abilities and knew that she un-nerved him, although she hadn't figured out why. "Good! Somehow I thought you and I would be working to the same ends. Although, Destiny was never bought with that objective in mind," Catherine speculated absently.

Grace looked down into her mug of coffee, and Colin cleared his throat nervously. "What objective was it bought for, Ma'am?" Colin asked respectfully.

Catherine looked at the downcast head of Grace and the nervous movements of the man opposite her, smiling briefly. "Adam, my husband, bought it as a sanctuary for our son and himself." She spoke quietly.

Grace looked up at the last words spoken by her boss and she noticed the faint lines of strain around the eyes. "Whom did they need sanctuary from?" She couldn't help herself; she just had to ask.

Catherine gave a weary laugh, got up from her chair and walking by Grace, she put a hand on her shoulder and gently squeezed it. "Would you believe, ME!" She answered and walked out of the door to her study.

Colin looked at Grace; neither of them had any words to counter that statement, both deciding some things were better left unsaid, for the moment at any rate.

Grace decided when she glanced at the clock and realised it was 9 a.m. that maybe their guest would be a little hungry.

Walking towards the room they had given to Ms. Bardley the previous evening, Grace heard faint moans coming from within the room. Knocking on the door she opened it cautiously just in case the woman would be upset at the intrusion. Not hearing any protest from within, just the louder moans coming from the bed, Grace quickly went over to the prone figure in the bed and pushed back the covers.

The first thing she noticed was the flushed face of the younger woman and the small moans coming from her. Slowly touching her forehead to check her temperature, Grace gasped at the heat and realised they needed a doctor; the woman was most certainly ill. She gently patted Jace's cheek to get any response and the eyes fluttered open briefly but didn't focus at all. Making sure she was fully wrapped up, Grace left the room and literally ran down the hall to the study.

Without even knocking, she pushed open the large oak door and was glared at by Catherine who was talking on the phone.

Noting the agitation of her housekeeper, she realised that something was terribly wrong. "Look Paul, it appears I have an emergency here; can you get the information for me, for the meeting?" She listened intently to the speaker on the other end, but her eyes never left Grace's face the whole time. Shit, what the hell could be wrong?

"Great, knew I could trust you on this one. Have a good journey to Sydney and I'll see you there. Bye." Putting the phone back on its cradle she raised an eyebrow for Grace to continue.

"Ms. Bardley's ill!" Grace shouted at the woman in front of her.

"I'm not deaf Grace! What's the matter with her?" Catherine spoke patiently, but her gut did a somersault and her eyes glazed with concern few had ever seen from her.

"I went to her room. It was getting late and I thought she might want something to eat. Well, I heard moaning and she has a fever, her eyes are unfocused, she's got a high temperature, she...."

"Okay, okay Grace, I get the picture! Get hold of Doctor Simpson and I'll go and see her myself." Catherine spoke gently to the concerned woman.

"Yeah...yeah, I will." She turned to leave.

"Grace do it here." Walking towards the woman and the door, she lifted Grace's chin and looked into her brown eyes and smiled. "It's going to be okay Grace, hopefully this error of judgement, I've made yet again, won't kill someone this time!" She left Grace to ponder that particular comment.

Catherine strode off in the direction of the room that her guest was staying in. *'Of all the stupid things to do, I've gone and done it again! My bloody pride and arrogance has had a detrimental effect on someone else again. Will I ever learn? Obviously not.'*

Opening the door, she saw the state of the younger woman immediately; the covers were strewn all over the floor, obviously kicked off by the sick woman. Closing the distance between the door and the bed, she noted the sweat running down the small body and the fever she was held in. Picking up the covers, she put them back over the body in front of her, although that only served to agitate the woman more.

Using her not inconsiderable strength, she placed her hands over the covers and held them over the small body on the bed and stopped the struggling woman from kicking them off. "Hey Jace Bardley, this is for your own good here. Come on now, help me out and let me tuck you in." Catherine softly said into the ear of the thrashing woman.

Something, somewhere must have registered within Jace because as the words were spoken she suddenly stopped moving around so much. "Hey, that's my girl." Catherine smiled at the woman she had effectively pinned down.

From out of her fog of pain and fever, Jace tried to open her eyes. Looking into the cool blue eyes, she knew felt them touch something deep within her soul. Just why Jace didn't know, but she wanted to stay like this forever. *'Whatever would it take to see those eyes looking at me with warmth?'*

"I...I don't seem to remember you?" A distinctly fearful look in the green eyes peered into blue.

Catherine looked a little shaken by the remark, but smoothed the hair from her eyes. "I'm Catherine, you stayed the night! You have a fever, the doctor will be here shortly, just take it easy."

Jace knew she had a massive headache and was having difficulty breathing; her body felt heavy and ached in every bone she could think of, and some she couldn't. *'I spent the night? Why?'*

"I'm very tired..." Jace closed her eyes to the pounding that was going on in her head, but wanted so much to open them, and see the concerned expression in those incredible eyes again.

"Hey, go to sleep. I'm here, it's going to be okay." Catherine meant every word.

Jace mumbled, "Please don't leave me?"

Catherine looked at the now sleeping woman and put a hand over her own tired eyes. *'Somehow I couldn't leave you Jace Bardley even if I wanted too! Now what would you think of that Adam, some slip of a girl has managed to get under my skin?'* She sat down in the chair opposite the bed and waited for the doctor.

Doctor Simpson had never been called to the ranch house before. Previously it had been just the employees of Destiny that he'd attended, but this summons was rare and he didn't want to miss the opportunity.

He was shown into Catherine's study.

"Take a seat Doctor." She indicated the large chair that Jace had occupied the previous night. Had it only been those few short hours ago?

"Thanks." He sat in front of the woman who hid behind the recluse exterior she portrayed to everyone. Now she concentrated on him full of concern.

Blue eyes looked directly into his grey ones. He noted again what a beautiful woman she was and how the warmth in her eyes, made her almost glow. "Will she be okay?"

Doctor Andrew Simpson could have been as cold to her as she had portrayed to him and his fellow neighbours during all the years she had been in the area. But something had changed here, and he wasn't one to hold a grudge.

"She needs to be kept warm, have the medication in exactly the dosages I've said and rest for as long as it takes!"

Catherine raised her eyebrows at the statement. "Can she be moved?"

Andrew was taken aback by the remark; it wasn't something he had thought would be a problem. "Well, I wouldn't take that chance if

I were you; she could develop pneumonia if she's not careful over the next few days. Is that a problem?" he inquired.

Catherine turned her back on him and gazed out of the window. "It's my fault she's in this state. When she's able, she might want to move back to town and her colleagues. I thought I'd better ask."

Andrew saw the tenseness of her body, shook his head and moved out of the chair towards the person standing very rigid at the window. "She didn't exactly want you to leave earlier as I recall." He spoke quietly to her, as they both looked out at the rain soaked drive.

Catherine thought about that. No, Jace had clung to her hand like a leech, when she moved to leave the room with the doctor. In fact, the girl had whimpered and Catherine had knelt beside the bed and whispered to her that she would be back as quickly as she could. It had, for some unknown reason, worked!

"I suppose she didn't, but she's suffering a fever at the moment. Jace said earlier that she didn't remember me! Guess that's a good thing in the circumstances, wouldn't you say Doc?"

For some strange reason Andrew Simpson recognised a need emanating from this woman, that she wanted the younger woman in the other room to want to stay. He again shook his head of the fanciful thoughts. This woman didn't need anyone, or did she?

"Oh, I don't know about that. I think you should wait and see what the next few days bring before you think about moving her out." He walked back to the chair, picked up his bag and went towards the door. Glancing back, he noticed Warriorson hadn't moved, but she did looked as if her posture had relaxed a little.

"Thank you Doctor. Just let me know what the bill is and Grace she will take care of it immediately." Catherine spoke absently to the retreating figure.

"My pleasure. Ms. Thornton is one of my favorite neighbours; it will give me a chance to talk to her again." He smiled at the thought.

"Does she know that?" Catherine turned around suddenly.

"Does she know what?" He asked at her sudden attentiveness to their conversation.

"That you like her, maybe more than like?" Catherine turned her profile towards him, her left eyebrow raised in question.

"No! No, she doesn't know that I like her and like her a lot." He smiled wryly at her.

"Guess I'll be seeing more of you at Destiny then Doctor?" Catherine replied, never taking her eyes of the blushing physician.

"If that's an invitation, you might never get rid of me." He chuckled.

"Oh, well at least you have a profession we can use around here. It wouldn't be a hardship, now would it?" She flippantly replied.

Andrew Simpson was bowled over. This woman could charm a snake if she ever let herself go. It made him wonder just what kind of person could ever make her see anything other than this life of a recluse she had adopted.

"I'll be seeing you again Ms. Warriorson." He nodded his head as he opened the door to let himself out of the study.

"It's Catherine. Yeah, I suppose you will." She turned back to her observation of the ranch yard.

Grace was walking back to the kitchen after having taken away the bedding and now held the clothes of the young woman. The doctor arrived at that moment and she smiled.

"How did it go?"

He looked at the vision in front of him. For more than four years he had tried unsuccessfully to get a date with Grace. Now he had a chance and, as unbelievable as it might seem, the reclusive Catherine Warriorson had made it possible.

"Great! In fact, she's said I can come over any time and to cap it all I get to call her Catherine."

Grace looked at him, her expression one of astonishment and wonder. This was turning out to be quite a day!

"Well, I guess that's good. Catherine huh. Wonder what brought that on?"

"Ha! Well, I did say that I wanted to see a certain favorite neighbour of mine more often and she kind of agreed." He smiled openly at her.

"She did? Now who would that be, I wonder Doctor Simpson?" Grace asked him nonchalantly.

"Yeah, she did! You, my dear Grace, are by far the most favorite neighbour I ever think about. Can I interest you in dinner one evening soon?" He waited with baited breath for her reaction.

Grace toyed with saying no. She liked Andrew Simpson; he had a good sense of humor and seemed to appreciate people around him. It would be good to go out for a change. "Sure, it's a day for trying out new things around here, I think. I would love to go."

He looked as if someone had handed him a million dollars.

"Excellent! You don't know what that means to me Grace. How about Friday?" He quickly hugged her and they entered the kitchen just as Colin Montgomery walked in from the side door.

Grace noticed Colin and quickly disengaged from Andrew, but couldn't help the blush that stung her cheeks.

"Can I call you later to confirm?"

Andrew looked at her and smiled. "Sure, no worries, talk to you later." He breezed out of the side door, almost knocking Colin over, in his exuberance.

Grace looked over as Colin came further into the kitchen.

"What was that about?" He couldn't keep the slight frown from his forehead.

"Oh that! Well, Ms. Bardley is ill, so the doctor was over checking up on her." Grace answered the question, without really answering the underlying question that had been asked.

"I see." Colin looked back as the doctor pulled out of the ranch yard area.

"Do you?" Grace whispered.

Colin looked back at Grace and said he needed to see Catherine. Holding up his hand he strode past her and said he would go straight to the study.

Chapter Seven

Jace felt disorientated.

She looked around the room, which spun if she glanced around too fast.

'Hell, my head hurts.'

The doctor had been nice as well as handsome! Although not her type, he did have a very good bedside manner.

She remembered`Catherine Warriorson now! Her current health crisis was in part her fault, but she couldn't find it in her heart to blame the woman.

All she wanted was to have her back here in the room and looking at her with those ice blue eyes that held a warmth she would gladly drown in.

'She'd said she would be back! Why hasn't she come back yet!' Jace was being impatient, it had only been minutes since Grace had helped her with clean clothes and washed her up to make her more comfortable.

The doctor had given her an injection to help with the symptoms she was suffering from.

'Would Catherine want me to leave? She might. It isn't pleasant having a sick person around the house, especially one you didn't even know! Oh god, I hope she doesn't! I need...I want...hell I don't know; but she holds all the keys.'

A deep shudder went through her body as she thought of Catherine rejecting her. Suddenly it was all too much and she broke down in tears, soaking the crisp freshly laundered pillow under her head. Her eyes dropped and she slept as the fever and the drugs rapidly   gained   control   over   her   body.

Catherine watched her ranch foreman pace around the front of her desk. He was distracted over some dilemma. He had discussed the problems he needed her approval on concerning the ranch. She had expected him to leave. He hadn't!

He was a tall man, around six feet five she guessed; knowing herself to be six foot. So he had an advantage over her. She looked into his worried face, which looked tanned and a little weather worn. This was to be expected in his chosen career, she supposed. He wasn't exactly handsome, but had more of a rugged look about him.

She'd heard that he was popular with the local women, but none had captured his heart.

"You going to tell me what else is bothering you, or are you going to wear a track on the polished floor here?" Catherine finally asked him, knowing that she'd promised Jace she would be back shortly.

He looked at her and blushed at her regard and comment. "I...I need some advice! I'm sorry Ma'am, I shouldn't be bothering you with my problems." He walked towards the door with a dejected look.

Catherine was wondering what else was going to get her to open up today, because sure as hell she was doing more talking in the last twelve hours than she'd done in years.

"Colin, before you tell me what advice you need, there's something you need to stop doing, okay?"

He looked at her stunned. "What would that be Ma'am?"

"Exactly that! Don't call me Ma'am, all right? I'm not the Queen of England and never bloody likely to be. My name is Catherine, use it!" She didn't much care how that came out; it had been bugging her for years - his subservient attitude and the man was better than that.

Colin Montgomery was totally floored by the remark. She had never said anything about it before. In fact, he could have sworn she hardly ever listened to him most of the time. "Yes, Ma... Catherine," he smiled shyly at her.

"Glad we got that settled then. So what advice do you need?" Catherine Warriorson looked at the man and saw him debate his reply.

"I'm not sure if I can say it." He looked around the room, his face carrying a hurt look.

"Do I have to guess then? I'm not good at guessing games. I usually leave those to Grace, she's better..." Catherine noticed the hurt move to his eyes as she said Grace's name.

'Ah, maybe I'm better at this than I thought.'

"Colin, take a seat!" It wasn't a request; it was an order.

Colin complied, due entirely to not knowing what else to do.

"So, you finally worked it out that you're in love with our Miss Thornton?" She asked him gently.

He looked at her and noticed, instead of the usual ice in the eyes, they held a warmth and compassion that literally made her glow. Hell, she was a beautiful woman.

'Why doesn't someone come in on their white charger and take her away from all this past she ties herself to! She's way too young to hide away forever.' He would, had he not fallen head over heals for Grace.

"Yeah, I guess I did."

"So, what you going to do about it?"

"What can I do? The good Doctor appears to have taken the opportunity to court her and I can't blame her; she gets lonely here at times." He looked over her shoulder out of the window.

Catherine noticed the tensing of his body as he spoke and that he looked out of the window as a way out of his problems. Guess we all look out of this window for inspiration.

"Have you ever asked her out yourself?"

He looked aghast at her question.

"Colin it's something you have to do if you want her to know you're interested. How would she know any other way?"

"I guess she wouldn't," Colin laughed self-consciously.

"Is that all the advice you need Colin? Because I made a promise that I want to keep if possible. I need to get going."

Colin stood up and held out his hand; Catherine took it and chuckled silently. They shook hands and Colin disappeared through the door as quickly as he'd appeared. Smiling briefly she looked at the leather bound book on her desk and touched the title gently.

'Maybe for someone Adam, your sentiments might well work out.' She mused as she left the room to go and see her sick guest.

Grace couldn't believe it, now she was in a dilemma. For the past six months she'd been toying with leaving Destiny. Things had been okay, but she wasn't exactly challenged. Now suddenly things had gone from the old boring routine to nothing being sacred anymore. Guests turning up uninvited, Catherine's complete change in attitude, the doctor asking her out with permission from Catherine! Then there was Colin! Oh, yeah Colin; he'd looked so upset when he went to see Catherine, wonder what was wrong there? Now she didn't know what to think. Going out with Andrew Simpson was a good idea; she liked him. Catherine was finally thawing; or was she? Ms. Jace Bardley had brought that about, she was positive! How? There was a question that she wouldn't mind getting an answer to in the near future? Time would tell that's for sure and in this household, at the moment, it was being turned upside down and who knew when it would right itself.

She looked around the large kitchen, her domain!

Grace loved living at Destiny; it was home. She hadn't felt like she'd had a home for years until she came here, and then it hadn't happened immediately. The place just kind of grew on you and the people too! What would she do if anything happened to Catherine? She loved Catherine as a friend, if only the woman would let her in and maybe together they could heal some of her pain. It looked like it wasn't something she could do for her friend, but could Jace Bardley? Would she want to, that was more to the point!

'I hope you know what you're getting into Catherine, because I get the feeling that you haven't opened up to anyone in years, if you ever truly have!

She walked out of the kitchen and sat on the bench overlooking her garden and drank deeply from her coffee cup. *'Wonder what's up with Colin?'* She looked over her garden again and a peaceful look gave way to a pensive one as she thought about her friend.

Catherine walked quietly over to the bed that held the sleeping, if a little fitfully, Jace Bardley. Looking down at her flushed face and the obvious discomfort of the fever, she pushed away a stray lock of damp hair from the girl's forehead.

"I wonder why you hold my fascination Jace Bardley? It's not as if you would ever have been part of my usual crowd of so-called friends, even back when I was a student. Hell, you would have cursed me no doubt for my activities way back then. Though wouldn't you have cursed me when I took over from my father? I was even more of a devious devil than he had become. You don't look the insensitive type at all, you have such wonderfully expressive green eyes, and I wonder if you know that? Would you have wanted to meet me back then? Or would you have looked at my many vices and given up as so many have done! Except one! Yes, there had been one, and eventually two people in my life who cared about me, but I turned even them away from me in the end."

Catherine noticed the heavy breathing of the younger woman and moved closer to her and noticed the pallor, but she appeared to be stable. Hell, had she just spoken all that crap aloud, just as well the girl was asleep, she would wonder what was going on, some demented recluse, huh?

Her thoughts went to another person, a person this girl reminded her of.

'I understand in my heart why you didn't want our son ever to be involved with me Adam. I applaud your courage in standing up to me. You were never the strongest man I ever met, but you had a heart that had the courage of a lion. I never gave you the opportunity to show that side of your personality to me until it was way too late for both of us.'

Catherine Warriorson stood up from her cramped position by the bed and wandered around the room, noting the books and the pictures on the walls. It was decorated simply, but held a welcome to anyone staying in the room. *'I have Grace to thank for that!'* All the rooms had been decorated over the past three years.

All the rooms had been redone except the study. That had been left the way it had been taken over, just as Adam had wanted it to look. Catherine didn't mind, somehow it gave her a link to her late husband that she hadn't had in life. The only thing she had never really resolved was her pain over their son, who had been nearly five years old when he died.

She hadn't even seen him the last time she saw Adam. He hadn't thought it a good idea and she'd been too busy trying to get away, back to New York and her schedule. All she had now were pictures Adam had sent her of Lucas when he'd turned four, photos from the last birthday party at their home in London. He had been a happy child, bestowed with his father's personality, but definitely her looks. *'He would have broken so many hearts had he lived. He was such a charmer, even then. Had she been too busy again? Yeah another take over, another boardroom brawl another WIN! Now where had that been?'* There had been so many, it was impossible for her to remember them all.

Catherine's mind mulled over the time as she sat and watched the young woman in front of her, breathing heavily with the infection Jace had contracted. Her mind suddenly recalled the place.

Santa Barbara! California had been hot that time of year; it had been a push over really. The local publisher was being ousted by the large corporation; just another take-over. Can't remember the name of the guy who owned it, it hadn't even really been an issue to her; she needed a place close to LA, but not in LA. She got it, simple as that! What about all those take-overs? Now she had no one with whom to leave the extensive business. She was never likely to have another family. Adam had shown her that much about herself, she wasn't someone who could turn off the emotional cripple she had become over the years. Subjecting anyone to that now was out of the question! No matter if they did love her, she didn't have the capacity to return anyone's love. There again, where the hell would she ever find anyone gutsy enough to even try?

Grace looked in at that moment and noticed the pensive look crossing over Catherine's face. "Do you need a coffee?" She asked tentatively.

"I'd love a cappuccino, if you don't mind making me one Grace?" Looking at her friend in gratitude, her thoughts were haunting her badly today.

Grace smiled at the request. It would usually have been given as an order. "Sure, do you want some company for a while before I start lunch?"

"I'd like that Grace, more than you know," Catherine replied softly.

"Okay then, two cappuccinos coming up, heavy on the milk if I remember rightly?" Grace went out of the door smiling. Catherine's idea of a cappuccino was more like a café latte, but she never questioned the terminology. Grace often speculated what Catherine thought when she tasted external cappuccinos.

Catherine smiled at the retreating back. *'Maybe it isn't so bad to talk once in a while.'* She sat back down in the chair and gazed at the fevered face of Jace Bardley.

Chapter Eight

Grace had been good company for the hour they had been chatting, mainly about her visit to Sydney, and what to do about Jace Bardley should she want to leave earlier than the doctor ordered.

"It's entirely up to her if she wants to leave before I return Grace."

"Yes, I know, but she would be foolish to do so, it's bad enough she's fallen ill because of the weather here!"

"Aren't you forgetting something Grace?" Catherine raised that ever-formidable eyebrow.

"No, I don't think so! What do you mean?" Grace asked the woman who sat closely observing their feverish guest.

"It's not because of the weather, although in a way it is. It's because I left them out there on an exposed ridge in bloody terrible conditions. God only knows if there are others feeling the same way?"

Grace knew that plagued the woman sitting only a foot away from her. She looked so dejected, which was not something you normally associated with Catherine Warriorson.

"Well, I don't think she will blame you for leaving them Catherine. She did come back to see you after you laid down the challenge, didn't she? Does that sound like someone who is blaming you for her predicament?"

Catherine looked up at Grace and noticed her frown slightly.

"You know something Grace? For the first time in years, it's important for me to put this situation right. Though just how I'm going to do that is beyond me at the moment."

Grace once again looked at the small woman in the bed, totally ignorant to the conversation going on around her, and the restless woman who was gently pushing back the soaked tendrils of hair from her forehead.

"Maybe if you just do what you've been doing in the last few hours, it will work itself out. Ms. Bardley will still be here Catherine, trust me."

"I'm going to hold you to that Grace." Catherine got up from her seat by the bed, and moved towards the door. "I need to make a couple of calls, will you stay here for a little while longer?"

"Sure, it's no hardship." Grace smiled at her boss.

Catherine left the room and Grace turned her attention back to their guest.

'What hold do you have on her, Jace Bardley? As sure as the sun goes down everyday, something in you has awakened some powerful emotions. I sure hope you can handle it, and I pray she lets you!'

Jace woke up from a very haunting dream. It was elusive to say the least, but she was sure it held someone with the most hypnotic blue eyes she'd ever seen in her life.

Opening her eyes, she noticed a small bedside light switched on at a table close to the bed. A tall woman was seated close by and was reading a book, a leather bound volume that looked like it had been well read over a number of years.

With the small movement in the bed, the woman looked up from her reading and Jace held her breath as she gazed into the hypnotic blue eyes from her dream.

"Hey, how do you feel?" A low gravelly voice asked, the eyes never leaving her face.

Jace couldn't answer. She was trying to decide if it was due to the fact that her throat hurt and felt dry, or the concern in those eyes; which held her captive.

Catherine noticed Jace had difficulty answering and suddenly realised she might need a drink. "Do you want a drink?" She went over to the tray that held water and the pills the doctor had prescribed.

Taking a glass and a couple of the pills she walked back over to Jace and knelt beside the bed. Never taking her eyes from the small vulnerable woman huddled in the bed, she gently motioned for Jace to take the glass.

Unsuccessfully, Jace tried to sit up, but the room spun and almost made her sick. Noticing the sudden change of pallor in the younger woman, Catherine put the glass down on the floor and reached for the woman in support.

"Hey, it's okay. I've got you!" Catherine spoke softly into the nearest ear.

Jace stared into the beautiful chiselled features of her host and smiled briefly as a wave of nausea came over her again.

Catherine held the slight woman in her arms with Jace's head gently lying on her broad shoulder. Noticing that Jace was shivering again, she gently laid her back in the bed.

"I'm going to help you drink this Jace. It might be uncomfortable, but you need to get some fluids back into your body and the medication the doctor left. Okay, you ready?"

Jace's green eyes looked trustingly into warm ice blue ones. Nodding her head, she waited to be pulled back into that strong embrace.

Catherine held Jace securely on her right side and put her head on her shoulder again, balancing the weak and weary woman as she put out her left hand to retrieve the glass of water.

'Damn how am I going to get the pills, they're in my right hand?'

Gently placing the glass next to Jace's lips she tipped the glass back slowly and saw Jace take her first sip. Eventually, with care, she drank enough to satisfy Catherine. Placing the glass back on the floor, she removed the pills from her right hand and looked back at the drowsing face still held close to her shoulder.

"Sorry Jace, but you need to take these pills too!"

Jace grimaced but opened her mouth a little for Catherine to pop them into her mouth, and then reaching for the glass of water she placed it back to Jace's lips for her to take another drink. "Hey that's my girl. You did well." Catherine smiled as she congratulated Jace on getting the pills and water down without difficulty.

"How about we both did well?" Jace replied quietly, looking back into the pale blue eyes, which she never wanted to stop looking into.

"Oh, I don't know about that! But, let's lay you back down, get you comfortable, then let you get more sleep. You'll feel better for it."

Catherine smiled back at Jace; something was definitely pulling her towards this woman and for the life of her she didn't understand it at all.

Jace pulled a face as Catherine laid her gently down and replaced the covers back around the slight form.

Noticing the change in Jace's face, she couldn't help herself; she needed to know what the woman was thinking. "Hey, what's the face for?"

Jace blushed as she tried to look away from the piercing glance.

'Christ I don't know how to answer that! I know what I'd love to say, but she definitely wouldn't be expecting that.'

Catherine saw the blush and that puzzled her. "You going to answer me?"

"I guess I was more comfortable in your arms than laying here in the bed." Jace closed her eyes as she spoke.

Catherine almost choked as she spluttered. "What.... what do you mean?"

Jace opened her eyes and saw that Catherine Warriorson looked really uncomfortable and wasn't that a blush seeping over her face?

"I.... I was having dreams when I slept earlier, but when you held me, I felt safe and secure. Weird I know, I'm sorry if I've embarrassed you."

Catherine digested this piece of information and briefly smiled.

"Are they bad dreams?"

"Not sure, they are sort of elusive when I wake up, but they sure tire me out. I don't feel rested at all."

"Do you often have dreams?" Catherine continued.

"Sometimes, but last night and today they just seem so persistent." Jace wanted to say that they all had one thing in common: 'hypnotic blue eyes', Catherine Warriorson's eyes!

Smiling briefly and looking away from Jace towards the window and the darkness outside, Catherine spoke. "Well, if you have any more dreams and I can help out, you just tell me okay?"

Jace smiled tiredly and closed her eyes at the pleasant thoughts that drifted through her mind.

"Thanks Catherine, I might just take you up on that offer."

Catherine looked out of the window and noticed Colin Montgomery pacing outside; he looked none too happy.

Turning, she noticed that Jace had fallen back into a somewhat more restful sleep pattern.

'Let's hope she stays like that! Not sure what Grace would make of me being used as a pillow for the young woman. There again, when did I care what people think about me! Must be getting soft all of a sudden.'

She quietly left the room to find a mug of tea.

Chapter Nine

It was close to midnight and Grace had gone to bed, the house had been secured for the night and only a light shone under the door of the guestroom inhabited by Jace Bardley.

Anyone looking into the room would notice the outline of a small person in the double bed, which was the centrepiece of the room. To the left of the bed was a bedside table with a small lamp illuminating the room with a soft glow. Beside that, a large comfortable chair was tucked next to the bed; residing on the chair was a tall figure, reading a book. The room was peaceful and anyone not knowing otherwise would think it a fairly normal scene; it looked so comfortable.

An hour earlier Grace had said she would spend the night looking out for Jace. She was concerned since Catherine had to leave later in the day to travel to Sydney and she needed to get some rest, not having much the previous evening.

"It's okay Grace, I don't sleep for long anyway. What's the difference if I sleep those short hours in a chair? Better one of us gets some rest, and you will have to take the watch once I'm gone."

Looking at Catherine and knowing the logic behind the statement, she backed off. "I'll get breakfast for the usual time then?"

"Yeah, sounds good to me. I need to leave by nine in the morning, so it will be ideal. Hopefully, our patient will be sufficiently improved by then."

"I hope so. I guess it will be a day or two before she feels well enough to cause you too much hassle around here."

Catherine laughed at the comment from her housekeeper and friend. "Oh, I think Jace Bardley attracts trouble Grace, it's a feeling I have about her."

"Is that good trouble or bad?" Grace laughed along with her boss.

"Depends who goes to her defense I guess."

"Would you?" Grace looked directly at Catherine and noticed she blushed slightly at the comment.

"Maybe. Then it would be bad trouble wouldn't you think?" Catherine grinned wickedly at Grace.

"Oh, I wouldn't say that. I get the feeling you two together would make quite a team!"

"You do huh? Now, why would that be exactly?"

Grace smiled wryly at her and walked towards her tall employer, who in the space of twenty-four hours had willingly let down no small amount of her defenses. Placing a hand on the woman's shoulder, she gently squeezed it.

"Because I think you have found a friend Catherine, however remarkable that may be. It might just be your destiny; don't define it, just let it happen. Maybe it will bring you some measure of happiness." Without waiting for a reply, she left the room.

Catherine was stunned by the comment.

'My destiny! A friend? Yes. Maybe in time I could call Jace Bardley a friend. We sure seem to have rapport. Happiness isn't in my realm of things to look forward to; but, a small piece of my heart is reaching out to touch the tender thought, a need so overwhelming it hurts.'

Suddenly, Jace started to thrash around in the bed and Catherine moved quickly and silently to the small body, obviously in distress. Pulling the covers aside, she noticed that Jace was soaked with perspiration and her clothes really should be changed.

Walking over to the dressing table, she opened the first drawer and noticed nothing that would be useful. The next drawer proved equally unsuccessful. So she quickly arranged the sheet over the woman and left for her own room. Rummaging around she found an old University T-shirt and a pair of towelling shorts.

Getting back to the other room as quickly as possible she noticed the sheet on the floor of the room, having been kicked off by Jace and her thrashing around the bed.

'Hell, she's going to hurt herself if she doesn't calm down.'

Gently taking Jace's shoulder she tried to wake the woman from her restless slumber, noting the fever had begun to take hold again.

"Hey Jace, I need you to wake up for a little while. What do you say?"

Not really expecting a response, she thought that maybe she would have to wake Grace to help her with the younger woman.

God, Grace will be asleep now; it's not fair to her. Surely I can do this alone!

Taking the bottom of the shirt Jace was wearing, she gently eased it over her head and carefully wrapped the sheet around her as she picked up the T-shirt and shorts she had dropped on the table when she came back in the room.

This woman was so slight in her arms. Catherine felt a slight tremor in her hands as she removed the sheet and noted the all over tan that Jace had acquired, probably in California. It certainly enhanced the beauty of the woman. Closing those thoughts, she carefully pulled the shirt over her head and down the body. It was so big it covered everything to her knees.

Not sure if she should bother with the shorts, she placed them at the end of the bed and gently laid Jace back down. The thrashing didn't stop and Catherine pondered that problem.

'Only one thing for it!'

Taking off her shoes and her jeans she climbed onto the bed and took Jace back into her arms. Her left hand gently stroked the blonde hair falling over her eyes, and her right arm snaked round her waist and held her tightly.

"I've got you Jace, just hang in there. Tomorrow it's going to be better; wait and see." Catherine whispered into her ear.

Jace, feeling the comforting arms around her, put her head down on Catherine's shoulder and the thrashing ceased. Arms that had been pulling the bedclothes apart, suddenly moved to clasp the tall woman closer and a sigh came instead of the laboured breathing of the smaller woman.

Catherine hadn't really known if her action would be welcomed, but it sure seemed to be working. Being a very private woman, she wasn't particularly comfortable with the closeness of Jace. It was something she'd always had difficulty with, especially after her mother had died. Now here she was with a near stranger, in her home, in her guest bed and being used as a giant pillow. Within minutes her eyes started to close and she felt very tired. She had become, in just that short space of time, comfortable! Giving in to her body's craving for sleep, she closed her eyes and dropped off into her own dreamscape.

Jace woke up and felt rested and secure. Her senses were telling her she was in a safe haven and that hadn't happened before.

Her head, although still rather fuzzy, didn't have the percussion instruments doing a warm up in her head. Well for the moment, at any rate. She glanced at the warm pillow she was nestled into and almost jumped out of her skin.

'Hades, how did this happen?' She wondered as she noticed the even breathing of the sleeping Catherine Warriorson. Her face looked younger somehow in sleep. Still the tension she seemed to carry around with her in her waking hours wasn't far away; Jace felt it as she lay still against this beautiful woman.

'Gods this is a nightmare!'

Then a voice inside her head told her she was being foolish.

'You're right; it's a dream and a wonderful dream. Even if I never ever get to experience this again, I will always cherish this moment. She is so lovely and so lonely.' Jace couldn't help the final thought filtering through.

Moving her right hand she gently pushed the ebony hair away from her lips, its length making Catherine almost eat it, as it had broken away from its usually restrained ponytail.

That gentle brush of her hand across Catherine's mouth woke the woman up. Looking around her, distracted for the moment, she then realised her position and looked into Jace Bardley's tender green eyes.

Smiling briefly, the blue eyes warming as she locked her gaze with the green one. "Hey, how you doing?" Catherine's voice was almost a growl. To Jace, whose senses had slipped into an almost sensual haze, sexy was the only word for it.

Jace swallowed several times and smiled. "A little better thanks."

"Great, do you need anything?"

Jace knew then and there that she was in love! Her heart was telling her and her head for once wasn't overriding the emotions.

"I would love some water."

"Okay, wait right there. I'll get it." Catherine slipped out of the bed, walked with fluid movements to the water jug where she filled the glass, bringing along a couple of the pills.

Jace had a chance to watch this spectacle and it had her heart pumping ten to the dozen.

'If I die now, looking at those legs and that toned body, I know I'll be in heaven.'

Catherine turned around and saw a look on Jace's face that, under normal circumstances, she would have said held desire. But the woman was ill, so the flush and the glazed expression in her eyes were probably more fever induced than anything else. Still, it made Catherine's stomach tighten a little at the thought. *'Christ I must be more tired than I thought; this kid is getting to me.'*

Walking back to the bed, she held the glass for Jace to take a drink and then passed her the pills. Taking them and then another drink, Catherine placed the glass back on the tray and went towards the chair, picking up a blanket along the way.

Jace was gutted. Somehow she thought that Catherine would come back to bed. A tear slowly rolled down her cheek at the loss, her heart tightened in her chest and all she could feel was pain.

Catherine looked at Jace and noticed the tears now tracking down the pale face.

"Jace, what's wrong?" Catherine went quickly towards the bed and touched the trail of tears on her cheek.

"Nothing, nothing I'm just tired I guess." Jace said tearfully.

"Is there anything I can do?" Catherine asked tentatively, not knowing really what to do. Sensitive stuff was way beyond her. It had always been that way. Adam had even been the one to talk to their son when he had hurt himself or something had upset him.

Jace just looked wearily at her and something in her eyes must have given a message to the concerned blue ones above.

"How about I get back into the bed, and you use me as a giant pillow and get some rest? You need it Jace."

Had the gods been smiling on her this trip or what!

"I'd appreciate that, but are you okay with this?"

"Sure, would you believe it's the best night's sleep I've had in years? But don't you go telling anyone that I'm the next best thing to a giant teddy bear okay?" Catherine winked at the young woman and chuckled at the thought.

Jace grinned at her and the tears stopped flowing.

"I promise you that no one will hear it from me." Jace was so happy she wanted to burst with the sheer joy of having this woman close to her. Settling back down on Catherine's shoulder she let out a deep sigh.

"Hope that's a good sigh Ms. Bardley. Can't be letting me think that my powers as a human pillow are waning now can we?" she laughed softly.

"Oh, it was happy." Jace silently thought: *'I'm so happy Catherine Warriorson, you have no idea how happy you make me; now to find a way to get you to stay in my life.'* With that, Jace closed her eyes and fell into a deep healing sleep.

Catherine looked down at the head resting on her shoulder and wondered about this woman.

'Has it only been a little more than twenty-four hours since we met? For some reason I feel that the small blonde in my arms has been in my life so much longer than that! Yet how could it be?'

Nothing had ever felt this good to her before, caring for this woman was something she was happy to do and her heart welcomed the challenge.

Yet..........her life couldn't be complicated by this friendship. *'What was it Grace had said? It was my destiny. Don't define it! I guess only time will tell on this one, but will I have the time?'*

Closing her eyes as sleep once again claimed her from her thoughts, she considered that what she'd said to Jace was true. It had been years since she'd slept that well, and no bad dreams either!

Both women slept peacefully, held in each other's arms.

Chapter Ten

Grace Thornton started the day much as she usually did. She went straight to the kitchen and put on the coffeepot and the kettle for tea. One thing never changed in this house, Catherine's two mugs of tea every morning when she got up. If she had to do without it for any reason, she was grouchy all day; and a grouchy Catherine Warriorson was a very mean woman to be around. Then, too was the fact that instead of a cup, which you would expect a woman of her up bringing to be used to, a very large mug was her preferred utensil and woe betide anyone who made a comment about that. Setting the oven to automatic, she made a pot of tea, poured a mug for Catherine and went in search of her boss.

'Probably she's curled up as uncomfortable as hell and grouchy with it on that damn chair!'

Quietly opening the door and going in, she nearly dropped the mug as she saw where her employer was sleeping.

There, sleeping peacefully with her arms around a small blonde woman, Catherine Warriorson looked relaxed, a small smile played around her usually tense features. The blonde was snuggled so far into Catherine's shoulder; you would think she was a permanent fixture.

This was a sight that made Grace happy. She wasn't too sure if it was going to make Catherine happy, but somehow Jace Bardley might just make it work.

'Something tells me you're going to try to run from this Catherine. But, oh I wish you wouldn't; you are so right together!' With that thought firmly entrenched, she quietly exited the room, shutting the door softly behind her. Seconds later she made a loud knocking noise on the door to announce her presence to her employer.

Catherine heard the knocking on the door; woke up suddenly; and realised that her position in the bed did look a little compromising, although Grace probably wouldn't say anything. Mind you, what was there to say? *'I was only comforting the girl, right? Right!'*

Gently disengaging herself from Jace's hold, she moved quickly to the chair and dragged the blanket over her before calling for Grace to enter.

Grace almost couldn't stop the smirk from coming to her face as she saw the flush on the face of her boss, and her discomfort.

"Ha! Tea, what a mind reader you are Grace. I was just thinking about coming down to the kitchen and getting a mug."

"Oh, well glad I could help. You sleep any in that chair?" It was a hard battle to stop herself from laughing.

"Oddly enough, I really slept very well, surprised the hell out of me!" Catherine glanced at the still sleeping Jace and a smiled played around her face. *'My young friend, I have you to thank for that.'*

Grace looked at Jace and went over to touch her forehead. "She's not got such a high fever this morning, did she have a good night?"

"Actually I had to change her clothes at one stage and she likes making mincemeat out of the bed clothes. But, all in all, I think she got some rest." Catherine looked at Jace and saw the more regular breathing and felt relief at the change for the better, especially as she was leaving shortly.

"That's good then, so the fever might have broken. Doctor Simpson will be over later today to check up on her. So when you ring from Sydney, I can update you." Grace spoke almost absently.

"Is it Jace, or you the good doctor is coming to see?"

Grace laughed, "Probably both, think I might invite him for dinner, if it's okay with you that is?"

Catherine laughed along with her friend. "Hey, go for it Grace. You never know when the chance might arise again. Anyway, I'm away and while the cat's away, as they say."

"Somehow, that expression doesn't quite cover our relationship." Grace turned to leave the room.

Catherine heard a change of emotion in the comment. "Grace, that comment wouldn't cover me at anytime. I don't go in for relationships, we both know that."

Grace looked back and her eyes strayed to the bed and the blonde sleeping there, once again innocent of the conversation around her.

"Maybe if you found the right person you might change your mind." A wistful look came across her face.

Catherine locked her blue eyes on the brown ones of her housekeeper and friend. "You're too good for me Grace, do you know that?" She tried to lighten the emotional charge that was being created in the room.

Never letting her eyes leave Catherine's face, she walked over to her and gently put out a hand and stroked the high cheekbones.

"Oh, Catherine you are way to hard on yourself. Love can come knocking on the door, even if you don't want to answer it. But once you do, it's very powerful and a wonderful feeling. I do so hope you let it in one day."

For once, Catherine was at a loss for words. Then she took the hand that had caressed her cheek and held it in her own. "Has it been knocking at my door long Grace?"

Jace Bardley took that moment to open her eyes and move around in the bed. Although she hadn't opened her eyes earlier, she had listened to the discussion between these two women and something in her subconscious didn't want to hear the end of this conversation.

Both women looked at Jace. Grace quickly exited the room for the second time that morning, saying she would get breakfast ready.

Catherine was relieved in a way that Jace had awakened when she did; the conversation she was having with Grace had taken a turn into a scenario she had never considered.

Christ, her only real relationship had been with Adam, well maybe there had been one other person, but she chalked that up to the drugs. She hadn't considered the possibility of being in love with another woman.

'Grace is a friend nothing more! I know that, hell I haven't got it in me to let love into my life, not now, not ever! Then to further complicate it by falling for a woman is not an option, not in this lifetime anyway!'

Looking directly at Jace, she smiled. "Hey sleepy head, do you want anything to eat? You look a little better this morning."

Jace wanted to do nothing more than watch this woman all day and all night; but hearing the earlier conversation, she figured it wasn't going to be easy to stay in her life. Never mind try to get a relationship going.

"I think I could eat something, I do feel better this morning. Thanks for being a great shoulder to sleep on."

"You're welcome, just don't mention it to too many people, or they might want to try it." Catherine chuckled.

"Oh, okay then, our secret. So, the shoulder is my private pillow then?" Jace didn't realise she had asked such a loaded question, until her words sunk in and she caught a guarded expression on Catherine's face.

Catherine considered the question and realised Jace was just playing along with the banter, or was she?

"Well, I guess you could say that, but only if it involves a bad dream, okay?"

Getting up from the chair, she picked up her shoes and jeans and made for the door. *'Hell, I hope Grace didn't notice the discarded clothing.'*

"I need to get a shower and a change. I'll get Grace to prepare you something to eat and I'll be back before I leave."

Catherine was out of the door before Jace could answer. In a very small voice she whispered, "You're leaving?"

The room never answered her.

Grace came back in to see Jace about ten minutes after Catherine had left her. "So, you want some breakfast? What can I make for you?" She asked cheerfully, and then noticed the tears that the younger woman tried to hide. "Jace, are you okay?"

Jace couldn't believe the woman in front of her. She obviously loved her boss; yet, she was being so gentle with her. Then again, Grace didn't know that Jace loved the woman also.

"I'm fine, really. But, I think I'll skip the food. Suddenly I've lost my appetite," she trailed off unhappily.

Grace pondered this for a moment and then sat on the bed and looked at her. "Wouldn't have anything to do with a certain Ms. Warriorson leaving later this morning would it?"

Jace was poleaxed at the direct and so obviously correct assumption. "How did you know that?" She couldn't keep the incredulity out of her voice.

Grace smiled and placed a hand on the woman's arm. "Because she told me that she'd just mentioned it as she was leaving your room. Guess you weren't expecting it and you like her, I suspect."

"Yes. I like her. When will she be back?" Jace hoped her voice didn't reflect the yearning she felt in her heart.

"She has business in Sydney and will be back in three days; it usually goes pretty fast." Grace tried to make light of it.

"Will she be expecting me to still be here when she gets back?" Jace wanted to know that above anything else.

"Oh, I think if you weren't here when she got back, she would be very angry."

"You really think so?" Jace started to think that maybe keeping Catherine in her life wasn't going to be as hard as she thought.

"Oh, yeah! Doctor Simpson said you needed to stay here until you felt better; or you might have a relapse or something. Catherine wouldn't be happy about that!"

Jace looked crestfallen at that admission.

"I see. So it's really because of the doctor's orders."

Grace saw the sadness in the eyes of the younger woman.

"No, no I think she likes you also, and wants to get to know you better, if she can. Although the doctor did say you need the rest. So, when she's back you need to feel much improved and maybe you two can become better acquainted."

"Thanks Grace." Jace replied a little happier.

"You're welcome. So what do you want to eat or Catherine will have both our hides?"

"I'll have toast and a boiled egg if that's okay."

"Sure, I'll be back later with it. Or better still, I'll feed Catherine and then send her in with it, how does that sound?"

Jace Bardley's face fairly beamed at the last comment.

"Guess I know which choice you made there." Grace laughed as she moved away from the bed and out of the door, almost colliding with Catherine on her way back to the kitchen.

Catherine looked at Grace and raised her expressive eyebrows. "Everything okay?"

"Oh, yeah, everything's fine. I was wondering about getting a door bell here; just might save the door knocker." Grace muttered with a smirk on her face as she went into the kitchen and Catherine diverted to the study.

"Doorbell? Doorknocker? What the hell sort of comment was that!" Catherine shook her head and went inside the study to make sure her papers were all together before placing them in her briefcase.

Catherine had her breakfast with Grace and Colin as usual and they went over final instructions for the next three days.

Colin was a little agitated, but knowing the reason, Catherine ignored it as best she could. Although she noticed Grace kept giving him interesting looks from time to time.

Then, she proceeded to take Jace her breakfast. They didn't talk much, but it felt comfortable to them both just being together.

"Why do you go to Sydney?" Jace asked in between eating her toast and eggs, thinking it strange.

"Oh, it's business that doesn't have anything to do with the ranch holdings. I have other interests; so, twice a year we get together to discuss the next few months." Catherine volunteered as she absently checked her watch. It was nearly nine and Colin would be coming to take her to the airfield for the trip to Christchurch.

"What is your other business?"

"Publishing." Catherine answered without thinking, and then looked at Jace. That wasn't something she wanted anyone to know about. Even Grace didn't know anything about her other business dealings.

"Publishing? Isn't that a little different from ranching?" Jace wanted to know as much as possible about this woman.

"Yes, family interests. Look I have to go, Colin's on his way over. I'll see you in a few days, okay? Don't give Grace any trouble and I might bring you a present. Get better, Jace." She then absently bent down and placed a kiss on her forehead.

Jace was upset at Catherine's preoccupation but she felt better with the feather light kiss she received. It was a start.

"Safe journey Catherine, I'll miss you."

Turning back from the door Catherine locked her blue gaze into a green one and smiled, it was a warm happy smile.

"Thanks, I'll see you when I get back." With that, she left the room and within minutes the car was pulling out of the drive, heading for the local airport.

Jace Bardley was, without a shadow of a doubt, hopelessly, head over heels in love with the woman who had just left the house. How on earth was she going to manage three days without seeing her? It would feel like a lifetime.

Chapter Eleven

Catherine arrived in Sydney as scheduled. She had taken a private helicopter from the local airport to Christchurch. Fortunately, she only had to wait an hour before her Qantas flight took off. The flight itself was six hours and she went first class. Wealth had its advantages, and travelling first class was one she definitely indulged in on the few occasions she travelled these days. It was worth the money to get extra legroom and the wider seats. Those factors and the improved service on board made it all the more beneficial.

During the flight, she had indulged in orange juice and reading the financial times. Her mind drifted to the events and conversations with the two women currently in her household.

'I can't believe that I slept the night holding a virtual stranger in my arms and it never bothered me, well only initially. For some reason it was familiar to me. Odd, so very odd! I know that we've never met before. I would have remembered wouldn't I? Yet, when she touches me I crave the feel of the contact..........I look into her eyes and see...what?' Glancing pensively out the window, Catherine was reluctant to answer the questions she posed to herself.

'I need to get a grip on this before something happens that neither of us wants. I know she's the friendly sort, maybe a little too friendly, but haven't I encouraged that! Grace said she was upset that I was leaving, but why? Hell, I don't know what to think of this situation. I've never come across it before!' God, there never had been a time that anyone had actively pursued her friendship, quite the opposite in fact. Now, here was a young woman who must be at least ten years her junior, not only looking towards a deep friendship, but possibly more.........or was that her over active imagination. *'I hope it is, because Jace, I can't be that person for you! That is something I'm very sure of.'*

'No! The reclusive Catherine Warriorson is afraid to answer her own heart! Adam would have smiled and maybe he is smiling at me now. But, I still don't believe in your soulmate theory, that is just way over the top for me.'

After the lunch was served and eventually cleared away, Catherine mused over her relationship with Grace. *'I know she's a friend, she offered me her friendship from the first day. We kind of drifted into an easy superficial friendship. Nothing too deep, no secrets have ever been exchanged between us, we've only indulged in mutual companionship and she is good company. I couldn't think of living on the ranch without her. Yet, might that soon be a possibility? Hell, she's got two men after her now and I think I know which one she will chose. Or is it just that it's more convenient for me to think that way? This morning's conversation was strange, almost a confession of something buried between us. She would have answered me honestly if Jace had not awakened at that time. Would I have been equally as honest with her? No! I doubt I would have shared her honesty.'*

Later, she finally got through the customs procedures, always a chore in her eyes, but something even she couldn't escape. She picked up her small suitcase, briefcase and laptop computer and put them on a luggage carrier and moved out of the airport arrival's lounge to the taxi stand.

Half an hour later she arrived at the Hilton Hotel, which was situated in Sydney Harbour and had a wonderful view of the bridge and the mooring of an old sailing boat. It was the replica of the Bounty, which was used in the movie 'Mutiny on the Bounty' starring Mel Gibson. Going towards the concierge, she was greeted by one of her Vice Presidents, Gareth Cuthbert, who was in charge of European operations and liked to wield his power at every available opportunity.

"Ms. Devonshire, how nice to see you again." He held out his hand, which she took and immediately knew one of the reasons she didn't particularly like the man. He had a very sweaty handshake something she couldn't abide. But, he was good at his job and she didn't have to do this more than four times a year. She would survive.

"Nice to see you also Cuthbert, is everyone else here?" She motioned for a porter to take her luggage.

"Yeah, Paul Strong arrived about an hour ago, he was the final VP to get here. Now that you're here, do you want to start early or wait until the schedule tomorrow?" He was never one to miss a chance at making brownie points with the great Ms Devonshire. It was legend that she loved the power she held, even if from a distance.

Closing in on the front desk she turned her blue eyes without any warmth and pinned him with a stare that would have had most people intimidated, but he knew her too well to worry about that, at least he hoped he did. "No, that's okay, keep with the schedule; but, Gareth good call." She turned away from him and spoke to the head clerk.

Within ten minutes she was kicking her shoes off and lounging in a soft leather two-seater pale blue sofa, waiting for room service to bring her tea.

Looking over the room, which was decorated in pastel shades to go with the furniture, consisting of two, two-seater sofas and a coffee table. Along one wall was a large entertainment system and the other wall had a desk with the phone and the modem ports. The next section of the suite held a dining table and eight chairs with a drinks cabinet. This led directly into the bedroom area, which housed a king-sized four-poster bed, a dressing table and another smaller TV set. A walk in closet was to the left of the bed and to the right was the bathroom, with a large sunken bath and an independent shower, bidet and toilet. She had also noticed in the hall was another restroom. Everything she needed, well more than she needed really, but it was useful if she needed to see any of her people alone. Right now, Paul Strong was the favored candidate.

Picking up the room phone she dialed his room, having obtained his room number from reception.

"Hello, this is Strong, can I help you?" A familiar masculine voice answered.

"Hi Paul, glad to see you made it early. How about a drink before dinner in my suite, say five o'clock?"

Paul Strong smiled when he realized the identity of the caller. I bet she hasn't even been in the room ten minutes.

"Sure, anything you say."

"Great, see you then." She didn't wait for an answer to put down the phone. Room service had arrived!

Paul looked at the receiver in his hand that had a dead tone. He laughed. She hadn't changed, that was for sure.

Grace had helped Jace to bathe and change her clothes. She was still far too weak to manage the task on her own.

Settling back into the now clean laundered bed, she watched Grace limp around the room, collecting the used glasses and water pitcher and making sure the furniture was back in its usual places.

"Grace, do you mind if I ask you a question or two?" Jace looked pensively at the woman who had turned from her task and was looking directly at her.

"If I can answer I will; go ahead, ask." Grace eyed her speculatively.

"I know it's personal, but how did you injure yourself?" Green eyes looked at her with sympathetic interest.

"Well, I could say I've had the problem since I was born," Grace saw the sudden flush of embarrassment and waved her hand at Jace. "No, I was in a car accident; my fault actually. Lucky to get out alive they say, but it left me less than whole. You can't count your chickens too much in this life."

Jace nodded her head in understanding. "Have you always worked as a housekeeper?"

"Hell, no! I was a rookie policewoman before this happened. It sort of stunted my chances. I needed a change of scenery before I did something stupid, so here I am." Grace looked at Jace to check her reaction. It was reflective.

"Interesting, you don't come across as cop material."

"Is there such a thing as cop material? Jace, I'm surprised at you! Didn't realise you had specific boxes for people to fit into." Grace laughed at the thought.

Jace looked embarrassed. "I didn't mean it like that, exactly! Only I figured you for a more gentle career, sorry."

"Ah, I see. So, have you always been a Publicity P.A.?"

"Yes, from college. Although, I had plans to join my father in the family publishing business. When I couldn't, I opted for this role instead," Jace answered quietly.

"What happened to make you give up your dream?"

"How did you know it was a dream?"

"Oh, just the way you said it."

"In my final year, he was taken over by a giant in the publishing business."

"It happens. So why not work for them or someone else for that matter?"

"Never! It was too painful and Xianthos never gave us a chance." She almost cried in remembered pain, recalling the situation vividly when her father told her they had lost the business.

"Xianthos? I've come acr□ss that name before, but for the life of me I can't remember where. Obviously it can't be very important." Grace shrugged her shoulders.

Jace decided it was a good time to change tactics. "Catherine left a book here called **There Can Only Be One Soulmate.** I've kind of glanced over it, but I noticed the name of the author. Is Adam Warriorson related to Catherine?" Jace looked down at the bedclothes and held out the leather bound book to Grace.

"It's okay Jace, I've read the book. I'm surprised she left it here, though. She's going to be upset when she finds out that she doesn't have it in her luggage." Grace absently said before answering the question.

"Why?"

"Oh, the book is very special to Catherine. She must have read it, God knows, maybe a hundred times! Adam was her husband."

It was a simple enough statement by Grace, but it caused Jace to suck in her breath as if in pain. She realised that maybe her dream of getting to know Catherine would be limited to a very long distance friendship. *'Hell, why did I think it could be anything else? She never gave the impression she was anything other than a very private person who would and did wield enormous power.'*

Clearing her throat from the sting of tears she could feel welling up. "You say was. Are they divorced or something?"

Grace smiled slightly. "Oh, well you certainly didn't do any research on this part of your trip did you?" came the gentle inquiry, not wanting to sound harsh to the still very sick woman.

"We didn't have time to do much research for this slot. Clarissa added it suddenly, and even Peter the director was shocked that we had to come here to film."

"So, when did you arrive in New Zealand?" This had piqued Grace's interest. Had Catherine been here, she would have been intrigued. Well, she would let her boss know about this later.

"Oh, about a week ago. We got some good footage of the surrounding area and some other ranches and their owners, but we had difficulty with this one, as you know. We didn't have the details of this area or of Catherine, just the name C X Warriorson. Guess we look kinda foolish to you all I suppose?" Jace asked sheepishly.

"To me, a little naïve maybe; but foolish no! Catherine, on the other hand, wasn't impressed with the situation. She had refused the permission and once she says no, she sure as hell means no!"

"Yet, she let me in, and even put me up for the night, and gods she's been so friendly, I don't really know what to think. But you haven't answered my question Grace, what's happened to her husband?"

Jace wasn't even sure if she really wanted the answer, but it mattered, oh how it mattered to her.

"Adam died in a plane crash along with their son Lucas, five plus years it will be now. Adam had just bought the ranch for him and the boy, but they never really had the chance to live here."

Grace noticed the look of compassion on her face when she mentioned Adam's death, but when Lucas was mentioned the sadness was profound. Grace continued.

"She actually likes living here, I think, but with Catherine you can't really tell. She keeps so much inside herself; one day it's going to be just too much for her to handle alone." Shaking her head she moved towards the door.

Jace thought about the comment. *'But, you're not alone Catherine. I'm here and going to be for as long as you want me!'*

"So Adam was a writer; was he a good one?"

"Why don't you read it for yourself and make your own mind up. One thing's for sure. He was a dreamer and that makes you wonder how they ever met. Catherine is logical and practical right down to her little finger." Grace opened the door and, as she pushed it shut, she heard Jace's reply.

"Yeah, good idea. A dreamer? Oh well, I'm a dreamer too!"

Grace smiled as she heard the comment and thought. *'Oh Catherine, you're going to have your work cut out for you avoiding this situation head on, that's for sure.'*

Chapter Twelve

Paul Strong arrived at his boss's suite at five promptly. You never, ever kept Ms Devonshire waiting. That was the first rule you learned and quickly, just as soon as you became an employee.

Paul had worked for the Xianthos Publishing Empire, for close to ul had worked for the Xianthos Publishing Empire, for close to twenty years. He had a degree in English literature and thought it would be adequate in a publishing house. Well, in most it would have been but Xianthos was different; from its very foreign name to its roots and finally it's original owner, Stewart Devonshire.

Paul recalled the man as being obsessive about the company, but never about his family. He'd heard that his wife was dead, and that an aunt in England was bringing up his two children. Quite common for lots of wealthy parents, but something in the way Devonshire spoke about his children defied that he never saw them. It was just another oddity of a very English gentleman, and Devonshire was that all right!

When he'd died, everyone wondered what would happen. There had been no natural successor. His only son was dead and his daughter, definitely the black sheep of the family after her continuous trips on alcohol and drugs, had finally ended up in prison. Not that that particular event had been given much publicity. Devonshire had managed to keep it under wraps to a degree, and he only knew because he'd been part of the clean up team that went to Europe to pay people off. Even he had wondered who would be the person to handle the vast and lucrative empire Stewart had built?

For a moment he was transported back to the day, he'd been in Stewart Devonshire's office.

"Strong I need you and at least three others whom you trust implicitly to make financial reparation to one or two prominent people who can initiate my daughter's release from jail."

Paul Strong had worked with the company for over a decade and worked diligently to gain his present position. This was a scenario out of the movies and his partner James would have loved the idea. He, on the other hand, wasn't happy at all. Why did Devonshire want to do such a thing? He didn't exactly come across as the loving, concerned parent type. It was common knowledge that the boss had a family living in England, beyond that little was known. He had been shocked inwardly to learn Devonshire's daughter was in prison. For what, he wondered?

"Sir, exactly why is your daughter in prison?" Devonshire gave him a glacial look and the dull red that appeared on his cheeks indicated his anger at being asked the question.

"My business Strong! I'm sure when you arrive in Germany you will find out. She didn't murder anyone, if that's what you're worried about! Not knowingly anyway."

"I'm sorry sir; it must be very distressing to have this situation happen to someone you love." Paul wished he hadn't said the words as a shutter immediately came down on Devonshire's face.

"I've been informed that she isn't safe in the prison. I want her out. Love has nothing to do with it."

Paul shuddered at the severe words, what kind of father was he?

"I see, in that case I'd better leave immediately."

"Yes, a good idea Strong. I want the right result without anyone knowing I had anything to do with it."

Paul nodded his head as he picked up the folder Stewart Devonshire had given him. Turning on his heel, he made for the door and his unusual assignment.

"Strong."

"Yes sir?"

"She's my little girl and no one, and I mean no one, does her harm if I can do anything about it. Make it happen." Devonshire dismissed him but not before Paul saw an expression cross the man's face. It had been tenderness.

"I will sir, count on me."

Shaking his head, he came back to reality.

Then that question had been answered and if they thought Stewart odd, well, at least he'd been a gentleman!

Ms Devonshire arrived on the scene within six months of her father's death, and proved true the old saying: 'better the devil you know.'

She had taken Xianthos to greater heights within the space of eighteen months. What she didn't do to get them the numerous take-overs were, to say the least, what legends are made from. Then, quite suddenly, her personal world had fallen from under her! No explanations, she was just gone! Many thought she had killed herself after the tragedy of the deaths of her husband and son, but she hadn't; she'd decided that it was time to remove herself from the world arena.

Within three months she had left him the largest role in the world operation and he had never let her down. His methods did not have the harsh backlash that hers had, as she made enemies …and kept them.

Now, five and half years later, she had asked a question that he hadn't expected. He'd thought the situation buried with her father, obviously not!

After knocking on the door, he was directed to enter.

Paul saw one of the most beautiful women he would ever meet. She had always fascinated him but she had never tried her charms on him, she valued him in the company far too much for that! Although he was glad, it could have turned nasty for him.

"Good evening Ms. Devonshire." Paul said, genuinely pleased to see her.

Catherine looked at the man who must be what? Maybe mid-forties, very handsome in a subtle sort of way, he had dark brown hair, greying at the temples, but that didn't detract from his masculine attraction. He dressed well too. Not ostensibly expensive, but a very good quality.

She held out her hand. "Great to see you Paul, thanks for doing the research for me." She lifted her eyebrow, knowing full well that he wouldn't have ventured near her if he hadn't.

Paul looked at the tall woman and noticed that she was dressed in a black leather skirt that fit snugly to her hips and reached just above the knees, with a white plain but expensively cut blouse. She was the epitome of a wealthy, beautiful woman but without the need to prove anything to anyone.

"Yeah, as always, my pleasure." He smiled at her.

He handed over a folder; she took it, glanced at the ownership rights and smiled. "Would you like a drink Paul?"

"Sure. Scotch and water thanks."

She motioned for him to sit and she prepared the scotch and water and a mineral water for her, speed-reading the documents enclosed, a particular skill of hers that annoyed a lot of her business associates.

"Right, so we still have sixty percent holding in the company and she has the other forty." It was an almost one-sided conversation; something that Paul had never experienced before or seen, to his knowledge.

A little perplexed, he answered. "Yeah, just as your father willed it."

Catherine looked up at the remark and suddenly realised she'd forgotten that Paul was in the room with her.

"Sorry about that Paul. I must be getting used to my own company too much." She laughed and the sound not only surprised him, but also made him aware that she was human after all.

"We still invest heavily, as my father wanted?"

"Well, to the tune of twenty million dollars as of the last financial year. Do you want me to drop the level?"

"No! Not yet at any rate; the bitch is up to something and I want to know what."

Paul looked at her with some concern; he didn't understand the conversation. "I'm sorry, but I guess you've lost me."

"I still have the right to veto everything from the original idea to the final tape and the staff, right?"

"Oh, sure. We never have, so far! It hasn't been worth the time, and you made it clear that you didn't want any of our resources to have anything to do with the project. Is that still the case?"

"To put you in the picture Paul, the good Ms Hudson, decided to set the hounds on me and dig me out of hiding. Done not very subtlety I might add, but effective nonetheless. She sent a kid to do a grown up's job and maybe she punched to many of my buttons this time around. She's going down this time, Paul. The hell with my father and what he wanted. Now she gets this particular Devonshire in her bed, and believe me, it won't be the happy ride she had with Daddy! Oh no, not this time. This time she's going to have to fight to the death!"

Paul looked shocked, he knew that she wanted her life now to be reclusive. He'd always secretly wanted her to come back. This situation was interesting to say the least.

"I thought your father made it plain that you couldn't interfere with her or the shares he'd given her, unless she chose to sell them to another party?"

"Well, there's more than one way to skin a cat, Paul. I thought you would know that by now, especially if someone crosses me!" She quirked that expressive left eyebrow at him and smiled a very wicked looking smile.

"Sorry, guess I'm getting out of the habit of having you around to remind me." He took a chance on her mood and wasn't wrong.

She smiled openly this time, and motioned her hand to the bar. He accepted the gesture.

"So who is the kid she set on you?" He asked more out of trying to find conversation than any real interest.

Catherine gave him a veiled look and she quirked her lips. "Well, not just the kid really, a whole crew to be precise. Peter Adamson is the director, have you heard of him?"

Catherine hadn't particularly been interested in any of the other members of the crew that she'd seen on the ridge. Jace Bardley had been the only one with guts to call her at her own game. Now she was interested in where this Adamson guy fit in.

"Actually, yes I've heard of him. He's a very good documentary director, very professional and this doesn't fit his profile somehow!" Paul frowned at his thoughts.

"How come you know so much about him?"

Paul appeared discomforted by the question and looked down at the rug at his feet. Not quite sure how to answer her, but knowing that he would have too eventually.

Catherine watched him gulp down the second drink. Now that was unusual! Not only did he seem nervous, he looked embarrassed; only God knows why?

She walked over to the drink's cabinet and got him another drink, guessing that might settle his nerves.

"You going to answer me?" she grinned. That particular retort was becoming a habit. What was happening to the people around her?

He looked up at her as she walked right up to his chair and offered him the drink, taking the empty glass away without any comment.

"I have a friend..." Paul spoke the word almost as a caress.

Now Catherine knew why he wasn't too pleased at the turn of the conversation. Obviously this could drop his ladylove in the cart.

Funny she had never asked or even been remotely interested in his personal life, even way back when she often took executives to her bed. Her mind drifted to a pleasant feeling of holding a very small soft body close to her all night! *'Christ, get those thoughts out of the gutter Warriorson. She's just a kid and you can't go there. Not now, not ever!'* She continued smiling at the thought of Jace, but she realized it had become impossible for her not to now.

Paul noticed the change in her facial expression and he could have sworn that she was thinking good things; maybe she had finally found someone, at last!

"He lives in LA, and knows the film crowd very well!" Paul listened for the penny to drop with his boss and awaited the outcome. He had never been sure if she had any feelings either way about the sexuality of anyone; but as with everything else about her, she was hard to find anything out about at all.

She had been married and had a son. She loved the boy; that had been obvious to anyone. His picture had always been on her desk and it changed as soon as she got another. He fondly recalled her expression; it softened to tenderness without prompting. Adam, well that had been another story altogether. He couldn't remember any rumours flying of her taking a woman to her bed, plenty of men, but women no!

Catherine wasn't sure if she was supposed to learn something from the fact that it was a man! Suddenly she realised what it was all about, as the penny finally dropped; this caused her to laugh outright.

Paul saw this as a derogatory comment on his choice of mate. He got up from the chair and coolly walked towards the door.

"Well, if you've finished with me now, I'll see you at dinner Ms Devonshire."

Catherine was stunned. *'What the hell have I done to bring on this reaction? Oh, shit I laughed. But I wasn't laughing at him! No, I would need to laugh at myself with the thoughts that went through my mind a few minutes ago about Jace.'*

"Wait! Paul, hold on there! I've not finished, sit!" It wasn't a request it was a demand. He did exactly that.

Catherine walked over to the chair that was directly opposite the one Paul had dropped into at the demand; she sat and directed a very powerful ice blue gaze at his grey eyes.

Several seconds later, she released his eyes and smiled. "You know something Paul, I know absolutely nothing about you other than what you do in the company for me. Guess that's a little remiss of the boss wouldn't you say?"

"In the circumstances, no! You're a very busy woman," he wondered where the questioning was going.

"Paul, you know more about me than anyone else I know! Maybe you think you don't, but let's face it, I've no family. Well none that want anything to do with me! I'm a virtual recluse, in a country that has taken me in without question. Although, I suspect my money is the leading factor there. I frighten the hell out of my neighbours, my business associates and probably most of the people who meet me! Do you know how that feels? No scratch that, I never wanted to belong anywhere anyway. Hell, I've experienced most of what the world has to offer, especially in my sordid past. So, are you going to tell me a little about your personal life?"

She wasn't sure if that had been the right approach, but recently she had put her reclusive nature on hold and opened up a little to the world.

Paul looked at her and a faint smile crossed his lips. He couldn't believe what he was hearing: the mighty Ms Devonshire was actually interested in him! Not on her personal level, but on his!

"James Thompson, that's my partner." He blushed as he said the phrase, looking shyly at the stoic woman in front of him and seeing the slight smile he carried on. "We've been friends since you found out about your father's other passion. I'm sorry I had to mention that."

Catherine nodded her head in acknowledgement.

"We met when you sent me to LA to sound out the company. He had worked for Union City Productions and gave me some of the low down you needed. Guess we just clicked. But, although we can't be together all year round, we have built a life together. He knows Clarissa very well. Peter is a friend of both of ours; we met him at a charity ball about five years ago. He has a thing about the Publicity Guru at UCP."

Catherine knew just whom he meant when he said the Publicity Guru. She didn't want to sound eager but needed the information desperately.

"So who's the Publicity Guru, certainly way off track if they came looking for me?"

Paul had been with this woman for the last eight years and knew when something was important to her and this certainly was!

"Jace Bardley."

"Would you believe she's the kid sent to help track me down?" Catherine looked at him closely for his reaction.

"Oh, that's a surprise. Jace is a good kid. She's great for the studio. Since she became Clarissa's aide, the studio has most definitely received better publicity and people really like Jace. James says she's the brightest star in that place; if I didn't know better, I would be jealous." Paul laughed and then noted the closed expression on his boss's face.

"I'm sorry if I offended you?"

Catherine was trying to decipher all the messages going to her brain at once. *'Jace is being courted by the director, had been hired by my enemy, and is sleeping in my house! Could it get much more complicated? So what do I feel about it all? Nothing! Oh, get real Catherine! That isn't a word you can remotely use in this situation. No way, you feel! What do I feel? I haven't let anyone into my heart ever! Well, maybe that's an exaggeration, there was Mother and Lucas, but that's family. Then there had been Adam, even if that had been for different reasons and her greatest achievement and failure, Lucas her son.' Now she was thinking about Jace being added to those that she cared about! Get a life Catherine, everyone around you dies! It's a fact of your sordid existence. Did you think for one moment that you wouldn't have to pay and pay for the rest of your life? Don't let that bad old heart of yours convince you otherwise; it's way too late for you, accept it!'*

Shaking the desperate thoughts away, she answered the pensively waiting VP. "No, no you never offended me Paul; quite the opposite in fact, you made me re-evaluate a few things in my life at the moment. So have you met the very bright Ms Bardley?"

Paul sheepishly nodded.

"Oh, so what do you think?" She hadn't wanted to sound to eager, but she couldn't help her sudden interest. Here was someone she did trust and he knew the woman who was making her re-evaluate her life.

Paul immediately knew from the stance of the woman and her piercing gaze that this was important and not for business reasons.

"She's all that people say; but she has integrity, is totally honest - and that's something in Tinsel Town. How she manages to keep her sense of humour working for Hudson is beyond most people, but she does. Jace is Jace, you just have to love her." His eyes never left the gaze that he was held in.

Catherine didn't want to hear that; she wanted Paul to give her some reason why things couldn't possibly work out! He hadn't. He had just told her all the things she had wanted to ignore.

"A paragon then?"

"Oh no, not Jace. Hell, she is so naïve sometimes it hurts to think that one day someone like Clarissa is going to debauch her; and with Clarissa, that could be trouble!"

"What about someone like me?" Catherine didn't know what to expect, she was just trying it on for size.

Paul looked at the suddenly tense woman and a thought flashed through his mind, but he quickly dispersed it as absurd. "You! Well, if she had you in her corner, then I guess she would remain naïve from most of the hurt in this world, if you could possibly do that!"

Catherine wasn't expecting that! In fact she had convinced herself she was worse for Jace than Clarissa.

"What makes you say that?" Her heart was screaming for answers.

Paul looked her squarely in the face.

"Because you care! Unfortunately for some they can't see that depth. If you ever wanted to, you might just convince them. Anyway, if Jace had you in her corner, I know she would be okay." He smiled and then looked down at his watch it was almost seven. "Guess we have to go."

Catherine looked at her watch and noticed that for once she might even be late. "Yes, better go ahead Paul and let them know I'm coming. I have a call to make." Just as he opened the door, Catherine softly said. "Paul, thank you. When we are alone call me Catherine, okay?"

Paul blushed at the comment.

"Yeah, no problem, my pleasure. Catherine."

He walked out of the door to the elevator and thought. *'Jesus, just wait until James gets a load of this; the great Ms Devonshire has all the symptoms of being in love and with guess who? That is the shocker!'* He entered the elevator smiling.

Catherine saw the door close and picked up the phone and dialed home.

Jace had fallen asleep after reading the first three chapters of the book, which under normal circumstances she would not have been able to put down.

Why hadn't she ever come across this book before? It had 'classic' written all over it! Yet, it was something that had been written over thirty-five years ago and left on a shelf until someone found it by chance. Well, this chance opportunity was one she wasn't going to miss!

One thing she had noticed, which made her grimace in disgust was the publishing company, none other than Xianthos! It was a wonder they ever had the brains or sentiment to discover such an author. Time was a great healer they say, but the pain and bitter taste hadn't gone. She hated Xianthos and its' owner the ever-resourceful Ms Devonshire.

'That woman shouldn't ever come into close contact with decent human beings, because sure, as hell she wasn't decent; certainly not in her business dealings at any rate.'

'Now how did you meet this man, Catherine, because it certainly must have been some match? Wonder if Grace can fill in any of the gaps? Maybe not, I should just keep my nose out of it right? Oh, right!'

Grace looked in on her charge later in the day and noticed that she held the book close to her chest, obviously doesn't want anyone to remove the book and lose her place. *'She must find it very enlightening, as I did.'*

Jace did look better and that's all that mattered.

Now, she had to think of something to cook for the good doctor. *'Oh well, that shouldn't be too hard.'* Smiling she left the sleeping Jace to her dreams.

Around five the phone rang and she knew who it was, as ever Catherine would be checking up! "Hello the Warriorson ranch, how can I help you?"

"Grace how is our patient?" Catherine almost growled at her housekeeper.

"Well, thanks for the greeting Catherine, but Jace is sleeping and looking much better." She couldn't help but smile.

"Hey, I'm sorry Grace, how are things with you too?" She answered sheepishly.

"Fine, Andrew will be here at seven, so everything's on schedule."

"Hell Grace, I didn't know you put your love life on a schedule; Christ what next?" Chuckling at the other end.

"I'll have you know working for you all this time, means my whole life is a schedule; so, what do you want to do about that!" Grace was also smiling the banter from her boss, most unexpected but welcome.

"Oh, give me a couple of days and I'll work it out. So she is really on the mend then?"

"Yes, Catherine. You're worse than the doctor, she's doing well, but you're not going to like something."

"What's that?" taking the defensive at her end of the line.

"You left the book behind and a certain Ms Bardley can't get enough of it!"

There was silence at the other end.

"Are you still there, Catherine?"

"Sure, I didn't realise I left it behind. It's the first time, guess my mind was preoccupied." *Yeah with a small green-eyed blonde that I had just slept through the night with.'*

"Is it okay for Jace to read your copy, I can get it back and give her the paperback I have?"

"I didn't know you had a copy Grace, why didn't you mention it? You could have read mine anytime."

"That's okay. I thought maybe it was a family heirloom or something."

"In a way it is, but.... I would have let you read it Grace. As for Jace, let her read it, I'll be interested to see what she makes of it."

With that, the doorknocker on the ranch sounded and Grace excused herself for a few minutes, knowing her discussion with her boss hadn't been completed.

A motorcycle messenger held out a box, measuring around three foot long and two-foot wide.

"For a Ms Bardley, can you sign?"

"Sure, thanks." She closed the door on the retreating back of the messenger. Putting the box down she went back to the phone.

"So what's going on?" Catherine asked.

"A box has arrived by messenger for Jace, wonder what it is. It's from Christchurch."

"Well, when you take it to Jace, I'm sure you will find out. Now, what else is new?"

Grace informed her of the conversation with Jace as Catherine listened intently but refused to comment. Details about the ranch were soon completed and Catherine wished Grace a good evening.

"Hey, don't go doing anything I wouldn't, okay?"

Grace laughed loudly "Oh, does that give me plenty of rope then?"

"Oh yes! Believe me you would hang yourself hundreds of times over. Got to go, see you in a couple of days."

Hanging up the telephone, Grace wondered about the remark, but smiled as she noticed the box. *'Well let us get this show on the road.'* She picked up the box and went towards the guestroom.

Chapter Thirteen

Catherine was weary after her dinner with her five VP's, although the meeting earlier with Paul had been enlightening. For once, she had taken the opportunity to find out some personal details about her senior executives, which had totally floored them. Well all except Paul, of course, who noticed that his normally stoic boss was actually taking the time out to make small talk? It was really turning into an interesting meeting.

Gareth Cuthbert, her European VP, had been married to Victoria for ten years and had the usual two point four children. That's how Catherine viewed it at any rate. He was quite happy to push them into a boarding school as soon as possible, so that he didn't have to worry about his image. She come across that before? This more than anything else made her dislike of the man credible in her eyes! He was a pompous, arrogant, English, middle class bore wanting to elevate himself to the next rank. *'What the hell, he can be a pompous arrogant upper class bore, for all I care, just so long as he does the job and does it well!'*

Eduardo Forencio was her South American VP. He was swarthy, good looking and single, loved to flirt with the ladies, but always managed to keep out of the final reaches of any one of them. He managed to stop himself the fool by coming onto her as she asked him about his personal life. In Catherine's eyes it was amusing and she enjoyed a little flirting; well she had years before at any rate. Come to that, in the old days she would have done more than flirt herself. He would have been a prime candidate for her bed! Funny how things change, now she found it laughable.

Tito Yashimo her Asian VP, a small compact Japanese, always listening but rarely was given to any mad spurts of creativity. He had a wife and son and appeared happy with his lot in life. She'd always had difficulty making small talk at the best of times and with the Japanese she found it impossible. It was a straightforward list of facts. Oh well, better than getting your ear bent.

Constance Waverly she was the African VP, African descent with a touch of European blood in her heritage. She was a small bubbly woman, who was happy to be single, although she was somewhat cagey about whom she dated. Catherine hadn't wanted to pry, but she was interested in the VP possibly because she was the only other woman at the table. She knew that to have advanced this far in the organization meant that a private life for the woman was virtually impossible. Although, why she should think like that when she had the power to do something about it was a matter of indoctrination, she thought. *'Weird.'*

Paul Strong was by his own admission happy in a gay relationship that had lasted about eight years to date. He got looks from all around the table when he mentioned James and was being scrutinised by Constance at regular intervals.

All in all, it was a very regular crowd, nothing to write home about, as they would say.

Now she was glad she had a few hours without the constant boardroom niggles. That was one part of not going to a regular office that she hadn't missed, the 'in fighting'.

Letting herself into the suite, she glanced around the room and noted it's elegance and style, but something was missing. Something that she hadn't realised she needed until yesterday and that something was companionship. Sitting down on one of the sofas she tugged her shoes off and wondered if Jace was awake? It was after all only ten in the evening at home, probably the good doctor was still around as well! Maybe that would cause too many questions. When had that ever mattered to her! Yet, she didn't want to make Jace feel uncomfortable in the house. No, far from it!

'Guess I'll leave it until I get back then.' She mused and then suddenly grinned as she recalled the earlier conversation with Grace.

Jace couldn't believe it!

Here she was recovering from a virus in the home of the reclusive C X Warriorson and being waited on by her staff. Not only that, but around late afternoon, Grace had arrived with a parcel and a relatively large one too!

"What's this Grace?" Jace asked as the woman put the parcel on the bed.

"Well, you better tell me, because it's just arrived and it's addressed to you personally and came by direct messenger as well."

"But who, other than Peter and the crew, knows I'm here?"

"I don't know. Would Peter have sent you a get well present?"

"Does he even know I'm ill Grace, I've not told him?"

"Yeah, Catherine sent a message to him at the hotel. She told him to cancel your room for the rest of the week. So yeah, he certainly knows." Grace remembered the phone call she overheard last evening, between the Director and her employer and it hadn't been cordial. To her ears it sounded very hostile. Anyone would think they had purposely got Jace ill, or did he think they were kidnapping her or something?

Catherine had finally agreed that Peter could visit tomorrow and she guessed he would certainly do that. Pity, Catherine will still be away.

"Maybe it's from him." Jace answered her own question absently. For some strange reason she felt lonely. Without the presence of Catherine Warriorson the place just wasn't home! *'Oh no, did I say 'home', what on earth is happening to me? If she finds out she's going to run me off the place, being ill won't stop that.*

"How about you open it and see? Do you want me to leave?"

"That's okay, Grace please stay. You never know, it could be alive in here." Jace smiled at the friendly woman, who sat gently on the bed and helped with the unpacking.

Jace reached inside the box and her hand touched something, very soft and wonderful to the touch, grasping further inside she pulled at the object and out tumbled the largest Tasmanian Devil she had ever seen.

It had a wonderful mischievous grin on its face and held in one of its paws a screwdriver and, in the other, a hammer. It had covering its body a light blue shirt and black trousers, with a red and grey tie hanging loosely round its neck. A caption on the shirt said, 'I can fix anything!' Nothing on the toy was made of anything other than soft materials. It was the most huggable toy she could have ever wished to own. Her tears ran unashamedly down her cheeks and Grace had to laugh at the sight of her small guest, being almost enveloped by this huge toy that portrayed one of the most devious characters in the 'Looney Tunes' camp.

"How about I get you some tea Jace, while you rummage in the box for a card or something?"

She left the happy, but obviously emotional woman to look for more clues to the identity of the sender. However, Grace had a really good idea who it could be, and it had nothing to do with a film crew!

Jace couldn't believe it, she was overwhelmed and in her heart she knew the identity of the sender. "Catherine I'm betting on you. I hope I'm right," she whispered into the ear of the giant Taz.

Finding what appeared to be a card towards the bottom of the box, she extricated it and hardly dared look.

Made out in a strong bold script, it read:

Jace,

Sorry, I had to leave you to your bad dreams for the next couple of nights. I'm hoping this cuddly toy can be my substitute. He appears to be in the position to fix things if you wake up in trouble. Although, I suspect he could wipe you under the table on the food issue given the chance. But given his reputation, I would think again about giving him that chance!

Anyway, sleep well Jace, and let your dreams be good ones.

Catherine

The tears that she had shed previously came again in a flood and it wasn't until Grace came back with the tea that she tried to stop them.

Grace had seen many tears in her lifetime and she knew that these were the products of someone who was happy.

"So, you found out our mystery toy sender?"

Jace looked up and choked back another sob; it really was too much this crying for no reason business.

"Yes."

"Well, you going to keep me in suspense?"

"Catherine sent him to keep me company during the night." Jace answered, not wanting to look up and see the hurt, which the words could possibly inflict on the other woman.

Grace started to laugh heartily. Jace looked up astonished.

"So the old recluse does have a heart after all." Grace merrily said. "Strange choice in a night-time companion though, don't you think?" Chuckling at the sight of Jace giving the giant Taz a sympathetic hug.

"It doesn't bother you, that she's sent me a present?"

"Why should it? Hell Jace, I love the woman as a friend! If you have finally got through where so many of us have tried and failed; then the best of luck to you." Grace watched the emotions pass over Jace's face and she smiled.

"I want to be her friend! I need to be her friend! Something inside me can't seem to stop thinking about her! Does that make any sense to you, because it sure doesn't to me? It confuses me, the emotions she brings out in me Grace. I'm just hoping I don't do anything stupid. At times all I want to do is hold her hand and just be there!"

Grace pulled the woman into her arms for a short hug.

"Hey Jace, watching you with Catherine is a gift, one that I hope she doesn't decide to be stupid about. There is nothing in your feelings for Catherine that can be anything but honest, and from the heart. Just give her some time to reconcile herself to having you around. But don't push her too hard Jace. Something this fragile could break so easily and there would be no coming back for a second chance with her. There again, she sure isn't the same lady who woke up at the start of this week, that's for sure. Looking at that present though, maybe she still is our Catherine under there. It sure wouldn't have been my first choice, more a Pooh bear."

Jace hugged Grace harder and sniffled into her shoulder.

"She helped me sleep last night, when the fever got too bad and I was dreaming." It was an explanation of sorts.

"Yeah, I know. You look pretty cute together too!" Grace couldn't stop the smirk from appearing on her face.

"How...I mean when...does she know you know?" Jace stuttered through the sentence.

"Actually no, she doesn't. For now it's our little secret okay? I get the feeling Catherine wouldn't want the fact known that she's a big mushball under that entirely stoic ambience she gives off to the world. What do you think?"

"That's just what she said." Jace laughed and wiped her errant tears away.

"Great, so Andrew will be here in about an hour. Think you can eat something for dinner?"

"Yeah, I'm starving, all this emotion is certainly giving me an appetite," Jace answered enthusiastically.

"Why is it, I think you might just have always had a large appetite?" She left the woman alone with that rejoinder.

"Wonder what she means by that Taz, I'll have to ask her when she comes back later." With that, Jace settled back down into the covers and snuggled up to the soft toy. It wasn't Catherine but she had sent him, so it was better than having no one in the bed at all. In a strange way, he gave off a feeling of safety. Now don't go using that hammer on me at any time will you Taz, or you might just have to explain yourself to a certain tall, dark and beautiful woman and we know how you would react to that! She smiled and her eyes dropped in fatigue.

Grace watched Andrew Simpson drive away from the property and waved as he passed by the ranch houses at the bottom of the drive. It had been a good evening, all told.

Andrew was very entertaining and had enthused over her cooking abilities and organizational skills administrating the household. He'd pronounced that Jace was doing very well and his first assumption that it would be a week for a full recovery was now muted to another day in bed. Then, she should be in a position to leave, if she wanted to.

Jace looked at Grace with the air of someone who had just been given a death sentence instead of being told they were actually fighting back an illness quicker than anticipated. "Don't worry Andrew, Jace has a date with my indomitable employer and woe betide her if she doesn't keep it! Right Jace?"

Andrew looked amused at the colour that seeped into Jace's cheeks at the comment. "Yeah, well I guess... It's not a date, but she said she would see me when she got back..."

"Okay, sounds good to me. Has the good Reverend told you who you're getting in our little community program yet?" Andrew changed the subject quickly, noticing how uncomfortable the conversation was making Jace.

Grace laughed, and smiled at Jace. "No, but I figured he'd send someone up here if she's away. What better time? So, give Doctor Simpson or I might just have to do something drastic to make you talk." She teased him.

Jace watched the inter play and smiled. Grace really was a great person and if she wanted the doctor it looked like she just had to crook her little finger at him.

Andrew smirked. ÓOh, now that sounds like a challenge, I might just take you up on my dear Miss Thornton." He looked at her as she patted him on the cheek.

"Maybe another time, so come on, who are we getting?"

Jace was puzzled what on earth were they talking about. "May I ask what you're talking about?" Not sure if she would be let into the conversation, she had to ask. She was after all a guest, even if maybe a little unwelcome at first.

Grace and Andrew looked at each other and smiled. "Ah yes, I forgot it was the night you arrived, so you won't know what were talking about, sorry Jace." Grace looked apologetic.

"Ms Warriorson, has agreed to take part in a local community project," Andrew volunteered.

Jace still looked puzzled.

"Yeah, but the project is about kids who have had a bad time and people who have the means are taking them in and trying to offer them a new life. The Reverend believes in friendship and love in a very positive, giving way." Grace supplied the rest of the information.

"It doesn't sound like something Catherine would volunteer for, not that I know her that well. It just kind of wars with her reluctance to interact with other people." Jace spoke softly.

"No, it's definitely not Catherine. She unfortunately said the wrong thing at the right time or vice versa, which ever you want to call it. She has passed this task entirely over to me. So, really it's my friendship and love the kid is going to get." Grace smiled sheepishly.

"But if she agreed to it, why shouldn't she get involved with it!" Andrew said in a mildly irritated tone.

Grace put her hand on his arm to settle the conversation. "She was pre-occupied at the time and the Reverend got lucky, I guess. So, Andrew who am I getting?"

He smiled at the woman who he imagined would always defend her boss, no matter how wrong she was. "You heard that the Patterson's got killed in a car crash three months ago?"

"Yeah, tragic for the family. Hadn't they both been drinking at the time and someone else died also?"

"Mmmm, so you do keep up on the local news?" He was surprised.

"Hey, just because Catherine wants her privacy, doesn't mean the rest of us live the same lifestyle. Don't judge others by one experience; that would be very dangerous, especially around here!" Grace flashed him an angry look.

Andrew saw the look and almost thought he'd blown it with this wonderful woman he'd lost his heart too, she was just so easy to love. "I'm sorry Grace, I didn't mean it the way it sounded." He looked shamefaced at her.

Never one to let things fester, she smiled. "Carry on, the suspense is killing me."

"Anyway, yes Joan Simeon died too. She was a wonderful woman." He sighed at the thought; she had worked in the town as the seamstress for over six years after her husband had been killed in a freak accident at work, on this very ranch. "The Patterson's had a son, Jacob. He's ten years old and very wild. No relatives to speak of, and even those that are related don't want him, too much trouble they say."

"Okay so we are getting wild Jacob Patterson, great! Catherine is going to love the local people that much more out of this little episode. Not!" Grace pulled a face. "So, when do I have the pleasure of meeting young Mr. Patterson?"

Andrew smiled. "Actually that's not the only thing." He noticed both women look at him, one in interest the other with, was it evil intent? "Because you have the resources, you get two of them?"

"What? Two of what?" Grace almost shouted at him.

"Kids."

"Come on and tell me, it can't get any worse. Now can it?"

Andrew sort of edged for the door. "Lisa Simeon, she's seven and definitely has no family." He held the doorknob in his hand ready to move quickly if he could.

Both women looked at him in astonishment. Maybe it just did get worse!

"That sounds like a bit of very insensitive planning to me Doctor," Jace said in a very small voice.

"Yeah, I know, but the Reverend insisted, said it was the best for both kids and Ms Warriorson too."

Jace looked at him. "Do you believe that?" She asked gently.

He shook his head and looked anywhere in the room except at the two women.

Grace let out a breath that she hadn't known she held. Jesus, Catherine is going to go ape when she finds out, and who could blame her. I somehow don't want to be the person that tells her, but guess it's going to have to be me.

Jace looked at the drawn face of Grace, which had visibly sagged at the information. "Tell you what Grace, how about I tell Catherine? I'm not going to be here much longer, and well, if she gets mad, she gets mad at me."

Grace glanced at the younger woman, knowing that Jace didn't want Catherine to have any thoughts other than good ones about her. The offer was tempting. Oh, so tempting. "That's okay Jace, thanks for the offer, but I think I'd better do it. Although, I might need the support."

"Anytime." She glanced at Andrew who had lightened up a little at their conversation.

"Go and sit on the porch or something you two, I want to read some more of this book." She smiled at them as she settled down, with the book and Taz snuggled next to her.

"Good idea." The two left her to it.

After that they discussed just about everything under the sun except the new visitors. Now here she was at midnight, contemplating Catherine's reaction to the new additions to the 'family'. It wasn't a pleasant thought. Her eyes strayed towards the foreman's house and she noticed a dark figure outlined against the white decking of the veranda. She looked away and considered her options. Tomorrow was another day and today had been exciting enough as it turned out. She wasn't prepared for any more problems. Problems?

Chapter Fourteen

Catherine was winding up the two-day session with her VP's; the business was doing very well. Her influence was hardly needed these days. Her reputation just worked for her; that was all.

It was time to consider some changes though, and her assessment of her executives, although veiled, had been very thorough.

"Well, another session has come to a close. I'm very pleased with the way things are developing around the world. In two months time, I'm going to want some changes in my VP's; can't let you all get to complacent in your roles, now can I?"

All faces turned to her in shock. They hadn't expected it and to at least two of them it wasn't something they wanted to do.

"I'm going to change all of you around. So if you're not happy with that, I suggest you start getting your résumés out in the market place, because it's going to happen! Is anyone around the table against the idea?"

Paul Strong had been as surprised as anyone at this change in events, but he could see the logic. Now who was going to be the fall guy between Gareth and Tito?

Gareth moved around in his chair and looked a little pale around the gills. Tito looked upset. Constance smiled, and Eduardo just took it all in his stride.

Tito got up from his chair and addressed the chairwoman of the company. "You just said we had done wonderful things with our different market places, why?"

Catherine looked at the little man and knew he was nervous. She smiled, but the smile never went to her eyes. "Don't you think it's a good idea? Wouldn't a VP posting to New York for instance, be a good move for you Tito?"

"I...I think it would be, yes it would, but my family?" He stuttered and ended on a weak note.

"Guess you're looking to quit the company then? Oh well, you win some you lose some." She stared at the other people round the table. "Does anyone else have something to say?" Silence.

"Well, that's wonderful. I wish you all a pleasant journey back to your own parts of the world, and I'll be in touch personally." She got up to leave, then turned around.

"Paul, before you go, I need to speak to you. Say in ten minutes?" She left the room without an answer to her question.

Paul looked around the room and realised they thought he knew something. "Hey guys, I don't know what's going on; maybe I'm going to be the first transfer, who knows?" He shrugged his shoulders.

"I think she's right, we are becoming complacent in our own backyards. What we need is change, she's giving us the opportunity before she has to replace us." Constance spoke decisively.

"Oh, it's okay for you! Your piece of the world is shit, if we didn't bail you out every few months, you would be on your arse out of here," Gareth said with venom.

"Well, if you think like that Gareth, guess Paul might just mention it to Ms. Devonshire that you could do better in my role! I wouldn't mind a piece of Europe for a change of scenery." Constance had never let the European VP score points off her. He was always ready to stick the knife in someone's back and it was not going to be hers. She hated his existence. One day his time would come. He was a pompous ass who still thought there was a bloody British Empire, and an arrogant bastard!

"Wonder where she will send me!" Eduardo chipped in, not really that interested; anyway it would give him new opportunities with the women.

"My family will not move Paul. So, I guess I'd better consider tendering my resignation," Tito said sadly.

Paul knew what it meant to Tito. Hell he was going to have to talk fast with James on this one, maybe he would need to find another position also!

"I have a meeting people, I hope everyone has a safe journey home." He left the room and heard the squabbles from the hall.

Arriving at the suite, he noticed the door was ajar, so he tentatively walked in.

"Oh! Paul, great, my bags have just gone down. They are getting me a taxi to the airport, so I'd better make this quick."

"Fine, no problem." Paul was surprised at her swift exit from the hotel. She usually spent a couple of hours winding down, by walking along the quay.

"I want you to consider taking over as World President. It's a new role, more money, and you will be in charge of the rest of the VP's. I don't need the answer now, but by this time next week, okay! Then you get to sort out the other VP's I hope, if not I will! You get to choose your base of operations also! If you have any questions just e-mail me, or call me in a couple of days. I have to go Paul, safe journey." She walked by him and smiled. "See you soon."

He watched the retreating back of his employer and wondered what had hit him. He sat down heavily on one of the sofas.

"My God, I think she just asked me to take over the empire!"

Grace watched as the hired car arrived, and a very nervous Peter Adamson got out of the car.

"You must be Mr Adamson, Jace's friend, welcome to Destiny." Grace held out a hand and smiled.

Peter didn't expect this cordiality, especially after his altercation with Catherine Warriorson. What next! "Thanks, yeah, I'm here to see Jace, how is she?" He deposited the luggage that Jace had left at the hotel on the porch steps.

"She's doing really well, actually. She got out of bed specially for your visit, s□ please come this way." Grace eyed the luggage in some amusement.

He followed her into the house, which was in a traditional style, but with all the conveniences that modern technology could offer. They walked to the study, where she opened the door. Jace was seated in one of the large armchairs.

"Hey, Jace how you doing?" He smiled, happy to see her basically in one piece, although she did look pale.

"Peter I'm fine. Thanks for coming to visit; how's everyone?"

"They're good, and want to know when you will be back with us? You know you're the life and soul of the party, Jace." He sat opposite her as Grace left them to their chat.

"She seems nice?" He indicated Grace's retreating back.

"Yes she is," Jace answered softly.

"They treating you okay Jace, if you want out of here, I'll take you, no problem. That bitch Warriorson can't keep you if you want to go!" Peter blustered.

"NO! No, it's not like that at all. They have been marvellous to me Peter. I couldn't have been in safer hands." Jace responded with gusto.

He looked at her and shook his head not understanding why she was so...protective. "Well, if you change your mind you know where we are staying and the number."

Jace smiled and they talked about the footage and what Hudson wanted, and briefly, when she would be ready to leave. The filming group had planned to leave on a Sunday flight back to the States and had tentatively booked her a seat.

Jace looked down at her hands, which she clasped together tightly. "That's in four days time. I guess I will be taking the flight Peter."

He noticed her subdued reply. "You don't sound very sure about it. Have you got a reason to stay here?" Had she met someone in such a brief period of time?

"I'm sure," she replied.

"Oh, well that's good then; can't have my best girl stranded here in this out of the way country now can we?"

'If only he knew that this out of the way Country as he called it, would forever hold my heart.' Jace winced at the words that flowed in her head. It sounded so melodramatic, like a lovesick teenager.

They talked for a little over an hour. Then Grace noticed that Jace looked tired and scooted her back to bed. She assured Peter that if he needed to come visit, to just let her know, as she couldn't see a problem with another visit after Jace had rested for a while.

"Thanks, I appreciate you looking after her."

"No problem, we all like Jace here."

"Even the recluse!" He couldn't help the sarcasm in his tone. Something about the woman just set him off.

Grace laughed, "Yeah, even the recluse." And as he walked away she thought. *'If only you knew, the recluse might actually more than like her.'* She walked back into the house and her schedule.

Grace was pacing. Definitely pacing.

Jace smiled wryly at the somewhat awkward pacing with Grace's limp. She had been up a couple of hours, chatted briefly with a very subdued Colin Montgomery. *'Now what was wrong with him? He had seemed so happy that first night she arrived; now, he looked like his best friend had died!'*

Something was very wrong here, but she couldn't quite put her finger on it, maybe Grace might open up a little. Then again, she had almost bitten her head off earlier, so perhaps not...!

Going over to the coffeepot, she noted the time at ten and knew that Catherine was due back around ten in the evening, twelve hours and she would be home! *'I just can't help that feeling of finding my home when she's around, could that be such a bad thing? What would Catherine say? Then again, I'm not likely to find out. I'm going to be leaving the day after tomorrow. Maybe that's for the best, for both of us!'* Her heart begged to differ.

"Grace do you want a cup?" Jace offered quietly.

The pacing woman looked up in surprise, she hadn't really noticed that Jace was in the room with her. "What? Sorry, you asked me something?"

"Yes. Would you like a cup of this excellent coffee that a certain party I know makes really well?" Jace bantered back to try and alleviate the tension in the woman.

Grace smiled briefly; Jace was a really good woman. Pity she hadn't been here from the beginning, maybe things would have been different. Oh well, no use crying over spilt milk. "Thanks. Yeah, I would love a cup." She watched the younger woman silently make the beverage.

"You want to talk about why you're so up-tight?" Jace prodded her shamelessly.

Grace laughed outright at the attitude of this woman whom she had met, what was it, four days ago? "Yeah, I think I do! Thanks."

"No problem. Is it Catherine?"

"Some of it yeah. But it's those kids we're getting after lunch. I think it's immoral that they should be put together. Hell, his parents were responsible for her parent's death and they want them to live in harmony, and to cap it all off, under Catherine's roof. God knows she doesn't want anything to do with this herself. I know she won't be happy about this situation."

"Why do you believe she won't accept this responsibility?" Green eyes looked into brown in question.

Grace snorted. "Something in her past I guess. She was really mad when she found out about what she had let herself into. Can't blame her really, now that we have the facts. But I could do with her support and somehow I don't think that's going to happen!"

Jace looked into the coffee cup she held and sighed. "Maybe she will come round to the idea. Hades, she came around to me!"

"Oh, come on Jace, this is different."

"How? Tell me."

"You know her husband and son are buried on the property?" Grace looked directly back into the green eyes, which suddenly took on a shadowy effect at the mention Catherine's deceased family. *'Of course she didn't know, you dummy! She didn't even know Catherine had been married until I mentioned it.'*

"No, I didn't. Is it far away?" Jace asked in quiet interest.

"Actually it's Cutter's Ridge. She wanted them to see the best of every dawn and sunset that was on the property for eternity. There is no better place than that particular spot."

Jace gasped at the sheer thoughtfulness of Catherine Warriorson. It was like something out of a gothic romance novel; so you do believe in romance after all! "How do you know that?"

Grace sucked in a breath and let it out slowly. "She got drunk one night. I'd been here about a couple of weeks and she was way over the top, told me it would have been what Adam, her husband would have wanted."

"No wonder, she wasn't happy that we were filming there. But, I don't recall seeing any evidence of a burial place?" Jace was unhappy that there would be footage that ultimately might upset the woman she cared about.

"Oh, Catherine wouldn't have been happy about you filming any place on the property. Unless you know where to look, it's a hidden place. Only Catherine, Colin and myself know for sure; other than the local burial agency and the Reverend that attended the final placing of them to rest. The Reverend is now deceased and the others, well they don't divulge that sort of detail, bad for business," Grace spoke matter-of-factly.

"Does she go there often?"

"No, only on certain dates, which I surmise to be anniversaries of some kind. Catherine hasn't been that forthcoming and she kicked the alcohol binges over three years ago."

"Guess she won't be happy that I know about this then?" Jace was upset at the thought.

"Oh! Jace haven't you realised yet? For the first time since I met her over five years ago, she has actually done something for someone and thought about that person beyond her own needs! Nothing, do you hear me, nothing you find out about her will harm her, you will see to that!"

Jace got up from her chair and went over to the other woman and simply hugged her. "Do you know what that means to me?" Jace asked tearfully.

"Oh, god Jace, your not going to cry on me again are you? Whatever would people think?" Grace said flippantly.

"Not much around here I guess." Wiping her eyes, she smiled at the other woman.

"Well you're not wrong there!"

Getting up from her chair, she hauled Jace along with her. "So any ideas, what do kids eat?"

Jace laughed loudly and punched Grace playfully on the arm. "Do you have any cookbooks, preferably with desserts in them?"

"Oh, way to go Jace. If I didn't know better I would think you were a kid yourself." She joked back as she went to retrieve a cookbook.

Catherine was waiting patiently for her personal flight from Christchurch to her local airport to be approved and she would be on her way. She was early. It was only three in the afternoon and usually she arrived well after midnight. That's exactly what Grace would expect. At this rate, she might be home by dinner.

'Funny I've never really wanted to get home this fast. I wonder what has gotten into me this time?' A demon voice that she knew too well prodded her to answer her own question. *'Yeah, I know, I know, Jace!'* She sighed in resignation.

Although, wouldn't she be going home soon and wasn't home, to Jace, the most hated place that Catherine knew in the world. *'Hell, I've run from that place for years, and now it comes and pays me back a hundred times over. Guess you just can't tempt fate too much, huh?'*

She hadn't contacted home since the first evening; so, she didn't know how Jace was doing or how she had received the gift she'd sent.

'Catherine you're going soft!' She smiled to herself at the thought.

Hell she hadn't bought a soft toy since Lucas was a year old! Then she had been relatively happy in a complacent sort of way. Adam had given her the stable lifestyle she had wanted when her brother had died. He had also given her security in not only his love, but also his home and little did she know his business interest too! They had been happy those first two to three years, as happy as she had ever been, since her mother had passed away.

Then her father died!

That had been a shock; he couldn't have been more than fifty-eight if that! She then learned through the lawyers in New York that Stewart Devonshire had passed all his possessions over to his one surviving child, subject to a couple of minor details that she had to uphold.

Well one of them had been easy. Adam, she then found out was a shareholder in the Xianthos Empire, a third shareholder no less!

She wasn't to try and oust him in any way and she had to consider any of his suggestions, just as her father had done in the past. They had argued long into the night on many occasions, once she had taken over the reins, about that part of the will.

Then there had been his involvement with Union City Productions and the young and very shrewd Clarissa Hudson. Oh, that was one fight she had run away from, not because she was scared, but more because her father had wanted it that way. Hudson had made no bones about the fact that she was willing to let Catherine into her life on much the same terms as her father. Only, she wasn't her father, and the thought of sharing anything, never mind her bed with someone as totally devoid of emotion as Hudson, was definitely not an option.

She had done, to the letter, what her father wanted and in many ways her frustration at that fiasco and any other that transpired was heavily aimed at Adam! He hadn't deserved it, hadn't understood her change in personality. But, had it been a change? Wasn't it something she had always been, but he had tried to soothe the image and create a person he wanted rather than what she was. Then her son had become a pawn in the game, games she never lost! But she HAD!

One day she literally turned her back on her family and had done exactly what her father had done all those years before. What did they say 'like father, like daughter'? She had closed her heart to feeling and held everyone she loved at a distance.

Now she was considering, she was certainly thinking about a certain Jace Bardley more than she should, that was for sure. *'What the hell, it was only a toy!'*

She closed her eyes and blinked back the solitary tear that threatened to fall.

A movement to her left made her open her eyes and she noticed the pilot of her personal helicopter coming closer, he looked relaxed. *'Good, that means we're getting out of here.'*

She cocked her head to one side as he spoke.

Grace watched as the Reverend's car drew up the long drive. She was standing next to Jace on the porch. Both women were a little nervous.

Jace for the life of her didn't know why? The day after tomorrow everything would be all over, and she wouldn't see the ranch or its occupants again, she assumed.

The Reverend got out of the vehicle and went around to the front passenger door and opened it. He spoke at length towards the occupant of the front, and then a young boy jumped out of the vehicle. He looked to the entire world as if he had been dealt a lot of difficulties in his young life.

Next, the Reverend went to the passenger door in the back of the vehicle and was handed a doll. That made Jace smile. Soon, a small girl crawled out of the vehicle.

Grace watched in fascination. She was now the responsible adult for these two children; and hell, she didn't have a clue.

Jacob Patterson, was a gangly ten-year-old, who obviously grew out of his clothes quickly from the look of his worn and short attire. He had black hair and a sullen face, although his hazel eyes looked more mischievous than wicked.

Lisa Simeon on the other hand was totally opposite. She had bright red hair and a smile that shone out of her pale blue eyes; in later years she would set many a hearts a flutter that was for sure. She looked delicate because of her size, but her stance gave the opposite view. She looked like an eight-year-old handful!

Jace looked at Grace and grinned. "Guess this is it, better go meet them Grace."

"Yeah, okay." She swallowed hard, and then moved off the porch towards the Reverend and his young charges.

Within a couple of short hours, they had retrieved the personal possessions of the kids and shown them into their respective rooms. Neither child had much by way of personal items; it was plain to see that they had been brought up without the luxuries of life. One, because his parents were irresponsible it would appear and the other, because that had been all her lone parent could afford.

Both children looked a little scared and intimidated by the ranch and the women to whom they had been introduced.

Lisa held onto her rag doll as if it were a lifeline.

Jacob looked sullen the whole time and just scuffed his feet, which, hadn't gone down too well with Grace on her freshly polished floors.

When the Reverend left, Jace went to make some drinks so that Grace could get better acquainted.

Something inside of Jace wanted to welcome these children too! It was, after all, Catherine's home, but she was herself an interloper. What could she possibly achieve by confusing the kids even more? *'Oh Hi, I'm Jace but don't get too friendly because I'm going the day after tomorrow.'* It would be like a slap in the face, not only for them but for her too!

She went towards the next room; peeking inside she saw the three figures, all with very tense body language.

Chapter Fifteen

Catherine steadfastly drummed her fingers on the arm of the seat that she occupied, waiting for one of her ranch hands to collect her from the local airfield. She'd called Colin directly on her cell to give him an e.t.a. He was late!

Perhaps something was wrong at the ranch? She'd been waiting almost an hour. Surely Colin hadn't forgotten? He hadn't mentioned anything in particular being wrong, although he had seemed somewhat subdued on the cell phone. Catherine had put that down to the connection. Grace would have called if things had taken a turn for the worse with Jace. Wouldn't she?

Catherine elevated herself from the chair and strode around the small waiting room. One of the operatives at the desk looked pensively at her and seemed to want to make conversation but thought better of it. Mrs. Warriorson didn't exactly look in the best of moods.

Catherine scowled at the weather, which appeared to be moving towards stormy conditions much in league with that of earlier in the week. A smile flashed briefly across her profile as she thought of the outcome of that particular storm and what, or should she say whom, it had deposited at her front door.

Turning back towards the chair she heard a vehicle approach, and glanced out of the window to observe a green Land Rover stop immediately outside the building as close as possible to the door.

She took in the tall appearance of her ranch foreman. *'So, Colin opted to come himself, interesting.'*

Colin walked swiftly to the door and as he entered shook off the droplets of rain that had landed on his hat. He walked towards Catherine's bags and nodded to her.

Catherine was amazed! He would normally have been bending over backwards to explain why he was late, but not this time, this time he just looked grim.

"Are you ready Ma'am?" He had reverted back to his subservient role again verbally, but his actions gave an entirely opposite reflection.

"Yes, let's go home before it gets any worse." She followed him out of the door of the airfield office not bothering to acknowledge anyone as she left. He swiftly pulled open the passenger door of the vehicle for her and then went around the back to stow her luggage.

She discreetly watched his profile as they pulled away from the airstrip and contemplated her next course of action.

She could just leave it and stay silent? She could discuss the weather and try and get a response? She could ask about the ranch and get him to review the last couple of days? No, none of the above! Nope the best course of action was definitely the direct sort, nothing else would get a response that she was sure of!

"Okay Colin, why do you look like the end of the world is nigh, and why were you late?" She didn't look away from her observation of the passing fields out of her window, her remarks suggesting a bored interest.

He shifted uncomfortably in his seat. His jaw clamped shut, and then he opened it again, but nothing came out.

"I haven't all evening Colin, so spill it!" She growled at him, now becoming frustrated with the situation.

He turned briefly to face her and then appeared to derive a decision. "I'm late because I needed to attend to something for Grace and all the other boys were out taking in the stock prior to the storm." He answered grimly.

Catherine pondered that answer for a few seconds. "Must have been an important task Grace wanted you to complete, if it meant keeping me waiting. Did she know it would do that?"

"Yeah, she knew." He answered knowing full well that Grace didn't know it personally affected Catherine.

This certainly wasn't turning into a pleasant drive home, not withstanding the fact that it was now pouring down rain. "So, did you get the task completed?"

"Yes," he answered tersely.

"Good. Would that be the reason for what's bugging you?"

He didn't answer.

The drive was like asking twenty questions and receiving replies to only a few of them and those replies making only partial sense.

"Guess Grace has some explaining to do when I get there, you're obviously not very forthcoming." Catherine drawled in frustration.

He remained silent, and the rest of the journey was taken up with the sounds of the approaching storm.

Grace had taken about all she could handle with the boy and he'd only been on the ranch for less than half a day!

When she'd sent Lisa to retrieve him from his room for the early meal she prepared for the children, she wasn't expecting the young girl to come running back shouting he was gone.

Jace had gone to take a nap. She had looked exhausted by the time she'd helped with the children's possessions, and then helped Lisa to get settled in her room. Grace had promised to wake her when Catherine was due to arrive home. Jace reluctantly left Grace with the two new residents of Destiny.

Beating a quick detour to Jace's room and getting her out of bed, both of them scoured the house but couldn't find the boy. The weather was closing in too, great!

"Jace, we can't let him stay out all night, we have to find him?" Grace said her voice a pitch higher in her anxious state.

"I know, I know, but what about a group of the men searching for him outside on the ranch, he can't have gone far." Jace tried to placate the apparently frazzled looking woman in front of her.

Grace sighed, she hadn't wanted to ask Colin, he had been very grumpy for the last couple of days, but what choice did she have? Taking the cell, she'd called Colin and explained the situation, he had said that he had to leave on an errand for Catherine, but Grace had overridden that. Explaining that Catherine would want him to find the boy first.

Grace had flitted around the kitchen making some cookies, because she didn't know what else to do!

Jace had taken the small girl and sat her in the corner of the warm, homey kitchen and told her a story about dragons and knights and fair maidens. The little girl had been enchanted, but she too looked worried, especially when the rain became intense.

Half an hour later Colin walked in almost frog-marching a very stubborn boy in his wake! They both looked very bedraggled and Colin looked none too pleased.

"Is this what you're looking for?" He held the collar of the shirt that Jacob was wearing. The young boy was looking decidedly sullen and uncooperative inside the shirt.

Grace smiled in relief. Both Jace and Lisa chuckled quietly in their corner of the room as they saw the state of Jacob.

"Yes, that's exactly what I'm looking for. Thanks Colin." She turned twinkling brown eyes to his grey, but he never returned the warm glance, he just turned on his heal and left.

Grace had been perplexed, but was so relieved at having the boy back that she dismissed him out of her thoughts for the moment.

"Jacob why? Catherine isn't going to be happy about you wanting to run off."

Jacob turned his hazel eyes to her and shrugged in defiance. "What will she care, she doesn't want us? We heard about her in the orphanage!"

Jace looked at him and then back to Lisa, her small charge, looking sadly at the floor. Grace turned her glance to Jace and silently asked for help.

"What did you hear Jacob?" Jace asked him gently.

He looked at the smaller woman and then to the little girl. "She will tell you the same." He pointed at Lisa, taking a defensive stance at the question.

Jace took Lisa's small left hand in hers and gently squeezed in understanding. "I guess as the oldest you have the prerogative to explain it to me?" Jace asked him surprising the young boy with her gentle rejoinder.

He looked at her with a defiant expression, but became mesmerized by the green eyes that looked directly at him with warmth. Not at all like the others; they just hadn't liked him, but she wanted to listen. "They said."

He was stopped as Jace countered. "Who are they?"

"The people who run the place, the man in charge, I heard him!"

"Okay Jacob, what did they say?" Jace gently tried again.

"They said that Mrs. Warriorson wouldn't want kids around the place, she hates kids! Maybe she would have us work on the ranch, but not as part of the family!" He rushed through his tirade.

Jace looked at Grace, who was looking at both children with a mixture of pity and surprise that adults had let the children overhear that type of insensitive comment.

"Mrs....Warriorson isn't used to children, Jacob. Maybe that's why people have gained the wrong impression. When you meet her she might just prove you wrong. Why don't you give her a chance? Just as she's giving you one," crossing her fingers, she said the last sentence.

Jacob looked around the kitchen and scuffed his foot against the floor, making Grace cringe at his abuse of the highly polished sheen.

"Maybe I will!" He looked at her with a frank gaze.

Jace smiled briefly. "Glad to hear it! Now young man, I think a change of clothing might be in order, and then we can all eat. Don't know about you but I'm starved." She laughed and smiled down at Lisa, who grinned back at her and nodded.

Grace laughed and looked at the boy, who for the first time in over five hours since he'd arrived at the ranch actually smiled, if only briefly. *'Well, that's got to be a start, let's hope Catherine is in a good mood when she comes home.'*

Jace left Lisa with Grace to help with the final preparation for dinner and led Jacob off to his room to replace his wet clothes with a set of dry ones.

Clarissa Hudson had talked to Peter Adamson about the filming in New Zealand. He had been a little cagey, but then admitted what had happened to Jace and she had laughed. Peter privately didn't like the woman, but on a professional basis she always gotten the funding for the obscure projects. He'd often wondered how, and now he had a very good idea.

"She's actually on the recluse's property staying as a guest?" Hudson asked him again, her tone calculating.

"Yes, it happened by accident. We thought Warriorson was a man. Jace went to confront him, and it turned out to be the woman who left us on the ridge in a storm." Peter sounded peeved that he had to explain the situation to Hudson.

"Oh well, it looks like Jace might get our coup after all, maybe a private interview with the reclusive Catherine Warriorson?" Clarissa was amused and surprised that her PA had gone to such lengths to make a point.

"Jace is ill, she might not get the interview. Warriorson is away!"

"Well, you said she was coming back with you Sunday, so I guess she's not that ill!"

"What more do you want us to do?"

"Nothing, your job is done. Take a couple of days off, see the sights. I hear there are some marvellous places to visit if you're scenically minded."

"What about Jace?"

"Oh, Jace is fine exactly where she is, believe me this couldn't have worked out any better. See you in LA, Monday." She disconnected the line.

Clarissa was a tall willowy blonde, she was thirty-three and had the intellect that made her a very powerful woman within her own defined realm. The only fly in her ointment was Xianthos and, in particular, the owner herself.

'Oh, I've been looking for you Devonshire and now I've found you, well paybacks were always a bitch and you spurned me! We could have been great together. But, oh no you took the noble way out. Not Daddy's spoils, you were too self-righteous. Must have been that ineffectual person you called a husband who caused that particular trait to surface! But I know better. Daddy told me of your exploits and your prison term. Baby, if you don't take me up on my offer this time, I'm hanging you out to dry.' She laughed loudly to no one but herself, the sound echoing around her sparsely furnished office.

"My Dear Jace, you have been a godsend, and oh, how I'm going to enjoy what you bring to the table this time." She walked out of her office into the midmorning sunlight. LA this time of the year was really quite wonderful.

Catherine grabbed her laptop and bolted out of the vehicle as it glided to a stop outside the ranch house. She left the rather morose ranch foreman to struggle, or not, with her bags. All she wanted to do was retreat inside from this god-awful weather. Running as if she was being chased by a tornado, she stumbled into the front door and whisked away the droplets of rain from her face.

It was only seven in the evening and she heard unfamiliar voices in the kitchen, did she hear children? Placing her computer on the hall table she walked quickly to the kitchen. Opening the door she looked around and saw what could only be described as a very cosy, domestic scene.

Grace was surprised at seeing her boss walk into the kitchen looking somewhat sodden and not a little up tight. *'Oh shit!'* she thought before she spoke. "Catherine, I didn't expect you until later?" was all Grace could mutter!

Catherine looked at Grace and saw her surprise; she then glanced across at two children, a boy and girl, who looked at her in equal parts awe, fear and defiance. Then her heart flipped a beat as her glance rested very briefly on Jace, who looked flushed but good. Jace looked equally as surprised as Grace. *'Hadn't anyone informed them I had arrived in the country for god's sake? I'm going to have an interesting conversation with Colin!'*

"What the hell is this? Alice's tea party?" She couldn't help the frustration of the last hour or so being transmitted to her voice.

Grace looked at the children and smiled briefly getting up from her chair.

Jace frowned at the sharp tone of her 'friend'.

The children shrank back into the chairs they were seated in.

"No, no it's definitely not that; unless, you're the mad hatter of course? Then again maybe your bursting into the room would give that impression." Jace stated blithely, trying to bring some light relief to the conversation-taking place.

She ignored the look she got from Grace although she thought it might be one of relief. Instead she concentrated on the ice cool stare she received from those remarkable blue eyes.

Lisa giggled at Jace's comment and Jacob laughed outright; then both children looked down at the table, not daring to gauge the expression from their new guardian.

"Oh, so we have appreciation societies too do we? Anyone care to tell me what these children are doing in my house?" Catherine said sarcastically, pointing a slim finger in the children's direction, with all tact blown out of the window.

"Yes I could, but maybe it would be better if you and Grace talked privately and I'll take the children into another room." Jace turned her gentle green eyes onto the impaling blue ones.

Ushering the two children out of the kitchen, she snagged the cookie tray as she departed, leaving the two women alone.

Catherine blinked several times as Jace left with the children and couldn't help but smile as she saw her take the tray.

Grace seeing the look realised that all wasn't such a lost cause. "Do you want tea, or something to eat before we start?"

Catherine still had her gaze on the closed door, her attention leaving with the departed blonde. "Yeah, whatever," she answered absently.

Grace had seen lots of emotions pass over Catherine's face in the past five years but she was totally thrown by the look she saw today.

It was a mixture of censure, puzzlement and happiness. Jace had completely outsmarted her and in such a very nice way.

"She's something else isn't she?" Grace said tentatively.

Catherine wiped an errant drip of rain from her eyes and turned to Grace and smiled, all her frustration now dissolved. "That's for sure. How is she? She looks good," Catherine asked turning her attention back to Grace.

Grace carried the teapot over and poured them both a drink. "Jace is well on the way to recovery. In fact, I don't know what I would have done without her today."

Catherine looked at the milky substance in her mug and a tense expression came across her face. "Did Adamson try to get her to leave?"

"Not exactly, the film crew is leaving on Sundiy, she's going with them, but she would have told you that! I'll miss her." Grace added, knowing that although her friend might think the same she wasn't likely to ever say it, not to her at any rate.

"Oh, well, I guess I was expecting that. You obviously have taken a shine to her over the last couple of days?" Catherine replied still a little absently.

"Yes I have, she's like a ray of sunshine and today especially with the kids. Well, that's another story."

"Yes, so what's with the kids?" Catherine looked mildly interested, the welcoming tea soothing her previous agitation.

Grinning, Grace passed her a hot pastry and proceeded to inform Catherine of the present situation.

Jace scanned the contents of the lounge, she hadn't been here before and plonked the children in front of the large twenty eight inch TV screen, or it could have been larger she didn't really know. It certainly would have dwarfed her apartment living space.

Jacob had resisted until he saw the Simps□n's were being screened and he sat in front of the set. "You'll go all goggle eyed if you watch it that close Jacob, come on sit here it's a good distance for you."

He looked at her, and then back to the screen. "No."

"Well that was sure to the point." Jace said under her breath. "Come on Jacob, Lisa is sitting in a chair."

He snorted at that and looked at the little girl, who was having trouble staying awake. "She's nearly asleep that's why." He pointed out.

Knowing that Rome wasn't built in a day she shrugged. "Well, if you end up with glasses then don't blame me!"

He looked at her and smiled, it actually made him look boyishly handsome. He remained seated on the floor but moved towards the chair and sat with his back against it. Fifty-fifty trade off Jace thought.

Moving over to Lisa who was struggling to stay awake, Jace gently picked up the small child and sat in the chair with her pulled her on her lap. The sleepy child smiled and snuggled next to Jace. "My Mom used to do this, when I was tired." The child said matter of factly.

"You miss your Mom honey, a lot I would think?" Jace cradled the child to her chest.

"Yeah, she would always tell me stories before I went to sleep. No one in the place we were at did that, they were all too busy," the child explained.

'Well, not tonight! And not tomorrow either, if it was the only thing she could do for these kids she would tell the child a bedtime story.'

"Well, my dad used to tell me stories too when I went to bed. Do you want me to tell you one of his tonight?" Jace smiled at the child.

The child looked at her in total innocence and trust. "Yes please." Then she snuggled deeper into Jace's chest.

"Good, because I think I would like that too." Jace's own nostalgia with the situation evident in her voice as she hugged the child closer.

Jacob watched the exchange furtively.

Catherine was moving round the kitchen in agitation. "I can't believe he would do that!" Grace had just explained all the facts to her boss, it wasn't going down well, but she'd known that would be the response anyway.

"Well, neither did we! But he has, and we have them, and that's the long and short of it." Grace said in resignation.

"For gods sake that's insensitive to both those children, does he expect them never to know the outcome of that night? I'm going to see him tomorrow and get this mess sorted out." Catherine paced around the room.

"Maybe you should talk to Jace?" Came the quiet rejoinder.

Catherine looked at her with a steely glance. "Why?"

Grace tried but failed to stop the blush as she said the next words. "Because, she's important to you, and I think you might value her opinion!"

Catherine couldn't stop the faint colouring of her skin as she frowned. "She's..." no more words came.

Grace looked at her and saw the frown. "Do you know how you feel or what you want Catherine?"

Catherine glanced around the comfortable kitchen and sighed. "It would be easy to say my life as it was, but that's not possible any more! I want what's best for us all." She simply stated.

"Then you better think fast, because she's out of here at the weekend." Grace said bluntly, sometimes you just had to take the bull by the horns and this bull was sure stubborn at times.

"Yes I know that! But... Grace I'm not good at relationships, hell I don't even know if she wants my friendship?" There was a heartfelt sigh at the end of the sentence.

Grace paused at Catherine's shoulder and placed her hand on it in understanding. "Why don't you go and change, and then see what Jace is up too. You might be surprised about her reaction."

"Maybe, but you're right I could do with some dry clothes. Hell, what's up with Colin these days, he was very strange on the way back here?"

Catherine changed the subject, and the action brought a wry smile to Grace's lips.

Grace looked down at the table and shrugged. "Beats me!"

Catherine glanced back at Grace, now she knew the reason. *'Jesus, the man hadn't even attempted to ask her out he had just left the field wide open for the doctor! Guess that's another thing I'm going to have to solve at a later date.'* But first, her own affairs, or rather lack of them!

Grace watched Catherine leave the kitchen. *'It was kind of strange Colin's reactions these days, but it didn't have anything to do with me, I haven't been near him for the last couple of days. So, I definitely wasn't to blame for his mood.'*

Catherine changed quickly and headed towards the lounge where she could hear the TV. Walking into the room, she smiled softly as she saw Jace sitting, or was it lying comfortably in a chair with a small redheaded child snuggled happily next to her. The child was almost, if not asleep. Jace was tenderly stroking her hair. It was quite the loving picture and the tall woman sensed a very warm feel surging through her body and was experiencing an unusual lump in her throat.

Then she saw the boy, he was watching some cartoon on the TV his hands where tucked under his knees, he was smiling at the antics of a dog and cat; she didn't know which cartoon it was. He looked relaxed, he had dark colouring very much like Lucas, and he was about his age, or the age he would have been had he lived. That brought a sharp pain to her chest and she without realising it let out a gasp as the recognition struck her.

Jace looked up and saw the anguish on Catherine's face and where she was looking. *'Had her son looked like Jacob, perhaps a little? What a traumatic event it must be to lose a child and one so young too.'* She turned her head towards the woman and smiled, hoping in some small way her understanding would help.

Catherine looked at Jace as she turned and saw the warmth in those green eyes. She smiled back and moved over to her. "See you have a handful there?"

Jace smiled and kissed the child's red locks above her chin. "Yes, she's tired but I think she wants to stay up with Jacob."

Catherine looked at the boy engrossed in the cartoon. "Well, it's almost nine, do you want to call it a day for them?"

Jace hesitated and then nodded. "The cartoon is almost over anyway."

Waiting for a few minutes, they watched the end of the cartoon, Catherine from her elevated standing position and the others from their chair or the floor respectively.

Jace started to struggle up with her precious cargo. Catherine noted this and stooped down. "Let me." She gently scooped Lisa up and put her over her right shoulder. The child was asleep and never moved.

Jace acknowledged the support and smiled. "I thought you'd left this to Grace?"

Catherine smiled. "Mmmmm, I suppose I did, but then again you are a guest and this is my house. I have other responsibilities now don't you think?"

Jace laughed quietly. "Oh, Catherine I think you just made an under statement there."

Catherine raised her left eyebrow and grinned. "You think so?"

"Yes I certainly do!" Jace responded.

"Okay, so what about the boy?" Catherine moved her head towards him.

"He's going too!"

"Fine, he can bring up the rear. Which room doe{ Little Miss Alice here have?"

Jace smiled at the slowly retreating back. "She's got the one next to mine."

Catherine turned back slowly and met the green gaze. "That means he's next to me?" her voice held amazement.

"Yes, I guess it does, do you have a problem with that?" Jace looked as if she wanted to laugh loudly at the affronted look on her friends face.

"No, no it will be fine, for now!" she disappeared through the door.

Jace sighed and looked at the boy who was clearly tired, but didn't want to succumb to his tiredness. "Come on Jacob time for bed, maybe you can stay up later tomorrow."

He scowled at her, but got up nonetheless and followed her out of the lounge.

Jace watched Catherine open the door of Lisa's room, and as she went into the room she saw the tall woman place the small child gently on the bed. Jace picked up the rag doll the girl carried everywhere with her and placed it close to her pillow.

Jace looked at Jacob as he watched the settling of his new 'sister', he wasn't sure if any of it was real, maybe he would wake up tomorrow back in the orphanage, maybe he wouldn't.

'Somehow, this is all going to work.' Jace just knew it, she felt it, there weren't any words that could adequately say why she felt that way, but it was going to be okay, for all of them!

Colin had stripped off his wet clothes for the second time that day!

He was annoyed with himself for letting things that he couldn't do anything about affect his relationship with his employer.

'Christ, I almost bit the boss's head off in the car. Added to that I haven't adequately apologised for being late and I blamed Grace for it too! I don't know what's wrong with me these days?'

He walked over to the dresser and got out a pair of faded denims and a very old sweatshirt, pulling them on, he sauntered towards the window that looked out onto the drive and towards the main house.

Colin wanted to kick himself, he knew what his problem was, and he just wasn't prepared to acknowledge it fully yet.

He had been a shy child, his parents had tried to bring him out of his shell, but it hadn't worked. Then his mother had died of a fever when he was twelve, leaving him and his father to carry on with their small holding and not much more. His father had continued to mourn his wife's death and it was no surprise that one day he'd had an accident with his shotgun. Colin had been alone since he was sixteen.

He then moved around the Islands, first the North and then finally settling on the South Island and experience from various holdings.

He was now thirty-six years old, with a very stable job and all the responsibility he wanted. What he hadn't acquired was anyone to share it with! Now, when he thought he had found the right person, it was all going wrong, he had no special skills like the Doctor. He wasn't good when it came to talking, so being romantic just wasn't something he'd ever experienced. Now he was watching, as the one person he wanted in this life was slowly moving towards a different direction and that direction didn't include him in any way!

Catherine was right; I should have asked her out! But is it way too late for that, after all the boss will have explained to Grace that I blamed her for being late, would there ever be a time I could ask! He hung his head in silent remorse for his bad attitude towards Grace.

Then he sat down in his chair and closed his eyes as a single tear cascaded down his strong profile. He wiped away the tear. *'Men aren't supposed to cry, we're supposed to be the strong ones, but wasn't that all bullshit! We feel love, pain and anguish; sometimes it's just the right time to let it all out.'* He tried to stop the continuing trickle of tears but his heart wouldn't let the emotional turmoil cease.

The room darkened but he remained in the chair, letting his desolate mood take over.

Grace sat in one of the easy chairs in the lounge as she watched Jace try to keep awake. She knew the blonde woman was tired after the full day they had, even the hour she had managed to steal before being woken abruptly hadn't helped.

Catherine was smiling as she too watched Jace try to chase away closing lids of sleep. "You know you didn't have to read a story to the child Jace, it's not something I want them getting used to." Catherine said gently.

Jace smiled. "Oh, I enjoyed it. My dad used to always read me a story when I went to bed; it sort of shut out the bad dreams. I think both these kids may well have bad dreams Catherine, you need to watch out for them."

Catherine looked at the green eyes that pierced her blue glance with a look of sympathy and compassion for the children. "Well, that's going to be Grace's domain. I'm certainly not going to tell any children's stories."

Grace smiled at Jace as she responded. "Okay I'm game, but I'm still going to need your support with them!"

"I told you Grace, that tomorrow I'm going to see that idiot who left us in this mess, I should have it cleared up by the evening!" Catherine gave an exasperated sigh at having to solve another problem forced on her. She turned her eyes to the window and the storm lashing away at them.

Jace looked aghast at the comment and looking towards Grace for understanding of what had been implied Jace receive a shrug of the shoulders only. "What kind of comment was that suppose to infer?" Jace quickly pushed all thoughts of sleep from her mind.

Catherine was surprised at the angry tone Jace used. "Why, the bloody Reverend of course. He's going to have to re-think this situation. What else do you think it means?"

"You're going to send them back!" Jace shouted at the woman standing at the window.

Catherine looked at her and pinned her with an icy look, outraged that she was even questioning her it. *'Wasn't it her home?'* "Yes, that's exactly what I'm going to do, what did you expect?"

Grace had hoped that Catherine would see it differently when she saw Jace with the kids, but obviously she hadn't. Now the blonde looked devastated as she looked at the rigid back in front of her. "I had hoped you would have compassion for them, they have lived through enough heartache already. To have you throw them back into the sea again without giving them or YOU a chance, is more insensitive than anything the Reverend has done already!" Jace's green eyes began to fill with tears.

Grace shifted uncomfortably in her chair and wanted nothing more than to leave the room, but she also wanted to hear what Catherine would say to that little outburst by the obviously upset blonde.

Catherine saw the tears in the green eyes and she almost fell to her knees before the young woman to ask her to forgive her for hurting her. But she couldn't! This was something she felt strongly about. "I'm sorry if you think that my actions will result in even further insensitivity, that isn't my aim. If you'll excuse me I have some work to do tonight, goodnight." She walked out of the room without a backward glance.

"She's just going to leave it at that!" Jace spoke quietly to Grace, anguish clearly written over her expressive face. "Why is she running away from me?"

Grace came over to the chair that Jace was huddled in and put a hand on her shoulder. "I was kind of hoping you might have swung her round in the kids favor, but.......... Jace, come on let's get you to bed you look exhausted and I'm a little drained myself. How about we try again in the morning, you never know she might change her mind overnight, stranger things have happened, and keep happening in this house."

They walked towards the stairs and Jace glanced at the door to the study and wondered not for the first time, what made Catherine Warriorson tick. She certainly was a mass of contradictions.

Catherine noted that it was two in the morning; she hadn't achieved much by way of work either! Her mind had been numbed by the shocked and surprised look on Jace's face when she had voiced her plans on returning the children! *'It's not that I wouldn't be prepared to have a kid here on the ranch, but this situation was wrong, morally wrong!'*

'Oh, yeah! And what do you care about what's moral or not? Where do you get to be the savour for peoples morals, it's laughable and in your case sad!' Her inner voice depreciated her arguments. *'You of all people have thrown morality, scruples and honesty out of the door more times then you can count. Suddenly someone who could stand for morality, who has scruples, who is honest, wants you to reconsider your stance and you walk all over her. What sort of friend would you ever be?'*

Catherine watched the thunderstorm and shook her head at her thoughts. Whispering to the empty room. "No friend, no friend at all! Jace will be better off without me and shortly that's just what's going to happen."

Getting up from her chair she switched her desk lamp off and went into the hall and up the stairs to her room. Walking by the room occupied by the boy, she heard noises, which had nothing to do with the storm raging outside. This, she knew was a storm raging from within, pain of the most demanding sort, which only someone who had experienced it first hand would ever recognise. She did!

It would have been so easy to just close her mind to it and move on by but that wasn't what she was all about not now. Knocking softly she opened the door.

There under the blankets was a ball of small humanity, moving to take away the covers and showing the bundle underneath, she saw the child's eyes take on the expression of a wounded animal, hurt and sadness all mirrored there. Slowly she sat at the edge of the bed, not wanting to scare the child anymore than he already was. Taking his hand she softly stroked the palm to try to quieten the storm that raged. "Hey it's okay, it's only the storm." She tentatively tried to blame the storm for his distress, knowing he wouldn't want to look like a baby in front of her.

He hiccoughed, and looked into her ice blue eyes with his frightened hazel ones. She continued to look directly back at him and smiled, her eyes gently indicating her understanding of the pain. She moved her hand to his unruly hair and smoothed it back. "You know tomorrow it's going to look a little bleak out there, but then the sun will eventually shine again you know."

Suddenly he looked at her with a trust she had seen recently but from green eyes. *'God what was she doing, this was becoming a regular thing for her, whatever would people think? They could think you might actually care!'*

"You going to be able to sleep now?"

"Yes.... thank you." he smiled tentatively back at her.

"You're welcome kid, let's get this bed straightened up, or you might catch cold too!" she said brusquely but softly to take away any perceived sting.

"My name is Jacob, not kid, and it's Jake to my friends." he offered her a hand.

She looked at the boy and the proffered hand and couldn't help the chuckle that escaped.

"Well Jake, my name is Catherine, pleased to meet you." she shook his hand solemnly as he settled back down.

"Goodnight Jake, see you at breakfast." She watched him close his eyes and noted that before she shut the door he was asleep.

Closing the door, she retreated to her own room and went to look out the window. The stars tonight were obscured by the stormy conditions, but she knew they were there and it made her smile.

'Guess it's not so cut and dried as I thought, maybe there was some mileage in having the two kids here, god knows it couldn't be worse than the orphanage now could it?'

She slowly went over to the en-suite bathroom and started to peel away her clothes, it had been some night. *'All I really wanted to do was spend some time with Jace and get to know her better. Hell of a way to do that, she thinks I'm some sort of monster now! I wonder if she sleeps tucked up to that soft toy I sent her?'*

She went to shower before getting into bed and trying to dismiss the thoughts of what it would be like to change places with that particular soft toy.

Chapter Sixteen

Grace was waiting for Jace to appear for breakfast, the kids had arrived a few minutes before, and although a little shy at first were now settled down to orange juice and cereal. They occasionally glanced her way and she smiled at them, the little girl had a very infectious smile, just like Jace.

'Maybe if Catherine saw that...oh what the hell, she only ever saw what she wanted.' Grace thought with frustration.

Catherine was in the basement exercising.

Jace rolled in at that moment, waved hello to the kids and said 'hi' to Grace, then sat in her usual seat opposite the head of the table. "So is our fearless leader up yet?" Jace knew the answer to that one without Grace turning back and laughing at her.

"Oh, okay just wondered if she'd changed her mind, you know 'stranger things have happened' syndrome."

"Jace has anyone ever told you that you are way too chirpy in the morning?" Her new friend quipped back.

"Nope, because actually I'm not usually. Quite the opposite, but something here brings out the best in me," she supplied with a warm friendly look.

"Can I guess what that might be?" Grace smirked and received a backhand from the blonde playfully.

"Please, not in front of the children!" Jace laughed, and winked at the two sets of eyes that were watching the banter in fascination.

"Okay, where is she?" Jace quietly asked Grace, her eyes sparkling mischievously at the children.

"She's in the basement working out, always does when she gets home from a trip, and she's been down there over an hour so she should be through shortly." Grace supplied.

Jace frowned, then her face cleared and a smile came unbidden over her expressive face. "Hold the breakfast for me, I need to see someone." She got up quickly and moved towards the door to the basement.

"Jace, she doesn't like to be disturbed, and what you see might make you...." She trailed off as the blonde disappeared down the steps. *'Guess she'll find out for herself.'*

Jace hadn't heard the last comment or she might have been tempted to listen further. She was fascinated though at what sort of exercises Catherine would do. Opening the large oak door, she emerged into a room that held a couple of bench presses, weights, bike and rower. Then she noticed a punching bag and from there, Jace saw her target.

Her jaw dropped.

Catherine stood on a wooden floor, obviously specially put down for aerobic exercises, but she wasn't doing that. In one corner was a stereo system that was pounding out 80's tunes the quality excellent. The song currently resonating out of the speaker system, '*When the Going Gets Tough*' by Billy Ocean. However, it was the woman in question that made Jace stare.

Catherine was wearing tight fitting navy cycling shorts that accentuated all her lower body parts, and a cut off T-shirt that did wonderful things for the woman's upper body. Her rhythm as she responded to the tune was overwhelming. She was swaying and dancing and moving as if the music was part of her blood stream. '*Erotic and very sexy*', came to Jace's mind and stayed there.

Jace sat by the side of the punching bag, wondering what had hit her; '*punch drunk*' came to mind.

She watched fascinated as the hi-fi pumped out further tunes, '*La Bamba*' by Richie Valens and then carried on through Culture Club's '*Generations of Love*,' it was the movements the raven haired beauty made to the Stranglers '*European Female*' that made Jace gasp for air. Seeing shoulders move and sway in fluid grace and her hips grinding to the music, and if she ever moved like that on a dance floor god's help who was dancing with her, it was just sex on the move! '*Did she even know how she looked?*'

Suddenly Jace moved a fraction, causing Catherine to turn in surprise. Shocked to find someone else in the room with her.

Catherine was covered in perspiration, beads of moisture evident on her upper lip and forehead, her hair was damp and the clothes she wore had dark traces of moisture all the way down her back. Jace noticed the predatory look and the animal magnetism that sparked from her.

Catherine was involved with the music but crooked her finger at Jace, without thinking Jace moved towards the finger as if hypnotised, as Infinity began the intro to '*Only You*'. Jace was danced around and was obviously being played with by a very sexy, tall, dark and beautiful woman, who mesmerised her.

The song pounded out.

"*Looking into your eyes, I see only you, can you see only me and how I love you?*"

Catherine touched Jace's cheek as she traced a finger from her eye to her chin. Always moving to the beat and the flow of music around her.

"Dancing with you close to my body, do you feel what I feel?"

Her hand moved from the chin to her neck and traced the collarbone.

"Watching the moonlight and the stars glowing, do you glow like I do for you?"

The hand then moved in a sweeping motion around her body without touching her physically but making her tingle with anticipation.

"Thunder crashes out a tune, lightening illuminates the gloom."

Her hand moved to her back and traced a line from her shoulder down to the curve of her hips.

"Going to sacrifice my will, if you listen to me speak of love."

A hand lightly traced down her chest to her taunt abdomen, Jace was on fire.

"You're the power behind persuasion, you succumb to this liaison."

The touch then travelled lightly down her thighs as Catherine moved fluidly down to an almost kneeling position all in time with the music.

"Holding my cheek close to yours, I feel the pulse of your soul and know it's only for me."

Moving languidly up Jace's body with a movement that didn't touch but spoke volumes, she gradually moved away as the last beat of the music slipped away.

Catherine bent close to Jace's ear and spoke in that low sexy growl that Jace loved. "I think by the look of you a shower wouldn't come a miss, you appear a little hot!" A small smile appeared, which gave her a rakish expression.

With that the music changed to Dire Straits *'Twisting by the Pool'*, not waiting for an answer to her observations, she shot off making several cartwheels across the floor and landed precisely next to a medium sized indoor pool.

Jace watched in awe and fascination as Catherine nonchalantly peeled off the T-shirt and the shorts and leaped into the pool totally naked. Coming up to the surface at the other end of the pool with no idea obviously, what she had just done to Jace's body and mind with that little show of exhibitionism.

'Great Zeus! She just made me turn into a puddle on the floor with that show. God's what would it be like if she really meant any of it for real!' Jace turned and fled the room. Opening the door and running up the short stairway, she cannoned into Grace at the top.

Grace held her shoulders as she noticed the heightened colour and raspy breath. *'Way to go Catherine, it works every time!'* "Oh, so she saw you did she?" Jace couldn't speak she just nodded her head.

"She's quite something when she exercises wouldn't you say? For such a big body she can sure make moves that make the old heart rate pound a bit!" She chuckled at Jace's glazed look.

Jace finally managed to choke out. "A bit! Grace have you seen what she can do to music?"

"Ah, that good! Well, if you ask her I'm sure she won't mind you joining her, she asked me once, I only lasted about ten minutes."

"Why?" Jace asked with interest, the glazed look almost dissipated.

"Well, she moves far too fast for me, and it is just so difficult not to just watch her move wouldn't you say? Then again she made me far, far too hot to continue that on a regular basis, you need a cold shower afterwards." Grace laughed as she recalled her first sight of the tall sexy woman dance around the room. Catherine had wanted to help Grace with her leg exercises and had thought it a good therapy. It wasn't the therapy that quite went with leg exercises that was for sure.

"That's exactly where I'm going, a shower definitely! Maybe a cold one at that!" She left Grace behind.

Grace smirked at her back. *'Catherine didn't know when she was onto a good thing, such a pity.'* She went to make fresh tea; Catherine would be up after her swim shortly. She just knew she would have a large grin on her face when she finally arrived.

Catherine dressed leisurely after her swim. She had gotten a bit carried away with Jace, but she thought the blonde had looked like she was enjoying the attention and it had been ages since someone else was involved. Actually, it always made it a little bit more exciting for her. Mind you, with the way Jace looked after they'd finished that particular routine, maybe it had been too much for her; she was still recuperating after all.

'No, Jace hadn't needed to do anything, I made all the moves, it felt good to lose all that tension of the last couple of days. Hell, it had only been a dance after all and only exercise too!'

Smiling as she climbed the stairway, she walked into the kitchen and found Grace lounging against the breakfast bar watching her enter.

"What!" Catherine asked as she noticed the smirk on her friend's face.

"Nothing! Did you enjoy your workout?" She turned to pour her a mug of tea.

"Yes indeed, you know me, I like to get rid of the tension caused from being a few days away from here." Catherine said quietly.

"Our guest join you for a workout too?" Grace watched the smile fade slightly from Catherine's face and an expression, of was it pleasure passing over it, then she looked down at her tea as if she was embarrassed.

"She was watching mostly, but I let her kind of join in on one session."

"I bet you did! She looked kind of flushed when she returned up here, looks like you haven't lost any of your skill in that area." Grace laughed at her friend, who coloured up slightly.

"Now Grace, whatever do you mean by that?" Feigning innocence.

"Oh, as if you don't know! I needed a cold shower after watching you workout, I'm scared to death to do it again, I might faint next time."

"I would catch you before you fell Grace, never fear of that." Catherine said seriously.

Grace looked at her and smiled warmly as the blue eyes looked back at her with a similar expression. "I know, but I'm not giving you the chance of dunking me in the bloody pool if I did."

"So where is Jace? Come to that`where are the kids?" Catherine asked with interest, changing the subject.

"Jace is getting a shower," they both laughed at that. "The kids are having a tour round the property, seems Colin is in a better mood today, said he thought it might help them settle in." She waited for the woman to retort with an angry comment.

Catherine looked out of the window of the kitchen. Almost talking to herself she said, "It looks bleak out there today."

Then the door opened and Jace walked in. She looked at Grace and smiled and then to Catherine as she sat opposite her. Her cheeks coloured slightly then she spoke. "That was one of the most fascinating shows of exhibitionism by a person I have ever seen in my life!"

Catherine gave her an amused look. "Oh, you didn't like it? Helps me to get rid of the tension. Too bad, I'm not giving it up."

Jace looked at her and realised that this woman really didn't know the effect she had on people, certainly with a display like that! "I would never ask you to give something up you really liked doing. Anyway when did I say I didn't like it?"

Catherine smiled broadly. "Good. What's for breakfast Grace." she once again swiftly changed the subject and they had an amiable meal together.

The two women watched as Catherine got into her Land Rover and headed out towards town, neither had approached her on the forbidden subject of the previous evening.

"What do you think she's going to do Grace?" It was a whisper.

"What she does best I guess, intimidate the good Reverend until he backs down, then we get a change of kids." Came the resigned voice of one who had known the woman longer.

"I don't think she wants to do it!"

"Why would you think that?"

"Because before she left, she was watching the kids closely as they went round the corral." Jace answered.

"So, what difference does that make, she watches everything around here, you should know that?"

"Her eyes weren't cold Grace, she looked at them in anguish, especially when she looked at Jacob."

"Oh, well it must hurt her still, when you think her boy would have been his age and from the pictures I've seen of him, he would have looked like her, so the dark looks of Jacob would stir memories. She's not totally devoid of emotions, although she can give that impression." Grace glanced at Jace, puzzled at where this was leading.

"Oh, I would never call Catherine Warriorson devoid of emotion. Maybe cut off from her emotions some, but never devoid of them. I think she wants to let them stay, but she has a principal to uphold and she's going to do that no matter what, even if it might cause her pain." Jace smiled wearily.

Both women saw the children approaching and Grace smiled tenderly as she saw Colin Montgomery being led hand in hand with a chatty redheaded small girl, who kept giving him a big smile, every time she looked up.

The boy was walking amiably along too, his attitude in stark contrast to yesterday, almost as if overnight some strange miracle had happened to him.

Colin brought his charges into the kitchen. He looked at Jace and smiled briefly. Giving Grace a cursory glance, he whispered something to Lisa and she gave him an unexpected hug, he looked embarrassed.

Jacob watched as the big man blushed. "You can't let girls get to you Colin, they're only trouble."

Colin looked bashfully about the room trying to find a spot on the wall he could look at, instead he turned to where Grace was watching him. "Trouble son? Yeah I suppose you could say that! Now behave yourselves, the both of you, I have work to do!" He walked out of the door that led to the porch.

Jace laughed loudly. "Well Jacob, in what way are we girls trouble, huh?"

He looked around and realised he was alone in this one. "Ah, well...I guess sometimes anyway," he trailed off.

Lisa took pity on him and walked around to him and put her small hand in his slightly larger on. "Jake is going to be a rancher too, when he grows up," she proudly said to the others in the room.

"Oh, well that's nice. Colin's training you young then?" Grace asked him in interest.

Jacob looked at the little girl and shrugged, but didn't drop her hand.

"No, Catherine will!" He stated importantly.

Grace looked perplexed and Jace was astonished.

"Hey, who said you could call her Catherine?" Grace finally asked in surprise at his use of the name.

"She did!" He said proudly.

"Does that mean I get to call her Catherine too?" Lisa said excitedly.

Jacob gave Lisa a long-suffering look. "Not unless she says, but I'll ask her for you." He said and Jace watched fascinated as he squeezed the smaller hand.

'Oh, Catherine if only you were here to see this, it is so special.'
Jace couldn't help thinking as a tear threatened to fall.

"When did she say you could Jacob?" Grace persisted.

"I'm not lying if that's what you think?" He looked at her with the sullen expression of yesterday.

"Hey, I'm sorry, no I never thought that Jacob, come on if she did, she did okay? How about some flapjacks, one of my specialties?" Grace was upset that the child thought the way he did, but it was very odd, very odd indeed.

"Well, I'm up for that, I don't know about you two!" Jace answered with a grin.

They all rushed forward towards Grace and the goodies.

"I'm not happy about the situation!" Catherine almost shouted at the smaller man seated in his office, in an annex of the church.

He shook his grey-haired head and gave her a sympathetic smile. "I know it's two children and that must have been a shock, but you do have the resources," he said quietly.

"No! No, that's not it at all! I could take on the whole bloody orphanage if I wanted too!" She said in exasperation.

"Is that an offer?" He looked directly at her and smiled.

"No!" She had wanted to get this over with as soon as possible.

"Pity. You're not happy about what exactly?"

"Why? Why those two kids!"

"Because they need each other and I believe you might find you need them also!"

"That's about the most stupidest comment you have ever made to me yet Reverend! You're insensitive to the potential explosive situation here obviously." Catherine was angry she wasn't winning this encounter.

"No, believe me I'm not. I trust you and your particular 'skills' can defuse it before it ever gets to explode." He said quietly but with conviction.

Catherine looked at the older man at the desk and she recalled Adam's strong resolve when he'd wanted something so badly, he had often won her over by his quiet patience to get a point across. In the early days at any rate. "That's a big responsibility for anyone to take on."

He smiled happily. "Yes but you're up to it, you have never backed down from a challenge, so my sources tell me."

Catherine raised an expressive eyebrow. "Oh, and who might that be?"

"I'm a man of the cloth Mrs. Warriorson, that would be betraying a confidence and I'm not about to do that!"

"You're not Catholic, I'm sure it wasn't a confessional." Catherine dismissed his remark. *'The damn clergy had more rules and regulations sometimes-mere mortals didn't have a bloody chance!'*

"No, you're right I'm not Catholic, but we still uphold confidences." He continued to smile at her.

"All right, so what happens next?" She finally asked turning her back to him and looking out of the window.

'Gotcha!' He laughed to himself.

"Well, depends on you really. Obviously we will check up on the children at intervals, quite frequent at first and then less often as they settle in. If you want to adopt them later, well the way is clear." He waited for her answer.

Catherine stiffened when he mentioned adoption, which was definitely not an option! "Okay, well I guess that's it for now," she turned to leave.

"Oh, just one other thing Mrs. Warriorson, that lovely young American lady who was in your home when we brought the children over, is she going to be here permanently? She was excellent with them." The Reverend looked at her and noticed her change of expression from one of impatience to a tender smile and then she masked it as suddenly, making him wonder if he had actually seen any change to her visage at all.

"Jace? No, Jace is a guest, she's going back to America on Sunday." The tone she used was one of practised indifference.

"A pity, a great pity, she would have been an asset to you, especially now." He held his hand out in a gesture of the conversation finally ending.

She took it and shook it briskly, opened the door and left.

The Reverend smiled at her retreating back, this had gone better than he had anticipated.

Catherine got into the Land Rover and considered her options. *'Not many, no she didn't have many options. Hell, we'll just have to get on with it! Wonder if Jace wants a career change, nanny for instance?'* She smiled at the thought as her mind did a double flip and another thought took over. *'A nanny for the kids, or would it be a personal nanny for her! Oh yes, I could think of one thing for certain you could do for me every night Jace that's for sure.'*

With her thoughts firmly in the gutter she revved up the engine on the vehicle and started for home.

Chapter Seventeen

The house was quiet when Catherine arrived back home, she for some reason felt lonely.

Walking around, she spotted that Grace had made preparations for dinner but it was as yet un-cooked. There was no sign of Jace or the kids. *'Is this how I will feel when Jace finally leaves tomorrow, has the young woman got so under my skin that it wasn't a home without her in it?'*

She went into the study and sitting at her desk picked up the Wall Street Journal from the pile of financial newssheets that lay there. Glancing through it, but not really taking any notice, she was restless. *'Would Jace consider staying longer if I asked? I could arrange it! I'd only have to deliver a message via Paul to Hudson, and there would be nothino Hudson could do about it!'* There again Jace had a right to chose what she wanted to do with her life, it would be just manipulation on her part and then what would happen to their friendship, it wasn't exactly past the fragile stage yet. Friendship a general purpose kind of word to use for how she felt about Jace, but that's what it was surely? Yes, that's what it was, she'd never felt this strongly about anyone before, but that's what it must be, that's the only thing it could ever be! Or was it?

She turned as she heard a knock at the study door and the particular young lady in question peered into the room, and then smiled as she saw exactly what she was looking for. "Ah, so you're back?" Jace walked further into the room.

Catherine smiled and got up from her chair and walked towards the other woman, they stood together, eyes gazing green into blue. "Yeah, about half an hour ago. Been anywhere interesting?"

"I took the kids to see the horses, they love them."

They continued to look at each other, trying to gauge which of them should start the conversation; they both wanted it out of the way.

"So.... well, did it...what I mean is..." Jace stopped as a long slim finger touched her gently on the lips.

Jace was mesmerised by this woman for the second time that day. "It's fine Jace, they get to stay. We'll work it out." Catherine answered the question softly.

With that Jace couldn't help herself she hugged the woman hard and put her hands round her waist. It almost felt to Catherine as if she had finally come home.

"Hey, I didn't know it mattered to you that much?" Catherine smiled her chin resting gently on the top of the blonde head.

"Yeah it did and to Grace too!" She replied tearfully.

"Then it looks like my household is going to be happy tonight, do we need to celebrate?" Catherine disengaged herself from Jace but for some reason felt bereft when she did so.

"That's an excellent idea, come on lets go and tell them." Jace clutched at Catherine's hand and pulled her along.

Catherine gave the young woman a tolerant glance, and allowed herself willingly to be pulled to wherever Jace wanted, if it made her happy, nothing else mattered.

Catherine was listening to Jace tell Lisa a story from her chair by the window in the lounge. Jacob was half listening to Jace and watching a rugby match on the TV. The story winning him over as she weaved the tale of two friends who lost each other in a forest, then had to go through various meetings with other forest dwellers before they were united.

When Jace had finished, Lisa was almost asleep, fortunately she had been bathed and in her night attire prior to the story telling. Jacob was told to go and clean up, he scowled briefly until Catherine gave him a stern look and he retreated.

Turning back suddenly he said to Catherine, "Will you come by and say goodnight?" his tentative question made Jace turn towards the other woman in the room in surprise.

Catherine turned a shade pinker as she saw Jace look closely at her. "Sure, give me a yell as you get into bed, okay."

"Yeah." He ran up the stairs with a happy smile.

Jace moved in the chair ready to take Lisa to her room. "Here let me?" Catherine stated as she picked up the small bundle.

Jace stretched as she let go of her precious cargo. "Thanks, but I could have done that." Came the protest from the blonde.

"I know you could, but why bother when you can let me?" Came the low response. Both women looked at each other and smiled as they made their respective ways to Lisa's room.

Settling the child in the bed, Jace pushed the covers to her chin and tucked them in the side of the bed. Bending down she gently placed a kiss on the little girl's forehead.

Catherine watched in fascination and wondered what it would feel like to have those lips kiss her, then shook that thought from her head. Impossible! Catherine moved to the back of the room, as Jace made certain the child was asleep.

She turned and left the room and went back to the lounge with Jace following behind a few minutes later.

"I left the door ajar a little, just in case she has any bad dreams and needs someone."

"Yeah, good idea. Wonder how Grace is getting on with her date in town?" Catherine mused as she sat in the chair next to Jace.

"Oh, knowing Grace she will be having a great time, she's a very fun loving woman that one!" Jace smiled as she thought of her new friend.

"I know, she thinks you're wonderful too!" Catherine watched Jace look at her in confusion.

"I guess it's mutual then," Jace's face turning pink.

"Yes, most definitely." They then sat in companionable silence for a few minutes.

"What time do you leave tomorrow?" Catherine hadn't wanted to think about Jace leaving but it wouldn't go away and not acknowledging it only made things worse.

Jace looked at her friend, this wasn't exactly how she had envisaged spending their last few hours together, although she hadn't known what to expect.

"Peter is due to pick me up around ten in the morning, we have a coach waiting at the hotel to take us to Christchurch."

"I see. What time is your flight to LA?"

"I'm not sure but I suspect around six in the evening, funny we get the day back when we get home, passing the international dateline and the time zone differences." Jace spoke softly, giving Catherine the information she requested.

"Will you ring me...us, when you arrive home?"

"Sure I'd love too, but it might be at a strange time here."

"You know us by now Jace, it's up all hours around here!"

"Do you ever come over to the States?" Jace held her breath as she waited for the answer.

Catherine pinned Jace with a warm blue gaze but then looked away.

"No, no I never go to the States!" She answered tiredly.

"Is there any reason for that? You travel, I know that much about you! Do you have interests in the States?" Not sure if she was over stepping her limit on the friendship line, she waited.

"I have extensive interests in the States, but I leave it to other people to cover it! They no longer need my skills shall we say."

"What if I said I needed your skills, would you come to LA for me?" Jace didn't know how she had dared pose the question and what she really expected to gain by it, but it was way too late to take it back now!

Catherine turned to look at Jace and with her heart hammering in her chest she put a hand out and stroked a finger gently down her face.

"Do you know what that means to me, you're wanting to have me in your life?" was the soft reply.

Jace couldn't breathe, so she certainly didn't answer immediately. The gentle touch on her face was doing far too much damage to her senses.

Then she finally gained control of her vocal chords. "No, tell me what it means to you Catherine?"

Catherine smiled, she looked very beautiful and entirely too sexy, for Jace's peace of mind. "I haven't wanted to be in anyone's life for quite sometime now, for you to ask me and for me to consider it, well let's just say it's a milestone in my life."

"So, will you come over?" Jace wondered if she should quit while she was ahead.

Catherine shook her head. "I'm sorry Jace, it's just not possible anymore, not for me!"

Jace looked in anguish as she saw the pain of old memories flicker over Catherine's face just as she was about to ask what was behind the memories.

"I'm ready for bed now!" Came a reedy, young male voice from the staircase.

Catherine looked at Jace in apology and shrugged her shoulders as she exited the room to say goodnight to the boy.

Jace watched the retreating back and knew that the subject would be dropped; it wasn't as if they were anymore than friends, now was it? How could she keep on at a subject that obviously upset her friend?

Gods, but I love you Catherine Warriorson, whatever it takes, however long it takes! I'm going to be there for you and one-day maybe you can love me too! You're far too important in my life to let you go and I'm not going too, not now, not ever!'

When Catherine came back in the room, Jace held the leather-bound book she had borrowed and read, and offered it back to her.

"Have you finished it?"

"Yes, it was a classic. Your husband was a romantic." Jace looked for a reaction from Catherine, she received a shrug, not what she had expected.

"Yeah, well he believed in the eternal love principle I think."

"You didn't share that concept then?"

"Ah, no not exactly, I married him for security and stability when things got rough. I guess I loved him in a way, but not how he wanted or needed to be loved." She smiled briefly and looked out of the window.

"So, you're still looking for your soulmate?"

"Somehow, I think that doesn't apply to me Jace, I can seriously say I've never been in love, never will be, I'm not capable of the emotion."

Jace gave her a sad look from those green expressive eyes. "You're wrong Catherine, there's always someone out there for everyone, you just haven't found them yet, but don't ever give up looking."

Catherine looked at the anguish written on the expressive face, her words sounded familiar but she couldn't quite grasp the memory. "So you believe in the concept of a soulmate?"

"Yeah, I do. Until I'd read the book I hadn't quite put a name tag on it, but it says exactly what I believe in." Jace accepted once again the subtle change in direction of their conversation.

"Well, you and Adam would have gotten along fine. I hope you find your soulmate Jace, and it's not too long in finding you." Catherine smiled wryly.

Jace linked her hands with her friend's and smiled. *'Oh Catherine if only you knew, you're my soulmate and one day you will realise it too!'* "I hope so too!" she replied as they spent the next couple of hours talking about Jace's job and the ranch, it was all trivial stuff but it made both women feel happier, until they finally felt exhausted enough to leave each other's company and go to bed.

Leaving each with their thoughts and dreams and expectations for the future.

Chapter Eighteen

The house was very calm considering that everyone seemed to have been up for ages.

Grace had arrived home sometime in the early hours but still managed to get up at six in the morning and start the day. Fortunately, it was Sunday so she had managed to stay in bed that extra hour later that they all indulged in on the ranch. She had almost dreaded this morning wondering how Catherine would react when finally Jace left, not to mention how Jace herself would react. Certainly it had been an interesting few days; never more so for the constant state of flux the household had been under ever since Jace's arrival on the property. Yet Grace was pleased, it had been a rough road for Catherine the last five years. Having little knowledge of what Catherine had been like prior to her time here but if her penance had been loneliness, then she had certainly received her fair share of that. Now things appeared to be changing, Jace had opened up Catherine's eyes to other possibilities Catherine might not know it yet, but it was working.

Grace hadn't been in the kitchen more than ten minutes when Catherine arrived. She slumped down in the chair by the table and looked at her friend. "Have a good night?"

Grace smiled at the rather terse phrase. "Yes, Andrew took me to a barn dance it was excellent, with lots of people and everyone enjoying themselves."

"I'm pleased, you going to make a habit of going out every Saturday evening?" Catherine asked her casually.

"Would it matter if I did?" Grace eyed her thoughtfully.

"I guess not, although I might have to find someone to baby-sit."

"Ah, the kids! I kind of forgot about them, will you be going anywhere on a Saturday evening?" Grace couldn't help it; she knew damn well that when Catherine was on the ranch she never went out, so her response would be interesting.

"Yes, the kids! You don't really expect me to be the bottle washer and nappy changer do you!" Catherine sounded and looked petulantly at her.

"I wasn't aware that they had that requirement, unless something happened last night and you haven't told me about it yet?" Grace eyed her with interest and a smirk.

"Figure of speech." Catherine did look a little embarrassed at her description.

"Just out of interest, how come the boy calls you Catherine? I wasn't even aware you had talked to them on an individual basis."

"I...Well...he, Oh, it was a deal we struck that's all; I get to call him Jake which suits him better."

"I see, what about Lisa, is she going to have the privilege too?"

"Yes, Jake asked me that same question when I put him to bed last night."

Grace almost dropped the teapot and mug, which she was about to pour for Catherine. "YOU! You put him to bed?"

Catherine raised an expressive eyebrow. "Yes, is that a crime?"

"Is what a crime?" Jace Bardley sauntered in and smiled at the others in the room.

Both women looked up and in unison said, "Nothing!"

Jace laughed and shook her head. "Okay, I get the picture not in front of the guests, huh?"

Grace chuckled and motioned her hand to the coffeepot and Jace nodded her head.

Catherine gazed deeply into her mug of tea.

"Penny for your thoughts?" Jace asked Catherine.

"What?" Jace smiled gently at the woman opposite her.

"A penny for your thoughts, you do look deep in thought, just an old saying."

"Oh! Yes, a penny, a penny for your thoughts," Catherine said distractedly.

"You seem a little distracted today, anything wrong?" The younger woman persisted.

"No, no I'm fine." Catherine gave her a small lopsided smile but it was very clear it was an effort for her to maintain it.

Not wanting to push the woman, she turned her thoughts to Grace. "Grace, how did you get on with lover boy?"

"Oh, come on Jace, he's just a friend, but we did have a good time." Grace smiled broadly at the chatty young woman she looked happy this morning, which she hadn't expected.

"Great, so fill me in?" With that the two women talked about the dance and various other topics, Catherine remained silent throughout, glancing on occasions at the animated blonde in front of her.

At seven, Colin arrived and as the two women were still chatting about Grace's exploits the previous night. Catherine deemed it a good idea to go to the study with him and they would finish breakfast there. Grace shrugged her shoulders but didn't say anything.

As they left, Grace smiled wryly at them. "You know that's the first time in over five years that we haven't sat down together for breakfast if we are all on the property."

Jace frowned. "Well, looking at them, I suspect they will either both come out of there smiling or with even longer faces than when they went in." She then giggled at the thought of the frowning man and the stoic woman. *'Wonder if they'll ended up with indigestion.'*

Grace starred after them and smiled. "You could be right about that Jace. Although you know she's sad because you're going."

Jace let her cheerful visage drop a moment and sadness appeared on her own face. "I know I feel the same. Actually Grace I probably feel worse. But she knows I can't stay and she can't leave so we have to do this."

"Yeah, but at what cost to you both?"

"Oh, I'm going to try and pursued her to come to LA and visit."

"She hates LA!"

"What! What ever makes you say that?" Jace gasped at the words.

"Because she once told me it had bad memories for her, something to do with her father, but beyond that she didn't say." Grace saw the pain register in her new friend's face and felt sorry for her.

Jace looked devastated. One of the reasons why she felt so happy was because she was sure that she could persuade Catherine to visit but maybe it wasn't ever going to happen. "Hey Jace, keep asking maybe one day she will put that episode in her life away and you will see her."

"I will!" she whispered.

Grace went over to the oven and brought out some cookies. "For the journey later, we can't have you starving on your way to LA."

Jace got up from her chair and hugged the other woman. "I'm really going to miss you!"

"The feelings mutual." Grace hugged her back.

Jake walked slowly into the kitchen and didn't know if it would be better to leave the room and come back in or just make a noise.

He coughed indiscreetly. *'Women!'*

Both women turned and gave him a tearful smile. "Ah, great another victim for my cooking." Grace pulled out a chair for Jake to take and she patted him on the shoulder.

He looked at Jace and raised his eyebrow. *'Hades! Was he related to Catherine? He certainly had that mannerism down pat.'* Jace wondered in fascination.

"You have a problem with that eye?" Jace asked him.

"No! But I wondered why you have to leave today?" Jake sounded interested.

"I am on assignment for my studio, by chance I caught a chill and Catherine allowed me stay here to recover, but I need to go back home." She patiently explained.

"You don't like living here?" Jake asked her in concern.

Jace glanced at Grace and smiled tearfully. "Yeah, I like it here, but it's not my home Jacob. I live in America my career, family and my friends are there."

"You have friends here too!" He protested.

Jace looked over at Grace, who eyed her with compassion it couldn't be very easy for Jace to answer his very logical, but painful questions. "Yes, I hope so!"

"Then you could stay here, Lisa will miss you!" The boy pointed out to her.

"She will soon forget me Jake, it's only been a couple of days and people forget." Her heart dropped at the thought. *'Please gods don't let Catherine ever forget me.'*

Little did they realise but Catherine had been listening to the conversation and her heart was pounding at the injustices of having met someone who could fill a void in her life, but it was being torn away almost as quickly as it came into being. "What if she doesn't will you come back to see us?" A low, gravelly voice, which would always send Jace's heartbeat racing, sounded from the doorway.

Jace looked deep into ice blue eyes, which held a question in them.

'She's telling me something and I don't understand what! So help me just say the words Catherine if you do I would stay with you forever.'

"We will have to see, I guess next time I have holidays available." Jace wondered how she managed to control the emotion in her voice.

"Holidays right, I tend to forget about them." Catherine ventured further into the room and stood by Jake's chair.

"Yeah, you always do! It's a wonder Colin and I don't sue you for lack of them." Grace tried to temper the emotional charges that were evident in the room.

Catherine smiled, "Okay, I won't answer that, it may incriminate me at a future date."

Pulling away from the table she looked out of the window. "Not as bleak today what do you think Jake?"

The boy was obviously smitten with Catherine because his grin was so warm when he looked at her and answered the sullen look completely gone. "Yeah, definitely not as bleak, it really is getting brighter."

She looked back at the boy and gave him a brief grin in return.

"I'm going to take Tralargon out for an hour, I'll be back before you leave Jace." With that she left the room for the stables.

Jace was dismayed she'd hoped that Catherine would spend what little time she had left here with her but that wasn't to be. "I think I'll go and check up on Lisa, see what she wants for breakfast." Jace left the room quickly tears very close to the surface.

"Is Jace mad at me Grace for asking her to stay?" The boy asked innocently, a little worry seeping into his eyes.

"Don't worry about it Jake. It's a question she wanted to be asked unfortunately you're not the person she wanted it to come from!" She patted his arm and gave him some sausages and bacon with hot buttered toast.

Catherine walked beside Tralargon on Cutter's Ridge her hair being whipped back by the steadily worsening wind; it really wasn't a good day to be up here at all. "But it's where I first met you Jace Bardley and for my sins it's where I left you to suffer with your friends."

Her inner voice continued. *'If you hadn't you would never have had her in your life as you do now!'* Catherine looked at the landscape; even in this wild weather it still looked a fascinating scene.

"I know that!" she spoke into the wind.

'So, why are you letting her go?' The nagging voice continued to taunt her.

"Because it's the best thing for her! I'm not into long term relationships, it just never works."

'Admittedly you never let yourself have a long term relationship before you arrived here but what about Grace and come to that Colin?'

"That's entirely different they work for me." Catherine turned her face towards the south-facing ridge and watched a waterfall cascade into the running stream below.

'Jace indirectly works for you!' The insidious voice still plagued her.

"I know! This is different she doesn't know that! I want to keep it that way." Turning towards her mare she vaulted up on her back with practised ease.

Catherine turned her head and shouted into the increasing wind.

"Because god damn it, I LOVE HER!" the cry from her heart pierced the wind but there was no one around to hear it and it carried ineffectually over the ridge.

The voice had done its worse or best it all depended on your point of view.

Catherine galloped off down the ridge back in the direction of the ranch she had something to do.

Peter Adamson arrived exactly as promised. He helped Jace with her bags and then went to wait inside the car as she asked him too.

He knew that something had changed with Jace but he didn't know what! Maybe, when she got back home it would all fall back into place?

Jace hugged Lisa and told her to ask Grace for a bedtime story from time to time! "What about Catherine too can't she tell me one on the nights Grace can't?" It was such an innocent childish question. MCatherine had her back to the door on the porch and just shrugged

Catherine had her back to the door on the porch and just shrugged her shoulders. "Maybe." It was a very noncommittal reply.

Jace whispered something into Lisa's ear and the little girl smiled and nodded.

Jace went over to Jacob. "Hey Jacob don't go trying to out do Catherine in the horse riding skills just yet will you she might get mad." A gentle-teasing note came from the blonde's voice.

He gruffly held out a hand to her, as she took it he said. "It's Jake and I won't, well not this week anyway."

Catherine smiled briefly at his comment. This kid certainly wasn't what they had been told to expect.

Jace looked tearful and muttered, "Thanks Jake."

Turning to Colin she looked into the grey eyes of the tall rangy man.

"Thanks for everything Colin I don't think you know exactly what bringing me here meant to me in the end?"

He smiled at her and then held out his arms and she ran into them and was held in a very tight friendly hug. He whispered into her ear.

"Oh, Jace Bardley I think I do." He then gently let her go.

That left Grace hovering.

Without a word they both hugged each other and the tears that threatened fell profusely. "You know what I'm going to remember the most about you Jace?" The emotional voice said next to her ear.

Jace looked into her brown eyes. "What?"

"Your kindness and your compassion, but above all that, the tears! I've never known anyone who can cry so much!" Her eyes twinkled with humour tinged with sadnuss.

"Oh, gee thanks." Jace looked towards the car and saw that Peter looked a little agitated.

"I'd better get moving thanks for looking after me Grace."

"Anytime my friend."

Catherine didn't move from her position by the door, it didn't look as if she was going to either.

Jace smiled tearfully at her. "Thanks for your hospitality Catherine and your caru."

Catherine shuffled her feet and all eyes were on her response.

"No problem Jace, I hope you have a safe journey home." Her voice sounded bored.

If this was a let down then Jace was positively deflated what did she really expect. "I'd better go." She turned away and rushed down the steps towards the car.

Seconds later she heard the pounding of those same steps and a hand clutched at her arm. Jace looked into the ice blue eyes of the woman she loved and once again was unable to understand the message being relayed.

"Why can't you tell me?" Jace asked softly.

Catherine swallowed her throat felt dry. She suddenly hugged the younger woman to her. "Thank you for offering me your friendship," she said fiercely, her chin resting on Jace's head.

Jace whispered into her chest. "I want to offer you so much more!" was the anguished response.

Catherine felt a tear drop on the blonde head. "I know! It's just too late for me Jace."

"Why? Why too late?" the anguished response drifted in the air between them.

Catherine didn't answer and she released Jace and propelled her towards the car as Adamson thrust the passenger door open.

Jace wasn't given the opportunity to say more.

As the car turned to leave Jace saw Lisa run up to Catherine and place her small hand inside the larger one. Catherine looked down in surprise but didn't remove her hand then Jake joined on the other side.

Jace smiled a bittersweet smile and tears began to fall even faster if that were possible.

Peter Adamson looked at the figures gradually getting smaller as he left the property behind. *'Jesus it felt as if he was watching an episode of 'Little House on the Prairie'. You just couldn't understand events in life some days.'*

Catherine bent her head to the small fair-haired child and asked her what she was doing.

"Jace said you would be sad. So, she asked me to hold your hand because she couldn't do it herself."

"I see, did she tell you that also?" she glanced at Jake once again a faint memory refused to take shape at the action of these children.

"No, but you looked like you needed it!" He replied with sincerity.

"Great, what I need is a drink! Who's game for a milkshake? I want the lime one!" She turned and walked back towards the house with two children hanging onto her. Discussing the merits of Strawberry, Chocolate and Banana flavoured milkshakes, but definitely not a lime one!

Grace had watched the events of the last two minutes enfold and it broke her heart. "She never gave Jace a chance Colin!"

Colin looked at the crying woman beside him and his heart went out to her. "Maybe she thought it was too late."

Grace eyed him dubiously. "Oh god Colin, it's never too late to take a chance on love!"

"Do you really mean that?" He asked forgetting for a moment they were talking about Catherine.

"Yes! Of course I do!" She strode back towards the kitchen.

Colin watched her go and put a hand to his chin thoughtfully as he went down the steps towards his house.

The American Airlines flight to LAX was on schedule.

Jace had the window seat next to Peter, he had insisted.

After the flight levelled off Peter tried to make conversation with Jace. "I talked to Hudson a couple of days ago. She asked about you."

Jace didn't look at him she watched as the plane flew further and further from her heart's desire. "She did that was nice of her." She replied absently.

"Not really, you know Hudson she thinks you might have a scoop for her. Have you?"

"No!"

"Well, I guess that was to the point. But she's going to insist on something for the background on the story. You have spent the last seven days under the recluses roof she'll expect something!"

Jace turned her head to him and noticed he was only trying to let her know what was going on with Hudson. "She's not a recluse, she just lives quietly."

"Jace, I don't know what's going on believe me if I didn't know better, I would say you've fallen in love. I also don't need to know, but if you need a friend's shoulder to cry on. But Hudson's a bitch and she will want something from you!"

"Peter, don'v worry I can handle Hudson."

"You haven't fallen in love have you Jace?"

"If I had, would it matter?"

"I don't want to see you hurt Jace, I care about you. I sometimes think you live in a world some of us mortals never get to see."

Jace for the first time since getting into his car on the ranch, smiled and then laughed at the comment. "Oh, Peter what a load of garbage, I'm a mere mortal too."

Peter smiled at the change in his friend. "Then I'm glad because I wouldn't want any thunder bolts coming over our heads about now, not when I'm thirteen thousand feet in the air." He chuckled and entwined his hand in hers.

"So tell me what's she really like?" He wasn't sure she would even answer him.

She turned her head back to look outside and this shielded her face from his view. "Oh, you know what these so called recluse figures are like all silent, angst and tragedy." Jace smiled at the explanation that certainly wasn't Catherine Warriorson.

"Is that so! How well did you get to know her?" Peter's interest was piqued.

"I guess as well as anyone can. But I did become friends with the housekeeper. Now that's a fun loving woman if ever there was one."

Peter noted the change in her voice she wasn't deliberately hiding anything but something wasn't being said. "Yeah, she did seem happy when I met her."

"You would have loved her Peter she can organise, cook, oh boy can she cook! She has a kindness in her heart that you don't see often in this lifetime she's quite simply a good friend to have."

Peter laughed loudly. "Hell Jace if I didn't know better next thing you're going to tell me is you're in love with the woman!"

Jace smiled and continued to look out of the window. "Would that be so wrong?"

Peter went silent and tried to see her face and expression as she made the comment. If nothing else Jace's face was expressive to the point of almost conveying the words themselves. "No, no it wouldn't be wrong. Are you?"

Jace waited a moment or two before answering. "Not with Grace no!" Silently she added: *'I'm hopelessly in love with her boss though.'*

"I'm pleased to hear it, what would your parents have had to say?" Peter said mockingly.

"My parents? Well, I wouldn't know. It's not a topic usually open for discussion between us." She laughed and turned back to him.

Peter smiled she really did like him and he had been a good friend for much of the five years she had been in Hollywood. At times it had been tough, she didn't exactly come across as the most sophisticated on the block. She had found out early that making the right friends and ones that were friends not the pseudo plastic type that was the key in LA. They kept you out of trouble and she had been able to maintain a lot of her original views on life because of that!

Peter was one of those friends.

Another was James Thompson he was the PA to the owner of Paragon Pictures and they had originally met after she'd hounded him for some information on Union City. Now he was a good friend she also liked his partner Paul Strong, he wasn't in town much having a high profile job and lots of money if James's presents were anything to go by but they were happy. She'd had dinner a couple of times in the last eighteen months with them; Paul was the strong silent type reminded her of Catherine in a way and James was the gregarious one, very like her. It made her smile, as she thought of Catherine in a domestic situation and with her as a partner.

"So, would your parents approve do you think?" Paul asked, noting she had gone silent on him.

"If it made me happy it would make them happy." Jace answered him finally.

"There would be no one that they would disapprove?" Peter was making frivolous conversation he knew it and Jace knew it but it helped to pass the time.

Jace had to think about that she didn't have any enemies that she knew about, neither did her folks but if you put things in context there would be one person they probably wouldn't entertain. "Oh, there would be one person they probably wouldn't approve of."

Peter almost choked on his scotch and soda that he'd just received from the steward. "Really! I hope it's not me?"

Jace smiled. "Peter, no way are you in this person's league, and not for the obvious reason either."

"So spill it Jace who is it? You have me really interested now."

"Devonshire, the owner of Xianthos Publishing Corporation and other holdings if I'm not mistaken."

Peter looked at her and wondered if she knew that Xianthos was the major shareholder in Union City obviously not by her vehement statement. Not a good time to let her know either just let sleeping dogs lie.

"Why her? What connection do you have with her?" Well this was a turn on Jace actually might have her own skeletons in the cupboard after all.

"Me personally none! I've never met the woman. But she bought out my Father's business in Santa Barbara about six years ago. We thought she would let him stay in the company but they tossed him aside as if he was a piece of garbage. I'll never forgive her for that!"

"What made him sell in the first place?"

"He had no choice he was putting me through college and had mortgaged the company. It had never done that well but it made us a living and I was going to join him that summer after I'd graduated. We had time to make some money before my sister needed to go to college she's ten years younger than I am. They called in the markers I guess."

"I'm sorry Jace."

"Thanks, dad works for a small publishing house in Santa Monica now they live on the outskirts of LA. With my sending them part of my salary and his savings, we should be in a position to send Lucy to college next year."

"That's very commendable Jace, is that why you work for Union?"

"Yes, I don't always agree with Hudson's tactics, but she pays well and I think I'm helping in some way to give the place a better image."

Peter squeezed the hand he still held. "You know if you got involved with someone, say someone like me then you wouldn't have to stay and be a lackey for Hudson."

Jace smiled at him gently. "Is that a proposal?"

Peter cleared his throat and with red stained cheeks he answered. "If I said yes would you consider it?"

"Oh, Peter you are so good to me I don't deserve you! But the answer to your question would be no." She sighed as she turned away from him once again.

"Well, I'm going to keep trying you know maybe one day you might actually consider it."

"Peter, that wouldn't be fair to you would it?"

"Jace, anything you offered me would be enough."

She turned for the final time and touched his cheek. "I love you Peter, but I love you only as a friend and I know that's all I can ever offer you."

"Well, I know people who have thought they loved as friends and have married and been very happy."

"Not me!"

"Well, I'm going to stay around a little while longer if you don't mind, you never know and what the hell, I like you."

Jace turned to face him and kissed him on the cheek. He blushed and punched the button for the steward he needed another scotch!

Jace moved the seat into the reclining position, she wanted to sleep and dream about Catherine and possibilities. Funny isn't it how Xianthos had reared its ugly head. Hades, it would be so ironic if she ever met Ms. Devonshire never mind had a notion to fall in love with her. No she had met her 'soulmate', Catherine Warriorson was most definitely that candidate, no one and nothing was going to stop her from making it a reality!

Sleep came to Jace and in it she saw the tall dark haired woman riding into the sunset, holding on to her waist was a smaller blonde woman.

Oh, if only dreams became reality.

Catherine had helped all day with the children; it had given her something to do, to help her stop thinking about Jace. It hadn't deterred her thought of the young woman at all.

'Hell, I almost told her!'

Grace had taken Lisa for a bath and was settling her into bed with a st□zy. *'I wonder what we have in the library that would entertain a seven-year-old?'* There again Jake wasn't immune to the stories either. Catherine had watched him the previous evening gradually relinquish his interest in the TV to a good storyteller and Jace had definitely been that! Tomorrow she would take a look after all, Grace might not be around forever.

The way her household was going, she was going to lose all the adults and have them replaced by kids! That made her chuckle and she wondered what life would be like with lots of children around the place. *'I miss you Jace Bardley, and you've only been gone half a day!'*

Jake was ensconced on the floor watching some trivial program on the TV he was a strange boy. Sullen one moment and then he could be so charming.

'I think I need to arrange schooling for them! Funny given the circumstances of a week ago, I would be sitting in the study pondering, which take over would give me the most profit! Now I'm contemplating bedtime stories and schools. Can your life change so drastically over night and you have no control over it?' Yes, hers had dramatically done so.

"Where are you now Jace how, far away from home are you?" she whispered into the room not loud enough for the boy to hear.

Colin was acting strangely. She needed to take him aside and talk to him about it. He was far too essential to the ranch and to her to allow him to leave because he was lovesick. No, he would come out of that. It was in his hands to do something about it anyway. Why on earth hadn't he taken her advice?

'Maybe, it's because I never took my own advice and admitted the same to Jace. Because he's probably as scared of making that kind of commitment as I am!'

It was time to get the boy to bed, he seemed to have some sort of crush on her, in time it would disappear, it always did but for now it served its purpose. Jake would go to bed on time and that's all anyone wanted at the moment.

Chapter Nineteen

Jace clutched the business card to her as she relaxed on the sofa in her apartment. Anyone watching at the moment would think she had a precious jewel in her hands rather than a perfectly ordinary business card. She had arrived home about an hour before, all thoughts of sleep departing as she opened her hand out and glanced at the card for what must be the hundredth time in the last ten minutes.

Catherine X Warriorson
Destiny Ranch
South Island
New Zealand
Tel: 03 443 7711
e-mail: Souless@nz.com
Private: 03 443 6669

Jace had smiled when she saw the private number, it reminded her of the Omen movies. Then she had pondered the e-mail address and wondered about that too, she was definitely going to get her to change that addy.

'I wonder when she will trust me enough to tell me what the X stands for?'

Now she was home. Well, it was a place to live, at least. Home, to her, had changed drastically in a short time frame. It was impossible to exist for five minutes without thinking of a certain beautiful woman who had by chance- a miracle of a chance-made her want so much more than the current lifestyle she had and it all centered on that particular stubborn raven-haired woman.

Jace knew she had been ready to open her heart to her, but Catherine just hadn't been ready for that but it was only a matter of time. *'I want her too much to let the past interfere forever. What haunts you so much that you won't allow yourself to experience love Catherine?'*

When she looked at the time, she realised that it was some unforgivable hour in New Zealand and although Catherine had said call well, it wouldn't have been fair. But e-mail well, that was another thing altogether. Oh yes, definitely a communication plus of the nineties.

Jace went over to the computer on a desk at the end of her lounge area and turned the power on. As she waited she mused to herself. *'Wonder if you can develop a love affair over the net? Not something I've tried before but you just never know! I'll never know unless I try especially with the challenge of the woman in my thoughts constantly.'*

Jace sat in front of her console and went into her server. Nothing ventured, nothing gained. Jace requested a new mail message format.

Paul Strong had discussed his predicament with his partner and both had come to the same conclusion, he had no choice.

The 'Great' Ms. Devonshire as she was affectionately called within Xianthos was finally bailing out of the buoyant ship; although the reason usually was a sinking ship this certainly wasn't the case here. It was something that Paul had wished the opposite of he wanted her back on board. She was wonderful at the corporate raiding and the eternal boardroom battles that seemed these days to constantly fill his day. Yet, he had coped, more than coped, if the business reviews and Devonshire herself were to be believed. He was the obvious choice for the job. No one else came close except, possibly Constance Waverly. She was good but hadn't gained enough experience yet. New York would be a good move for her.

Hell, he'd just made the decision hadn't he by promoting Constance to his position which certainly would make some waves.

Constance was the only woman in the top executive level and she was African decent with a touch of European, some people still had issues with the colour of a person's skin or orientation. Guess he was a prime example but the boss lady was in charge for now. At no time had it become an issue in fact he doubted that she even considered those aspects as part of the equation. Hell, he knew she didn't because he'd had to explain his own situation well, surprise of all surprises she was obviously batting on the other wicket these days also!

Although, if you ever asked Constance about her roots she was adamant that the part of her that was European was very well diluted and only a trace remained. Only the name bore any resemblance to the old colonial regime. She had clearly inherited some of the traits of her British ancestry, however, these traditional legacies had not been detrimental to her career in any sense of the word.

Paul looked at his neat and expensive apartment layout in New York and smiled as he thought of James's untidy, meandering house in LA and the peeling external paint and the old furniture.

'Hell, you're going to have to change some of that when we live permanently together James! Well, guess that takes care of the home base too.' He smiled and picked up the phone to call his employer.

Catherine wandered around the house in a daze. She had spent the day taking Jake and Lisa around the ranch in the Land Rover. She knew that Colin had taken them on a tour it had only been a small tour of the surrounding area of the house, but this was different. Grace had provided a picnic for them and her friend had made sure there was everything in the basket needed for both Catherine and the children.

Grace had seen the emotional strain evident with Catherine's need to get away from the house she had been so restless. *'What better way than a picnic and children who were lonely too!'*

It was also evident that the children had seen another lonely soul searching for something, the holding of her hands as Jace left was evidence of that fact. *'Funny how kids could be so receptive to emotions.'*

Lisa had mentioned at supper just why she'd held Catherine's hand it brought a lump of emotion to the surface, which eventually gave way to a splash of tears. Her boss and friend looked so lost and alone now, surely she must see it herself and do something about it.

Grace had obligingly made the picnic and suggested that as it was a reasonable day not raining and cold they should search out a place that held the beauty of Destiny in it's palm.

Catherine had smiled briefly at the suggestion. Grace was being less than subtle, Christ she was being bloody transparent. *'I gotcha Grace, Cutter's Ridge.'*

They had left shortly after and Catherine marvelled at how these kids so easily let someone into their lives. Yet, should she be surprised, they were lonely without family and needed someone to love. Hadn't she experienced exactly the same feelings with a certain Jace Bardley, only she had let it fly away without a care! Without a care, oh no, not this time. This time Catherine cared far too much for the young blonde woman who was constantly in her thoughts. She had not had one moments peace since she had remained silent and allowed Jace to leave Destiny without her speaking up and telling her how she felt. Without a care, no, she definitely cared. *'So why am I not doing something about it?'* She questioned herself silently.

Colin knew that he had a one off shot at asking Grace out and trying to get her to see him as more than the ranch foreman. He was nervous but after the comment she made about Catherine and Jace Bardley he saw the ideal opportunity that he hadn't dared thought would appear. He had a shot and he wasn't going to let some clever educated Doctor get in the way of love! Well, his love for Grace at any rate he needed a chance and if it was the last thing he did in this world he was going to ask her out. Whatever the outcome or the embarrassment if she refused there was no better time than now.

'Why are you thinking about it and not using the opportunity to do something about it. For sure as hell the good doctor didn't waste any time did he? Go for it man this might be your only chance.'

Colin looked over at the main house and saw Catherine leave with the children there was no better time then right now.

Peter Adamson had arrived at the studio building earlier than normal, Hudson wanted a meeting as early as possible and he obliged.

Walking into the small headquarters of Union City Productions, he passed the small office layout that Jace Bardley used. She hadn't turned up yet but there again it was only six in the morning.

He sauntered by her pine desk and noticed that she had small trinkets on the side, also a number of small dragons depicting various stages in their development from the egg through to a fully fledge adult breathing fire. All were less than three inches in height but they had comical expressions and appeared to be made out of porcelain. He smiled as he went by. Jace was such a softy at heart; you could almost see the child in her expressions at times.

He wondered again how it was possible for one so naive to have broken through to the reclusive C X Warriorson then again they were talking about Jace, she could get through to almost anyone he was very confident of that.

He knocked on the inner door and a voice called for him to enter.

Clarissa Hudson looked away from the window and turned to the man who entered her office. He was a good-looking guy in a homely sort of way, not her type at all. Then again her type wasn't the norm, she was interested in tall, muscular, dark haired and powerful men or women and it didn't really matter to her, which gender it turned out to be. Her biggest disappointment had always been Devonshire, the daughter. She had miscalculated and it had proved a bitter blow to her ego when she had been turned down.

Devonshire senior had been a good lay for her; he had never known that she had secretly hoped to have both father and daughter in her bed. That hadn't happened yet! But her time was coming and it appeared that Jace Bardley now could play an important role in bringing the reclusive Devonshire back into her clutches and into her bed.

Time to get a plan of seduction into operation because sure as hell that was the only thing she really wanted from Devonshire, and this time she was going to get it. She had the ammunition and was prepared to use it! "So Peter, good trip back?"

Peter looked at his boss and he saw the cold beauty. She never gave away any warmth. He had seen more warmth from Catherine Warriorson in those brief minutes with Jace, as she was leaving, then he had with Hudson in all the years he had known her.

"Yeah, it was a good journey back, the weather here is so much better."

"Glad to hear it how's our star interviewer?"

Peter wasn't a fool he knew who she referred to. "Jace is well, she appears to have recovered from the virus she had over there."

Hudson smiled; at least he wasn't trying to be evasive. "Good, when she comes in I'll get her to share some of our recluse's secrets with us, it should round out the documentary with, shall we say, that personal touch."

"What if she doesn't want to say much about her days at the ranch?"

"Oh Peter, it's all in a days work. Of course she'll want to share some titbits with us, why wouldn't she? Surely there isn't any reason for her to ever see the recluse again is there?"

Peter knew that Jace wasn't going to talk much about her time on the ranch, but he had no way of helping her out of this situation. Only she could do that. "Maybe, maybe not. Guess we will have to see what she brings to the table."

"Yeah, won't we just!" Clarissa said in a laid back tone.

"Jace doesn't know that UCP is part owned by Xianthos does she?" Peter noticed Hudson starring for a moment.

Leaning back in the chair that she had just sat down in, expecting the director to leave, she looked him in the eye. "Why do you ask?"

"Because if she did, Jace wouldn't be working here! How did you keep it from her? Jace hates the Xianthos Corporation."

Clarissa laughed hollowly. "Yeah, well our Jace has some strange views. I know of her particular dislike of them; sure, she said so at the interview. But she's good at her position here. Why tell her something that doesn't really affect her. I made sure she never saw anything that was related to Xianthos and let's face it, unless you go digging, you really don't see their name on anything. What she doesn't know can't hurt her is my motto."

"So, when she finds out who Catherine Warriorson is, you think that's going to help you keep her?" Peter smirked at the look of shock on the producer's face.

"How the hell did you know that Catherine Warriorson is also the Great Ms. Devonshire of Xianthos?" This was a surprise. Hudson was impressed the director hadn't looked that bright!

"Something Jace mentioned jogged a memory, so I checked up on an old photo library shot. Low and behold, the article was about Devonshire and the death of her husband and child, one Adam Warriorson and son Lucas. Guess I'm not dumb. I can occasionally put two and two together. Jace, on the other hand, can't stand so much as the mention of the name. So she hasn't bothered to find the face behind the reputation, which is a pity for her really because I think she likes Warriorson." He hadn't intended to mention that Jace liked Warriorson but it had just come out. It was the only way he knew of, getting someone else to be the one telling Jace the truth, he really hadn't relished the task.

"I appreciate the candour Peter. I'm sure, at some stage, it will be my pleasure to enlighten Jace about her new 'Friend', but lets see how things go first shall we? I don't want to lose a first class assistant without just cause, now do I?" Hudson purred.

"No, I'm sure Jace is becoming invaluable to you in many ways." He turned away and headed for the door, feeling as if he had betrayed Jace in some way.

"I'll see you later with the rushes." She dismissed him and leaned back in her chair.

'Oh life was certainly looking up. God almighty, it looked like the stoic bitch that ran Xianthos, so efficiently and without mercy, had actually been taken in! God, it was delicious, just the thought of it. So she wasn't immune to the charms of women after all. I always knew she had a soft spot for the ladies; wonder if I can exploit Jace to my advantage. That wouldn't be too bad, especially when Jace finds out the true identity of Catherine Warriorson. Hell, I don't care about that either!' She smirked to herself.

Musing over the blonde PA in the outer office, her thoughts drifted along another path. *'So she likes green eyes does she. Well, contact lenses would solve that problem for me. Maybe I should think about making an appointment with my optician. Oh yeah, excellent idea.'*

She made a note in her diary for her secretary to make that call.

Chapter Twenty

"No! Colin said I could go first, I want to!" Lisa's childish voice rose as she confronted Jake at the paddock where the ranch horses were stabled.

"Short Stuff, you can't ride yet; you're too young. Colin said he was going to teach me first!" Jake shouted back at the younger child.

Lisa pulled a face and then started to cry.

Jake looked at the little girl. They had lived on the ranch for a month now and although it had been strange at first, they had settled down to a routine. Although it came with a strict upbringing it also had the benefits of having horses and people who appeared to take a genuine interest in them. Now he had upset Lisa, again! Grace was going to be mad, she always seemed to take the little girls side, no matter if it was the wrong side at times. He couldn't really complain though, Catherine usually took his side when it was a full-blown argument. He liked Catherine, she understood him.

He sat down heavily next to Lisa and looked into her blue eyes, now very tearful; she really was such a baby. But she was their baby so he had better make it up to her. "I'm sorry Lisa." He looked down at his toes as he waited for her reaction.

Lisa gulped back a sob and looked at the dark boy next to her that she had to come to call family. He wasn't any relation to her but he did look after her, even if he made her cry. He was a boy after all! All boys made girls cry at times, didn't they? Her mother cried when she talked about her father but she had never met her father, so she often wondered why. "Why don't you like me Jake?" It was a childish statement, but the boy was hurt by the accusation.

Hazel eyes turned to look into blue ones and he knew that was a mistake. "I do! Whatever gave you that idea?" He answered sullenly.

"Because you're always angry with me." Lisa said quietly.

ause you're always angry with me." Lisa said quietly.

"No I'm not!"

"You are! It reminds me of Catherine when she's mad at something."

"I'm not Catherine!"

"No, but you love Catherine and you want her to love you too, so you act like her - to me anyway."

Jake didn't have an answer to that particular question. He yearned to love but people always went away when you loved them.

"I don't love Catherine, she's just...Catherine. Lisa, how old are you?"

The boy looked at the younger child next to him.

"I'm seven. I'll be eight next month, want to buy me a present?" She smiled at him with a grin that showed that one of her front teeth was missing. She'd lost it earlier that day and was waiting for bedtime so she could put the tooth under her pillow so the tooth fairy would come and leave her a dollar!

"No! Yes, but.... Oh girls." He looked away from her blue gaze and studied the grass beneath his feet.

Lisa smiled and wiped the tears away. "One day can I call you brother?"

Jake looked at the girl and saw her for the first time in any sort of clarity, but she wasn't his sister. "No!" He said forcefully, and then tempered it with, " but you can call me a friend."

Lisa started to cry again, it didn't make sense. "Why not my brother, we live together now?"

"Because I'd rather be your friend than your brother," he simply said.

Catherine watched the scene and heard the conversation from her position on the hill, which had an advantage of being very close to the paddock, but they couldn't see her. "Well, that was an interesting conversation Tralargon, wonder why the boy doesn't want a sister?"

She had watched the kids get over their initial fears at being in a strange place and they had developed a rapport with Grace, Colin and the rest of the ranch hands that defied explanation. It was almost as if they really did have the Warriorson name, because sure as hell, everyone thought of them as being her family.

'Do I? It was an interesting question and one I haven't considered in any depth, maybe I should. What do they think of me? Hell, I don't know really. The boy- he's my shadow. I always try to get rid of him when I can; the girl- well she's so clingy, not something I'm used to or wanted to get used to either! Jace would kill me for thinking such thoughts. That woman has managed to get me to read stories to them at bedtime and had convinced me that going to the movies was a good idea. That taking them to town for clothes might be an icebreaker. Oh yeah-such an icebreaker, Jake had almost had a fight.' Well, he was in a fight but she had to stop it and promise

the locals that it wouldn't happen again. It hadn't, she hadn't taken them again! Funny thing was when she told Jace she had laughed and wished she had been there. *'Oh, how I wish you were here Jace Bardley but...'*

Rounding the corner on Tralargon, she reined the mare in front of the startled children. "You two arguing again?" the softly spoken words drew the attention of the two children.

Jake coloured up but remained silent.

Lisa looked at the formidable woman on the horse. She really wasn't so scary, she read them good stories at bedtime and tucked them in. "No, we were talking." Lisa replied finally.

Catherine raised an eyebrow and smiled at the sheer audacity of the girl. Oh, she was going to be some handful in the years to come that was for sure. The child almost reminded her of her brother Lucas. "Good! So what you doing here then?"

Jake responded this time. "Colin said he would teach us to ride."

Catherine quirked her eyebrow, "Colin is teaching you both?"

Jake realised that he had included Lisa in the statement. "Yes... maybe!"

"Good, I need you both to ride."

Lisa looked at the beautiful woman on the horse. "Why?"

Catherine laughed at the small child who now reminded her of a certain Californian. "Then we can all go riding together."

Jake smiled, Lisa looked at Catherine with a beguiling look from her blue eyes. "You mean like a family?"

"Well, I suppose." Catherine was a little perplexed at the question. This child was almost as precocious as Jace when she riled her over the e-mail, for her attitude.

Lisa walked up to the horse and the mare dwarfed her but she never looked intimidated. "Will Jace come back and be family too?" There was an almost pleading look to those innocent eyes.

Catherine was taken aback by the question, stunned and not able to say anything, it was far too raw a question to answer, and she therefore continued to stare at the child with a blank expression.

Jake looked at the expression on Catherine's face and answered for her.

"Lisa, Jace doesn't want to come back; she lives in America!"

Lisa shook her head. "Oh, I know Jace wants to come back, she said so!"

Catherine was astounded by how quickly things could get out of hand with children. Her brief sojourn into motherhood had never gone as far as being in the company of older children who could ask questions and direct ones at that!

"Jace, has a job to do in America she has family and friends we can't expect her to want to come back here, now can we?"

"Yes we can!" Lisa said forthrightly.

"Why?" Catherine asked the child in the direct tone the child had used on her. *'Christ, this was worse than any boardroom manoeuvre she had ever been involved in before.'*

"Because she loves you!" Lisa continued her defiant stand. Catherine blushed and turned her head towards the stable and the movement of others. Taking a deep breath, the raven-haired woman was thanking anyone who was listening for giving her a distraction to that very revealing comment.

"Well, seems as if your coach is ready, better get your behinds down there or we won't be getting those family rides going will we?" Catherine glanced towards Colin as he sauntered towards them.

Colin nodded his head at the boss.

"Better get th... My family, riding soon Colin or they will think I'm neglecting them." With that comment she cantered off towards the hills.

Colin looked at the slowly receding figure on horseback. "She misses Jace." Lisa supplied to the puzzled ranch foreman.

Colin smiled at the two children. "Maybe she does at that. Let's get you two educated shall we." He looked again at the far distant spot of his boss.

It really was time she considered asking Jace back, would be the best for them all. He took a hand of each child and they went towards the horses.

Grace had been going over her dilemma in her head since breakfast. It wasn't getting any clearer either just more complicated.

Andrew had asked her to marry him!

Colin had asked her out a couple of times but she had been unable to go for some reason or other invariably associated with the children.

He hadn't seemed to mind although he tended to stay away from the ranch house if she had been on a date with Andrew. For some reason fate was certainly taking Andrew's side in the romance stakes; she had always been free when he asked her out.

She walked over to the laundry room and picked up the articles of clothing that the children had left from yesterday's school sports day. She and Catherine had gone to the event, it had been fun to watch the kids compete and especially when it came to their kids.

Catherine had been so proud of Jake when he'd won the long jump, and commiserated with Lisa by buying her the largest ice cream cone she could get her hands on when she tripped in her race. Lisa had never left her side after that and the number of people who had watched them and commented that it appeared that Warriorson had finally found something worthwhile in her life. Grace had smiled at the comments but she had been proud of Catherine too. At no time did she give off one of her steely ice blue glares, which frighten people, especially when they talked disparagingly about her and she heard them. That woman's hearing was uncanny.

Reverend Stott had talked to Catherine and Grace about the possibility of them taking on long term guardianship of the children, Catherine didn'v comment just smiled briefly and excused herself to watch Jake run the relay.

Oh, Catherine was changing. That much was for sure and Jace's consistent e-mails everyday and the odd phone calls they indulged in were clearly the main reason for it. *'I wonder when Catherine will finally let go of her reasons to keep Jace at arm's length?'*

The kids had settled in quite well and they appeared to have developed a routine. It irked Catherine at times Grace could see it in her face but, after talking it over with Jace, she appeared to get over each particular problem.

Collecting the clothes and putting them in the washing machine she glanced over to the paddock area where the kids had wandered to see Colin.

Once again her thoughts went over her own problems. *'I guess I should talk to Catherine though why I should amazes me it's not like she's much use when it comes to an affair of the heart! Although who else can I turn too for help?'* She became thoughtful and a little pensive.

'Maybe I should take a holiday and go home for a week or so? It wasn't as if I've taken any holidays in over three years. So, it surely couldn't upset Catherine too much. Yeah, my sister would be happy to see me and maybe the parents too.'

Going back into the spacious kitchen, she looked around at her home. This was home! It was where she was happiest and the thought of leaving here and ultimately Catherine just wasn't an option. Not one iota. Destiny be damned, she belonged here it was just a matter of defining which path to her destiny she wanted to take.

Jace had had her fair share of warding off Hudson. The woman was almost demonic with her fascination of Catherine. The final rushes of the film had been approved and now the dialogue was being put together. The whole process would be complete in the next couple of weeks.

"Well, at least Hudson would get of my back when it was all complete." she thought out loud as she went over to Peter Adamson's office.

Knocking on the door, Jace paused a moment and then went inside.

Peter was pouring over some stills and he obviously hadn't heard her knock, which was often the case with Peter when he was engrossed in film.

"Fancy a drive to the beach?" she quietly approached his desk.

"Yeah, great idea." He grinned and got up from his chair and came up next to her and took her arm in his and they left the room.

An hour later, having eaten at a tiny bistro, which had the most delicious Tiger prawn dishes she had ever come across, they went for a stroll on the beach. Jace kicked off her low healed shoes and walked barefoot in the sand. Peter looked at his sneakers and decided to leave them on.

"Has Hudson been bugging you again?" Peter finally broke the silence. They had walked for over five minutes without a word from Jace and that was unusual.

Jace glanced at him and gave him a wry smile. "Now whatever makes you say that?" she took his arm and tucked it under hers.

He laughed, "Because my dear Jace you never go out to lunch unless Hudson gets to you and I'm afraid this is about the fourth time in the last two weeks. What does she want?"

Jace pulled her free hand through her blonde hair and looked out onto the Ocean. "She wants whatever I can tell her about Catherine Warriorson."

"So tell her, and get her off your back."

"It's not that easy Peter. I get the feeling it's not about the documentary; it's more personal. I can't really explain it."

"Maybe Hudson wants her to invest in a movie?" Peter smiled cynically Catherine was by definition already doing that.

"I don't think so. She seems to think that Catherine and I have a relationship of some kind but I don't understand how she could possibly think that!" she sighed in exasperation.

"I know where she got that idea." Peter cleared his throat self-consciously.

"You do?" Jace looked at him with a green trusting glance.

"Me." He looked down at the sand covering part of his sneakers. Jace clutched his arm and pulled them to a stop. "Why?"

"She asked me how I thought you and Warriorson were getting on. I said well, you appeared to be getting friendly. Guess it's from that conversation. I'm sorry Jace." He didn't dare look at her.

"I see." Jace looked out to sea and her face became wistful.

"I would never knowingly hurt you Jace." Peter tried to explain his actions.

"Oh, that's okay Peter. I am Catherine Warriorson's friend but it's personal and not for Hudson to exploit!"

"She can be very persistent you know."

"Yeah I know, but I can be stubborn too!" Laughing softly she grabbed hold of Peter's hand and ran towards the steps leading off the beach.

"Better get back before she sends a search party out for us."

Catherine was watching Lisa chat amiably with Grace about everything under the sun; she was a veritable chatterbox. It brought a fleeting smile to Catherine's lips and then she took a sip of her tea. Glancing to the outer kitchen door she saw Jake enter he was muddy as usual.

'Hell, that boy got mud in places that didn't even see the light of day how he did it amazed both Grace and herself.'

She watched him shrug out off the warm outer coat they had purchased on that fateful trip to the town two weeks ago. He hadn't wanted her charity and conveniently ran out of the shop and ended up in a fight. She'd bought it anyway, and now he sheepishly wore it when the weather turned really cold. He kicked his boots into a far corner and walked in stocking feet into the warm kitchen.

"Jake, you're back?" Lisa announced excitedly. For some reason this child had taken a shine to the often-sullen boy Catherine needed to broad the subject with him about not wanting a sister.

"Yeah." Was his only reply he seated himself opposite Catherine at the kitchen table.

Grace looked at the boy and saw his set expression. "Soooo, what have you and Colin been up to today?"

It was Saturday and with no school Colin often took the boy out on the ranch showing him various parts of the operation. Lisa was always invited but she had opted instead to help in the stables, she loved the horses they didn't always love her but she didn't seem to mind when she got the odd nip or two.

"We went over to the small farm that the Henderson's run."

"Oh, that was a good idea." Donald Henderson had three boys; one certainly would be about Jake's age. "Did you meet the boy's?"

"Sort of." He looked around the room feigning nonchalance.

Catherine had been watching the boy he certainly didn't look happy and usually after a day with Colin he was more likely to be in good spirits. "What sort of answer is that Jake? I suggest you answer Grace properly." Catherine growled at him.

Jake looked at her and saw the impatience in her eyes. "Yes, I met the Henderson boys."

Grace looked at the boy and then to Catherine. *'Really those two had such a similar range of expressions and answers all pretty sullen, stoic and uninformative.'* She chuckled at the thought of them being in the house together without her and it made Catherine glance her way in question.

"Did you have any time with them when Colin talked to their Dad?" Grace asked him continuing her placid interrogation.

"No, not really, they didn't like me!" He said off-handily

Catherine nearly choked on the tea she had just drunk from her mug.

Grace looked at the boy in compassion and thought she had better go over and see Colin and find out what had happened.

Lisa was the surprise. She left Grace's side and went over to the boy.

Putting a small hand on his dark head she stroked his hair and smiled into his sullen face. "That's okay Jake. I like you." It was said with all the ingenuity of a child who wanted only to show affection after seeing someone hurt.

The boy jerked away as he realised that a tear threatened to fall and embarrass him. Boys didn't cry!

"I like you too." He said quietly and got up and went to his bedroom. He didn't spare a second glance for the little girl or the two adults in the room.

"Well, what do you make of that?" Grace said to Catherine as she came back from settling Lisa in the lounge to watch some cartoons.

Catherine had a hand on her chin and was looking out of the window of the kitchen towards the foreman's house. "Don't know but I'm going to find out. Is Colin due over here anytime tonight?"

"No, I was going over to ask him before I went out with Andrew."

"Do you think that's a good idea, you know how he gets uptight when you're going out with the good doctor?"

"Maybe you're right. It just seems that every time he asks me out something crops up and we never have had a date yet!"

"Why didn't he ask you tonight?"

"I guess because Andrew usually does; this is a weird situation." Grace gave an exasperated sigh.

"Do you want to go out with both of them? Doesn't seem your style somehow Grace." Catherine pointed out seriously.

"Oh, and what would my style be? Wait around forever and never give love a chance like someone I know?" Grace wondered at times how she hadn't been fired from her job when her tongue got out of control. She waited expecting fireworks from her boss.

Catherine tensed at the barbed comment aimed her way. "Each to her own," was her only reply.

"Catherine, I need to take a holiday preferably as soon as possible." Grace finally broached the subject that was on her mind finally.

Catherine looked at her friend and housekeeper. *'Hell, Grace hadn't left the ranch in what? It must be over three years. Was it something she'd done?'* "When did you want to go?" Came her forced reply.

Grace smiled at her boss she knew that her tone held guilt and a touch of anxiety.

"How about next Friday? I can get to Auckland by jeep Sunday."

"Do you want to take the helicopter? I'm not planning on going anywhere next weekend." Catherine offered.

"No, it's okay. I need the time alone that the drive will give me. However, thanks for the offer Catherine."

"How long will you be gone?"

"I'm not sure. Definitely a week perhaps two, can I call you when I get there?" Grace knew she was being evasive and that it would concern Catherine, but she just didn't know the answer to that question herself.

"Yes, okay ring me when you know. I guess I owe you on the holiday front." She smiled briefly.

"Do you want me to arrange for someone to come over, cook and clean while I'm gone?"

"I never thought about it. Yes, I suppose the kids wouldn't want to sample my cooking; they might find that the orphanage fare was far superior." Catherine chuckled at her lack of skills in that particular area.

"Don't kid yourself Catherine, the children would eat anything you put in front of them because you made it! They worship the ground you walk on." Grace saw the blush rise to Catherine's cheeks.

"Oh, come on Grace, you are exaggerating again. They think you and Colin are great, I'm just here to pay the bills." She said self-depreciatingly.

"Well, you tell that to a certain boy who will want you to tuck him into bed tonight and I'm betting if you then asked him what the problem with today was, he would tell you." Grace gave her a punch on the arm.

"Okay, that's Jake but what about Lisa? She will most definitely miss you." Catherine shied away from another attack from her friend.

"Ah, I never said they wouldn't miss me but Lisa loves your stories you know. She waits patiently for you to collect her after her bath. That kid lights up the sky with her smile when you come into the room."

"Yes, okay Grace, now you can pull the other finger. Who the hell are you going to land me with this time? If I recall on the previous occasion, it was a teenager who nearly broke every appliance in the damn place. Cost me a fortune to replace everything when you got back." Catherine raised her eyebrows to give menace to the words.

"Oh, you intimidated her that's why. Catherine you have such expressive eyebrows, did you know that?" Grace chuckled as the said eyebrows danced towards her forehead.

"Rubbish! She was so, so stupid. What the hell have my eyebrows to do with anything?" Catherine spluttered indignantly.

"Catherine, you have a very primitive ambience about you did you know that? The girl had a crush on you and you never have understood that part of your physical presence. What I wouldn't give to have a little of that ambience myself." Grace gave her a cheeky grin.

Catherine laughed loudly, surprising herself. "Christ Grace, I think you do okay on your own, what with two men after you already. Having a simpering teenager in tow would be even too much for you, I suspect."

"Oh Catherine, I don't know. It could get interesting."

Catherine raised her left eyebrow. "One thing I know about you is that you're not interested in girls. Lots of other things but you're definitely not interested in women, on a physical front anyway; a very good friend but nothing more!"

Grace blushed slightly. "What makes you say that? It's not as if you know me that well. We haven't exactly shared our personal secrets with each other now have we?" She said defensively.

Getting up from her chair she touched a finger down the right side of Grace's cheek. "Do you respond to my touch Grace as much as you would with say Andrew or maybe Colin?" The voice had a low resonance that sent shivers up Grace's back.

Grace pulled away from the heat of the touch. She wasn't going to be some kind of experiment for Catherine. "What are you trying to prove here Catherine?" She rasped.

"Nothing." She dropped her hand and walked towards the door that led into the hall. Grace was unable to see the expression on Catherine's face as she turned away.

"I'll be in my study for the next hour or so, if you have trouble with the boy when it's supper time give me a shout." She left the room.

The atmosphere fairly bristled with electricity from the same woman who had just left.

Grace watched her leave. The woman was lonely it showed in every facet of her life these days and she knew the answer to her loneliness it was a petite blonde, green-eyed Californian. *'Maybe she should ask herself the same question.'*

Grace picked up the cell and called home, she had plans to make.

Chapter Twenty-One

Jace immediately logged onto her computer as she entered her apartment; it was a ritual these days. How long had it been now? A month. Yeah, a good month! Although it hadn't been easy she had fallen into the usual routine at work and managed to leave her personal disappointments at home. At least most of the time except if Hudson hounded her on the subject of Catherine, then it became almost unbearable.

'How do you tell your employer NO, I'm not going to rat out my friend? Especially when she is the love of my life? No, guess I couldn't very well say that, I haven't discussed my love with Catherine yet, never mind mention it to my somewhat focused boss.'

The server prompt pulled her from her reverie and she entered her name and password. Bingo! It immediately told her she had e-mail.

A couple from her sister who was home for the holidays and making her mind up about which college she should attend. There were also a couple from her favorite websites; which consisted mainly of fan fiction. *'Hell, it's better than going to the library!'*

She chuckled when she remembered trying to explain to Catherine that it was a very good way of reading stories about subjects you were really interested in. Catherine had come up with some very stubborn arguments and she hadn't been at all happy with Jace's continued use of the medium. They hadn't actually argued about it but it ran close. *'She was a little too uptight about it; it must be her age, or her objection to the idea.'* Jace chuckled again.

Then there was her favorite e-mail sitting there as usual Catherine's. Jace hadn't managed to get her to change the addy, Catherine had just replied. *'It served it's purpose and suited her.'*

Taking off her jacket, she went to her kitchen and retrieved a bottle of banana milk; it had been a Hades of a job to find some in LA. But it was one of Catherine's favorite drinks and somehow just having it in her refrigerator gave her a sense of Catherine in her home. Grimacing as she took the first taste, it always was a bit of a shock at first; there again, Catherine didn't have a sweet tooth, not like she did, and how she had a sweet tooth!

She settled down into the chair next to the desk holding the console and she punched read.

Jace,

Well, it's been one of those days here again, eventful!

I'm wondering if you decided to leave on purpose when you did because you knew what was going to happen. Guess not huh?

Grace wants to take a holiday. Nothing wrong in that but.... she hasn't said when she's coming back! I'm a little worried. Hell, no I'm very worried maybe she won't come back, what will happen then? I rely way too much on her for my peace of mind around here. Any suggestions?

Jake was strange again today!

That kid certainly knows how to keep us guessing. He went over to one of the smallholdings with Colin today. They have three boys, should have been fun for him, he said they didn't like him! Kid was upset. I guess tonight he's going to have to open up or it will fester inside him and with that kid it's not good. Lisa on the other hand is different; a Jace in training, I might add. LOL

Lisa likes the boy. They argued today about trivial stuff but the conversation took on a serious note at one stage. She wanted him to think of her as a sister he said no only as a friend. Got to talk to that boy I guess. She's not afraid of anything Jace she talks to me just like you do with all that innocent warmth that helped to make me see you as a friend.

Jace looked at her console and a silent tear fell as she read about the trials of living on Destiny at the moment. *'Oh, I wish I could be there with you through this Catherine, but we both know it's impossible, at least for now, until you learn to trust me!'*

That girl child is going to break someone's heart one day, that's for sure, but she has a compassion that goes beyond her years. Must have been something her Mother taught her, because sure as hell, she doesn't get it from around here!

I've decided to set up a fund with regards to this type of project. I haven't told anyone about it yet, guess I'm sort of bouncing it off you at the moment. But I thought I would invest in the scheme in the name of my son. I know it's only money but in some instances people want to help but don't have the funding, I can make that happen or rather Lucas's memory can! I want your advice on that one Jace? If you could, it's something you would be better qualified to advise me on than all the lawyers I know. I need someone with a heart.

'Did this woman know what she was saying? Catherine has a great presence about her at most times. There is also a latent power just waiting to be unleashed. Yet, when it comes to matters of the heart and the concern of others, she has the naivety of a five-year-old. It is both endearing and sad. I will gladly hold your hand if you ask me, my friend. Zeus, help me, I would hold your hand forever if you would only let me inside!'

Colin hasn't got past first base with Grace, seems that every time they make a date something comes up! I'm not sure that Grace wants to go past the friendship she has with Colin, although I'm not sure she finds the good Doctor quite what she's looking for either. Hell, what do I know! Maybe she should talk to you Jace and get some sympathetic advice.

Well, guess that's my day! What's the score with you today? I'm hoping it's been far better than the strange one I had. Too much emotional crap is a hard taskmaster for me.

I'm going to wish you a good night Jace and I'm hoping happy dreams. How's my stand-in, by the way?

Oh no, I can't make it this weekend in LA, but keep trying. It makes me feel that you want to see me again.

Take care, my friend. I think of you frequently.

Catherine

Jace couldn't help the tears that she shed; it was as if there was a well inside that kept filling up when she read messages from this special woman.

'Oh, my friend, you're going to be fine believe me, you will survive this initiation into parenting again. I know you don't want it, you're too afraid of failing...again! But you won't this time! This time you have people who want to see you succeed far beyond what you

think you're capable of achieving. I know you have the strength of character to get through this wall you've erected around yourself, you will do it and without help. Because that's the only way Catherine you are ever going to accept this destiny that has fallen into your lap, and I hope you decide it's worth the effort.'

Jace stood up and decided to order a Pizza, and read the rest of her mail and maybe indulge in a little light reading of net fan fiction. She was going to tease Catherine with that later. Then she would answer her friend.

Catherine,

You know my friend; I have never come across anyone quite like you in my life before. You make me feel so...so proud to be your friend and someone you want to confide in, I feel very honored.

I think Grace needs some time away from the ranch Catherine. It's not necessarily anything to do with you; maybe her love life is getting more complicated than she wants. It's not easy to choose a man over you!

Now, don't go getting all upset with me for that last remark, I know it's true, Grace certainly does, which is why she needs to be alone or at least with people who have no influence over this decision. Let her go Catherine, and hope that when she comes back she's made the right decision for her, not you.

Hey way to go, what a great gesture a fund in Lucas's name, what are you going to do, have one of your lawyers administrate it, so you can still be seen as the reclusive owner of Destiny? No way are you the same woman that they perceive you to be Catherine. You need to accept your changing role in the community; I hope you do, you might enjoy it.

When are you going to take the kids to town again? Don't' shake your head now; we both know you enjoyed that trip it's just a matter of you getting the confidence to go again! LOL

Okay you can shout at me when you see me in the flesh.

Jake sounds as if he needs a friend. You don't need me to elaborate; you're a very intelligent woman.

Lisa, oh Catherine, what joy that girl is going to bring you! She sounds as if she can already twist you round her little finger. LOL

I hope Colin can accept the decision that Grace makes in the end, but you might lose him Catherine, it happens.

Well, what sort of day have I had?

Nothing exciting! Nothing, that compares to your adventures.

'No way am I going to tell her about Hudson bugging me, she'll give up eventually and Catherine will only get protective. Mind you, I wonder if it would bring her over here in my defense?' Jace smiled reflectively at the thought.

'That is one thing I can be certain of, as my friend you will try to protect me, but who protects you my friend, who will you let protect you against the tides that seem to ever change in your world?'

I had lunch today with Peter. Do you remember him? He is the director of the documentary. We are at the final stages of the production, should be ready for final grading next week. I might go over and watch it; hopefully it will bring back good memories. Because Catherine I have more good memories in those few days with you, than I have of the five years I've worked in LA. Kind of sad to you I guess, but look at it from my point of view, I met my best friend!

I'm also reading my fan fiction; some of the authors are really very good. You should try it one day!

Guess that's me for now, also Catherine.

So when are you coming over to take me to dinner? You know I'm going to keep asking in the hope that one-day you just might agree. Is it wishful thinking on my part Catherine? Oh well, you can't blame a girl for trying and what wouldn't I give to see those fantastic blue eyes of yours looking into mine again. Okay, so I love your eyes, going to sue me? (G)

Love you my friend. Hang in there.

Until tomorrow!

Jace

P.S.

Don't forget to read a story to Lisa for me and give her a big kiss as she goes to bed, you can with Jake also if he will let you. (G)

She closed out the entry and touched the screen with a feather light touch as she sent it to its destination. Catherine would probably be in bed or working in the study. Who knew with her?

'Hope her pep talk with Jake went well, they are very alike at times it makes you wonder how they do react to each other on a one to one basis. Grace my friend, I hope you work out your problems and oh, how I wish I could help you.'

Shutting down the machine she walked over to her bedroom and stripped off her clothes and headed for the shower. It was at this time in the evening when she knew that her soul was missing its other half, the longing called to her. She constantly struggled with the image, but for now, she had to force herself to ignore it.

Grace managed to get Jake to leave his room for the evening meal. She hadn't wanted to use Catherine as a big stick, although she would have done so if necessary.

Grace had the dubious pleasure of watching Jake consume his meal in silence, which he frequently did; and noted that he smiled occasionally when Lisa made some silly remark, which she was apt to do. Little Lisa appeared to be the only one at the table talking constantly.

Colin hadn't wanted to eat with them; he'd decided to go into town with some of the other ranch hands.

Catherine had joined them but she was silent most of the meal except for the politeness of a please or thank you during the meal.

Grace chatted along with the youngest child as she talked about the horses and her day, she then held out her tooth for everyone to look at.

Grace smiled and watched Catherine grimace at the exhibition during a meal, but she held her thoughts to herself this time.

Jake merely looked at the girl and shook his head at her.

"It's for the tooth fairy Grace! I'm going to put it under my pillow and when I wake up in the morning she will have left me a gift in its place." Lisa smiled showing the gap between her front teeth. It made the child look even more endearing than she already was.

"Well, I guess that's a good idea. Wonder what she will leave you as a gift?" Grace tried to gather the information out of the child so she wouldn't be disappointed. Neither Catherine nor herself were exactly aware of the particular type of gift kids thought appropriate these days. *'Hell, in her day it was a nominal coin to get some sweets with, which was ironic when you thought about it.'*

"Oh, you can't ask that Grace, it's a secret, between me and the fairy!" The child said in an excited whisper.

Grace laughed out loud as she glanced towards Catherine, whose expression hadn't particularly changed through the dialogue.

"What do you think Catherine?" It was a direct challenge, Grace had to get this woman as involved in them as the children appeared to be getting involved with Catherine, it couldn't be one sided, it had to be a two way street.

Catherine looked at her, raising the ever-faithful eyebrow.

'One of these days she's going to lose it!' Grace couldn't help the grin that appeared at the thought.

Catherine looked at her friend and wondered vaguely why she was grinning like a Cheshire cat. "Can't remember a time when I lost any teeth so I wouldn't know what a tooth fairy leaves behind." She hadn't meant to speak solemnly, it just happened.

The others in the room all looked in her direction.

Lisa scraped back a chair and walked over to Catherine, whose tall frame in the chair made the child look small next to her.

A small hand tugged at hers and she reluctantly gave in to the pressure exerted by the child. She felt a small object being placed on her open palm. Then the small hand gently closed her long fingers over the object and the child moved back to her chair. She didn't know where to look or if it was even prudent to observe the object in her hand.

She eventually looked at Lisa, who winked at her and smiled. Then she carried on with her dessert.

Grace looked at Catherine expectantly.

Jake had a wicked gleam in his eyes he knew exactly what the girl had done.

Catherine made a move to get up and said she would have her tea in the study, and that she would be back later after they had their baths.

Walking out of the kitchen Catherine briefly opened her hand and saw the small pearly white tooth nestled in her large hand with blood congealing inside the root cavity. At first she couldn't understand the significance of the act. Then it dawned on her. *'Lisa wants me to experience the tooth fairy? What have I ever done to deserve this un-reserved love and affection from this small child?'* A tear tracked its way along her left cheek as she swiped it away and placed her hand over her eyes briefly as she went towards the study.

Grace watched the emotionless features of her friend and boss, as the child had surprised her, but she like Jake knew what the child had done.

"Why did you give Catherine your tooth Lisa? Now the tooth fairy won't know it's yours." Grace gently smoothed a lock of the red hair away from the child's face.

Lisa took a few minutes to think about it as she scooped more ice cream into her mouth, spitting some out from the gap in her teeth at Jake who was nearest to her as she explained.

"Catherine has never had a visit from the tooth fairy and she's old now. I will have another chance another day, I'm still young and all my big teeth haven't got here yet." the child patiently explained to the adult.

Grace was touched by the generosity of the child she enfolded her in a big hug. "Thank you Lisa, you might never know how much that means to her, but thank you anyway." Lisa smiled her toothless smile.

"How about more ice cream for you two. We can't let a gesture like that be wasted now, can we?" The children both agreed by nodding profusely, although Jake moved his chair out of the reach of Lisa.

The house was relatively quiet; Grace had left minutes before to drive into town to meet Andrew for her evening out.

Lisa was tucked up in bed, after a nice hot bath and a story session that had started with a short Pooh Bear story, and ended with the start of a largely unknown work of short stories by various European authors. Jake listened with half an eye as he always did to the stories, as he watched a rugby match on the TV at low volume.

Then he had silently switched off the TV as Catherine was asked to read stories that she read as a child. "Oh, come on now Lisa, that was a long time ago now, you won't want to listen to those surely?" Catherine blushed a little as the child looked at her with a steady blue gaze.

"Did your mummy read you those stories?" the child retorted looking into her ice blue eyes.

Catherine had to blink several times as she realised what the child had asked her. *'Had her mother read to her as a child? Yes.*

The ones she remembered the most had been the numerous short stories from all over the world, although in actual fact, it had been just European authors. She hadn't known that until much later though. Even Lucas had listened to them when he was old enough. In the end it had been me reading the stories to mother and Lucas, when our mother became too ill to read to us. Then, I just read to my brother to ease the hurt of mother's passing.'

"Yes, yes she did Lisa. I guess you better give me a minute to find one of them." Catherine left for the study and walked right to the books. She had found them when she had been foraging for reading matter for the child earlier. She had leafed through them fascinated that they still held her attention after all these years. Tucking the first book under her arm she went back to the lounge and now Jake was seated with his back against the arm of the chair that Lisa sat patiently waiting for Catherine to return.

Settling back into the chair with Lisa folded onto her lap and sinking into her chest as she always did in the evening, usually ending up asleep, but at least she never had any bad dreams.

The book had seen better days that was for certain, but it hadn't lost any pages so she suspected it would hold its own then her expression changed as if she'd thought of a better story.

"The first story concerns a young boy called Jacob!" Catherine smiled briefly at the boy as he looked at her in surprise she continued with Lisa looking expectantly at her. "And his younger sister Lucy," she winked at Lisa who gave her a crestfallen look. "Sorry misread that, she was called Lisa and the youngsters adventures to find a new home back in the dark ages when there wasn't TV, cars and computers!"

Chapter One
Jacob Salt held tightly onto the hand of his younger sister Lisa Pepper as they were settled into the back of the hay wagon that would take them and their meagre possessions to the nearest town. Jacob was thirteen years old and now the man of the family, having recently witnessed the tragic flood that had swept away their family home and the rest of the family in a matter of minutes. There had been nothing he could do, it had happened suddenly the bursting of the banks near their cottage. There had been one thing that had stopped him following his father and step mother, that had been the sight of his sister holding onto the back of a donkey and crying as if her heart would break. He had to look after her and see that she

was well taken care of; they would have to leave the farm and go to the nearest town.

"Will we find a nice family to offer us a home Jacob?" Lisa looked into her older brother's grey eyes with complete trust, holding his hand in hers; she tightened her grip waiting for the answer.

"Yes, we will Lisa, don't you know that no one ever splits up the salt and pepper pots, they belong together." He chuckled at her puzzled expression.

"What do you mean Jacob? If we weren't called Salt and Pepper someone might take you away from me?" Lisa dropped the hand she held and threw her arms around his slight shoulders and cried into his neck.

Jacob had always considered it a huge joke the fact that his father had married a woman who had previously been married to someone called Pepper, and her child Lisa was called Pepper. He was sorry he had teased his sister, she was still upset over the accident and he hadn't the heart to tell her he didn't really know what to expect when he got to the local town, he'd never been there himself before. "No one will take you away from me Lisa, we are going to stay together, I promise you."

The rest of the journey in the hay wagon, went remarkably well, the old wagon master had felt pity for the two orphans having had agreed to take them to the town, although he doubted the boy would be in a position to honor his promise to keep them together. There was nothing but difficulties ahead and unless you had funds, there would be only hardship and misery to follow. He continued to listen to the young man soothe his sister. If there was a God up in heaven, maybe he could answer a prayer today for these unfortunate children.

*

Kate Cook watched the sun set over the tall spire of the town church and sighed once again at her loneliness, she had agreed today in principle to marry the widowed landowner Simon Iron, but she hadn't decided exactly when. Kate really felt that something else was out there waiting for her, but in all her thirty years she had yet to find it. Having been the only daughter of the local Mayor, she had been given privileges that others in this age could not anticipate. Her father had died two years previously, leaving her tidy sum, with this inheritance if she so wished, meant that marriage did not have to be her lot in life. However, she was lonely and

Simon was older yes, but at least he would be company for her. "I wonder if there really is something or someone out there that needs me?" She walked away from the window and proceeded down to the dining room for her evening meal, alone!

*
Jacob didn't like the smell of the town it reminded him of rotting meat and vegetables, that they kept in a compost heap at the farm. There was also another smell that he couldn't quite name, but it too wasn't pleasant, wrinkled his nose as he passed by a hole in the floor that had an iron cover over it, the smell was particularly bad when they crossed one of those areas. He held onto Lisa's hand tightly, exactly as the old wagon master had instructed him, he would not lose Lisa in this horrible town.

Lurking nearby a wizened man with a long ragged beard and small pin points for eyes, starred at the children in speculation, maybe there was money to be earned yet this day, the man pondered as he stroked the matted beard and smiled with evil in his dark eyes. He had heard the old wagon master tell the children to be careful, that he would be back in a week if they need him again. If he had anything to do with it, they wouldn't ever see the man again!

*

Catherine noticed that Lisa was almost asleep at the end of that particular chapter; guess it bored them. "Time for bed Lisa, you too Jake." She turned her eyes to them in anticipation of her thoughts.

Both children looked at her with hopeful eyes. "Can we have the next part of the book tomorrow Catherine?" Lisa pleaded. Jake nodded his agreement to the question.

Catherine was astounded; she'd thought they hadn't liked it! "I guess so, did you like it?" she asked tentatively.

Blue and grey eyes both shone excitedly up at her and they both smiled.

"Right, tomorrow night then, we have a date with a another chapter of this book," she chuckled, swinging Lisa over her shoulder as she got up from the chair. The child giggled at the action.

Jake smiled at the two females, one rather tall one and the other tiny swung nonchalantly over her wide shoulders. He followed them out of the room.

"I'll catch up with you shortly Jake," Catherine remarked as she headed for Lisa's room.

"Sure," he replied and sauntered along to his room.

Putting Lisa down gently on the bed, the child suddenly put her arms around Catherine's neck and hugged her. "What's that for?"

"Just because," the child replied.

"Because what?" Catherine questioned.

"Because I can, and you read me such smashing stories," a toothless grin followed the words.

"Ah, give me a break Lisa; next time you can read." Catherine feigned annoyance but was secretly pleased at the compliment.

"No! You're the best Catherine, I like your voice, cause it makes me feel all warm and safe. Now, don't go forgetting about the tooth fairy you gotta remember to put it under your pillow when you go to sleep okay?" Lisa said seriously. The child placed a wet kiss on her cheek and snuggled into the soft bed cuddling her rag doll as she closed her eyes.

In all her thirty odd years she had never felt so lost for words this child had a knack of leaving her emotions raw, but she felt good too.

Tucking in the covers she looked once again at the child and quietly said goodnight. Leaving the door ajar slightly, as Jace had done that first night. You just never knew if the young girl might need her during the night.

Now for Mr Sullen.

Jake lay in bed he had a football magazine on top of the bedclothes, and he looked up at her pensively as she entered. *'Unusual'*, she thought.

"Hi, Jake. You going to enlighten me about your exploits today?"

Catherine asked in quiet interest.

He turned his hazel eyes to hers, and she could see the finely disguised hurt in the look. "What exploits?" he asked finally.

"Okay, I believe you mentioned that the Henderson boys didn't like you so give! Tell me why?" If the kid wanted forthright she had no problem with that.

He frowned at her; he really did use some of her expressions. It made her chuckle silently. "We go to the same school they called me a charity case and if I thought because I was living here with you it made me better then them now, that I wouldn't be welcome there or at any other boy's home either." He paused there for a little while and waited for her reaction.

She looked at the dark skies, filled with bright stars then turned to face the dark haired boy. "You know Jake, children can be cruel with their words. I think you have realised that in the short time you have been here, especially when you talk to Lisa. So it's not hard to understand that other children say cruel things to you. Is it?" Catherine spoke softly to the boy.

"Lisa is different, she's my...my friend."

Catherine glanced his way; he had difficulty trying to say exactly where Lisa fell into his world. "Yes, I think she is your friend. But you don't want her as a sister, am I right?" *'Hell, why not get two issues with this kid out of the way at the same time. It certainly gives me a headache all this emotional stress, there are times like now when I could really use a certain Jace Bardley at my side.'*

Jake looked at her and his expression changed to one of chagrin.

"She's not my sister, just as you're not my Mum!"

"True." Catherine paused and stroked her chin in thought. "My son would have been your age Jake. He died along time ago and if he had been alone as you are, I would like to think that he would have a friend like Lisa to help him with his challenges in life. I also would hope he would accept her as his sister also!" She waited for the boy to answer.

"Why?" He asked as his hazel eyes stared at her blue ones.

"Because Jake, family is important and if you feel that you have a family behind you it takes away the pain and hurt of just about everything, even snipes by boys like the Hendersons."

"Friends do too!" the boy replied obstinately.

"Touché Jake! But, what better thing to have a member of your family as a friend too!"

"That would be good too, I suppose. Can I think about it?" His face clearly showing he was concentrating on her words.

"Sure, we have plenty of time. And Jake, you're not a charity case take it from me, living here isn't any picnic. You might want to request a transfer one of these days when it gets too much for you," she winked at him and moved towards the door.

"That story you told was different tonight, did you change the names on purpose?" He surprised her with his statement.

"Now that's for me to know and you to find out." She quipped back at him as she turned to leave.

"Would you have read that story to your son?" He watched her turn to him again and she looked at him seriously.

"Unfortunately not Jake I was always too busy making money. But he had a good father, and he would have read to him every night, just as Lisa likes to have stories read to her." This time she left the boy with a whispered goodnight.

"Goodnight Catherine, I hope the tooth fairy brings you what you want." He snuggled down in the bed and picked up his magazine, feeling a little happier with his day. *'I wonder what happens next in that story, will that strange man capture them or will the lady come to their rescue?'*

Catherine heard his wishes and she glanced down the stairs to the silent and empty rooms below. "Oh, I somehow think that's an impossibility this time around." She shrugged her shoulders and went down to her study, and the business messages of the day she would tackle in her customary way.

Chapter Twenty-Two

Jace wasn't going to get away with it today! She had found things to do that kept her out of the office when Hudson was there, and in the office when she wasn't, it seemed to work. Except today, no today she was caught! Hudson had requested her presence and she wasn't going to take any excuse, not this time.

Jace entered Hudson's office. When she'd called her on the intercom; it had been a very brusque request. *'Hope she's not in a bad mood.'* Jace thought as she went through the door.

Clarissa Hudson was sitting in her large office chair it was black leather and essentially suited the woman. She did exude a dark power, almost evil in it's intent at times, or so it appeared to Jace.

"Ah, Jace. Glad you could finally set some time aside to see me!" Hudson said the voice dripping with sarcasm.

"Your time, your money." Jace said with a small smile.

Hudson watched her closely and waived her to the seat in front of her desk. "Yes, glad you realised that!"

Jace dropped down into the seat knowing this wasn't going to be a picnic.

"So, have you finally remembered some interesting details on Warriorson for the documentary yet?" It wasn't a request it was a demand.

"No." Jace looked directly into the hard expression of her boss.

"Why not?" Came a sickly sweet reply.

"It wasn't anything to do with the company when I was a guest on the ranch. It would be a betrayal of her privacy if I revealed how she lives and the people she has around her." Jace answered confidently.

"Come, come Jace, don't be naive! Catherine Warriorson will know that we will want you to tell us something about her! Hell, she will expect it!" Hudson said in an amused tone.

"Well, I disagree. She doesn't expect that of me!"

"I'm afraid that if you don't tell me something, particularly the facts, then as you know in this town, things kind of slip out of proportion to the event." Hudson looked at her nails as she spoke.

Jace looked at the woman. *'Was that a threat?'* "I'm sorry, forgive my stupidity here but exactly what do you mean by that?"

"As I said before, naïve maybe, but certainly not stupid. You are a very intelligent woman, I'm more than happy to have you on my team's side." Hudson continued her examination of her fingernails.

"I wasn't aware there was an issue with sides here?" Jace looked confused.

"Didn't you? Mmm, well it would appear that a line has been drawn Jace; you need to decide which side you want to be on." Hudson eyed her discreetly, curious to see her reaction.

"Why do I need to be on a particular side? It's not exactly a major issue here, you only need about thirty seconds of dialogue, is it so important?" Jace was dumbfounded. It didn't make sense this obsession of Hudson's about Catherine. *'I'm going to have to ask Catherine if she knows Hudson, maybe in her past.'*

"To me it's important Jace, let's just say I'm fascinated with the legend." Hudson said almost in a whisper.

"Legend?" Jace asked her puzzled.

"Ah, too young, I forget sometimes. Let's just say Ms. Warriorson has a background that is legendary; I wondered if she has changed in anyway." Hudson smiled at the younger woman and noticed her puzzled frown. "Times change Jace, she's probably nothing like the woman she was, but tell me does she still have that expressive eyebrow action that literally is one of the most powerful weapons in her arsenal?"

Jace paled, Hudson did know her. "I wouldn't know the difference would I; I've never met her before?"

"No, but I have! Indeed, on several occasions. Does she still put the fear of God into people?"

Noticing Jace wince at the term, she smiled. "Guess she still does, wonder if she still pulls that hard nosed bitch front she used to do when we knew each other?"

Once again Jace's facial expressions gave her away. "Can't say I blame you for not wanting to say much about the cold-hearted bitch, you never know if she might retaliate. Does she have anything on you that she could score a point off you Jace?" This time Hudson looked at her directly and noted the sudden swallowing and the pale visage getting paler.

'Oh to be young and in love.' Hudson chuckled silently.

"She...she wouldn't do anything to make me upset, I know her! She wouldn't, she knows I...I value her friendship." Jace whispered at the room, it was suddenly becoming oppressive. *'God, how well had Hudson known Catherine, and when and where?'*

"Guess you need to get some work done Jace, but remember where your pay check comes from okay?" Hudson inclined her head to the doorway in dismissal. "Oh Jace, in this town and our industry try to remember one thing."

Jace looked up at her and wearily got up from the chair. "That would be?"

Hudson looked at her with a cynical smile. "Why, never be gullible Jace, you might never know when it could come back to haunt you."

Jace paled even more and thought. *This woman was a manipulator, Peter had been right, she wouldn't give up; but I haven't given any damn interview either, so that was something to be thankful for at least.'*

Leaving the room she picked up her purse and headed for the canteen, she needed a coffee and how!

Hudson looked at the dejected Bardley leave her office and as the door closed, she allowed herself a large grin and a small laugh.

"Oh Catherine, how you still manage to charm people to your side of the camp, and now without the mantle of Xianthos to help in your enticement. It will give me great pleasure in using what Jace didn't say! As a background to the story and eventually you will have to do the evil deed yourself and admit whom you really are to her, saving me the task in the long run. I'm sure Jace will be happy to know that her...friend as she calls you, is really her number one enemy! How appropriate for you both; she gets a lesson in life, and you get a touch of your own medicine. I love it, just love it." She spoke icily into the empty room.

Grace had packed as much as she wanted for the trip home, if she needed anything else she would buy it there. Her sister Alison had been ecstatic over her visit, after all it had been three years since she'd been home, and they thought she had forgotten them.

Recalling the phone conversation.

"Hell Sis, we thought that you had finally decided we weren't good enough for you anymore. What with living like you do at that big ranch and with a rich recluse?" Alison had laughed when Grace had snorted her disgust at the comment.

"Sure, how on earth could I forget you Ali, you wouldn't let me anyway, would you?" She laughed herself at her sister's infectious laughter, it reminded her of Jace in some ways, as they were both about the same age.

"Mom was pleased that you're coming home."

"Good, it will be good to see her too, what about Dad?"

"Gracie you know Dad, he never says much, but I noticed him look at your photo when I mentioned it."

"Which photo? Thought he'd got rid of them, when the police thing went out of the window."

"It's the one you had taken about six months into the training, guess he kept one or two huh?"

Grace smiled at the thought of the picture, she had been happy then.

Her Dad had been proud of her, he had been a police officer himself, but due to a heart problem had retired earlier than expected, three years ago. He had never forgiven her for the car accident and the waste of her career, what she did now was not fit work for his daughter, or that's how she had viewed his continued silence over the past five years, guess sometimes you don't need words.

"I remember it well. Who has the pleasure of putting me up?" She asked, knowing that her sister no longer lived at home.

Alison laughed at the question. "Boy, you sure have a chip on your shoulder Gracie. Come on now. Mum and Dad would be furious if you didn't go home, she got your room ready so you have to go."

Grace was surprised, more than surprised, the last visit hadn't gone too well and if it hadn't been for Ali's influence, she would probably have said things she would have regretted later. Mind you there would always be a second chance, Ali wasn't going to be there this time around.

"Okay, well I'll see you Sunday Ali, don't go getting into too much trouble before I get there, love you. Bye for now."

"Love you too Gracie, see you Sunday, bye."

Cradling the cell in her hand she hadn't noticed Catherine walk into the room silently. Turning she noticed the strange smile on the woman's face as she watched her from the door.

"Okay, what's so funny Catherine?"

Catherine moved from her leaning post at the door and walked closer to her friend. "I've never heard you talk to your family before, do you often?"

Grace smiled briefly and went over and put down the cell on the kitchen table. "No, no Ali, Alison my kid sister has been travelling abroad, she's an engineer, works on rigs and such stuff. Clever kid about Jace's age." Seeing the fleeting sadness in Catherine's eyes she looked away and went over to put on some tea.

"Interesting profession, obviously she likes it?" Catherine said conversationally.

"Yeah, she does. Took my Dad ages to come to terms with it especially after... Well anyway she gets around now." Grace kept her back to Catherine.

"After?" Catherine was never one to miss a change in subject.

"You know you could just ignore that and ask me when I'm going to leave." Grace smiled wanly at her friend and boss.

"I could! But nooo... where's the fun in that!" She returned a brief smile and sat at the table; tea looked a good possibility and she knew once Grace was gone she wouldn't be in the kitchen much until she got back.

"After I dipped out of the police, my Dad was loathe to believe that his other daughter would finish her chosen profession."

"Your sister is her own person what happened to you was an accident, surely he didn't assume she would be as f...." She didn't finish the sentence.

"Foolish is the word you wanted to say I believe." Grace supplied for her.

"Yeah, foolish. Because sure as hell my friend, you certainly were in that car that night." Catherine never released the stare from the other woman's eyes, essentially taking any of the sting out of the words.

"I know, and would you believe good old Dad has never forgiven me! Hell, I was his eldest child and following in his footsteps. Now, he thinks I'm a waste of space, doing a mediocre job for some recluse who has more money than sense." Grace laughed as she said the words pouring them tea.

"Maybe your Dad is right, you could do better than this Grace." Catherine had pondered that very same thing about Grace recently.

"No! I couldn't Catherine. This is my home for as long as you want me in it! I'm happy here with you and now with the children, it's going to be interesting times." She locked brown onto blue in a sincere look.

Catherine placed a hand on the other woman's. "You know I think you're right Grace, it certainly is going to be interesting times."

"Yes, so don't go doing too many interesting things while I'm gone will you?" She chuckled as they sat there in friendly companionship.

"Okay, just don't stay away too long will you?"

"No, no I have something to come back too now haven't I?" she said softly.

"You never needed to go away to find a reason to stay here Grace." Catherine replied solemnly.

"I know, but some things need to be cleared up, and I can't do it here. Do you know you're too much of an influence?" She smiled at the colour, which appeared on Catherine's cheeks.

"Christ, that's just what Jace said." Catherine tried to laugh off the embarrassment that the two most important women in her life seemed to have the same opinion of her.

"I always knew Jace was an astute woman. Pity some others haven't got the same perception." She moved away quickly as Catherine jabbed her in the arm.

"Get out of here Grace, you're going to make someone an interesting wife one day!" She got up and walked towards the outer door.

"I'll be back before you go, in about an hour okay?" Catherine smiled and left her friend to her final leaving preparations.

"Interesting wife indeed! Maybe she should think about that herself."

Grace chuckled as she cleared away the tea mugs and went to her room to get her things together.

Chapter Twenty-Three

Paul Strong had started all the necessary procedures to ensure Catherine's plans for a World President of Xianthos coming into operation without too much controversy with the various personnel and departments.

He had received the internal memo from Catherine to all VP's about her plans; it had clearly stated his new role, which placed him in charge of Xianthos. Catherine wouldn't interfere, unless it meant that Xianthos was under criminal suspicion or that the market lost faith in the President.

He had practically run the company for the last five years anyway on the more sensitive issues, so she had great faith and would tell the market so in a rare interview in the coming months. She had also stated that he would be the person to move if he thought to fit any VP's into new positions, especially the New York role, which would be perceived as his second in command.

Paul had considered the options he had, but primarily he needed to act on Catherine's last discussion with the other VP's; it was very appropriate how she had rearranged positions and responsibilities, just another of her many skills.

He was going to move Gareth to Africa, he'd been far to out spoken of late and what better way to see if he could actually put his money where his mouth was, or rather, Xianthos's money back into the Corporate pocket.

Constance had done well there; she had turned round what had been a big loss of seventy million a year to a meagre five million. How she had done that was amazing, sometimes he thought that she should have the new role, but he did have the more sophisticated experience with the major clients. If she continued in New York the same way she did on the African continent, she would easily oust him in about five years. He smiled at the thought.

'Hell, he had enough money from the bonuses alone to retire now, but it was always a challenge and the last five years had been exactly that.'

Then there was Eduardo. He was definitely the candidate for Europe without a doubt! Anyway he would love the new scenery, especially the European females.

Tito wouldn't necessarily have to move, he could put the new person in the South American position, certainly closer to the two senior executives if things went wrong! Yes, that would work. Might cause problems with Gareth, but he would be the only one. He didn't want to lose Tito, he was a very fine man and it was his decision after all.

Now, the new candidate for the VP position was certainly something he had to consider well; the selection would have to take into account every senior manager in the corporation, which seemed to have produced several highly qualified applicants for him to consider.

The phone rang in his office.

"Strong."

"Sorry to bother you Paul, but I have Catherine on line one and Gareth on line two, which one do you want to take first?" Celeste Johnson asked, she'd been Paul's aide for over ten years and he had never known anyone like her for efficiency, in his life.

Paul smiled.

"I'll take line two first, Catherine will wait." He smiled as he thought of his boss, she knew that the corporation came first and the day to day operations was his call.

Celeste smiled at her boss's tone; she knew that he was smiling. Catherine rarely called during normal office hours it was unheard of.

"Ms. Devonshire, Mr. Strong has just taken a call from the European VP, would you like me to get him to call you back?" Celeste had met the woman a few times in her career at Xianthos, she was formidable but entirely fair in her dealings, or so it had always appeared to her.

Catherine looked at the time, if she put down the phone it might be another hour before Paul rang back and she would be bathing Lisa.

"I'll wait, thanks Celeste."

Celeste was surprised at her waiting. "What's the weather like in your part of the world Ms. Devonshire?" It was better than the piped music, and no way was Celeste going to subject the owner of Xianthos to that!

Catherine was a little surprised that Paul's aide would try to converse with her, how times are changing, but at least it would be better than listening to the piped music. "Very cold, we had frost this morning, could be some snow on the way."

"Well it's just started to heat up here, in the seventies, so quite comfortable at the moment. My kids love the hot weather, wonder where they get it from sometimes." she said cheerfully.

Catherine smiled and thought of her two charges and wondered what they thought about the season changes. "Yes, kids appear to like hot weather, must be the thought of open spaces, holidays, swimming and generally getting up to mischief I would think." Catherine said in a relatively talkative way.

Celeste was surprised, she hadn't expected much of a response to her chatter. She knew Ms. Devonshire's background and that her immediate family was all dead including her only son.

"You have any children on the ranch?" It was open speculation.

Catherine wondered if the aide was being nosy or just making general conversation. She decided on the latter.

"I've got a couple of kids staying with me at the moment, only ever seen them with the cold weather. It will be interesting to see what they get up to in the summer months."

Celeste was amazed, should she say more or not? What the hell you only live once! "My son Richard, loves going boating with his father in the vacation time, but Gayle my youngest, she likes nothing better than sitting in the sun doing nothing in particular."

Catherine laughed at her description. "How old are your children Celeste?" she couldn't remember exactly how old Celeste might be, maybe mid-thirties, more or less, she didn't know, it had never been important.

"Richard is eighteen in a couple of weeks, goes to college next fall. Gayle is sixteen and making my heart stop from time to time with the number of interested young men who seem to want to get to know her. Guess you just never get over being worried about them, do you?"

Celeste said, forgetting whom she was talking to for the moment.

Catherine mulled that one over. "No, I guess you don't Celeste, but so long as they stay safe, what more can any parent ask?" She spoke solemnly thinking about Lucas.

A light going out on the console indicated that Paul had finished his conversation with the European VP. "Well, it was wonderful to talk to you Ms. Devonshire. I will put you through to Mr. Strong now, bye."

Catherine smiled, "Bye for now Celeste, oh and next time I'm on the line call me Catherine and let me know how you're getting on with your children." With that she waited to be put through and a male voice answered.

"Sorry to keep you waiting Catherine, Gareth is getting up tight about your recent memo." Paul laughed softly at the remembered conversation.

"I'm sure you will handle it Paul." Catherine spoke with disinterest.

"I'm sure I will, so what can I do for you today, it's a little unusual to hear from you this time in the day?" Paul was curious.

"I had a snippet of information passed to me confidentially, that Hudson is ready to go for release of the documentary. I want access to it prior to release. No ifs or buts' just send me a copy of the tape. If you have any resistance, just get the lawyers involved." Catherine spoke in a demanding voice.

Paul looked at the intercom thoughtfully, he had known that Catherine would get at Hudson eventually, but to suppress the documentary would only bring her even bigger publicity. "You going to veto the documentary altogether?"

"Ah...Paul, now why would you think I would be that malicious?" She laughed, and it came out as a low throaty expression that made the hairs on the back of your neck stand up.

"Not malicious, just payback on your terms." He ventured.

"The answer to your question is no, they can show everything except Destiny. It really is as simple as that."

"Okay, I should have it to you by courier within the next five days."

"Fine. Oh, and Paul tell Hudson if she doesn't co-operate I'll personally come over and sort the issue out!"

"You know she might just take you up on that threat."

"If she does, then I guess I'll get to kill two birds with one stone. But believe me the other bird is far, far more important than Hudson." Catherine said in a gentle tone.

"Never thought I'd see you in LA?" Paul was surprised at the turn of the conversation.

"Who says I will be yet! I'd rather conduct any of my business anywhere else in the world, but it appears that affairs of the heart Paul, sometimes ignore your preferences." Catherine spoke in a casual tone.

Paul was once again surprised, so she did have a relationship with Jace Bardley, interesting. "That they do Catherine, that they do!"

Catherine was answering a question in the background.

"I have to go Paul, Grace left this afternoon and I have the dubious pleasure of bathing a seven year old tonight, no rest for the wicked it would seem." She laughed and waited for his response.

"You will miss Grace, she's a very fine asset to you on the ranch."

"An asset Paul? Really, you say the nicest things about people. Although you're right, I will miss her. Hell! I miss her now and she's only been gone about three hours. She's a good friend," her voice wistful.

"I better let you go, I'm going to contact the VP's tomorrow and let them know my decision on the global areas. Obviously, I will update you tomorrow also." He immediately went back to business efficiency mode.

"Great, do what you have to do. Bye." Completing her call, she placed the cell phone down on the desk.

Paul glanced back at the intercom. *'Wonder exactly how Jace Bardley feels about Catherine? Can't say I've ever seen her quite so laid back as she is at the moment. Love must agree with her.'* He chuckled at the thought of his boss in love and the object of that love, was so different from her that it was almost ludicrous.

He pulled out his personal diary and rang UCP direct.

Chapter Twenty-Four

Catherine sat alone in the lounge and glanced at the book she had recently put down after reading to the children again. *'I wonder what my life would have been like if Lucas and I hadn't lost mother when we did? Wonder if Lucas would still be alive? Father might have come home more often and they would have been a family. Strange how mother always had a sense of the future and she knew deep down she wasn't going to be around to see our future.'* Catherine idly thumbed through some of the pages of the book, and a small smile appeared as she read pieces that brought back her own memories.

Twenty-three years earlier:

The rambling house, in a fashionable district in London, was alive with laughter and people enjoying themselves in a party-like atmosphere.

It was Elena Devonshire's thirty-fifth birthday and just about everyone who was anyone in the publishing world was there. Stewart Devonshire had made sure his wife would enjoy the day in every way, he loved the woman to distraction, and she was his whole world. Even his children came a pale second to her and his business a necessary evil, he wanted Elena to have everything money could buy and he worked hard to achieve just that.

It was late afternoon and several of the guest requested that Elena do one of her party tricks, her two children were fascinated, it was their first grown up party and they had loved every minute of it.

"Please, you flatter me." Elena blushed as she eyed the numerous people sitting in various places in the large dining room.

Stewart came over to where the children sat with their nanny. "Your mama is very talented children. What will it be a song or some of those fortunes she tells from time to time?" He spoke into Catherine's ear but loud enough for Lucas to hear too.

Both children looked at their father and smiled brightly. "Oh, I want a song daddy, mama sings nice songs." Lucas said in a loud voice, so that those seated close to them, laughed out loud.

Elena looked over at her family and knew that a conspiracy was a foot.

Stewart glanced down at his shy, gangly ten-year-old daughter. "What about you little princess, what do you want mama to do as her party piece?" He smiled at his daughter; she was at times difficult to get a sentence out of if she wasn't confident about something.

Ice blue eyes looked into his blue-green ones and smiled. "Fortunes daddy, she could tell fortunes." She continued to look earnestly at her father.

Elena looked over at her husband.

"My love, it appears Lucas wants you to sing, but our little princess here wants you to tell fortunes. Your choice." He laughed and the other guests joined in.

Elena looked at her two expectant children, noting the excitement on her son's face and the quiet anticipation on her daughter's often-emotionless visage.

"I think I will not chose, I will sing a song for Lucas and tell some fortunes for my friends. There is a catch to the fortune telling though, my dear daughter will also get her fortune told, she requested the party piece after all." Elena noticed her daughter blush and gulp at the same time; she was so very shy that one.

Sometime later after a song and several fortunes being told, Elena was tiring and Stewart said enough was enough and the children had to go to bed. Elena rested her hand on husband's arm. "No, I have one more to do and I will do it as she gets ready for bed, heh little princess." Smiling at her daughter, who had looked both relieved and a little disappointed by her father's announcement.

"Okay, my love, but don't take all night, we still have a party to finish." He pushed her gently towards the children making their way up the stairs to bed.

After her bath, Catherine looked into the brown eyes of her mother and waited.

Taking her hand and turning over the palm she looked at her daughter and spoke softly. "Catherine there will be times in your life that appear as if the god's themselves are out to defeat you, but take strength my child that you will survive and you will be the stronger for it. You will suffer tragedy, but I see a great, wonderful sense of peace that will be hard fought for and it will bring you a lasting happiness. Don't ever give up on love my daughter, because you have a great capacity for it, but the darkness that is in our ancestry will rear up and try to defeat it. Always remember that there is a one true love out there for everyone, and you will have that Catherine, but you may have to sacrifice everything that you hold dear to your heart to achieve it. Take council from a brown haired, brown eyed foreigner in the future, she will steer you towards your goal. But never fear daughter, I will always be there to hold your hand in the darkness that comes and goes, it is my destiny."

Elena looked into the ice blue eyes that held fascination and wonder, but also pain at the statement her mother had made. "Mama will you always be there to hold my hand in the darkness, even when I'm older?" Came a tentative question.

Elena smiled wistfully at her elder child, so solemn this one, so full of promise and yet so full of tragedy too! "Oh yes, never fear Catherine, no matter what, I will definitely hold your hand, you just need to think of me and I will be there, it is my destiny. Just as you will have a different destiny marked for you one day." She gently pulled the covers over her daughter as she got into bed.

"I love you mama, never ever leave us." It was the plea of a child not yet ready to consider the consequences of the journey of life before them.

"I love you too Catherine, never ever forget that!" Elena kissed her cheek and left the room.

Catherine wondered what her mother meant by all those words, it was far too much for her mind to understand. Mama would tell her again when she was older, for now it was sufficient to know that she would   always   have   her   mama   near   at   hand.

The present:

Catherine wiped a tear from her cheek as the memory invaded her space, her lonely life; one she had purposely sought was now closing in on her.

'Had her mother been right? Was there a person out there who could bring her peace and love? Sometimes I've wanted to believe in Adam's theory of soulmates, never more so than in recent weeks but... Yes, there always seems to be a 'but' in my life. I cannot let the past go; it darkens my doorstep too often to think about trying for a life with someone new. I cannot take another round of deaths of people I love, it would break my heart all over again, and only this time I'm not sure I would ever survive it! Mama if you hear me, I could do with a hand to hold about now!'

Catherine looked again at the book and placed it on the fireside table, knowing the futility of her childish thoughts.

She closed her eyes and wondered what Jace was doing right about now.

Jace had arrived at her parents around dinner, it was rare she visited them during the working week, but today had been difficult to cope with and veiled threats by Hudson, just set her on edge.

Seeing her mother in the kitchen, she went in to greet her.

"Mom, what's for dinner?" Jace happily hugged the surprised woman, who was the same height as her daughter, but much more heavily proportioned.

"Jace, what made you come out here tonight? Not that it isn't good to see you," said the smiling woman as she smiled green eye to green.

"Can't a girl come and see her family from time to time huh?"

"As the girl in question is my eldest daughter, absolutely. It's good to see you Jace, you haven't been here for over two months."

"I've been out of the country, I told Dad, when I rang him last."

"No worries my dear, come on let me see if you've lost any more weight with this job in Hollywood." Her mother gently chastised her daughter with a twinkle in the eyes.

"Oh Mom, it's not that bad and anyway I caught a virus over in New Zealand," she held up her hand as her mother tried to get a word in.

"It's okay Mom, no harm done, I'm fine. I was well looked after, you would have liked the people I stayed with at the time." Jace pictured her mother getting to know the stoic woman she'd lost her heart too, it brought a smile to her face.

"In that case I'd better feed you up then; come on your Dad and Lucy are in the study, talking as always. She's nearly as bad as you for talking constantly, only she doesn't have your persuasive skills with your Father." Tugging her eldest child along, they went towards the study.

There in the chair, at a much used desk sat a grey haired, ruggedly handsome man of about sixty; he generated confidence and happiness about him. He was conversing with a five foot eight inch young woman who had his blue eyes and blonde hair from her mother. At fifteen she was challenging her father to something with all the enthusiasm of youth.

"Well you two, we have a guest for dinner." Her mother pushed Jace into the room.

"Jace." Came two voices simultaneously. Both rushed forward to hug her in welcome.

"It's great to see you Jace, have you got a holiday it's the middle of the week?" her Father asked in interest.

"Oh come on Dad, Jace never takes any holidays, that place must owe her weeks and weeks," Lucy replied for her sister.

Jace ruefully looked at the two and smiled deeply, this was her family home, and she knew that she would always be welcome here no matter what happened in her life. "No holidays but I guess I was feeling kinda lonely." Well it was true; she was lonely now without Catherine.

"Looks like a decent meal wouldn't come a miss either Jace." Her father looked at the fashionably slim woman in front of him.

"Ah come on Dad, I've just had that conversation with Mom; let's catch up on some gossip until dinner arrives."

They talked for about half an hour and then during dinner.

Lucy helped her mother to clear away as father and eldest daughter went into the lounge to await them.

Jason Bardley looked at his daughter with concern. Although she had been talking, it had appeared to him to be somewhat subdued conversation on her part. "You going to keep an old man in suspense Jace?" her father asked with a grin across his expressive face.

Jace turned to her father and returned the grin. "I never could keep anything from you could I Dad?"

"Never, so come on what's worrying my little girl?"

"I guess it's work mainly, Hudson has been a little vindictive of late, she's not the easiest to work with but recently she's been more difficult. She called me naive today, maybe I am. But what she wants I just can't give her that information, no matter how trivial it might be! Does that make any sense to you Dad?" she said in a quiet sad voice.

Jason looked at his eldest daughter, he knew that losing the publishing business six years ago had broken her heart; it had been something she had always wanted to do ever since she had started to walk and gone to the office on occasions with him.

She'd said that one day 'Bards Publishing' would publish a book she had written. Then the bubble had burst and he wasn't even sure if she wrote in her journal anymore, never mind the book she'd always dreamed of.

Jason had always known his eldest daughter had an almost idyllic lookout on life; she never judged anyone always looking for the best in everyone no matter the circumstances. But it was also going to hurt her one-day. All he wanted was an opportunity to be there when it did, and help with the disappointment. Maybe this was that time.

"Jace, you have an understanding of people that can be both a gift that hurts or brings great joy. Sometimes it's perceived as naïve, then again it can be a strength too, all depends on who you talk too." Her father looked at her intensely. "That's not all though is it Jace?"

Jace shook her head and returned his stare. "No, I've met someone Dad. Only thing is I know I love them but they don't seem to want to take a chance."

Jason had wondered when it would be that she would fall in love. Jace had never given much time to romance always saying it had to be that special person before she wanted to play in that arena. There had always been the odd skirmish with the boy next door and the couple of college friends; certainly in the last five years or more nothing or not anything she was willing to admit to.

"Wonderful news Jace, is it someone we know?" he asked gently.

Jace rose out of the chair and walked over to the window. "No, you wouldn't know them. In fact they live in New Zealand. We sort of became friends when I had to stay at the ranch to recuperate after catching a virus. Strange how the fates have put a distance between us, almost as if they're on her side." Jace whispered barely audible.

Jason wasn't sure if he'd heard right 'her side'? He had always brought his children up to respect other people's beliefs and choices in life but he was a little surprised that his daughter had chosen to become a member of a minority group. Which frequently went through the mangle at any available opportunity at the hands of bigoted and small-minded people. "You say she doesn't love you? Why would that be Jace?" he asked concerned.

The young woman turned to him and realised she had let it slip that the love of her life was a woman! "You know something Dad?"

"What would that be daughter?" He bantered back.

"Have I told you recently how much I love you and how well you brought us up?" She said a tear welling up in her eyes.

"Well, come to think of it not recently." He smiled and held out his arms for her to come into a much-needed hug.

"Oh Daddy, what am I going to do, she's so... so out of reach. Not just the distance physically but mentally she just wont let go of the past, and although I know she likes me as a friend I'm not sure if she even wants a relationship beyond that! Hades, she was married and had a son, so maybe it's just my hormones Dad." Jace spoke thickly into her father's shoulder.

"Jace, I've known you for what?' he smiled at the rueful look he got from his daughter. 'Okay, all of twenty-five years and this is not your hormones Sweetheart. Although you might have to consider, that your friend doesn't have the depth of love you have for her, you are going to have to come to terms with that and respect it. Can you do that Jace, can you just be her friend and not want more than she's willing to give?"

Jace looked into her Father's concerned face with tearful eyes. "I love her dad, if all she can give me is friendship, I have to live with that and I will. Because I can't live with the thought of not having her in my life at all, just the thought of it hurts too much!"

"Then Jace, you are going to be okay. Hell! Who in their right mind wouldn't love you in the end? Just give it time, and they say patience has it's own reward, you never know Jace, yours might just be...sorry you never did say her name?"

"Catherine, her name is Catherine Warriorson," she said softly.

"Well, your reward might just go by the name of Catherine." He smiled and held his daughter in a warm comforting hug. At the same time thinking that the name was familiar and an echo of the past in some strange way.

"Thanks Dad, I'm really pleased I came home. I always know you're there for me!" Jace said thankfully.

"We are all here for you Jace never forget that! Now come on let's dry those tears your mother and sister will be coming in soon and you know what it's like if they pick up on juicy gossip." He laughed into her blonde hair.

"Yeah, like I'd never get home this side of next week," she laughed along with her father. Somehow everything was going to be all right. It was just a matter of a little faith.

Chapter Twenty-Five

Paul Strong wearily got up from his chair, putting a hand across his brow. *'That woman was the very devil incarnate,'* he thought as he'd concluded a very interesting conversation with Clarissa Hudson.

It was late and he wanted to get home and pack, before heading off to LA on a late evening flight. James would be excited at his arrival, it was going to be a surprise and how! Especially, when he told him the whole story. He smiled in anticipation of his partner's response, and picking up his briefcase and switched out the lights as he left his palatial office. On his way down from the thirtieth floor, which was the executive level he mused over his conversation with Hudson.

"Clarissa Hudson speaking," answered the sweet tone of the woman who was anything but.

"Clarissa, this is Strong from Xianthos in New York, have you got a few minutes to talk?" Paul spoke in a brusque tone.

Clarissa started out of her chair in surprise, that the most powerful person in Xianthos, other than the owner herself was calling. *'Now I wonder why?'* She smirked, as she knew damn well.

"Sure Paul, go ahead," never one to miss an opportunity.

"I have a request from Ms Devonshire. She wished to look at the new documentary by Peter Adamson, prior to it being released."

Hudson smiled, "Now that is an interesting request, this is the first time she has ever taken an interest in UCP, I'm flattered," she said sarcastically.

"Well don't be! We won't beat around the bush, you know as well as I do why she wants to see the tape," Paul snarled into the phone.

"Touchy subject I see Paul, pity she couldn't have come up with a much better disguise to remain anonymous. I'm only the Producer, not the Writer or Director of the documentary."

"I think you did a good job in steering them directly into her path."

"Me? No, I suspect she shouldn't have taken one of the team into her home, if she didn't want to feel any repercussions." Clarissa felt quite pleased with herself; this conversation was heading right into her hands.

"So you are saying that Ms. Bardley is instrumental in some of the 'facts' on the tape involving the Destiny ranch." Paul was puzzled; he didn't think Jace would give any information, not if she was involved with Catherine on a personal level, but then....

"Let's just say, Jace knows who pays her salary every month." Hudson stated simply.

"Well, that would be Xianthos then wouldn't it!" Paul answered scathingly.

"Oh, petty point Paul, she works for UCP not Xianthos, she knows that and is very happy with the situation."

"The fact remains that I need you to send me a copy of the tape, when will I see it?" Paul had digested the information.

He heard a faint laugh at the end of the line. "Don't worry Paul, you will see a copy on your office desk tomorrow evening, I will wait for the almighty Ms. Devonshire to stick her two pennies in, but then it gets released!"

"Leave it with your secretary tomorrow by lunch, I will get it picked up. Have a good day Ms. Hudson." He put down the phone.

Paul contemplated the conversation; he could warn Catherine about the comments made by Hudson regarding Jace and her participation in the tape. Then again, it could be nothing and he would have looked a fool.

The doors opened and he stepped out into the lobby noting the evening sky with its multitude of colours. He smiled and headed out of the swinging doors.

Colin glanced at his boss, who was lounging negligently over the railing to the paddock, watching the two youngsters with their riding lessons.

She looked relaxed and very beautiful, although if you looked deeply enough into her eyes you could see the veiled sadness held there. Not many-dared look into her eyes, so few people would ever see it. He had! At breakfast that morning they discussed the ranch, it's opportunities at length, being interrupted only by the motherly figure of one Doris Gladstone, the woman who was helping out until Grace came home. He had looked at her and saw the sadness there, not very far from the sadness in his own he suspected. Unrequited love was one hell of a burden to carry around, for his part anyway.

"They're doing well Ma'am," he said politely as she glanced around and saw him looking at her.

"Yes, I noticed." She answered quietly and went back to her observation.

"Jake is a natural you know, once he's told, it's as if he's always known how to do the exercise. Were you like that Ma'am?"

Catherine turned to him and bit of an angry retort. "I thought I told you to call me Catherine?" she responded.

He looked flustered and nodded. "You did, guess old habits."

She shook her head, "No, not old habits, just stubborn men I think, and the answer to your question is yes."

He pushed his hat back on his head and regarded the girl on the pony, she had a toothless grin plastered on her face as she tried but failed to catch up to Jake on his larger pony. "Lisa is a little different as you can see." He smiled. He'd been enchanted by the little girl from the first time he'd met her.

"So I see, I wonder how she's stays on the pony?" Catherine also smiled briefly at the sight of the little girl pushing the pony forward but slipping continuously in the saddle.

"Diamond likes her I guess."

"How old is the pony?"

"Oh, he's the eldest one on the ranch, was going to retire him but thought he might like to get to know one more rider before he gets his rest. Not sure now if that was a mistake or not." He laughed at the thought of the old pony and the excited child that first day out.

She'd pulled at his mane and tail as she executed various stages of falling off the pony, he'd even pinched her back at one stage, but she never looked scared and he'd eventually nuzzled her at the end of the session.

"Will he stay the course do you think?" Catherine asked with interest.

"Diamond?" he looked for confirmation and she nodded. "Oh yes, she has him eating out of the palm of her hand, quite literally." Colin laughed.

"Not the only one she has eating out of her hand I suspect." Catherine levelled him a wry look and moved away from the fence.

Colin turned crimson and pulled himself over the railings to enter the paddock.

"You know something Colin," she continued without waiting for him to answer but noted that he turned in her direction. "She has the same effect on me too!" Then walked over to the barn and her exercise with Tralargon.

He watched her body swing into action towards the barn, she certainly moved with power and grace; he shook his head from wayward thoughts.

Jace enjoyed the rest of the evening with her family; it had helped to talk to her Father. When she'd been a child it had always been Daddy she went too, even on the most diverse subjects including sex!   Her father had never turned her away, always explaining patiently what his daughter needed to know, although his wife had coached him on the questions she'd thrown at him about sex. Jace had been embarrassed, but laughed when he had explained that year she was home from college and they had been reminiscing.

'Now I've openly discussed my love for Catherine Warriorson. Funny it hadn't been has hard to say it, as I thought it would be. There again I was only talking to my Dad! Hades she had to approach the subject with Catherine, now that, was one wonderful but scary thought.'

Smiling, she contemplated the time in New Zealand and wondered if a phone call would be well received. "Hey, all that can happen is she's out!" Jace said out loud to her empty apartment and picked up her phone and dialed the number.

What seemed to be minutes but was only around thirty seconds the tone changed and she knew it was ringing.

Waiting.

Jace looked at her computer and she thought that maybe it would be better to just send e-mail.

Suddenly the phone was picked up and an unfamiliar voice spoke.

"Warriorson residence, how may I help you?"

"Ha.... I'm sorry, hello this is Jace Bardley is Mrs. Warriorson available?" Jace stuttered wondering who the stranger was at the end of the phone.

"Well, I will check. Is she expecting your call?" The woman asked Jace perceived her as being mature she had a motherly tone.

"No, no she's not but I'm sure she will take the call if she knows it's me." Jace almost pleaded with the woman.

"Be right back my dear." The phone was placed on the hall table Jace could just picture it.

Waiting.

She then heard solid footsteps making there way towards the area of the hall the phone was placed down in.

Jace took a deep breath; hopefully it was Catherine.

"Hi, Jace?" came a low voice which she immediately recognised and that brought a blush to her cheeks.

"Catherine, hi yourself." She giggled at the other end to hide her sudden nervousness.

"Look Jace, this isn't the best place to chat. Give me a few seconds to get to the study and we will talk, be right back." She placed the phone back down and Jace heard her moving down the hall. Calling to someone called Doris to put the phone back on the hook when she picked it up at her end.

Catherine rushed over to her phone in the study and picked the instrument up and Doris then put down the other phone. Hearing the click, Catherine cleared her throat of its sudden dryness.

'Jesus, was she nervous of talking to Jace? God I really must have it bad.'

"So Jace, what brings about this call? Not that I mind you understand it's great to hear from you! How are you by the way?" Catherine spoke very fast.

"Hey hold on catch your breath I'm fine, and you?" Jace smiled as she tried to picture the woman at the other end.

"I'm good, all the better for hearing your voice." Catherine said it without thinking. Now what would Jace think?

"Glad to hear that because I feel the same. In fact that was the reason I called, I wanted to hear to your voice. Stupid I guess." Jace smiled self-consciously.

Catherine smiled brightly at the admission. "No Jace, not stupid but its going to be costly for you." Catherine laughed to ease the tension.

"Yes, well for my best friend I can afford it."

"Best friend huh? Well, best friend, I guess that next time I get to call and we waste some of my ill-gotten gains."

"Sounds good to me what about Sunday, we could talk all day?"

"Please.... Don't you think I have things to do on a Sunday?" Catherine laughed and wanted nothing more than to do just that!

"Ah, almost forgot you have responsibilities. Speaking of which, how are the children doing?"

"Good, both appear to be settling in and they are both learning to ride so they can come for rides with me and Tralargon."

"You spoil them Catherine and I wouldn't wonder if you're not worse now that Grace has gone! By the way when is she coming back?"

"She called yesterday but she wasn't sure, just wanted to let me know that she arrived okay. I worry about her when she drives long distances, the leg gives her some pain from time to time, but she rarely says anything." Catherine said softly.

"You miss her don't you?" Jace was almost jealous. Hades she was jealous, at least Grace was in the same country, she wasn't.

"Yes."

"So, you going to come over and see me anytime soon?" Jace moved off the subject.

"Jace, you ask me on every e-mail and the answer is still the same. But I love the fact that you keep asking me." Catherine answered in a sultry voice.

"Speaking of which."

"Which?" Catherine said puzzled.

"Oh... love, I was thinking about love." Jace answered almost absently her train of thought scattering.

"I see. Any reason other than the fact that maybe you might have fallen in love?" Catherine cringed at the thought but asked anyway.

Jace went quiet, how to answer that!

She was so slow in answering that Catherine spoke again.

"So have you?" She went quiet at her end.

"Well, yes and no, really." Jace finally answered.

Catherine looked at the phone in her hand almost as if it was burning into her palm and frowned. "It is either yes or no. I'm not sure the object of your desire would like to be on the receiving end of a halfway statement."

"Have you ever fallen in love Catherine?" Jace already knew the answer to that.

"No, well maybe that's not strictly true." And added silently, *'Not now anyway.'*

"So, you have just used the yes/no scenario." Jace laughed at her end.

"I guess I did; do I know him?" Catherine asked quietly.

"Him? No you don't know 'him'." She answered equally as quietly.

"I see. Guess you knew him before you came here?" A sick feeling was building in the pit of her stomach and it was almost a temptation to finish the conversation now.

"I think I've always known the person in my heart, but I fell in love with them almost from the first time I saw their eyes look into mine -such beautiful eyes too! No, I met the person in New Zealand." Had she said enough? She hoped so.

Catherine tried to digest the information. *'Who on earth had she met here? Was it someone prior to Destiny, or was it on the ranch? Who had she responded too?'* Catherine was trying to decipher all the signals.

"Have you gone to sleep on me out there Catherine?" Jace chuckled she could almost hear the wheels turning in Catherine's head.

"What! No Jace, sorry, I was thinking." She said sheepishly.

"Must have been some thought you were having?"

"It was."

"Did you come to a conclusion?" Jace held her breath.

"No." Was the plaintiff response.

"When you do let me know will you. I'm always interested in your opinion especially about this particular person." Jace smiled and wished she had more time to tweak Catherine, it was late and she had to get some sleep. For someone as worldly wise as Catherine Warriorson, it sure took a hammer and chisel to get her to see the point!

"Oh Jace Bardley, never fear you're top of the list with the comments on the person you have fallen in love with, believe me!"

"I have to go Catherine, it was good to hear your voice."

"Same here Jace, sleep well."

"Behave yourself Catherine, and I lo...look forward to your call on the weekend," she finished weakly.

"Bye Jace, I..." Catherine had no more words.

"Yes, I know." Jace said softly as she hung up the phone.

Catherine stared at the instrument and became thoughtful.

Jace looked at her apartment and noticed how lonely it appeared, she headed for bed and sleep, which wouldn't come easily tonight. At least she still had Taz to keep her company, but who would keep Catherine's bad dreams at bay, she wondered?

Catherine sank back into the depths of the leather armchair behind her desk. Her hand touched the mouthpiece of the phone and she sighed heavily. *'I know you deserve to be happy Jace, but.... but I wanted to share that happiness with you! God, how I want that to be part of my new life; I guess creating a new life is okay but getting people to participate in it is quite something else! So my friend, who are you in love with?'*

Her head dropped onto the back of the chair and she closed her eyes to contemplate what Jace had said. *'How long were you in New*

Zealand Jace? Couldn't have been more than a couple of weeks and one of those with me!' Her face held a frown as she concentrated.

Suddenly her eyes blinked open in shock. "Oh God, how could I not see it! She loves ME!" The knowledge not only hit her squarely in the chest, but it made sense out of all the conversations that she'd had with Jace.

'What do I do now? I've wanted Jace to be happy; I couldn't possibly let her follow the reclusive life that I feel comfortable with. She's so young and is on the threshold of life, I'm just not the person you take home to the parents as a prospective in-law, hell, did I say that?' Catherine laughed at the thought.

'Jace why me? Why offer me your heart, I could only bring you unhappiness, if only you knew me, how you think you know me! Christ, but I so want to have what you're offering me and I would love you for eternity if I could make it happen.'

Glancing at the photos of her parents and brother and then her son she smiled. "You would want me to be happy, I know some things you just have to sacrifice for the pain you have caused in the past and I've done that for sure, especially to Adam and Maria."

A single tear trailed down the high cheekbones and splashed on the desk. "Maybe if I told her everything and Jace decides if she still wants me could I do that? YES!"

That would be the only answer she could ever give, better she was left the lonely one after she told Jace. Hadn't she chosen that particular scenario for herself anyway, now it would just hurt a little more but as with everything she would get used to it. At least Jace would have the chance not to be part of her dubious future, which no matter what always seemed to end in darkness. Now, that darkness potentially had the chance to take the one hope she had seen for a light at the end of her particularly dark tunnel.

'Funny I never saw myself as a noble person before now! That's one thing you have given me Jace, those children out there may thank you one day.'

Once again looking at the family photo she directed her gaze to the older woman. *'You know something Mama, I think I need that hand to hold again about now, any takers?'* She touched the framed photo and gently rubbed her finger over the silhouette of her mother.

Catherine arose out of the chair and left the room abruptly.

Catherine was fuming, her hand smashed down on the desk more times than she cared to acknowledge.

Doris had discretely removed herself from the study, after delivering the package earlier and the tea that Catherine requested, as she ripped open the parcel.

Stalking over to the video recorder, she placed the tape inside and set it running, full running time was sixty minutes, but she was only interested in the footage on Destiny, that would be towards the end of the tape she perceived.

The narrator was smooth, had a very cultured voice and made the scenery sparkle with life and information as each segment was described in detail.

Moving to the part depicting Destiny and its owner, the narrative changed, from being a compulsive piece of documentary film to adversarial. The mention of the owner of the ranch being a recluse, the breakdown of communications between the owner and the film crew, leading to them being left in a wild spot without protection on a stormy day and subsequently the illness of one of the party. This showed a picture of an arrogant, selfish landowner attitude to anyone that came within miles of the property. This, along with flashes of the arrogance of the English aristocracy in the previous centuries to colour the narrative, as well as the beauty of the ranch was hidden behind archaic policies and attitudes from its present owner, Catherine Warriorson. The adverse narrative depicted Catherine as a modern day tyrant.

The desk was now a punching bag and when she was finished, she wished she'd just gone down to the gym. Her knuckles were raw and bleeding and the curses streaming from her mouth, enough to keep even the most courageous away from her at the moment.

"What sort of fucking documentary is that supposed to be?" Catherine shouted at the now empty screen in front of her. Walking around her desk she noticed that her tea was spilt and most of her papers she had on the desk had been stained by the beige liquid.

"I can't believe she did this, she knew I would veto it, what the hell is she up too?" Catherine was speaking out loud, although in a much lower tone than when she first started the tirade.

"Jace hadn't given any bloody interview, of this she was certain, Hudson had used certain facts and twisted them to her own ends. Okay I get to clear this up personally Hudson, and not just the video." Catherine almost snarled at the thought of Hudson and her cocky attitude.

"Fuck you Hudson! I'm going to make you pay, and how." She headed out of the door; her hand needed some treatment and about now some hot tea wouldn't come amiss as well.

Thinking, she went to the kitchen, Paul would be in his office in a few hours, she was certainly going to enjoy that call.

Paul had always known that Catherine would veto the documentary, but she now wanted it all recycled, not just the piece on Destiny but everything and she wasn't up for any argument.

For the first time in years, he heard her voice take on the demon edge it possessed particularly when she was involved with nasty take-over deals. This wasn't a take-over but it was going to be nasty. He doubted that Hudson would take it gracefully, oh no, not the vindictive Hudson.

Could be an interesting confrontation though one super bitch against another and he knew whom his money would be on!

He smiled as he recalled James' face as he'd explained his new role and where he was going to have the headquarters. If someone had told him that a smile could literally transform a person's face, he wouldn't have believed it until he saw it for himself and he certainly saw that on the face of his partner. He chuckled and looked out of the window of the house that belonged to James, which he also called home, that is when he managed to get the time to visit.

It was Saturday morning and they had decided that today was going to be a day off from work, and they would just enjoy the day. Ending up having a long leisurely dinner at home, their time together was so short that going out was something they didn't contemplate unless it was absolutely necessary.

He wondered about Jace Bardley and considered his options; Hudson had implied things that Jace had said. But Catherine never mentioned any of that when she called, he had been right to ignore her jibes, if Catherine thought something was wrong she would deal with it in her way.

'Well James, I guess I'm going to make that call Monday and watch from a distance, the fireworks should be interesting. Next time we have a dinner party, I think a certain Jace Bardley should be invited, now that would be really interesting!'

He smiled and went in search of his sleeping lover who seldom got out of bed before noon on the weekends.

Chapter Twenty Six

Sunday dawned bright and early for Jace she was so excited! No, she was more than excited if her stomach was anything to go by.

'Surely Catherine would have realised the identity of her prospective lover by now! Yes, but would she admit it if it wasn't what she wanted too?' Jace frowned at the thought and her stomach did a somersault that had nothing to do with excitement. Walking over to her computer she switched on and waited for the log in prompt. Padding over to the kitchen area she retrieved the items to make coffee and set it up and then went back to log in the computer.

Wading through her messages that she hadn't collected for a couple of days she saw one from Catherine. Quickly opening it she smiled at the contents.

Hello Jace,

Thought I had better give you some indication of the time when I would call. How does ten in the morning sound to you? Okay, I'm going to go for it anyway, in the hope that you're at least awake and if not I get the privilege of being the wake-up call. Not bad for being thousands of miles apart, don't you think?

I have an appointment with the Reverend after our call later today, as it's Monday here; already things are in the normal routine. The kids will be in school so I haven't the interruptions; hope you get to read this before I ring.

Catherine

Jace smiled at the message, ever thoughtful, this woman tried to cover all the bases. That meant that the call would be in, Hades about now!

Snagging a cup of coffee she managed to get a bagel as well, just as the phone rang. Walking swiftly over to the instrument, she put her cup down and bagel on top of the cup and picked up the phone.

"Hi." Jace spoke softly.

"Hi, yourself Jace. How are you today? Did you get my message?" Catherine spoke in a low gravelly voice.

"Catherine I'm fine and you? Oh, and yes I got the message you think of everything." Jace laughed trying to picture Catherine at the end of the line, what would she be wearing? Was she sitting in her chair behind the desk or walking round the room?

"Yes I'm fine too! When did you wake up?" She pictured Jace having just got out of bed and being somewhat tousled and dishevelled.

"About fifteen minutes ago, haven't showered yet, I can do that later." Jace was now sprawled out on the couch with her feet up on the coffee table.

"Sounds good to me, want any help?" Catherine teased from her end.

"What! Help? Zeus Catherine do you know what you're saying?" Jace spluttered at the end of her line and almost kicked the cup of coffee over at the mere thought of the help involved.

"Guess, it wouldn't be a good idea then. Pity I'm very good with a sponge so the kids say anyway." She finished off a wicked smile on her face.

"Jake let's you near him with a sponge?" Jace was incredulous. What was happening here? Whatever it was, let it continue on forever.

"Well, no, not exactly. I have to chase him with the sponge sometimes when he comes from the stables. Lisa does though; she's a really pampered little girl that one." Catherine let out a soft sultry laugh.

Jace grinned and felt her heart beat faster at the sound of the laugh. "Let me get this right. Reclusive C X Warriorson chases dirty-faced boys around her stables with a sponge, then pampers little girls who can twist her round her little finger with a luxury bath. Does that about cover it?" Laughing at the mental picture it brought up.

Catherine looked out of the window and smiled. "Just about, I guess. Only it's not just little girls that can do that now is it?"

"You want to clarify that for me?" Jace asked quietly.

"Oh, I like to think my best friend has a quick intelligence and can work that one out all on her own." Catherine teased.

"Yeah! So, that means me then?" Jace replied.

"Means you what?"

"Means I can twist you round my little finger too!"

The silence that hung in the air was electric.

"Yes." One solitary word, that brought about a thousand and one scenarios and possibilities.

Jace sipped from her coffee and cleared her throat. "Have you come to a conclusion after our discussion of the other evening?"

Catherine moved back to her desk and sat down. Trailing a finger over the portrait of her deceased family she smiled sadly at the group that had been held for a split second of time. Had it been so long ago?

Jace waited patiently at her end not wanting to push her into something she wasn't prepared for.

"You know I thought long and hard about what you said and I know the answer. Can't say that I'm impressed with your choice though." Catherine spoke seriously a smile edging her lips.

"What! Catherine you're fooling me! Let me tell you..." Jace was spluttering at the other end.

"Hey, hold on Jace, let me tell you something first, you did ask remember?" Catherine spoke with determination.

"Right! Yes I did, carry on, sorry." Came the mumbled reply.

"Good! For your choice does feel the same way and is honoured beyond any shadow of a doubt about what you're offering her!" Catherine slowly answered the question.

"Catherine, do you really feel the same?" Jace responded shyly.

"Jace Bardley, I fell in love with you the night you entered my study in those ridiculously large clothes and those bare feet. Hell, who wouldn't have fallen for you!" Catherine admitted in a low seductive voice.

"I can't believe this is happening. Why are you so far away from me!" Jace spoke with passion; all she wanted to do was hug and kiss the woman that held her heart.

"Hey, listen Jace, I need to talk to you about lots of things and that can't be done over the phone or on e-mail. Grace isn't back for another few weeks and then I have a couple of business matters to take care of. Then I'm coming over to see you okay?"

"I don't need to talk Catherine, I need to see you, and touch you and let you experience exactly what my love means."

"Jace, talking is important, especially about me! I need you to know everything that I was and what I've done in the past. Then, if you still love me well, I think we can sort something out on a more permanent basis what do you think?" Catherine smiled at the thought of seeing the passion she heard in Jace's voice manifest itself just for her.

"Whatever you tell me Catherine will never shake this love I have for you, that much you have to believe!" Jace spoke with conviction.

"I hope so Jace, because I've never been in love before and this feeling isn't one that I want to lose, ever!"

"I promise you Catherine, whatever, and I mean whatever you have to tell me about your past, I will be there for you after all is said and done, you can count on me." Jace sounded as if she was trying to convince a child about going to the dentist, but then Catherine was a child in many ways when it came to the romantic relationship area.

"Good, that's one promise I'm going to hold you too. Let me say one thing though Jace it's important!"

"Go ahead I'm listening."

"If you hear what I have to say and then find you can't keep that promise, you have to tell me. Don't let me hurt you as I've hurt others in the past, you have to promise me that!"

"I won't do that to you..."

Catherine interrupted her. "Promise me!"

Jace had tears of happiness flowing down her cheeks. "I...I promise." She answered in a slightly hoarse voice.

"Excellent. Now, what do I get this little wonder kid called Lisa for her birthday next week?" Catherine realised that the emotions were running too high for the present conversation to continue being thousands of miles apart; she went on to more normal conversation items.

"It's Lisa's birthday? How old is she?" Jace knew when the subject had been closed, if only temporarily, she knew why and smiled through the tears.

"Eight on Thursday, Jake will be eleven in three months; so what do you think?"

"I think you should take her shopping and let her chose something herself. Okay, you don't have to take Jake too." Knowing Catherine would be putting on a face at her end.

"Oh, that kid will do as he's told or he doesn't get to ride Ruby for a day. That is the only punishment I can meter out the boy understands. He expects to be beaten I think when he rebels, not my style and certainly Grace wouldn't ever lift a hand to them. Guess his parents thought corporal punishment was the answer, at least he doesn't have to go through that sort of abuse again." Catherine meandered off and Jace had to stifle a chuckle as she thought of the stoic woman who most would assume that hitting a kid to discipline them would be right on target for her.

"You know, I think those kids are having a great time now, I know they will miss their parents from time to time, particularly Lisa. Catherine you have provided a stable background for them to be brought up in, to be whatever they want to be in the future. You should be proud."

Laughing at the thought she responded. "Let's get them to twenty-one shall we, then we can decide if they have enjoyed living on Destiny."

"Are you asking me to help you raise two children Catherine?" Jace asked, wondering if it was a slip of the tongue.

"Would you if I asked?"

"Yes."

"Then let's get that talk out of the way and we can work on that little scenario, okay?"

"You betcha! So you going to take Lisa shopping or have you something else in mind?" Jace changed the subject this time, although her heart was racing at the mere thought of spending the rest of her life with Catherine.

"Shopping is a good idea, next weekend sounds about right. Did I tell you that she gave me her tooth, which had fallen out to leave for the fairies?" Catherine's voice wistful as the memory came to hand.

"She did what!" Catherine explained the situation.

"Well, that child sure does love you Catherine to do something like that." Jace said in wonder.

"No! No I think she just felt sorry for me." Catherine spoke absently. *'Had it been love, or was it just a sense of sadness she had felt coming from me? Maybe I will never know for sure, but it made me feel really good.'*

"I think she loves you. What did you get under your pillow that night Catherine?" Jace teased.

"I never put it under my pillow," She said solemnly, very much as she had spoken to Lisa that day.

"So you never got to receive a gift that day." Jace said quietly.

"Oh, I got a gift alright Jace but I didn't need to put the tooth under any pillow, the child had already weaved her magic on me! She gave me back another part of my heart that day, a part that died the day my Mother died. She opened it up and I will never forget that again." Catherine said in an almost awed voice.

"Then, my love, you did indeed get a gift that day." A choked voice answered back.

"Yes, what have you got planned for the next week?" Catherine pushed on into neutral emotionless topics.

Her call to Jace had gone better than she had anticipated. At the end of the conversation, which had lasted about three hours all told, was with emotion, but a promise that held a future or hopefully it did.

'I hope you can keep your promises Jace, something tells me to trust you implicitly, but another part of me is holding back, what if you can't handle what I have to say, what then of Love?'

Her car was heading towards the suburb that held the Reverend's house, he was at home today, but insisted she come to see him there, after all she was doing him a favor. Parking the car in the large drive, she walked quickly to the front door and rang the bell.

Moments later the door was held open by a very distracted Reverend Stott, who looked like he'd been pulled through a hedge backwards.

"Ah, Mrs. Warriorson, I'm sorry for my appearance, the dog got out of the garden and I've been chasing him around the neighbourhood, just got him back. Come in, come in." He motioned her forward.

"Thanks." Catherine couldn't help the small grin that appeared and quickly left as the Reverend looked at her immaculate appearance in close fitting black cord pants and a thick twill blouse. Her leather Air Force jacket slung casually over her shoulder; leather hiking boots in brown soft leather finished off the casual but cool image. Her hair was held in a loose fitting ponytail, which hung in neat precision down the centre of her back. Ice blue eyes held a hint of merriment as she walked into the house.

"This way, Mrs. Warriorson, I think my study would be the best place for a conversation. Let me tell my wife you're here and she can bring us some refreshments. What would you prefer Tea or Coffee or..."

"Tea is fine, thanks." She followed him to the study and walked inside as he left her to talk to his wife.

She noted the large pine desk, with a green leather bucket chair and a multitude of books in the bookcases or stacked in corners of the room, it looked untidy, but had a comfortable feel about the place.

She walked over to the window and glanced out over the lawn and saw the vegetable patch, with its winter selection taking life, then the birdbath and stand that obviously saw activity at all times of the year. It was a typically average sort of garden really for this part of the world.

The Reverend returned a little more composed and glanced in her direction and smiled. "Do you have a love of the garden?" He asked politely.

"Not really, Grace my housekeeper likes to keep a garden. I'm more for the open spaces myself; the natural wonders of nature have always fascinated me. Although it's nice to see them, reminds me of back home in England." She finished in a reflective mood.

The Reverend, not one to miss an opportunity to know more about a person asked. "Do you miss England?"

Catherine smiled wryly. "Not really. I no longer have family there to make me miss it too much, but sometimes things bring back memories from time to time that are good. Are you a native of New Zealand?"

"No, I came over from South Africa some twenty-five years ago. My family still live in Johannesburg and I have visited occasionally, but, my wife is a true Zealander, she's a Maori. We met about twenty years ago and have been together ever since! Truly a match made in heaven, well, I think so anyway." He chuckled at his descriptive observation.

"Sometimes they can be!" Catherine said and smiled at him.

"So you have a proposition for me, or that's how I viewed our last conversation?"

"Yes, I have started a memorial fund in the name of my son Lucas, I want the funds to be channelled into this project and others like it. I was going to ask if you wanted to be co-executor along with Grace Thornton, my housekeeper. She doesn't know yet, it was rather sudden." Catherine spoke fast and with precision.

Suddenly the door to the study opened and in walked a large homely woman, who clearly was a native New Zealander, her brown eyes looked at her with warmth and her smile was both sincere and infectious.

"Mrs. Warriorson, welcome to our home." She held out her hand as she relinquished the tray to her husband.

"Thank You, I'm very happy to meet you!" Catherine responded with a warm smile of her own.

"I better let you get on with your business, if you need anything else please call me." She left the room as quickly as she entered.

The Reverend smiled at the fading back of his wife, as he looked at the woman in front of him, who had offered, what he thought, was a lifeline for his project. "Exactly what would I do in this role?"

"You, and Grace, decide who should benefit from the funds available. It can be in the form of grants to people for caring for the children, or funds to build centres or whatever you feel will benefit the project. I'm not concerned with the details, only the initial scheme of things. I'm sure Grace will be happy to help on that front." She picked up a cup of tea, these small cups never held enough tea for her.

"It's that simple? How much would the fund hold?" He asked pensively.

"Yes it's that simple. Value, well I haven't discussed it with my lawyers, but what is your funding to date?"

The Reverend looked down into his cup and sighed. "Not enough, but at least we are able to help a little and the generosity of people like yourself have made the project take flight." He answered obscurely.

"That didn't answer my question though did it? So, how much have you had in the coffers since the project started?" She continued in that train of thought.

"Just over twenty thousand dollars." He answered quietly.

Catherine looked at him with her ice blue gaze and the look was one of incredulity. "Is that all? Why haven't you asked people like me for donations, it's a good cause?" She finished a little abruptly.

He looked at her sheepishly. "It wouldn't have been right to ask you for money as well as making a home for the children, let's be fair now, you didn't exactly warm to the subject at first."

Catherine smiled at him and considered his words.

"You're right I didn't! Although I have had cause to review my original opinions. Even I can be wrong Reverend, lucky someone came into my life at the right time and showed me the error of my ways."

"Would it be too personal to ask who that would be?" He eyed her cautiously, not wanting to overstep the current good feeling he was getting from the stoic woman in front of him.

"Well, you have met her, she was the American guest I had staying when you brought over the children that day." Catherine said softly.

"Ah, Ms Bardley. Yes such a pity she had to go back home." He looked at her and noticed the tightening of a muscle in her cheek at the mention of her name.

"Mmm, well she made me reconsider things in a big way and it's working out, so her influence helped your cause. If ever you need to thank anyone for my help, she would be the one to thank."

"Will she be coming back to visit?" He asked tentatively.

Catherine smiled warmly at that comment. "Yes I hope so."

They both drank their respective cups of tea. "So when will the fund start?"

"The lawyers will draw up the papers and I need to get Grace onboard, she has my full confidence and she's a friend. My son's name will not be involved in anything underhand if she's involved." Catherine said in a forceful way.

"My dear Mrs. Warriorson, I can assure you of my integrity when it comes to handling funds. I have never been involved in anything crooked in my life." He sounded affronted and rightly so.

Catherine realised after she'd spoken exactly what she'd implied. *'Guess my tact went out the window.'* Stifling a chuckle she responded. "I'm sorry Reverend no slight implied, it's very important that my son's name is never tarred with any of the feathers that have inadvertently been attached to me in the past." She answered.

"So you have a past?" He looked at her and arched his eyebrow to the left.

"Reverend, I don't know anyone who hasn't reached their mid-thirties without some kind of past." She grinned at him wickedly.

"I take your point Mrs. Warriorson. When do you think we will see this extra funding?"

"I should think in a month's time. Grace is back at the ranch in a couple of weeks and I can contact the lawyers, the funds are available immediately, it's just a matter of transferring them as you see fit."

"Sounds like a plan. So how are the two children you care for?" He changed the subject.

"Well, that's another reason for my visit actually. You mentioned adoption last time I was here right?" She asked tentatively.

He was surprised at her question. "Yes, adoption is a very good possibility, if they want it too."

"Yes, I was going to broach it to them soon, see how the land lies if you know what I mean." Her face held a look of consternation, almost not saying the next words. "What would be your reaction if I started a relationship during the process? Would there be any restrictions to the adoption?" She knew she was treading a fine line here but what the hell!

"No, nothing that I could see or comes immediately to mind. Are you asking me if there are some relationships that are not welcome by the adoption agency?"

"Yes." Came the clipped answer.

"Then I would have to check for you, but I'm not aware of any. If the children are loved and cared for and are happy, what more can you ask for. Would that person equally care for them?" He asked gently.

Catherine got up from her chair and gazed out of the window, her back to the Reverend as she spoke quietly. "Oh yes, without a doubt that person would care for them, maybe more than I'm capable of myself. Love would never be a problem for that person, that much I can promise."

The Reverend had an inkling that she was talking about, but you never broached a subject as sensitive as that one without facts and especially not to the party in front of him. "Then my dear, have no fear. I have always believed that love conquers all."

Catherine turned to him, "Thanks." and went towards the door.

Reverend Stott got up from his seat and held out his hand. "Thank you, and I hope you achieve what you seek."

Catherine clasped his hand in a strong handshake. "So do I, will you thank your wife for the tea and I will talk to you later about the adoption, after I've spoken to the children."

She opened the door and walked down the hall with him following behind. Opening the front door she suddenly turned back and looked at him with a piercing ice blue stare. "Oh, I forgot to say what the value was, of the fund I mean." He looked at her with interest. "I was thinking ten to start with then see how that goes." She waited for his reaction.

He smiled happily. "Ten thousand dollars sounds good to me."

Catherine never once letting her glance be diverted she once again smiled wickedly at the Reverend as she continued. "No! No not ten thousand! I was thinking more on the lines of Ten Million dollars." She saw his face pale and she laughed. "That's, US dollars not New Zealand. Bye for now Reverend."

She left the clergyman open mouthed at the door; he was still there looking as if he'd been poleaxed as she pulled out of the drive.

"Guess money has its way of muting a conversation from time to time." She chuckled out loud as she turned off the road towards home.

Chapter Twenty-Seven

Catherine was somewhat frustrated at the events over the last month, especially after her admission to Jace that she loved her. She had intended to have the talk with Jace, then things would have been in the open and they would be either building a life together or she would be here on her own. Well, she was certainly still here on her own although it had nothing to do with Jace.

Circumstances had decreed otherwise, Grace hadn't returned after her three-week visit, her father had suffered a heart attack and died two days prior to her coming home.

Now she was waiting for Grace to ring and say exactly when she would be home. But was home Destiny? That had been a question that Catherine had asked herself time and again, without a definite answer. Plans that she had made, which included Grace had to be put on a back burner. Would she come back, or stay in Auckland with her mother? God, too many questions and no adequate answers, this had been aggravatingly frustrating for Catherine.

Jace had been supportive from afar, unfortunately it was evidently clear events Catherine had set in motion with Hudson had affected Jace. Hudson was being particularly obnoxious with Jace sending her to South America on some really weird projects, which often meant they talked less and less and only e-mailed sporadically due to bad connections in the places she visited. This would end soon, that was for sure, the need to be close to Jace, especially since they had both admitted their love was overwhelming. At times she wanted to get the next plane out of New Zealand and go and see Jace. But she hadn't, she had responsibilities. Kids! Who'd have them?

Catherine smiled at the thought and reminded herself that without them in the last month, certainly she would have gone out of her mind. *'Yes, I would have them, especially these two wonderful children of 'mine'. Maybe it was time to talk to them about adoption, it didn't have to be soon, it could be in a couple of years or never. I feel good about the prospect and I have never been one to pass up a chance that I perceive to be correct.'*

Walking over to the study window she saw a redheaded child riding around on a bicycle in the yard. She looked happy with the rag doll, which she had brought with her, sitting precariously on the handlebars. Catherine smiled wistfully as she recalled the trip into town a couple of days before Lisa's birthday.

"You don't like taking us to town do you Catherine?" Lisa stated and looked at her with inquisitive blue eyes.

Catherine pulled the Landrover into an empty parking spot in the centre of the town and looked over at the child in the back seat. Jake had opted to sit in front and he was looking at both of them with interest.

"Yes well, the last time I came into town with you two, we had trouble if I recall correctly." She looked at the boy who fidgeted at the remark and them smiled at the two of them. "I don't know about you two, but I'm always up for a challenge."

Lisa sent out a whoop of joy and Jake laughed.

They piled out of the vehicle, Catherine wasn't too sure where to take them to shop; she looked around when she felt a small hand tug at her larger one. Looking down at the blonde child she raised her eyebrow in question.

"We might have to cross a road." Was the serious rejoinder.

Jake scuffed his toes on the pavement edge and looked down.

"Okay, sounds reasonable to me." Catherine clasped the hand in a firm but gentle hold.

Jake walked along behind them and they all glanced in the stores although they never ventured into any one of them. Half an hour later they all looked at each other...

"Guess this isn't getting us any where is it?" Catherine looked at the two children.

"No." They replied in unison.

From time to time people looked at them and voices could be heard discussing what they thought was an interesting trio. Catherine smirked at some of the comments and thought. *'One day it's going to be an interesting quartet, let's see what they make of that!'*

Catherine didn't really know what to do, what would her two friends do in the circumstances? *'Ask the kids probably.'* "So, Lisa as its going to be your birthday, what do you want to see?"

Lisa looked at her with glowing blue eyes. *'One day that kid was going to bowl people over, that was for sure. Hell, she was doing it now!'*

"Can we see the bikes?" Her voice rose in anticipation.

Catherine looked at her puzzled at first and then saw the shop that her young charge was looking at. "Oh, bikes. Yes, no problem whatever you want." Catherine looked at Jake who smiled tentatively at her.

"Cool!" Said the young voice as she suddenly felt herself dragged towards the shop with Jake walking slowly after them.

Settling into the shop, she motioned Lisa to look around for as long as she wanted. Then she watched Jake from the corner of her eye; he was looking over at Lisa with a sad expression. *'Something was bugging the boy again. Hell, was this kid ever going to be anything other than complex?'*

Approaching him, she laid a hand on his shoulder and he looked up at her and smiled briefly. "What's with you?" Over the weeks he had lived on the ranch they had reached the conclusion that straightforward confrontation on a subject seemed to work the best for them both.

He looked sheepishly at her and shrugged his shoulders.

She quirked her eyebrow and he knew that only a verbal response would appease the woman in front of him.

"I can't buy Lisa a present." He solemnly said.

Catherine looked at him puzzled. "Why not?"

He shuffled around and then starred at her with his frank hazel gaze. "I haven't any money of my own." A simple statement, suddenly Catherine realised she had missed something else in the child rearing game.

Passing a hand over her hair in frustration she looked at the boy and gave him an apologetic glance. "I'm sorry Jake that's something we need to sort out when we get home. What do you need now?"

He looked at her and motioned for her to bend her head so he could whisper into her ear what he wanted to purchase for Lisa.

Smiling she looked at him and realised that the kid was indeed growing into a really likeable person. Reaching into her purse she took out several notes and passed them to him discreetly. "That enough?" She said huskily.

He looked at the wad of money, then back at her and gulped at the amount. "I'll bring you some change." He said as he went out of the bike shop towards the shop two doors down.

"You keep out of trouble, that's all I need." She smiled as he left with a big grin on his face.

They had bought the prettiest pink bike in the place, including every imaginable accessory, placed a basket to hold 'Sherry' the rag doll, or that was what Lisa had said at the time. By the time she had purchased everything and had them packed for transport to the car, Jake walked in with a large parcel tucked under his arm he was smiling broadly.

"Hey Jake what you got there?" Lisa asked him excitedly.

He looked at the little girl and smiled. "It's a surprise."

She looked at him and she smiled beguilingly at him. "For me Jake?" A soft voice asked.

He looked into the blue eyes and was l☐st. "Yes."

She smiled even more brightly, if that could have been possible and this time as they left the shop she held not only Catherine's hand but Jake's too!

Catherine decided they would eat at a burger bar. *'Well at least it was fast food and she didn't have to cook it!'*

So here she was, watching the child with her new toy and the rag doll didn't reside in the basket that was left for the puppy dog that Jake had bought for her. It was a brown beagle, look a like. It had been quite a scene when she'd opened that present. Tears had streamed down the child's face and the boy had looked embarrassed, although in a shy sort of way very pleased with himself. So he should be too! Catherine had been proud of him; he had actually thought about the present, and if she hadn't been too obtuse she would have realised that the children needed some money of their own, even if it was only a token sum every week or month.

Glancing towards the ranch drive, she saw a cloud of dust appear and she thought at first it was either Colin or one of the other men on the ranch. Her first concern was for the child riding the small bike around the drive. If it was a stranger to the ranch, they might not be aware of the small obstacle that rode merrily around.

Moving quickly she opened the patio door of the study and called to Lisa to move towards the house, the child did so and stopped her bike close to Grace's herb garden, propping it up against the porch steps.

Watching the vehicle approach, she at first couldn't gauge the vehicle then suddenly it came into view. 'No, it can't be!' She looked again at the clear image of the vehicle now. *'Good grief that woman hadn't even called to say she was coming.'* Catherine quickly went down the steps of the porch and waited for the vehicle to stop.

Hands on hips she looked menacing until you looked up into her eyes and noted the sparkle of warmth within.

The woman got out of the vehicle and slowly approached what looked like a very imposing figure to anyone who didn't have personal knowledge of the woman's stances.

"Good to see you Catherine." Choked a voice with sincerity.

Catherine didn't waste a second she rushed down the final step and pulled the woman into her for a hug. "Bloody glad you came home Grace." She held her closer as the other woman cried into her shoulder.

Pulling away she looked up into the concerned ice blue gaze and smiled wanly. "I figured arriving home would be better than a phone call." She managed to say with a break in her voice.

"Yes, I would agree with that, and we all are very glad to have you back, we have missed you Grace." Catherine said sincerely, knowing that at the moment, just holding the woman brought her a peace she had missed in the weeks Grace had been away.

Grace looked at her with tear-filled eyes and she smiled again. "Thanks Catherine, I missed this place and everyone."

"Good, come on let's get Doris to make us some tea." With that a little redheaded whirlwind descended on them.

"Grace? Grace you came back to us, we missed you!" A small girl wrapped herself around the younger woman. Catherine grinned at Grace and moved away so that Lisa could hug her properly.

"I missed you too little Miss Alice. What have you been up to while I've been gone?" She asked in a happy voice.

"I had a birthday Grace and Catherine bought me a bike, do you want to see?" Lisa asked as she pulled Grace towards the bike and it's residents.

Catherine laughed and motioned Grace to follow Lisa. "It's okay Grace. I'll sort out the bags and when you're ready, tea will be brewing." Grace smiled back at her boss and thought she looked different, something had changed and she wanted to know exactly what that was.

Later!

Catherine watched as Grace consumed her evening meal chatting amiably with the children. Lisa had never left her side since she'd arrived back and even Jake looked happy at the prospect of having Grace back in the fold.

Colin had briefly looked in and given Grace condolences over her father and then left abruptly, as she teared up at his concern.

Doris had made the evening meal and then left, she had enjoyed her work at Destiny and indicated that if ever they needed any help again just to let her know. Catherine had thanked her personally with a healthy bonus that had been very unexpected, but gratefully received.

Grace looked over at Catherine and smiled warmly at her. "Everyone seems to be happy and healthy here you haven't caused havoc while I've been gone it would appear?" She teased the older woman.

"Oh, come on Grace, now why on earth would you think that?" She smiled back at her friend.

"Just a thought, you appear happier now than when I left, any reason for that?" Grace pushed her luck.

Catherine quirked an eyebrow and then gave a brief grin. "Yes, a very good reason, I'll tell you about it later or maybe tomorrow, you look tired."

Grace accepted the truth in the statement. "Yeah, I'm tired it's been a long month all told."

Catherine pierced her with a compassionate look clearly sending the sympathy message without words. They both looked at each other at length and them turned away as Lisa began a story about 'Sherry' and 'Blacky'. Now that had been amusing trying to explain to Grace and making her understand that the brown beagle soft toy was called 'Blacky', at the time it had amazed both Catherine and Jake. Neither had the heart to ask Lisa about the name, just accepting it, even if it did make them chuckle every time she mentioned the dog. "I know I think an early night for us all wouldn't go amiss now would it kids?" her tone brooking no objection.

"Will you still read to us the next story though Catherine?" Lisa chirped in.

"Yes, you've only got the last couple to finish now." Jake added for good measure.

Catherine smiled at them and held up her hand. "You know when we are finished here, we will be on the third book, and there is a limit to how many books have been written."

"Yeah we know but you will finish it won't you?" The plaintiff voice of the girl asked.

Suddenly, Catherine got up from her chair and walked over to the small figure seated opposite her; looking down at her with a warm ice blue glance she stroked the blonde hair. "For you and Jake anything Princess." She then turned and walked out of the room.

Grace had watched the display of affection with fascination. *'Hell things had changed here and in a big way, maybe I'm not so tired after all!'*

Although both women had agreed they were tired, it felt good to just relax together after the children went to bed with a coffee and companionable silence around them.

Catherine was the first to break the silence. "I'm sorry about your father Grace."

"Thanks." She said simply.

"You want to talk about it?" Catherine asked gently.

Grace looked at the older woman and once again marvelled at the gentleness she sensed in her, which certainly wasn't around when she left. "I think I've done all the talking about it that I need to do, now I need to heal. My sister was a big help; Ali is staying around Auckland for a few more months to help Mum adjust. I think it will work out."

Catherine nodded her head and acknowledged the truth in the statement. "I never got around to talking about any of my families deaths with anyone, guess that's why I got myself into a mess in the end."

Grace looked at her directly and smiled sadly. "I wish I'd been there for you then Catherine, but its no use wishing for things that are firmly planted in the past, you have to look towards the future instead."

"Thanks Grace, you have been a good friend, I've genuinely missed you around here, it's been very lonely without you and the kids have missed you too."

"Ah, the kids only want my cooking or should I say cookies and you. I hazard a guess it was my tea-making skills that you missed?" She smiled at the thought.

"Well, I wouldn't go so far as to say that, but your skills in making cappuccino certainly rate high on my list of reasons to keep you around." Catherine gave a warm throaty laugh.

"Great, I knew I had a good reason to get myself back here." She smiled and continued. "You've changed Catherine?"

Catherine looked at Grace speculatively and grinned that lop sided grin that produced mischief in her eyes. "Yes, I know. Hopefully, it's for the better."

"The better! Hell, if you changed any more I might think we opened a sanctuary for do-gooders here on Destiny during my absence."

"Never that Grace! But it feels good to do something for someone else instead of for purely selfish reasons." Catherine got up from her seat and walked over to the window and looked out over the dark drive. "I think it could snow soon it's getting quite icy here in the morning."

"So, who or what is responsible for the change?" Grace persisted.

Catherine turned back and regained her seat next to Grace. "Jace."

"As simple as that huh?" Grace noticed the tenderness when Catherine said her name.

"Yes, it was really as simple as that! You once told me to listen to the knocking on the door Grace. I did and I opened it; you were, as usual in these things, right!" Catherine sheepishly smiled at Grace.

"You telling me what I think your telling me?" Grace was surprised but happy for her friend and boss she looked so relaxed.

"That I've admitted I love Jace Bardley, oh yes!" Catherine spoke the words almost in wonder.

Suddenly Grace pushed herself out of her chair and kneeled in front of the one Catherine sat in and placed her arms around the legs of her friend in a comforting hold. "Then I'm happy for you, does Jace know?"

Catherine laughed out loud at that question. "I certainly hope so! We obviously haven't been able to see each other since the admission but I'm going to see her shortly, now you're back that is."

"You're going to LA?" Grace was surprised at that.

"Oh, I know I don't like the place." Grace sent her a look that made her blush. "Okay, so I hate the place, I have business to attend to and of course Jace lives there for the moment, so why not kill two birds with one stone." Catherine said matter of factly.

Grace snorted at the last comment. "Jesus, Catherine, I'm sure glad you're not courting me!"

"What do you mean?" Catherine looked at her in indignation.

"Look, when the object of your desire is spoken about in the same breath as a business deal, I would be kind of upset."

She looked perplexed and thought about what she'd said a worried look appeared on her face. "I guess you're right again, but Jace will always come first, believe me."

Grace patted her hands that were clenched tight together on her knees. "Hey, I know and Jace knows. We both understand that you are a powerful business woman and at times relationships might have to take a back seat to that."

"It won't matter soon Grace, because I'm going to leave all the business dealings to others. I've already got that plan in operation.

Tomorrow we need to talk about something important I need you to consider. Tonight you're way too tired to give it your best attention."

"Well, that's something to ponder when I'm trying to sleep now isn't it." Grace answered feigning a heavy sigh.

"Do you want to know what I need you to consider now?" Catherine looked at her in surprise.

"No, leave it Catherine, after breakfast we'll talk. I need to make a call in the morning first thing, so I will attend to the breakfast but leave you and Colin for an hour or so, if that's okay?"

Catherine glanced at her and noticed the sadness appear once again but for a different reason. "The good doctor?"

Grace looked at her and a tear threatened to fall, eventually it slowly trickled down her cheek. Catherine wiped it away with one of her tapered fingers. "Yes," came a strangled reply.

"I'm here for you Grace, never forget that!" She gave her a long sympathetic look. Brown eyes looked into the ice blue ones above her and she smiled briefly.

"Yeah, I know and I love you for it." Getting up she slowly made for the door feeling drained.

"Do you know something Grace?" Catherine spoke quietly as she watched her move towards the door Grace inclined her head in question. "My mother was right she told me about you and how you would help me see what would be best in the future."

Grace turned in surprise. "I never met your mother. Didn't she die when you were a child?" What an odd thing for Catherine to say.

"Yes, she did, but she was a descendant of a long line of people who had the gift of prophecy. She told me about you when I was ten years old guess it's taken me a few years to see it that's all."

"Did the gift pass to you?" Grace was fascinated with this new facet of Catherine's life.

"I hardly think so, do you? Or I certainly wouldn't have made half the mistakes I've made in my lifetime so far!" She laughed depreciatingly.

Grace smiled back and shook her head. "Maybe you just needed to believe in the power of love a little more before you get the gift."

"It can be a curse and in my case, I would think it would be just that!" Catherine looked down at her hands, which now lay flat on the top of her thighs. "Goodnight Grace."

"Goodnight Catherine, pleasant dreams." She opened the door and left.

Catherine mused over the previous statement. *'Do I want the gift? No! Knowing the future would certainly be a curse having the things happens, as they do could be hard to bear at times. Actually knowing the outcome before hand and not being able to change isn't something my competitive nature would ever get to grips with. Had my mother seen her own death? Yet Mama had been so calm and serene about the gift she possessed. Surely she would not have been had she known how short her life was going to be? Questions and yet more questions and no one to answer any of them. Or was there someone? Yes! She might not want to talk to me but it is worth a call something to consider in the future, yes, certainly I will go to her and talk, it was time.'*

Catherine moved out of the chair and turned down all the lights, double-checking that everything was secure she walked up to her room.

Checking on Lisa as she walked by the bedroom, which most definitely belonged to a young girl. As she walked over to the bed and pulled the covers back over the child as they had been pulled off at some stage during sleep she swiftly glanced round the room. The floor had some clothes scattered around nothing too untidy, but one day it could be a problem. Then there were the few trinkets Lisa had been left by her mother, taking pride of place on the dressing table although there was nothing of intrinsic value. Catherine had been given Lisa's mother's rings and a gold chain for safe keeping until the child was old enough to appreciate them.

It was still very sparse for a child's room, the only toys being the original rag doll 'Sherry' that had been brought with her and 'Blacky' the brown beagle that Jake had bought her. She knew that the wardrobe was full of clothes; Grace had purchased most of them before she left.

Checking again that the child was sleeping peacefully she went out onto the landing and looked at the room that Jace had used, it was empty but she opened it anyway.

Entering the room she had the distinct impression that Jace was close by and her thoughts of the young woman she loved magnified accordingly. Jace had not only stolen her heart but also offered her a chance for a bright future with a happy family atmosphere, rather than the austere loneliness of the reclusive life she had opted for five years before. Looking round the room, it hadn't changed much since she had left, the bed was in the same position, the chair was pulled up close to the table and the table lamp was angled towards the bed.

Kicking off her shoes Catherine climbed on the bed and sank into its depths. Closing her eyes she imagined the smaller body of the woman she had grown to love within the circle of her arms. Catherine loved Jace in the short time she had stayed in the house and it had just gone from strength to strength after each message or call. Recalling once again holding Jace in her arms she sighed and opened her eyes knowing the futility of dreaming about things that couldn't take place at least at the moment. But, oh she hoped that would be over soon and that it wouldn't be a dream, it would be a reality.

Gracefully getting up from the bed, she left the room and its memories and headed to the next room and its closed door.

Jake hadn't had a nightmare for a couple of weeks and so they had agreed that he could keep the door shut. The boy had been embarrassed on the several occasions that he had been consoled by Catherine and realised that he had disturbed not only her but Lisa as well. Now he was getting his dreams under control, but Catherine suspected that they would surface again if anything upset the boy too much. She was not going to let that happen any time soon, not if she could help it.

Opening the door she glanced in and noticed the magazines strewn on the floor and the shoes kicked off haphazardly into a corner. He didn't have any toys or anything other than magazines in his room clothes of course but nothing personal. His parents hadn't left anything of value for him. To say he was impoverished was somewhat melodramatic, but basically correct.

She hadn't approached the subject of money after the visit to the town now Grace had come home she would ask her to deal with that small point. She smiled, as she looked at the peaceful expression on his face, it often held a scowl or sullen look about it, and only when he was riding Ruby or speaking to her or Lisa did he give a smile of any depth. Maybe with time, they would find out the depth of the hurt this boy had suffered, then again maybe not, no harm in trying though and she knew just the person who might have the right sort of c□mpassion for that task in the future.

Seems Jace had the compassion to tame the savage beast and some of the boy's hurt certainly mirrored some of her own. Time would tell.

She closed the door and headed for her own room, to find sleep.

Chapter Twenty-Eight

The long distance trips that Hudson pulled on her at short notice were frustrating Jace. For the last three weeks she hadn't been home longer than a day.

Now she was heading back. Hudson had been called away to New York, very strange, only for Jace it was a heaven sent opportunity to not only have a break, but also get back in touch with Catherine. If they had e-mailed four times in the last two weeks, that would be about all the joint interaction and that certainly wasn't enough for either of them. She missed the older woman with an intensity that threatened to overwhelm her at times. Her insecurities would often rear their ugly heads when she settled down for the night, and not being in a position to contact Catherine to calm her fears only fueled the problem.

Well, she was an hour from home, only she really needed to go into the office and check in there, if only for a short time. Walking into her office space an hour later she asked Agnes what was going on. Hudson's secretary was anything but informative, she could only say that a very important meeting was being arranged and very powerful people were involved. That really didn't say anything at all.

Looking over the mountain of mail she decided that maybe having a few days off wasn't going to work with all this garbage on her desk.

Wonder what was happening to Peter's documentary, he'd mentioned that there had been a hold-up, but she hadn't heard anything for at least the three weeks she had been away. Maybe now was a good time to find out what was happening with her friend and then she would get home and make that longed for call.

The room that Peter Adamson occupied on the property was compact and gave the impression that the director rarely ever entered it. That wasn't strictly true but he had always preferred to be on the set and marshal most of any project he was working on himself. Jace entered the room after knocking and hearing a muffled voice say enter.

Looking up from his desk Peter Adamson beamed when he saw whom his visitor was. "Jace, good god, has she finally let you come home?" He got up from his chair and gave her a hug.

"It's good to see you too Peter." She laughed into his shoulder as he hugged her harder.

"So what brings you into my office, thought you would want to go straight home and rest up, I heard she sent you to some rough terrain." He looked at her seriously.

"Yes she did, and yes I would like to go home. I thought I would catch up with the news before I went." Jace smiled at him and sat in the chair opposite his desk.

"Well, that could be tricky, exactly what are you interested in?"

"Have you got a release date for the documentary yet? Wasn't it held up for some reason?" She inquired.

Peter looked at her and a small frown appeared over his forehead.

"No it hasn't been given a release date, in fact the current edit has been vetoed altogether. Hudson won't change some of the dialogue and the person vetoing won't change their stance."

Jace looked at him in sympathy. "It was a good documentary Peter, the filming is superb as always, can't you pursuade Hudson to change the dialogue a little, if that's the only objection?"

"It's called internal politics Jace, looks to me like a waste of money and time, guess it's their money to waste." He stated bitterly.

"Do you know who the person is that's vetoing the project?"

Peter looked at her strangely and took a deep breath before he answered. "Yep, I sure do!"

"Going to share?"

"It doesn't matter Jace nothing can be done." He said resignedly.

"Peter, please tell me. If you don't I will find out from someone else. Is it such a big secret?" Jace spoke in a determined fashion.

He knew she would too! Nothing would get past Jace when she wanted information badly enough. What the hell, he had no love for Catherine Warriorson anyway.

"Ms. Devonshire the owner of Xianthos Holdings is the person behind the veto."

Jace suddenly paled and a strangled sound came from her throat.

"Devonshire? Ms. Devonshire is behind the veto? How can that be?" She managed to whisper finally her face clearly shocked at his admission.

"Obviously she has an interest somewhere and Hudson has stepped on her toes." He was sorry to see his friend upset. He knew how she hated the mention of the woman if only she knew who the woman really was!

"Peter, if it had been Catherine I could understand that! But where does Ms. Devonshire come into the equation?" Clearly puzzled at the revelation.

"Maybe your friend Warriorson has powerful friends?"

"But even if she did know Devonshire, how can she influence Hudson, it's an independent studio?" Jace was getting more confused by the minute.

"Jace, look I'm sorry. I never wanted to be the one to tell you certainly not after you told me about your dislike of all thing{ Xianthos. Devonshire can do what the hell she wants with the studio, she owns sixty percent of the holdings! Hudson keeps quiet about the set-up, she thinks that way she keeps the power plays all to herself."

Jace got up from the chair and her pale face showed the anguish etched there. "So I've been working for Xianthos all these years and I never knew about it!" It was a heart-piercing statement.

"Yeah, unfortunately you have had the pleasure of being employed at least in part by the mighty Xianthos holdings. Only good thing is the pay I suspect." He said scathingly.

"I need to go home and completely understand all the implications here Peter I...I will see you later." She walked like a zombie out of the door towards the car park.

"Jace wait up." He called as she got the door of her rental car open.

Looking round at him she waited for him to say more. "You going to be okay? You look kind of out of it. I worry about you Jace."

"Thanks for your concern about me Peter. I'm going to be fine I just need to get home, it's been a long month all in all." She climbed into the driver's seat and switched on the engine.

Peter watched her drive out of the lot and walked slowly back to his office. *'Hell, why did these women make life complicated for not only themselves but also all the others around them. At times like these he wished only men held the power to complicate lives. Then again, they made a fuck of a job of it also, most of the time. Thank god, I spend most of my time behind the camera, away from this shit.'*

Grace had arrived back on the ranch and was busy clearing up after feeding two hungry wolves or their two kids appeared that way to her.

"You two been eating while I've been gone or have you been saving it up until I arrived home?" The woman asked casually as she cleared plates into the dishwasher.

Both children looked at her and smirked. Finally Lisa answered her. "If we saved it up waiting for you, we would be dead by now Grace." The innocent reply echoed in Grace's eardrums.

Grace suddenly slammed the door of the dishwasher at the words and her hand caught in the top she gave out a scream of pain.

Jake ran up to her and pulled open the door and helped her to the basin to run cold water on it. "Lisa, Grace needs help find Catherine or Colin. Now!" The boy said quic{ly noticing the tears of pain streaming down the older woman's cheeks.

The girl clearly upset ran out of the kitchen to the stables shouting at the top of her voice for Catherine.

Catherine heard the commotion as she was talking to Colin about the horses and the new stock that was due in a week's time. "What the hell is that all about?" She muttered as she saw the child flying in her direction.

Catching hold of the bundle of child, she steadied her by the shoulder and pushed her long frame down to the child's level. "Hey Lisa, what's the matter princess?" Catherine spoke softly to the child.

Lisa gave her a tearstained look. "It's Grace she got hurt in the dishwasher and she's crying, Jake said we need you!" The child put her hand on the woman's larger one and started to drag her up and towards the house.

Looking at Colin who had a worried expression. "I'll deal with it Colin, if I need you I will call, okay?"

"Yes, I'll wait around to make sure." He said quietly his expression worried.

"Good, come on Lisa, let's go and make Grace better." Catherine suddenly lifted the lightweight child in her arms and strode off towards the house, her strides quickly making short work of the distance.

They entered the kitchen area and Grace was setting with a towel wrapped around her hand and a hovering boy looking a little upset.

"So, what have we got here then? Can't leave you for two minutes alone can I Grace?" Catherine tried to bring some light relief into the sober scene.

Grace looked up at her friend and boss and noticed that Lisa was held securely in Catherine's arms; she didn't look like she wanted to be put down either, smiling wanly she shook her head.

"I'm sorry Catherine. I did something stupid, tried to shut the door of the dishwasher when my hand was still in it. Jake here has helped me to put a cold compress on it."

"I can see that! So, do we need the doctor?" An expressive eyebrow rose in her face.

"No! No, it's okay Catherine; we can deal with it here. Should be fine soon." Grace spoke quickly and nervously.

"Right, well in that case you better show me the damage then."

"Oh, it's okay I will just keep this on for an hour or so and it will be fine."

"Show me!" Catherine lowered her voice to almost a growl. Slowly putting Lisa down she tweaked her hair and motioned her to a seat. Catherine swiftly walked around to where Grace was seated. Jake previously hovering beside Grace moved to the chair next to Lisa and sat down concerned.

Grace looked at Catherine and knew that nothing was going to stop her viewing the injury. Gently she felt Catherine un-wrap the towel and heard her suck her breath in as she saw the damage.

"For gods sake Grace, it's swollen already, you might have done some major damage, and you need to see the doctor!"

"Catherine No! I won't see him! Don't even think about calling him out. It's swollen and looks nasty but I can move my fingers so no breakages, it will be fine, let it be!" Grace implored her.

"Okay! Okay. I can see the problem, are you sure you can move all the fingers? Go ahead and try." Came the serious retort.

The fingers moved slowly and the pain clearly etched on her face but she maintained her control and satisfied the tall imposing woman in front of her. "Told you so!"

Catherine gave her a look that silenced her, and then she looked at the children. "Right kids, go tell Colin that everything is fine here. Grace is going to be okay and he can give you your next riding lesson now. Be back for lunch at the usual time, although it looks like it's my cooking for the rest of the day." Chuckling she saw the children each look at her and then each other and grimace.

"Hey it's not that bad!" Catherine said with a hurt look on her face.

They both laughed and headed for the door. "Kids." She snorted as they left. Turning back towards Grace she noticed the slight smile on her friends face. "Okay, are you going to comment about my cooking skills too?"

"Never, would I dare?" Grace smiling replied.

"Hmmm, not so sure these days with you Ms. Thornton."

Catherine walked over to the medicine cabinet, one of the few places in the kitchen she did know intimately. Selecting a bandage and sticky tape she proceeded to wrap the injury and make it more comfortable giving Grace a chance to swallow the painkillers she had found. "Guess this is as good a time as any to talk to you about the project I want you to consider, but first, how the hell did this little episode happen?"

"Lisa answered a question I posed, and she referred to being dead or the prospect of being dead, guess it threw me, I lost concentration for a moment." Grace said sheepishly.

"I'm sorry, I should have warned the kids but it sort of comes under the sensitive chat parts and I'm not much good at those." She noticed a quirk of an eyebrow from her friend. "I've not changed that much Grace!" She smiled grimly at the thought of bringing back bad memories to them.

"That's okay Catherine, I will tell them myself when I feel up to it. So what project have you got for me? You left me intrigued last night."

"Great. Well, for sometime now I've toyed with setting up a trust fund in the name of my son, wasn't sure what type of fund to have though. When this opportunity came around, it peeked my interest, once I was involved I thought why not help in this area. I went to see the Reverend and asked him to be a co-trustee, he accepted readily and I want to ask you to be the other trustee Grace?" Catherine wasn't too sure if Grace would accept but she was her first choice, her only choice really.

Grace starred at her and swallowed several times before she answered.

"You want me? You're going to trust me with a fund? But why me?"

Catherine smiled at the surprised face of her friend. "You are the only one for the role Grace. First I trust you implicitly and when it comes to anything with my son's name associated with it, I know you won't disappoint me. Second I can think of no one better suited to making sure the money will work for the right causes. Are those good enough reasons?"

"Thank you Catherine, for your trust and I will gladly help with the fund, what do I need to do?" She spoke with emotion.

"The lawyers are waiting for me to call for the transfer to take place, then it's up to you and the Reverend to get together and plan what you want to spend it on. I have advisors for you to call on at any time if you need to do so." Replied Catherine in true business like terms.

"Just how much are you talking about here?"

"Oh, I thought ten million US dollars and if that's not enough for the first year, I can be persuaded to increase it for a good causu." She laughed at the thought.

Grace nearly fell off her chair. "Jesus, Catherine, ten million? What the hell kind of number is that? You're going to trust me with that amount of money?"

Catherine laughed loudly at the spluttered words floating around the kitchen. "Well, I can make it more if you want? Why wouldn't I trust you Grace?"

"No, no believe me ten is quite enough to be going on with and thank you. Thank you for your complete trust Catherine, I know it's hard for you to completely trust people." Grace said with conviction.

"Well, glad that's settled then. Have you finished with the good doctor?" Changing the subject totally.

"Yes, I realised that I wasn't in love with him. I might have thought I was, but I think it was just running away from the truth."

"And that truth would be?" Catherine asked although she wasn't sure she was going to welcome the answer.

Grace watched Catherine move gracefully towards the kettle and switch it on. "The truth is I love it here on the ranch and the people too! Now, we have the kids, it's more reasons to stay and I found out that this is home Catherine, here at Destiny. Whatever happens in the future I know it's going to happen on this ranch and I will fulfil my own destiny here." She spoke with such insight and strength it threw Catherine for a few moments.

"You sound like my Mother when you talk like that! Seriously Grace, are you sure finishing with the doctor is the right choice? He was in love with you."

"Yes I know he was and it hurt to tell him, he understands my reasons and will remain a friend. I guess this place is all I need right now and a few friendly faces too."

"Then that's absolutely no problem, we can certainly furnish you with the friends and speaking of kids, can you arrange a personal allowance system with them? I think I'm being a little mean not giving them any personal income." Catherine smiled at her ignorance.

Grace laughed genuinely for the first time since she arrived home.

"You know, it's somewhat of a let down from being a trustee over millions to administering pocket money to two children, but I think I'll cope."

"Good." Catherine grinned and pulled on Grace's free hand and tugged her out of the chair. "Now I suggest you get some rest, let me worry about the kids for a few hours. Wonder if they will bring burgers all the way to the ranch?"

"Oh god Catherine, that would be priceless." Grace laughed again as Catherine's hand lead her towards the stairs.

"Go rest woman! I'll bring you some tea shortly now I have some calls to make."

Grace watched her move back towards the kitchen. *'If I wasn't seeing it with my own eyes, I would never have thought you could change so much, and in such a profound way, Catherine Warriorson. Falling in love has certainly been a catalyst for change in you my friend and we have a small, blonde, green-eyed Californian to thank for all of it. Way to go Jace!'*

She smiled and headed for the luxury of a little sleep, her hand was throbbing but the painkillers would kick in soon enough.

Jace arrived home and she threw her case and car keys into the apartment in a haphazard way, not really caring where they ended up.

'All these years I've been working for Xianthos and never suspected. What sort of publicity person am I? I didn't even know that the studio was sixty percent owned by another entity. Hudson had certainly maintained that secret well. Too well! Now, I have choices to make, but not many. Did Catherine know Devonshire? And if she did, how well did she know her? I hope you don't Catherine; it would break my heart if you told me she was a good friend of yours. How would you react to my hatred of her? Do I even need to tell you of my dislike of the woman we might never meet? Guess it's something for our talk when we get together, not over the phone or the e-mail, you need to understand my hatred and I can only do that if you're here with me in person.'

Slowly retreating to the bathroom she decided the best remedy would be a long soak in the bath, followed by a call to Catherine just to hear her voice, would be therapy enough for her.

Watching the bubbles grow in the bath she contemplated her options and wondered if James had any openings in his organisation she would call him soon and check out the possibilities.

'Catherine my love, I think we need to get that talk over and done with and soon. Before I just hijack a plane and come running into your arms without warning. Wonder what you'd think about that!' Smiling she stripped off her clothes and slowly lowered her aching body and mind into the luxury of a hot bubble bath.

Chapter Twenty-Nine

Catherine's phone rang; she had just completed her calls to Paul Strong and a couple of the other vice-presidents. Picking up the instrument absently she said a curt "Warriorson," and waited for the recipient to answer.

"Hey, with a welcome like that I'm not sure what to expect when we meet up again finally!" Jace laughed softly at the other end of the line.

Catherine nearly dropped the phone shocked hearing Jace at the other end. "Oh God, I'm so sorry Jace, I was preoccupied. Forgive me?" Her voice held a trace of anxiety.

"I will always forgive you, no matter what!" Jace replied mollified at her apology.

"I might hold you to that one day." Catherine said seriously.

"Nothing would give me greater pleasure. So, how have you been?" Jace smiled as her mind pictured Catherine in the study. It gave her a warm feeling in the pit of her stomach as she recalled every feature of the woman she loved.

"Good, and you?"

"All the better for hearing your voice. I've missed you Catherine." Her voice cracked a little as she said the last words.

"I've missed you too Jace." Catherine pictured the younger woman reclined on the sofa in her apartment, Jace had often described the scene to her in their numerous calls. "Grace came home, looks like I can arrange my trips away from here now."

Jace gave a small sigh of relief. "That's good news. How is Grace?"

"She's doing pretty well, although she had an accident today with the dishwasher, means I have the dubious task of cooking for us this lunchtime. Kids are a little sceptical about my cooking skills, I think Grace just laughs. Maybe she won't when she tries my cooking. It'll teach her not to lose concentration with the domestic appliances." Catherine smiled into the receiver. It was so good to hear Jace's voice, it warming her in more places than she wanted to admit too.

Jace laughed, "Guess you need some lessons, do you want me to give you some?"

Catherine raised an eyebrow even though there was no one there to see it. "I can think of other lessons I would prefer you to teach me than cookery!"

"I.... well.... Yes! I'm sure you could." Was all Jace could manage; she was completely floored by the suggestive comment.

"You know my love, there's no reason to be embarrassed; it's only a phone call. Wait until I'm in the same room with you, then you can take me to task over any comment I make, and in any way you want!" Catherine mellowed at the thought.

"I love you Catherine." Jace's voice took on a husky quality.

"And I love you too, my dear Jace. Are you home for good now, or has Hudson plans to send you even further afield?" It was difficult to maintain composure even with a phone call, and it really was getting too much taking the proverbial cold shower after every call.

"Hudson is away in New York, not sure what she has planned for the future, hopefully nothing as rural as where she's has been sending me lately." Her voice held the frustration she had been feeling recently.

"Mmm, well I hope she doesn't send you anywhere in the next few weeks because I would have to come and find you, now wouldn't I." Catherine growled into the phone.

"You say the nicest things Catherine." Jace chuckled at her end. Having Catherine come looking for her in any part of the globe sounded pretty romantic to her.

"Glad you think so. I've got Grace and the Reverend on board for the trust fund and the kids are settled. I was wondering..." Catherine stopped mid-sentence as she heard a giggle from the other end of the line.

Jace was intrigued, what had she been going to say? "You were wondering?"

"Ah, yes wondering." Then she said nothing more. Silence prevailed. They say silence is golden but to Jace, silence in this particular case, was intriguing.

Jace was happy the woman had completely lost her train of thought or it appeared that way. Over a giggle too! I wonder what else I can do or say that would bring on that reaction? "You going to tell me?" Borrowing an expression that Catherine used frequently to get answers from people.

"You sound like me!" Catherine was surprised but pleased at the banter she was being subjected to, it felt really warm and quite good inside.

"Is that a good thing or bad?" Jace countered.

"In this case good, but don't let it happen too often." Catherine retorted with mock indignation.

"I'll remember, you were wondering or don't you remember now?" Jace teased her gently.

"Yes, I remember, you don't get my mind to completely shut down Jace Bardley." Catherine let a light laugh finish for her.

"I hope I do one day." Was all Jace replied. She heard a sharp intake of breath at the other end, which pleased her very much, and brought a warm, glowing smile to her face.

Catherine left that comment for another day. It was getting way too hot in here, however it had nothing to do with the temperature in the room. "Yes, well I was wondering if I should adopt the kids or at least ask them what they think?" The tall woman changed the subject abruptly.

"Way to go Catherine, that's a wonderful idea." The happiness in her voice, made Catherine smile and realise that she had been right to think Jace would show the kids more love than she ever could.

"Glad you think so, because I sort of hoped that maybe.... well that you would.... I guess what I'm trying to say is..." Catherine was at a loss to finish the sentence without pushing her boat out too far.

"Yes." Came the solid answer from Jace, who was smiling broadly at the cell phone held in her hand. All she wanted to do was hug the woman at the other end and hold her close; probably more, but she would accept the embrace for a start; yes a start of something more intimate.

"You don't even know what I'm going to ask?" The tall woman at the other end was smiling equally as broadly.

"Yeah I do, you want me to help you raise two kids. Am I right?"

"Yes!" There was an almost inaudible sound from the other end.

"Does that imply you're going to make an honest woman of me?" Jace couldn't help the chuckle and the possibility of making the older woman blush. "Have I made you uncomfortable Catherine?"

Catherine was certainly blushing, she hadn't thought of making a permanent commitment well, not until she had spoken to Jace about her past anyway. Then again she hadn't really considered the possibility of a permanent statement of their relationship. *'Honest woman indeed!'* "Not uncomfortable, no." She muttered.

"So, are you?" Jace persisted.

"Am I what?" Catherine responded cautiously.

"Going to make an honest woman of me? Or will I just be the nanny?" After Jace said the word, she suddenly realised that she could have meant exactly that, they hadn't talked about a permanent arrangement together. Had she been wrong with her assumptions?

"Nanny? Now there's a thought! How about I answer that question when we see each other shortly?" Catherine refused to be drawn into the subject until after their talk.

Jace sighed heavily and a feeling of rejection took over. *'Maybe she did only want a nanny? What a fool I can be sometimes, I must be very tired to have pushed this far.'* "Okay, I look forward to it."

"You won't be disappointed, I promise you Jace." Catherine spoke in the low voice that sent Jace's senses reeling. Her feelings suddenly shooting back onto the exhilaration level.

"Glad to hear it! Please tell me Catherine, what else is happening with you and at the ranch?"

They talked about several issues, Grace, the doctor, Colin and the children. Finally Jace had to ask the question that had been plaguing her since Peter had mentioned Ms. Devonshire.

"How well do you know Ms. Devonshire of the Xianthos Corporation?" Jace nonchalantly asked.

Catherine found the question unexpected, and a little strange but she countered with a question of her own. "Why do you ask?"

"The documentary we filmed at the ranch has been vetoed by her I wondered if you had been influential in that decision?" Jace held her breath waiting for the reply and hoping she wasn't going to be too unhappy with the response.

Catherine thought about her answer, it wasn't the right circumstances to explain and tell Jace that she was Devonshire. That admission had to be done face-to-face, one-on-one, to gauge the reaction.

"Yes, I was influential in that decision; let's just say Xianthos owes me a favor or two."

"So, it was really you who vetoed the project?" Jace asked quietly, her heart beginning to race as she thought about the powerful friends that Catherine could weald if she wanted too.

"If you put it like that, yes." Catherine needed to say more. "She shouldn't have pushed me on this one Jace, I had already denied access to my property, she ignored me! Did you think I would leave it like that? I'm not a person that you walk all over and ignore!"

Catherine looked around the study, it was getting close to lunchtime and she needed to start something, those kids were always hungry.

'That, and you're scared to death she will think less of you, because of your show of what? Power? That was all it came down to in the end, petty power plays, because you hate Hudson's guts.' Her internal voice mocked her.

"No, no I knew that you would perhaps take a stand, but to stop the whole documentary being released, that reeks of something else." Jace answered in a quiet voice.

"And that would be?" Catherine answered her coldly, this conversation wasn't going anywhere, and it wasn't relevant to them personally!

Jace bit her lip as she heard the change in tone and knew that the woman would have a very cold expression especially in her eyes.

"Childish behaviour." She'd said it, and knew that it wasn't going to be something Catherine would take lying down.

It was a minute before she heard heavy breathing and a sharp intake of breath at the description. "Childish bloody behaviour! What sort of answer is that? Do you think I've been stuck here with kids too long Jace?" Was the scathing reply.

Jace was upset and knew that this wasn't how she had envisaged the conversation to go. "Never that Catherine, but...why veto everything?"

"Because I can!" Came the blistering reply. "I have lunch to prepare Jace, guess I'm going to have to resort to some more childish behaviour to tackle that problem. You want to say anything else?"

Jace could hear the drumming of angry fingers on the desk. "I guess not."

"Glad to hear it, I'll be in touch." Catherine replaced the receiver and pushed herself away from the desk, but then moved forward again and placed her hands on the top of the polished surface.

'Are you mad, what the hell have you just done?' Her head hit the desk as she closed her eyes at her own impatience and lack of understanding. 'That was Jace, the woman you love, not some bloody business associate who has rattled your cage. Get a grip on life Catherine or you're going to blow it all away, again! That is assuming you do love her. Yes! Oh god yes I love her.'

Jace was crying, it was a natural reaction; the tears felt justified. It had been a long three weeks, and now this!

'Why? Why did it have to end like that, it wasn't meant as a criticism? It was more of an observation. When will she be in touch? What if she doesn't get back to me? What am I going to do? I can't pretend anymore that I can walk away from this without being hurt, and it sure hurts now! Please call me Catherine, please!' Her mind pleaded.

Jace walked into her bedroom and flung herself on the bed and cried herself to sleep. Xianthos had a lot to answer for.

Grace had seen the gathering storm that threatened to fall in their paths any day now! Catherine Warriorson was a veritable storm front waiting to burst forth. She had been like that for days, in fact over a week. Nothing anyone could say brought a smile to her face, not even when the kids tried, and they had tried. She'd even stopped telling them stories, saying she was busy with work related problems and that she was going away soon.

That had upset them, particularly Jake. He was even having bad dreams again, but Catherine was way too busy to see that, she was always ensconced in her study and hardly past the time of day with anyone. There could be only one reason for this, Jace! Well if the storm front was coming, she was ready for it, Wellingtons, raincoat and all!

Catherine stalked into the kitchen that afternoon and sat heavily in the chair a scowl on her face.

"You know if you keep that expression on your face too much longer it's going to be permanent and you have a beautiful face Catherine." She was never one to miss an opportunity.

"What the fuck do you know?" Catherine angrily replied, it wasn't often she swore and certainly never to Grace.

"Guess you're not in a good mood, couldn't tell by looking at you?" Nothing ventured, nothing gained.

"What the hell do you want from me Grace?" Catherine pierced her with a cold look.

"How about what's wrong Catherine, friend to friend?" Grace smiled at her warmly; this wasn't the time to run from the problem.

"Nothing." Catherine replied sullenly.

"So, nothing is making you walk around as if the whole world is going to end at any time?" Grace tired the diplomatic route.

"Don't be melodramatic Grace." Catherine said scornfully.

"Okay I won't, if you tell me what's wrong?" Grace gave her a friendly smile.

Catherine ran a hand through her unruly hair; it needed to be in that damn ponytail. "I think my world is ending Grace." A desperate voice replied. *'Now, who was being melodramatic?'*

Grace looked at the untidy image of her usually immaculately coifed friend; smiling gently she said one word. "Jace?"

Looking up, Catherine smiled wryly for the first time in days. She nodded her head. "Have you argued?" Grace asked her quietly.

"In a manner of speaking, it was to do with the documentary, she didn't like my tactics, called me childish." Her voice held a hurt expression.

"Was she right?" Grace asked tentatively.

"I hope not! But I was rude to her and I don't know how to take it back?" Catherine almost blasted her anger at Grace with her question.

"You know, Jace might be feeling equally as badly and it's easy, how about you send flowers and then follow up with a call? In person would be better, but the phone would be a start." Grace felt suddenly ancient next to this vulnerable woman who didn't have the slightest clue about relationships.

Catherine suddenly got up from the table and went over and hugged Grace. Beaming she whispered in her ear. "I don't know what I would do without you Grace. You think that would work?"

"It would with me!" Catherine hugged her even harder.

Grace laughed loudly and the kids came in at that moment and stopped as they saw the tall, dark and recently usually angry woman smiling and hugging Grace. "How about tonight you take back your place of reading to our children here?" Her head moved to indicate the present children.

Catherine released Grace and a flush started at her neck at having been caught in a sentimental embrace. Looking at the children she sheepishly smiled. "Do you want me to take over tonight?" It came out slowly and quietly.

Both children exchanged a look and then they looked back at her.

"Yes please, Grace doesn't know how to make the right voices for the characters, especially the animals." Lisa piped up and then launched herself at the tall woman for a hug. "We missed you." The child spoke into her thighs, which was the highest she could reach without being lifted off the ground.

Jake just looked at the end of his shoes and a slow smile took over at Lisa's enthusiasm.

"I missed you too, Princess, I'm sorry to you both for my...my indifference." She looked at the boy with apology in her eyes.

Jake looked directly back and grinned back at her nodding his head at her apology.

"Well Grace, I'd better get onto that florist before I lose my nerve." With that she released Lisa and kissed her head, and on the way out of the door placed a hand in Jake's hair and ruffled it gently.

Grace was chuckling. "Was that easy or what!" She congratulated herself as she went on to get some cookies for the kids, before they started to fend for themselves, which would be worse than a storm brewing with Catherine.

Sending flowers half way round the world was easy, all you had to do was find an international florist.

'Okay, that's not a problem, just send a selection, yes that would work. She didn't know what Jace's favorite flower was anyway.' Smiling she picked up the receiver and called the largest florist in Christchurch and told them to arrange whatever they could as quickly as they could to get to LA, money wasn't a problem.

Then she thought about another option! *'Chocolates. All women liked chocolates, didn't they? Yes, except for you! Okay, but who could arrange that one?'* She scanned the Internet for an hour. Finally she selected what she needed. *'Now, that would certainly keep Jace in chocolate for.... depends on her appetite for goodies.'* That brought a smile to Catherine's face; she wished she could be there to see the said goodies arrive.

The next thing she needed to do was arrange a courier to get a personal message to LA to arrive in tandem with the flowers and the chocolates, calling her usual courier, she arranged for the person to arrive within the hour, this was way too easy she thought. Then it occurred to her, what was she going to say on the message? *'Hell, I'm no good with words, not romantic ones anyway. Screwing up romantic situations is more my line.'* Thinking about the problem, she put on the radio for background noise and heard a song that had words that explained the situation. What a coincidence.

Opening her personal writing drawer in the desk, she pulled out a handmade, pristine white piece of paper, with her personal monogram of the ranch on it. She hardly ever sent this paper out, usually only used for invitations to the ranch or close friends. Not that she had many of those, but it would have served that purpose. Now it seemed appropriate to send this message on something more fitting than a normal card or sheet of paper.

Picking up her Mont Blanc fountain pen, she penned the note that she hoped would help her make up to the woman who held her heart and her prospects for a brighter future.

Chapter Thirty

Jace had been walking around the studio or sitting in her office either moody or withdrawn. Peter had been called to Chicago to talk about another project and he had been away since the morning she came back on the lot, which had been two days after talking to Catherine. She hadn't been in the mood or capable of putting her personal problems on a backburner, now she had to, she had to get on with her life, what was left of it anyway!

Hudson had arrived back two days later and smirked at the obvious unhappiness of her publicity PA. Could it be, she wondered, anything to do with a certain Catherine Warriorson? *'Oh I hope so, yes indeed I do. Life is looking up for me at the moment, and another's discomfort always added to the euphoric feeling I'm having. Well, soon enough you're going to hear the truth about your little friend Jace. No! That's definitely the wrong word to use for her! No, you're tall, dark, sexy and very dangerous friend. I'm going to love every minute of that encounter.'* Hudson grinned evilly at the back of the young blonde and re-entered her office.

Jace had tried to concentrate on her work, she really had; but it was becoming intolerable. She needed to talk to someone about it soon and she didn't have a clue who she could confide in. Her Dad was away on business and Peter was still away, not due back until late the next week. Turning in her chair she looked at Hudson's door. *'God I must really be losing it, if I even think about discussing this problem with her!'*

Jace pushed a lock of her hair from her eyes and looked at the blank screen in front of her. *'Dare I send Catherine e-mail? No! She doesn't want to hear from me or she would have done something about it by now, wouldn't she? Maybe, she thinks I should get in touch first? No, she said she would be in touch; she's the one who got angry, not me! Why, why do I keep going over this, it won't help anything?'* Tears stung her eyes as she tried to stop them flowing.

Getting up from her desk she noticed it was five p.m. *'Hell, I might as well go home I'm not contributing much here at the moment.'*

Hoping that Hudson wouldn't come looking for her, she picked up her purse and car keys and headed for the parking area. The sun was still beating down as she exited the building and continued on her way. Pausing for a moment she looked at the simple colours that made up the logo for UCP, wondering not for the first time this week if the colours had any relation to Xianthos; maybe she would check tomorrow.

Climbing into her very hot Toyota coupe she turned the ignition and hoped the air conditioning would get to work fast, getting incredibly hot inside a car would only fuel her depressive state at the moment.

The car negotiated the final turn to her apartment complex and she locked the vehicle and ran up the steps to the building wing that housed her apartment and the prospect of a cooling shower.

Glancing at the corridor as she got off the elevator she noticed a man loitering half way down the hallway, he was wearing a uniform of some description. Quickly walking towards her apartment, she noticed a deliveryman was lounging on the wall opposite her door.

"Anything I can help you with?" She inquired as she put the key in the door. Wondering if she was smart doing that, you never knew who was hanging about these days.

The young man fairly beamed as he saw which apartment she was entering. "Would you believe, you sure can?"

Jace looked at him and noticed the name of a famous international florist on his jacket. "Then you better tell me?"

"Are you Ms Bardley?" He said quickly, pulling out his delivery sheet.

"Could be, who wants to know?" Jace answered with a slight smile.

"Your lucky day I guess, must have a really wealthy suitor, hope you have room, I'll be right back." He announced as he quickly levered his body from the lounging position against the wall and rushed towards the elevator.

Half an hour later, flowers surrounded Jace, flowers in every variety and colour of the rainbow and some that had nothing to do with the rainbow. It was spectacular and totally unexpected. One thing missing was a note or message of any kind.

Carefully walking around the living room, she negotiated an area of the floor that was covered by flowers and heard the doorbell ring. Approaching the door she was greeted by another delivery person, who asked the same question as the previous young man.

Sometime later she sat on her computer chair and contemplated the flowers and the boxes and boxes of chocolates from every known chocolate producing country of the world, it was awesome, but no note or message! She wasn't sure if it was someone's idea of a joke, but a lovely joke none the less. Or was it Peter? Or could it be the only person she really wanted it to be from, Catherine? *'It had to be Catherine, it just had to be!'*

Now she waited in anticipation, surely she would get some sort of message no one would go to this effort without at least some sort of note would they? Putting on a pot of coffee she felt her emotional walls beginning to break away again and this time it was for a happier reason.

Stepping over the flowers into her bedroom she picked up Taz and hugged him. "I know it's you Catherine, I just know it!" She whispered into the soft toy's ear, seeing only the wicked smile answer her.

Then the doorbell went again, she nearly crashed into a basket of roses at her haste to get there. Wrenching open the door she saw the courier and he handed her a plastic wallet and made her sign for the document and went on his way.

Glancing at the plastic wallet she noted the country of origin. "I just knew it!" She shouted in happiness and noted the surprised expression of one of her neighbours, who had been going into his apartment.

Closing the door with a faint blush on her cheeks, she held the wallet to her heart.

Grabbing a coffee she sank into her sofa and put her feet up on the arm of the furniture and gently opened the seal on the wallet. Gingerly opening it she extracted a pristine white envelope in what could only be specially prepared paper and if she didn't know better it looked like Chinese handmade to her. Putting the envelope to her nose she could smell the faint trace of fresh cologne, which was all Catherine Warriorson. Slitting open the envelope, she pulled out a matching piece of paper and slowly opened it out to see the flowing bold script that told its own story.

Jace,

Seems that words are not my friends on many occasions, and I wanted to tell you exactly how I felt. At times it's hard to find the right words, so I've taken the liberty of borrowing a few from a song. I'm sure the author or the singer won't mind in this instance. As you know I love to listen to songs, I can feel so much through them that I find difficult to voice on my own, so here goes.

Don't turn me away; I'll give anything to see you stay.

I'm lost and alone without you here with me.

I will be your lady if you really want me!

I need you to be the first sight I see, living fantasy as reality.

That's where I'm gonna be.

I would never break your heart my love is beating strongly here for you.

Please come home and collect it from me as only you can!

I hope you know the song, heard it today on the local radio station, kind of a fortuitous listening session for me. The rest of the lyrics mirror what I need to say to you Jace and I'm going to do just that very soon if you will let me? Please give me the chance to show you how I feel Jace that's all I ask?

I'm going to call, please don't hang up on me!

I love you,

Catherine

Tears streamed down the cheeks of the emotionally happy woman. It had been a maelstrom of torrential emotions as she read and reread the note. Her heart was so full of love for the woman who she knew deep down to her core was going to be her lover sooner rather than later it was their divine destiny. "I love you too Catherine." Smiling tearfully into the empty apartment as she looked over the array of flowers and chocolates.

The phone rang.

Picking up the cell phone on the coffee table she answered with a warm "Hi." Jace was far too overwhelmed at the events happening, it was all she could say.

"Hello Jace, I'm sorry!" Catherine spoke softly and not without an element of trepidation in her voice.

"I love you Catherine." Jace managed to utter before she burst into tears. Catherine listened to the woman crying and wanted nothing more than to get on the next flight and go to her, but it wasn't possible. Too many people still had to be dealt with before she could fly off at the drop of a hat.

"Jace? Jace are you okay? I'm sorry love, there is nothing I want more than to be with you and say that in person and I will as soon as I can believe me, I will!" Catherine wasn't immune to the emotional storm that was going on in LA.

"I...I love you Catherine! That's all that matters. That's all that will ever matter to you and I!" Jace was trying to control her tears and get her breathing under control.

Catherine breathed a sigh of relief and smiled briefly. "You forgive me to easily Jace, was it the flowers or the chocolates that helped me out here?" Catherine tried to lighten the tension.

"You know it wasn't either of those, it was your note. I loved the note and even if all you had written was 'I love you', that would have been enough! But when you get here, I'm going to make you listen to that song again and we are going to act on it okay?" Jace finally managed to get her vocal chords in full working order.

"Anything you say, I will be all yours to do whatever you want with, and you will be the only person that has or will ever get that promise." Catherine spoke with conviction.

"I've got to tell you this Catherine, I thought you had given up on me!" Jace gulped back a sob.

"Give up on you Love! Never! Nothing will ever be that bad that I will not want you in my life, nothing do you hear me Jace?" Catherine spoke with such conviction.

"Yes, but something might?" Jace whispered.

"No! You are my life Jace Bardley, without you I'm a shell that exists but has no meaning. When I think of you and what I've already achieved simply because you're behind me, no matter the distance between us, just think what I could do with you by my side!"

"Then I'm going to be by your side for the rest of your life. Think you can put up with me and my questions for eternity?" Jace was smiling happily, everything was going to be okay, and she knew it.

"Oh Eternity with you, well...? Guess I could try it and see what it feels like." Catherine chuckled at her end. This was one of the happiest calls she had ever made. No, it was the happiest.

Chapter Thirty-One

Catherine Warriorson had often wondered what it would be like to fall in love. Now she knew exactly what it felt like and the obvious elation the feeling gave you was nothing in comparison to the drawbacks like jealousy, anger, frustration and loss of control!

Now who was she kidding, even if the other emotions went into override she would still want to share this experience with Jace, it wasn't a decision she could calculatingly make any more, it was just there and not to be trifled with. No, being in love with Jace Bardley was the most important thing in her life, and she was going to make sure that if Jace wanted to share her life with her, then who was she to stop it.

'She said she would take the baggage whatever it was and I'm going to hold her to that! I can't foresee my life without her in it now anyway.'

Tonight she was finishing the last of the 'European Short Stories' she had started a week ago; those kids wanted at least three chapters a night, so it was easy to get through a book in a week. Nothing she had previously experienced in her life could have warned her of the dangers of becoming emotionally involved with these two children. She had let the defenses that Jace had casually brought down around her, remain down and let them in, not just to her home but to her heart also.

Catherine was waiting for them to appear, or rather the shout from Grace to say that Lisa was bathed and ready for her trip down the stairs, it had been another ritual, which had been broken because of her obstinacy over her disagreement with Jace. Now she was back in harness and the kids didn't seem to be any the worse for wear over her handling however badly of them. Except, Grace had informed her of Jake's nightmares and she had been visibly shaken, for she knew she had been partly responsible, no wholly responsible for their return.

"Okay boss lady, there all yours." Shouted a happy sounding Grace.

"I'm on my way." Catherine responded with a chuckle.

Making her way to Lisa's room she glanced at the next door and sighed heavily, it was almost time for her visit to Jace, almost.

Walking inside the child's room she noticed a few toys and trinkets that hadn't been around the last time she looked in. "Have you been shopping Lisa?" Glancing at the small redhead who was dressed in a nightdress with small teddy bears swinging from a half moon emblazoned on the material. Her dressing gown had a similar motif.

The child looked up at her and smiled her gap tooth smile, although the tooth had begun to peep through. "Grace took Jake and I shopping, we have pocket money now!" Her excited voice answered.

Catherine laughed at the remark and held out her arms for the small child to be lifted up and carried downstairs. For some reason they had developed this routine and neither one of them appeared uncomfortable with it. There is only one word for you these days Catherine 'SOFT' in capital letters. "Glad to hear it, looks like you made some good choices, tomorrow you can show me what you bought, if you want too?"

"Yes, please Catherine." The child hugged her tighter round the neck and planted a sloppy kiss on her cheek.

"Come on, let's get to the lounge before Jake reads the story before us." Catherine was slightly embarrassed at the display of affection, but deep down she relished the innocent contact and silently thanked whoever had let her have a second chance at motherhood.

They settled into the large armchair, Catherine seated with Lisa nestling into her chest and Jake at her feet resting his back against her legs. He didn't go much for personal contact but managed to settle into this pose comfortably.

An hour later the book was put aside on the coffee table and Catherine saw the yawns from both children, although Jake would never openly admit he was tired.

Two minutes later, Grace walked into the lounge bearing a tray laden with milky drinks for the children, a mug of tea for Catherine, she brought along her coffee also. It had been something they had agreed on after an hour of reading to have the bedtime drinks around that time, so that the story telling didn't get carried away, as it had one evening when Catherine had totally forgotten the time.

Grace settled down into the chair opposite Catherine and winked at her.

Sending her a raised eyebrow but having a grin plastered on her face, Catherine looked at the drowsy children and took a breath as she considered her options. No better time than this, she might as well get everything in the open. "Jake, Lisa. I need you to listen to me for a few minutes please?" She tentatively approached them.

Grace smiled warmly at them as they starred intently at the woman who had become almost an idol to each child in different ways.

"Okay." They both piped up at the same time.

"Good, good. I need to go away for a few weeks." Noticing they're crestfallen expressions and the quickly tearing up of Lisa, she held the child tightly to her and whispered in her ear. "Hey, it's not that bad, honestly." Lisa gulped and Jake continued to look at her with a hooded alm□st closed look in his eyes, mirroring old pain.

"I have to go to America and clear up a business problem but I'm coming back and hopefully, I will have a good surprise for you when I do get back." She looked at their faces closely and smiled at them with gentle understanding. "You will hardly miss me, for no sooner will I have gone but I'll be back, I promise."

Grace saw the sudden welling of emotion in her friend and continued in part for her. "Yeah, kids we can get the horse lessons finished, for when she comes back so you can surprise her and you can all go riding together as a family, what do you say?" The children looked in her direction and each gave her a small smile the question unanswered.

"What I really wanted to say was while I'm gone I need you both to consider something for me and you mustn't rush into making up your minds, we have plenty of time. What I want to ask is, if you will consider letting me adopt you both!" There she'd finally got it out and what a relief that was.

Both children looked at her in astonishment and wonder. "You know that I care about you and so does Grace. We thought that maybe you might consider becoming a real family here on Destiny, but I'll understand if you can't or if want to wait until you're a little older to decide. Like I say, think about it and let me know when I get back. No pressure, it's all up to you." Catherine finished lamely.

Lisa slipped out of the arm that held her and scrambled off her lap to stand at the foot of the chair, almost standing on Jake in her haste, he moved hastily aside for her. Looking into the ice blue eyes that had given them a new life even if she was a little quiet and austere at times.

"I can answer you now Catherine, but I'll wait until you get back. Might make you get back to us quicker?" The childish logic wasn't that far from the truth.

Catherine smiled at the serious expression. "That it will Princess, that it will." She then looked at the bowed head of the boy on the floor, only a foot away from her chair. She waited.

Grace was looking at the bent head of the boy and the pensive expression on Catherine's face. Suddenly he looked up at her and his hazel eyes held a fear that she didn't understand. "It won't make you my mother, will it?" He asked her directly.

Catherine was stunned by the question and a little sad at his objection to her taking the role even as a surrogate. "No, no I could never be your mother." She answered his question sadly.

"Then I will do the same as Lisa, when you get back I will let you know what I think about the idea." He got up from the floor and picked up his drink and walked towards the door. "Goodnight." He then left the room.

Lisa looked at the two adults in the room knowing that Jake hadn't meant to hurt their feelings. She placed her hand on Catherine's arm and got her attention. "He just gets upset sometimes about his parents, but he wants to be family, really Catherine." The child said earnestly, championing her 'brother'.

Catherine stood up to her six feet and picked the child up and swung her over her left shoulder and snagged her drink from the tray.

"Yes, I know Princess, now it's time for bed and let's get that show on the road before Grace gives us a hard time okay?" She glanced at her friend.

"Yeah, I should think so too! Keeping our kids up late, shame on you Catherine." Getting up from her seat she placed a gentle kiss on the child's forehead and winked at her.

Catherine entered the room a short time later and walked towards the window, peered out at the white sheet that was forming over the yard. "I think its going to be a hard winter this year Grace."

Grace moved towards the woman standing rigid at the window and she looked at the natural beauty snow held to the onlooker. "Oh, I don't know, something tells me that with luck this winter might be quite beautiful and full of surprises."

"Ever the optimist Grace."

"Someone has to be, thought I'd told you that before?"

"Yes, I think you did and perhaps you're right as usual."

"Jake will be fine Catherine, maybe he's just a little shocked at the speed you came to this decision? Hell, I am!"

"Why?" Catherine turned from her view of the growing bed of snowflakes.

"Come on now, when was the last time you did anything remotely like this?" Grace asked her knowing the answer already.

"I've never done anything like this in my life!" She replied enigmatically.

"Exactly." Her friend grinned at her lack of understanding.

"And your point would be?"

"I love you Catherine, the kids love you, and Jace loves you. But lady you sure have some baggage that you're finding difficult to shed and until you do, gestures like this, can mean everything and nothing, depends on your mood." Grace hadn't meant to sound critical of her friend's decision, it was the right one for them all, but she did have problems that she kept locked away and they needed to be aired.

"Yes you're right." A quizzical look appeared on her face. "Why are you always right about me Grace?"

Grace laughed at the look on her friend's face, and smiled broadly.

"Guess it must be something your mother passed onto me, who knows."

"Maybe, to answer the jibe, I'm going to tell Jace everything about me! My past, my present and how I want to spend my future. Then I'm going to tell you everything too! You deserve that much my friend."

Grace smiled warmly and put her arm around the taller woman's shoulders in understanding. "Bring Jace back with you, that will be all the explanation that will ever be needed between us Catherine. You're not a saint and I'm sure you've done things that I would personally abhor, but what you are today, far outweighs anything that has happened in the past. That goes for Colin too!"

"You know most of the time Grace, you speak for everyone on this ranch, myself included." She smirked at the blush on her friend's cheeks.

"No! Well, okay it's becoming a habit, I really must do something about that." Pulling the woman back towards her chair as they settled down to a few minutes of peace and quiet. "By the way when are you leaving?"

"Tomorrow evening, I have a flight out of Auckland to LA and then onto New York, it leaves at 11pm. I need to get to New York as soon as possible."

"Your business okay?" Grace asked, interested in the other world her friend was embroiled in but rarely mentioned.

"Yes, but I have a threat that needs to be resolved, once it is, I get to ask a certain Jace Bardley if she wants to come and live with me!"

Catherine looked bashful as she said the final words.

"Do I get the guest bedroom ready?" Grace smirked as she looked at the ice blue eyes of the woman in front of her, which held quiet joy at the prospect.

"Christ, I hope not Grace!" Catherine said with feeling.

"Good, I would need to have help soon, if you fill any more rooms." She laughed softly and drank her coffee, seeing the faraway look on her friend's face, but it was happy expression.

Chapter Thirty-Two

Hudson was happy; she'd finally received the call from Paul Strong that she had expected over a week ago. For some reason he had been unable to contact his employer. Now, he had confirmed the date, it was going to be in three days time at her offices as requested.

'I've finally got to her, she's on the run, if she wasn't, then she wouldn't entertain coming out of her exile for me! I thought throwing in the threat to expose interesting material to the media, might get the desired result. Especially now that she was involved with a certain employee of hers. It had been interesting to see Jace go from despair to the ecstatic all in the space of a few days. How will she react when she finds out her sworn enemy is also the woman she loves? Wonder if the sensitive kid can take it, this one she would bet her share of UCP that Jace couldn't hack it! Well, only three days to go before we find out, now that is some meeting that I'm looking forward to! You never wanted my bed, but I'm going to get you in it Catherine no matter what. Some naive blonde isn't going to succeed, not now, not ever!' Walking over to her desk she called for Peter Adamson to get his rear end into her office now!

Several minutes later a harried looking Peter Adamson pushed open the door to Hudson's office and noticed her negligently draped across her desk, viewing some stills of a new feature.

"You wanted to see me?" Peter spoke politely.

"Yep, I certainly do, now shut the door and take a seat." She directed not looking up from the stills on her desk.

"I've got the Xianthos people coming here in three days, are you going to be available to see them over your project?"

"Sure, who's coming from the Empire?" He asked with interest.

"Ah, well I could say it's a secret, but as you already know part of the story, the very reclusive Ms. Devonshire, or should I say Warriorson herself, will grace us with her presence. Also, Paul Strong their new President, appears he's taking over the reigns officially from her." The last she said with bitterness.

Peter smiled inwardly; he liked Paul Strong, and had met him over dinner with James on the several occasions, when he'd been in town. "Sounds like all the big guns are in town, but isn't that a little over the top for a project this small?"

"Let's just say I have my own personal agenda with Ms. Devonshire, so at some stage I want you to take Mr. Strong out of the room for me and show him the ten cent tour okay?" Her voice brooked no argument.

"Whatever you say, I just want to get a release date before I move on next month." Peter stated finally.

"Yeah, well no promises but I think I can wangle that one if you do your bit."

"If I don't?" He eyed her suspiciously.

"Then your reputation as a director might get a little sullied in the process of this deal, you catch my drift?" Hudson spared him a withering glance.

"Yeah I get the drift. What about Jace?"

"What about her?" Hudson was bored with the subject.

"She doesn't know her friend Warriorson is Devonshire, it will break her heart." Peter said in a quiet voice.

"Fancy that, I'm counting on not only Jace being heart broken but a certain recluse as well! Makes perfect sense to me." She smiled at him.

"You have a strange sense of perfection then, if other people suffering gives you any kind of thrill." He was disgusted at her and knew the sooner he could get out of her grips the cleaner he would feel.

"Quite so, but for Devonshire, nothing else would be appropriate. Believe me, she's no innocent babe in arms, I have proof of that."

"But Jace is!" Peter exploded at the injustices he saw for his friend.

"Oh Peter, she's a casualty of war, think yourself lucky, you get to pick up the pieces. Sounds like a good deal for you from my point of view." The vindictive woman eyed him speculatively.

"I don't want her that way." He knew that he was lying; he would take Jace on any kind of rebound situation, any kind at all!

"I don't believe you! Time will tell as they say and the time is getting ever closer." She gave him the dismissal look and he got up and left the room.

He heard her laugh as he passed by Jace's empty chair and went out into the sunshine of a beautiful Californian day.

Catherine walked into her building in New York; it was impressive by any standards and had the opulent designs of the twenties. Her father had chosen well when he'd purchased the deeds back in the late seventies.

She sauntered towards the reception area and waited in line for her turn with the receptionist, a tall brunette who had a smile permanently placed on her face, no matter what the situation. She was new or certainly hadn't been here when she left the building that final time over five years ago.

It gave her the usual rush of adrenaline as she waited and watched the numerous people coming and going in the area. At one time her father being the head of the company, had his picture plastered on all of the thirty floors, or at least twenty-nine, as there was never a thirteenth floor in any building. She had left them in residence until each floor had been redecorated over a period of time and now only one hung in the boardroom, along with her only portrait. She refused to have her picture strewn all over the place, it didn't matter if her employees knew who she was, all she asked was that they do a good job in the positions they held. Having people watch out for her, was a waste of energy and time and in her mind, time was money and she paid far too well to waste it!

Finally the receptionist asked her whom she wanted to see. The tall elegantly dressed woman noticed the badge of the very efficient receptionist, which clearly stated her name as Claire Fallen.

"I have an appointment with Mr. Strong." Catherine spoke decisively.

The young woman looked closely at her, and continued. "May I ask who's calling to verify it on my appointment sheet, pleasu." Then gave her a speculative look? The false smile was back, it amused Catherine and she gave a tight smile of her own.

"Certainly, it's Mrs. Warriorson." Catherine waited to see if there was any recognition of her name.

The girl scanned her sheet and looked perplexed. "I don't appear to have that name down on my sheet. Are you sure your appointment is today?" The girl asked tentatively, it wouldn't do to upset potential clients and you just never knew who was coming through the door unexpectedly.

Catherine's smile faded and she looked at the sheet from her elevated position, her stance giving off an angry message. "I'm sure! In that case I suggest you call Mr. Strong immediately and clear up the difficulty." Her tone permitted no argument. *'This wasn't good enough, was Paul letting things slip?'*

"Would you please take a seat, I'll call his secretary." The young woman spoke quietly to the seemingly pissed off woman.

Catherine glanced her way and gave her an icy stare and shrugged her shoulders then went over to the glass display panels that held information about the company. Her name was mentioned and there was a small photograph taken some eight years ago, when she had taken over from her father.

Celeste Johnson, Paul's personal aide answered the phone. "Hello, Johnson speaking."

"Hi Celeste, it's Claire at reception, does Mr. Strong have an appointment that he hasn't mentioned?" Came the quiet voice of the girl, she didn't want to upset the PA, especially if she'd screwed up.

"No, he didn't mention anything, why?" Celeste was inquisitive. Paul was usually very meticulous about appointments, something he had learned from the owner.

"I have a woman here who says she has an appointment and believe me she doesn't look the type you disagree with, not if you still want to be left in one piece that is." Claire said with a light laugh.

"Oh, don't tell me tall, dark and beautiful?" Celeste laughed along with the woman.

"You're right on target, but how did you know?" Claire gasped at the accuracy of her description.

"I didn't, but I know what you consider dangerous material. So what's the mystery woman's name?" Celeste chuckled.

"Warriorson, Mrs. Warriorson." Responded the receptionist.

There was a sound that could have been the phone being dropped, but quickly picked up again. "Are you sure about that?" Came a strained response from the other end.

"Yes, positive, why who is she?" Claire was intrigued.

"Claire for god's sake send her up immediately, no special passes nothing, do you hear me?" Said the PA in an authoritative tone.

"Well, that's outside protocol Celeste, surely she needs a pass, security will raise a fit with me and so will my boss." Claire was surprised at the directive.

"Claire get her a pass, make it one of the gold VIP ones okay, just put down her name and that should appease all the protocol you need. Don't waste any more time Claire, just do it!"

"Who is she Celeste, surely she's not that important that we break all the rules for her?" This was fascinating the woman it was a rare day indeed that anything rattled the Vice-President's PA.

"When are you going on break?" Celeste asked her.

"Actually in about two minutes, Connie is walking towards me now."

"Okay, get the pass, hand over the position to Connie and personally bring Mrs. Warriorson here and then you will find out first hand." Celeste smiled at her idea, she knew that Claire was discreet but speculation would be rife if it wasn't handled properly and Claire was excellent at handling this type of situation.

"You got it, see you shortly." Replacing the handset, she reached for the box that held the special passes, it would allow a person access to all levels, except for the Vice-President's office, his PA, the boardroom and the not in residence, Chairwoman's Executive Suite.

Claire passed over the position to Connie and said she would be gone about half an hour or less. Walking swiftly over to the tall woman looking intently but with a bored expression on her face at the history of the company.

"Mrs. Warriorson, I have your pass, please follow me, I will escort you to the executive floor." She smiled genuinely at the visitor.

Catherine quirked an eyebrow at the woman. "That isn't necessary, I've been here before."

"Oh, that's okay, it is my pleasure." Turning she motioned to the far side of the elevator bank, taking the furthest one from their position.

Catherine was surprised at the move and her face must have shown this.

Claire smiled briefly and said. "We will have the elevator to ourselves, and most people can't be bothered to walk the few yards to the end, but will wait ages for another if it's full. I could never understand that logic myself."

"Yes, I wouldn't understand that logic either." This time Catherine sent her a lopsided grin.

Getting into the elevator, Claire pressed the button of their destination.

"How long have you worked for Xianthos?" Catherine asked her pleasantly.

Claire looked at the woman and saw her interest. "Four years, straight from college; I'm working on an advanced degree in administration and hopefully I can get more experience in other roles."

"I see... working on reception won't be a good foundation for your degree?" Catherine arched her eyebrow in question.

"Perhaps not, but the company pays well and I need to do the studying part time, I'll work on that problem later." Claire replied confidently.

"Have you talked to your supervisor about it?" Catherine persisted; one thing she wasn't happy about was a waste of talent.

Claire laughed it was almost musical in its tone. "No, Mr. Reeves wouldn't understand."

Catherine raised an eyebrow. "Why not?"

"Well, he's old school. Thinks that women should be around for the more menial tasks not management roles. It happens." The girl replied without bitterness.

Catherine pondered the remark. "I thought this company was owned by a woman? Doesn't that sort of deflate his ideas?"

"No, why should it. Ms. Devonshire is only a figure head, men run the company, here in New York particularly." The door slid open as they reached the floor.

Plush green carpet swept up in front of them and she could see the familiar doors leading to the various executive personnel assigned to the floor. Immediately ahead was the Chairwoman's office, the only key except for a security key was in the possession of the Chairwoman herself. They walked briskly towards Paul's office area and his PA in particular.

"You do know your way around." Claire smiled at the woman who was way ahead of her.

Turning back she dismissed the woman's comment but nodded her head, turning the door of the PA's office she sauntered in, followed quickly by Claire. "Hello Celeste." Catherine greeted her.

"Ms. Dev...Warriorson, I wasn't expecting you." Celeste got up quickly from her chair, not knowing if she should shake the woman's hand or just find Paul Strong.

Catherine dealt with that problem, she held out her hand and shook the proffered hand that Celeste held out. "How are the children?"

"Fine and yours?" Celeste said in surprise.

"Good, it's snowing at home, they should be having fun at the weekend, Colin is taking them sledding."

"They will have fun, I'm sure. Paul is in a meeting until one p.m. with some clients, I can interrupt him for you?"

Lifting up a hand, she motioned for Celeste to sit down. "No, that's okay, I could do with a drink though, what have you got for me?"

Claire was watching in fascination, this was no ordinary VIP.

"Anything you want?" Celeste confidently answered.

"If they make decent tea, I'll have a mug. If not I will have a cappuccino." Turning she looked at the girl waiting by the door. "Miss... Fallen, what do you drink?"

Claire was surprised, but was outdone in the surprise stakes by Celeste, who looked at the tall woman with her mouth open. Catherine saw the look and laughed at the sight. "Better close that Celeste before you catch flies." She said casually as she walked towards the window, which had a good view of the city.

Claire looked at Celeste for guidance. She just shook her head.

"So, what are you drinking Miss. Fallen?" The voice asked again from her position at the window.

"Oh, expresso for me." Looking once again at Celeste. "Do you want me to go for them?"

"No, take a seat Claire, I will have them brought up." Picking up her phone she connected to the cafeteria on the fifth floor.

"Claire works for someone called Reeves, Celeste, get me his file and have him in my office in an hour." The tone was cold and determined, which surprised both women.

Celeste looked at the girl seated opposite her and her frown gave everything away. "Will have that in here shortly."

"Oh, I didn't mean to cause any trouble, it was only an observation." Claire didn't know what to say. *Which office was she referring to?'*

Catherine turned back to the occupants of the room. Sending the girl a stare that would silence the most antagonistic. "Have you known this woman long Celeste?"

"Yes, since she arrived about four years ago."

"Have you known her to be anything but honest?"

"No, she's a very honest and capable worker."

"Fine, then I'll take your observation and let's see if I make the same diagnosis." She gave a wicked smile and turned back to the window.

Without thinking Claire asked a direct question. "Who are you?"

Catherine chuckled in merriment. Celeste put a hand to her mouth and just cringed.

"Me? You want to know who I am?" As she walked towards the girl seated in the low chair, she didn't look much more than in her early twenties, it reminded her of Jace. Must be the girl's lucky day, giving her a mock menacing stare she answered. "I'm someone's worse nightmare, but I can also be their saviour too. Today young lady you're going to have a saviour." She walked up to Celeste. "When the drink comes I'll have it in my office, along with that file."

She passed the PA and went to the permanently locked door of the Chairwoman's office and pulled out a key, opened the door, entered and then shut the solid, decorated door gently behind her.

Claire looked on as she saw where the woman went; her face paled as the tall impressive frame opened the sacred door and went inside. "I just made a grave mistake here didn't I Celeste?" A small voice asked.

Celeste walked over to the girl and patted her hand. "No, not really. Trust me, she's not the bitch everyone thinks she is, whatever you said, if it's the truth she will see it also, so don't worry."

"Easy for you to say, you knew who she was. I'm right in thinking she's the Great Ms. Devonshire?"

"In the very flesh Claire." Celeste smiled at the devastated expression on the younger woman's face.

"She's very beautiful." Claire slowly lifted her head from its hung position and smiled weakly at the other woman.

"Yes, she is. The drinks are here, come on have that before you go back to work." Celeste picked up the mug of tea and the file she had received from personnel, and entered the other office, coming out a few minutes later with a smile on her face.

"She wants the office cleaned, said it's dusty and she hasn't enough clothes with her to have them messed up with dirt."

"Can't she buy more, she must be incredibly wealthy."

"I wouldn't know, she probably is very wealthy if the share prices of this company are anything to judge by. Catherine Devonshire is a woman you never second guess, too many people have tried and to-date no one has ever won that particular game with her, I doubt they ever will." Celeste went back to her desk and called Reeves.

Catherine had her meeting with Reeves, it was one of those times she really liked demoting people, he was pompous and his results over the last two years didn't measure up. He appeared to relish putting women in the background you could see that with the staff line-up. Men dominated all the senior positions and the women had lowly administrative roles. The turn over of female staff was incredible, especially as she knew that the company was one of the top-ranked for employee pay and benefits in the city. *'Wonder why personnel hasn't picked up this trend? Glad the girl was right with her observations, or she would have been looking for a new position herself.'*

Closing the file, she would write the report herself, as Paul wouldn't be back for another hour; so she turning on her laptop computer, which had been pulled out of the secured cabinet close to her desk and started the demotion paperwork. The place hadn't changed at all.

Her cherry oak desk with its royal blue blotter in the centre was empty, except for a small in tray of royal blue. Opening one of the drawers she pulled out a fountain pen and a cartridge, waiting for the flow of ink to reach the gold nib. She glanced round at the dark blue leather sofa, which adorned one side of the office wall. A cherry oak cabinet held her personal filing system and some stationery. A leather swivel chair designed for computer use was tucked away in the corner closest to her desk. Her leather executive chair had pride of place in front of the desk and she sat in its welcoming comfort. The small cabinet close to her desk, housed the computer and the communications system, her personal company cell phone sat in the drawer and would remain there.

Getting up she walked over to the window and switched back the blinds, the bright light of a sunny New York day spread itself over the room. She missed this! The total control she had when she came into this office, it was something she wondered if she could ever have given up, but she had and until now, she had never felt the nostalgia of the situation. *'I was bloody good at the role, even my father might have been proud of me in the end.'* The door was pulled open and Paul Strong entered a wide smile on his handsome face.

"Catherine, why didn't you say you were coming?" He went over and shook her hand.

"I thought I'd mentioned coming over, we talked yesterday?" Catherine looked at him in surprise.

"I thought you wanted a meeting at the hotel, not here!"

"I guess I never made myself very clear, but it's good to be here Paul."

"It's good to see you her also, I miss you around here you know?" He looked at her sheepishly.

"Thanks. Even if I was one of the most ruthless people you have ever work with huh?" She smiled at his sudden blush.

"Oh, I wouldn't go so far as saying that." He laughed self-consciously.

"You know if you weren't already taken, I might just ask if you would be interested in a date, you look real cute with a blush." Catherine teased the man that was going to be effectively the man behind the Empire she had forsaken.

He looked at her in surprise. "I would think that a certain party that holds your affection might have something to say about that too!"

"Yes, maybe you're right. Hate to say this Paul but I've kind of demoted one of your senior personnel, a man called Reeves, any objection?" She waited for his response with interest.

"Not me Madam Chairwoman, if that's what you want, I haven't a problem with it. He's been with the company for over thirty years, old school type."

"So why haven't you done something about it?" Catherine asked him with veiled interest.

"He managed to scrape in each year with passable explanations, I'm sorry." He looked at her for a chance to gauge her reactions.

"Who would be the prime candidate to replace him?" She sounded bored with the discussion.

"You have any suggestions?" He asked hopefully.

"Yes, but let's get on with the new line up here and in South America. Is Constance ready to take over here?"

"Yes, she's been over twice, she passed all her materials to Gareth last week and will be here tomorrow, before we go to LA. Enricho Garcia is the new vice-president for the South American operation. He's been with the company for ten years and was heading Eduardo's sales operation. I know he will be good for the role; he has the connections as well as the intelligence. He could do with some support for a few months though, but I'll tackle that one as soon as I can." Paul explained briefly.

Catherine digested all he said and smiled briefly.

"Time for lunch, you seem to have everything under control. I want Celeste's personnel profile on my desk when I get back, she will take over from Reeve!" Looking at the shock on his face.

"Come on Paul, Celeste isn't going to LA with you, so Constance can get her own PA, we need her in there Paul, it's our communications in the company; I want the right person in the position, and she is the right person. Clear it up for me, will you?" She smiled at his expression.

"Did I say I was glad to see you back?" He asked her with a wry grin.

"Something like that." She grinned back it him.

"Do I get to take it back?" He headed towards the door and opened it she walked towards him and placed a hand on his shoulder. "No!"

They headed for the elevator and the fifth floor; this was going to be quite a day, her first day back from exile and she was already making waves, what a wonderful feeling.

Chapter Thirty-Three

Catherine sank into the wonderful downy bed in the hotel room in LA. She was tired after her journey from New York and the hours she had needed to work to enable her to have everything covered. Now, reclining on the bed, she was tempted to just sleep the afternoon and evening through until her meeting with Hudson...but NO! There was an infinitely better reason to stay awake tonight, Jace!

Paul had taken the opportunity to spend some time with his partner, although he had offered to have dinner with her, she had declined. Hell, she had a much better candidate lined up for that festivity.

Picking up the phone she dialed the UCP office number given to her by Paul, and asked to speak with Ms. Bardley.

"Hello this is Jace Bardley, how may I help you?" A cheery voice answered.

Catherine found the voice totally enchanting. Smiling, she answered in a low voice. "Ms. Bardley how about dinner?" She waited for a response.

Hearing a thud and a scuffle she was a little surprised, was there a problem at the other end. "Hey, Jace are you still there?" Catherine asked in concern.

"Zeus, Catherine you surprised me! What do you mean dinner?" Jace was flushed and excited all at once, having recovered from dropping the phone.

"Well...I kind of thought that as a stranger in town you might take pity on me tonight." Catherine spoke in a low gravelly tone, and to Jace it was one of the most tantalising voices she would ever hear in her life, it consistently set her emotions on overload.

"You're in town?" Jace asked in wonder, if Catherine could see her eyes they would have been as round as saucers.

"Yes, I think a certain best friend of mine constantly invited me, so here I am." She chuckled at the complete surprise of her friend.

"You never mentioned it at all! Catherine if I didn't love you so much I would be furious with you!" Jace laughed self-consciously at her end.

"So, have we a date?" Knowing she was teasing Jace.

"Oh, my god, of course we have a date. Do you know how long I've been waiting for you?" Jace answered breathlessly but in a serious tone.

"Two months, three weeks and a day." Catherine said nonchalantly.

"Hades, I didn't realise you were counting, but I was going to say Forever." She laughed at the thought of Catherine counting the days since she had left Destiny.

Catherine this time was the one to be surprised and she let out a sigh as she sank back into the bed.

"Are you still there, Catherine?" This time Jace was concerned.

"Yes.....yes I'm still here. Guess I wasn't expecting that. What time shall I pick you up?" Catherine said quietly, still digesting the last snippet of information from Jace.

"How about I meet you at your hotel, and we decide where to eat from there?"

"Sure, but I still need a time?"

"I would take the afternoon off if I thought I could get away with it, but Hudson is having a strange day, so make it seven, okay?" Jace said abstractedly.

Catherine smiled at the statement regarding Hudson. *'Yeah with luck she might actually be rattled for a change.'* She continued with her conversation. "Great, I'll meet you in the lobby at seven."

"Until then." Jace smiled into the handset.

"Until then, bye Jace." Catherine replaced her receiver and shut her eyes, with one thought coming to mind, or was it a word?

'FOREVER!'

Jace was smiling. Well, grinning would have been a more appropriate expression. Everywhere she went on the lot she smiled, it didn't matter if someone was happy or gave her a sad story about their dog dying or that their grandson was in an accident or something equally distracting, she smiled. It was almost as if she had found a secret stash of a happy drug or something, people who knew her well, found her smile intoxicating and reciprocated. Others thought she was on a high and someone really should do something about it!

As Jace rounded a corner of the lot near her office, and the time got nearer to six, she suddenly jumped as high as she could and said out loud to no one in particular, "YES!" Giving the air a high five as she jumped. Her happiness wasn't going to be dulled by anyone, not even Hudson. She briskly walked into the building.

All sorts of thoughts went through Jace's mind as she went about her day, she couldn't believe that Catherine was finally here and she hadn't mentioned one word, not a one. *'Oh there is payback and how*

Catherine! I can't believe you have come over and to see me! I'm going to make tonight so special that you won't want to leave ever again, or at least not without me by your side.'

Jace walked by Agnes' desk and noted she had gone for the evening, which was always a good sign. Walking into the area that held her office space and also the internal door to Hudson's office, she noticed that the light was still shining under the door. "Hades, I hope she doesn't want me now!"

Jace went to her desk and sorted through any mail that had arrived in the interim of her absence. Nothing to worry about, she put them away in a secure place and closed down her computer, with that the door to Hudson's office opened and Peter Adamson was being hustled out.

"Ah Jace, glad to see you back! Wanted to let you know we have important visitors tomorrow and Agnes is on holiday, so I need you in the office to welcome them and stay until they leave." Hudson demanded not asked.

Jace glanced at Hudson and nodded her head, and then she noticed that Peter looked uncomfortable as she looked quizzically at him.

"Hi Jace, do you want to go out to dinner tonight?" He smiled at her wearily, his face telling her more about his trials with Hudson then a thousand words could ever express.

"I'm sorry Peter, but I already have plans." She replied softly, giving him a smile of understanding.

"Rain check then?" He tilted his head in her direction totally ignoring an impatient Hudson.

"Yes, look forward to it." Jace looked from Peter to Hudson.

"Oh, so you finally noticed the boss exists, how very kind of you!" Hudson said sarcastically and noticed Jace flush.

"Just remember who signs the pay check Jace, I think we have already had this conversation, and hate to repeat myself!" Hudson said maliciously.

"Yes, you have already told me that! Do I get to know who the special visitors are?" Jace looked directly at her boss.

"No!" Hudson said and strode past the two of them and out of the external door.

Jace watched her go and then looked at Peter in question.

He shrugged and walked over to her desk. "Is it a heavy date?" He asked her with interest, somewhat disappointed.

"Yes." She answered with a slight blush to her cheeks.

283

He noticed the colouring and managed to look a little contrite. "Guess it's none of my business, hope you have a good night." He walked towards the door.

"Peter!"

He turned to look at her.

"You're my friend Peter, thank you for asking." She smiled at him and collected her purse and car keys.

Peter left the building and Jace glanced at her watch. "Hades, I have to get home and shower and change and get to the hotel in...hotel...which hotel? Oh gods, I never asked. She's going to kill me, I never thought about it." She spoke absently to one of her resident dragons.

Sitting down on the chair, she looked at the blank terminal screen in front of her and wondered what to do. Putting her head on the desk, she closed her eyes and knew she had really blown it. Getting up slowly she noticed it was six-fifteen; and she needed to get home and changed, there must be some way she could find Catherine?

Walking as fast as she could, but without the spring to her step of earlier, she got into her car and headed home.

Catherine awoke from her sleep at five, not bad really, she certainly felt refreshed for her evening with Jace. Gradually waking enough to get out of bed, she stretched and realised she could have at least an hour in the bath before her engagement with Jace.

Walking over to the TV, she switched channels several times, and then decided that CNN was perhaps the best option for a foreigner, especially in the States, too many damn channels to choose from and nothing on any of them to watch. No, that wasn't quite true, if you liked a particular program you usually saw it first in the States. Not like at home, usually at least two seasons behind, assuming they didn't cancel it on the home run; now, that really was a pain. Fortunately with her resources, she bought up videos ferociously to combat that particular planning problem. Not only that, she hated Ad's and that was one thing the BBC was good at, no Ad's. Still she no longer lived in the UK and hadn't for a while now, so it had been purely nostalgia. Good nostalgia though!

Curling her toes on the thick carpet, she decided to run her bath and contemplate her evening.

Sitting in the bath relaxing, she wondered what she would say to Jace tonight. *Tonight was perhaps the right time to tell her everything, it would give her time to digest the information and decide if she really did want any sort of lasting relationship with me. Mind you, Hudson in the morning after seeing Jace upset wasn't a good way to have a meeting. No, think the explanation will come after the meeting with Hudson, at least she will know part of the story by then or at least the alter ego. Hell! I can't see any problem with Jace knowing that my business life went under the name of Devonshire, hardly a major topic of conversation. Yes, that sounds good to me.'* Sinking further in the bubble filled bath; she suddenly shot up!

"Oh Christ! I forgot to mention which Hotel I'm in!" Catherine spluttered as she spoke the words out loud and close to the bubble water line. Thinking fast she rushed out of the bath and grabbed a towel and moved into the recreational area. Picking up the phone, glanced at the time. "Gads, it's six-ten!" She speed dialed a number she had programmed into the cell phone.

After leaving a message on Jace's machine, she rubbed herself dry and sat down heavily on the end of the king-size bed in the luxuriously decorated suite. Suddenly weary at the thought that what she anticipated as a wonderful evening could easily have been a very frustrating one.

Catherine walked around the lobby in an agitated way; it was seven-twenty and still no sign of Jace. *'Hell, maybe she hadn't managed to get away from the studio?'*

Her back turned away from the main entrance; she failed to see Jace enter.

Jace looked around the lobby, noticed the woman who would always hold her attention no matter where she was or what she as doing. The tall, dark and quite intoxicatingly beautiful Catherine Warriorson was only yards away from her; she felt the magnetic pull of attraction so acutely it was almost breaking her apart. Walking over to the raven-haired beauty, Jace smiled at the anxious look she saw on Catherine's profile from the left side. "You know if you keep that expression on your face much longer it's going to stay for good and mar that beautiful face." Jace spoke softly to the woman whose back tensed at the words.

Turning, Catherine drank in the lovely sight that appeared like a spectre to her. It had seemed so unattainable, yet it was within her grasp at last. "Have you been talking to Grace recently?" Catherine nonchalantly replied, although that belied the true feelings she had coursing through her veins at the sight of the young woman.

"Hello Catherine." Jace spoke shyly her eyes never leaving the ice blue gaze she had longed for in the months of their separation.

"Hello Jace Bardley." Catherine couldn't stop herself from putting out a hand and gently touching Jace's cheek. *'She was definitely real!'*

Jace was entranced. This was the woman she had professed her heart and soul too, and all she wanted to do was drown in the emotions of being with her again. "I love you Catherine Warriorson." Her voice cracked at the emotion she felt at their close proximity.

Smiling Catherine gently grasped one of Jace's hands and pulled it towards her lips. "I love you more than life itself, Jace." The emotional charge around the two of them was electric.

They stood there, each absorbing the presence of the other; neither wanted to move.

"Where do you want to eat?" Catherine asked finally, her ice blue gaze tracking the green eyes with precision.

"Eat! You want to eat?" Jace asked in frustration.

"Well, there are alternatives to that of course. What do you want to do?" Catherine gave her a cautious look as she saw the frustrated expression on Jace's face.

Jace saw the concerned look from her friend and decided that eating was a start. "Okay, we eat. How about my place?"

Catherine's smile changed to a grin. "Maybe tomorrow. How about we have a meal here and we talk. What do you say?"

"Well, I guess we can. But wouldn't you rather go back to my place?" Jace look disappointed.

"Patience my friend, patience! Let's go and have something to eat."

Catherine saw the disappointed look and, disregarding anyone or anything in the vicinity to them, she dipped her head and placed a tender kiss on Jace's lips before gently taking the younger woman's arm and guided her towards the hotel restaurant.

Jace bemusedly followed, the feel of Catherine's lips imprinted on hers to savor. Tonight, was going to exceed her expectations of this reunion, without any shadow of a doubt.

Their dinner progressed easily, each woman talking about situations in their own world, and constantly passing tender glances across the table.

At one stage their glances had locked so much it had taken the waiter several clearances of his throat before he could get their attention. He looked the most embarrassed of the three, playing out that little scenario, when they finally noticed him.

As they concluded the main course, a dessert was offered and Catherine passed the menu to Jace with a smirk.

"What?" Jace grinned at the woman opposite her, whose face held such an expression of happiness it was hard to associate her with the stoic persona that could easily present itself to the world in general.

"Dessert for you, not me." Catherine gave her a grin.

"Well, I was kinda hoping that..." Jace gave her a wicked smile.

With Catherine's left eyebrow raised she looked quizzically at her friend. "Hoping?"

"Yes, hoping that the dessert I was going to offer at my home would be more to your liking." Jace looked down at her empty place setting and a blush became apparent to the onlooker.

"You do, do you? Now that's an offer worth considering." Catherine spoke in a low growl, for Jace's ears only.

"Is that a yes or no?" Jace asked breathlessly.

Motioning over the waiter, she spoke briefly to him; he immediately rushed to his station and grabbed their bill. He quickly sauntered back to them, with more haste than Jace had ever seen in a waiter.

Catherine looked at the green eyes of her friend and saw the sparkle of laughter at the action of the waiter; who had tripped in his haste to swiftly present the bill to Catherine.

Taking the bill from the man, she signed the paper with a flourish and looked him in the eye, unexpectedly giving him a wink, added something to the bottom of the bill, passed it back to him and saw his smile grow wider. Catherine then looked back at her dinner guest and smiled seductively. "Does that answer your question?"

"Yes." Jace swooned silently, giving a thank you to whoever was listening.

"Let's go then." Catherine got up from her seat and, with a speed that amazed Jace; she was behind her seat helping her up.

Jace looked into those ice blue eyes and the look she received almost sent her back into the cushioned seat to stop her legs giving out at the dazzling, sensuous glance.

"Thank you."

"My pleasure."

They walked out of the restaurant and through the main door into the cool night air. Catherine casually linked her arm in Jace's as they headed for her vehicle and the place Jace called home.

Chapter Thirty-Four

Glancing round the small apartment, she noticed arrays of flowers and smiled, knowing that they must undoubtedly be from her. She also noticed all the items of furniture that Jace had mentioned in their conversations and e-mails. Going over to the desk, which housed Jace's PC, she picked up a framed photo, which could only be of Jace's family.

Jace had gone into the kitchen to prepare some coffee and in all honesty to get her equilibrium back. Although she wanted this Jace had no experience whatsoever of how to seduce Catherine, other than with words and she had obviously done that already. Having read some revealing fan fiction on the Internet it had at least given her ideas, if not the courage to attempt them. *'Has Catherine experience with other women; I know about her taste in men or at least one man, but women? That was something different again.'* Pushing a hand through her hair she collected the coffee mugs and went back in search of her friend.

Hearing her approach, Catherine turned and smiled gently at Jace, she looked a little nervous. "Is this your family?" Her hand paused over the picture frame.

"Yes, my Mom, Dad and my sister Lucy. We're very close, I was over at the house a few weeks ago." Her gentle smile clearly painting its own picture.

"Your parents have done a good job in bringing up at least one of their daughters." Catherine looked keenly at Jace.

"My parents will be happy to meet you anytime if you say nice things like that about them, without prompting too!" A chuckle passed Jace's lips.

They each drank a mug of coffee in silence.

Catherine glanced around the room and then grinned at Jace. "I don't see any chocolate about, didn't I send enough; or wasn't it to your taste?" Catherine asked her in earnest.

"Don't go there, Catherine. I'm not sure if I should even allow you around me. You are so, so bad for me!" Jace chuckled at her friend.

Catherine moved closer to Jace. "How so?" Quirking her ever faithful left eyebrow.

"I must have put on ten pounds with all the chocolate I've eaten already, it was irresistible." Jace grinned at her.

"Irresistible huh? So it's all gone?" Catherine sounded disappointed.

"No! No, quite the contrary, in the kitchen you will find a cupboard called Catherine's chocolate cavern, trust me on that!" Jace gave her a dazzling, appreciative smile.

Catherine found something equally irresistible to her; bending closer to Jace she captured her lips in a searing kiss, leaving them both breathless when they eventually surfaced for air.

Considering her options, Catherine looked deep into green orbs that looked back at her passionately. She'd hoped to not have this conversation tonight. "I need to tell you some things about me Jace. Some are good, some are bad and to be honest some are downright disgusting. I need you to know everything about me." Her eyes never left the blonde and she could see conflicting emotions pass over the expressive face.

The silence became almost unbearable for Catherine.

Then, suddenly Jace moved to within an inch of her face and a dreamy expression came over her. "Can I show you something?" She whispered seductively.

"Sure." Came back the simple reply.

Capturing one of Catherine's larger hands in hers, she tugged her towards a room immediately left of the kitchen area; opening the door they entered Jace's bedroom.

Catherine looked startled at the younger woman and started to speak, a slim finger was placed over her lips to silence her. "Sit, I'll be back in a few minutes." Jace went through a door in the middle of the right hand wall; it was a small but comfortable bathroom.

The bedsprings squeaked a little as Catherine lowered her weight onto the bed and looked around at the very tidy but cosy room. *This isn't working we should be talking. She needs to know everything!* Her mind said, but her heart was thudding at the possibilities the situation was opening up.

The door to the other room opened and Catherine was hard pressed not to shout out at the vision in front of her.

Jace had dispensed with her clothes and stood before Catherine almost as an offering to the gods of the ancients. Her body was very well defined and it was clear that Jace worked out. Her tan, evidence of the part of country she lived in, the expression 'all over tan' popped into Catherine's mind. It made her skin look very healthy and quite magnificent.

Jace walked over to Catherine who couldn't keep her eyes from the vision getting closer and closer, speech was no longer an option, her mouth far too dry to utter one syllable. The super confidant Catherine Devonshire-Warriorson lost for words? She most certainly was.

Jace stopped within inches of Catherine, who sat rigid on her bed, smiling, her confidence coming back in leaps and bounds. Somehow she was in total control and it felt good, no, it felt wonderful. "I think I promised you dessert?" Jace huskily said, looking into ice blue eyes that held deep desire, or could it be 'fear'? No, it was returned desire.

Catherine hadn't recovered from the vision in front of her and she didn't think she ever would, her response was to nod her head.

Had Jace not been locked in a sense of complete sensual mist herself, she would have chuckled at the nervous anticipating movement of Catherine's head. Sensing it was up to her to make the first physical approach, as Catherine seemed incapable of any suggestive action for some strange reason. Her green eyes sparkled with the fire of rekindled need and unexpected passion, making her blush and chuckle silently. Placing her hands around the broad shoulders of her friend, she lightly turned her face to Catherine's for what started as a gentle exploration but ended up a passionate embrace, sending erotic shockwaves through both of them. Jace relishing this sensation, collapsed on top of Catherine and settling into her lap.

Cradling Jace's face in her hands, Catherine finally managed to speak, although it was rather hoarse. "Please, Jace we need to talk!"

"No! I need for you to know how I feel about you and the only thing that will do that is for you to touch me, not talk to me." Her emotions were evident in her words.

"Jace it's important to me that you know what and who I am." Catherine pleaded.

"I know what you are! You're the woman I love, what more do I need?" Several soft kisses were placed on full lips and she heard a low growl of protest.

"I love you too! But....." Catherine tried again, knowing her resolve was just about shot to hell.

"No buts Catherine, you're mine! That's enough for me, now stop talking and kiss me." Jace placed her inviting mouth tantalisingly close to the older woman's.

'I tried, I really tried, but ...oh hell, she's just too much for me.' With her resolve finally shredded to the wind, Catherine pulled Jace further into her arms as she lay on the bed and kissed her soft lips again, again, and again.

"You have too many clothes on Catherine." Jace finally whispered into her neck, Catherine's clothes already askew from their passionate kissing and exploring touches.

"I know Love, going to help me with that problem?" A throaty voice, close to the curve of Jace's left breast, eventually asked.

"I doubt you would try and stop me!" Jace began her task in loving earnest appreciation.

For the rest of that night only the sounds of two people very much in love could be heard, experiencing and professing that very emotion. Two souls celebrated and rejoiced in that love being satisfied again, having been reunited and claimed.

Catherine woke to find herself being held captive by a blonde wrapped tightly around her body, sleeping soundly. *'If this is the captivity of love, then I'm never letting it go!'*

Glancing towards the small bedside table, she noticed that it was five thirty a.m. *'Hell, I've got a breakfast meeting with Paul in the hotel at seven. I'm going to have to wake up sleeping beauty.'* The thought made her smile in anticipation

Placing feather light kisses all over the face of the woman who had so deftly and without apparent effort claimed her heart. Catherine felt Jace stir and she smiled, the smile becoming wider as Jace finally opened her eyes.

"Good morning, My Love. Are you going to wake me up like this every morning?" Jace looked at her with a sleep filled expression.

"Good morning to you too, and the answer to that one is yes!" A low growl erupted from Catherine as she said the final word.

"Gods, do you know how sexy you sound when you say things to me in that tone of voice?"

"No, but I'm sure you will enlighten me." A slow sultry smile settled on Catherine's face.

"Catherine, I think you can feel what you do to me with that voice, without any help from me!" Jace softly responded.

Catherine placed a hand in a strategic spot, her lips curled up in a wolfish grin. "So I see."

Laughing, she gently disengaged her hand from the spot in question and looked deep into Jace's glazed expression and it wasn't from any remnants of sleep either. Lacing her fingers with her younger partner's, she brought them to her lips and kissed each one reverently. "I have to go Jace. Unfortunately, business calls and somehow turning up at the hotel looking and smelling as I do wouldn't quite be in keeping with my image." She smiled gently at Jace, who looked disappointed.

"We could always cancel what we have on today and stay in bed?" Jace flushed at the thought of spending the entire day making love with this silky haired, beautiful woman. Catherine hadn't said but it was obvious to Jace early in the throes of passion that Catherine wasn't a novice in the art of making love to a woman, she was going to ask about that someday, but not today.

Tracing a finger down the Jace's cheeks, which had taken on a rosy glow, she gazed at her young lover and wanted nothing more than to spend the day in bed with her, but later. After today, then the way would be clear for them to do whatever they wanted.

"I want that also Jace! But today I have to keep to the appointments I've made, it's important to my future." Catherine noticed a look of anxiety on Jace's face. "Hey, my love, don't worry, it's just business and when I think about it, it's for our future. So come on, the sooner you let me up, the sooner I can finish the business and get back to you!"

Jace turned her face into Catherine's chest and the older woman felt moisture forming on her breasts.

"Are you okay Jace?" Catherine anxiously asked her lover.

"I love you Catherine." Jace turned her head slightly so that Catherine saw the tears she was shedding.

Tilting up Jace's head with gentle fingers, Catherine kissed away the tears and sighed softly into the face that would forever hold her soul.

'Did I really think that? She has my soul? Maybe, I do believe in soulmates after all! How ironic that would be!' Laughing, she caught Jace's surprised look as she leaned in once more and passionately kissed her hungrily on willing lips that had clearly been lovingly sought and tasted repeatedly the previous night.

Catherine had called a cab; she knew Jace had to be at the studio, so it made sense for her to make her own way back to the hotel.

Looking at the blonde who was standing a few feet away from her in an over-sized T-shirt with the familiar 'Taz' on the front. Catherine's mind flashed to the moment in Christchurch when she had seen the store with toys of all shapes and sizes. She had almost sent Jace an adorable Pooh Bear complete with the honey pot. Then she had tripped literally over the giant 'Taz', after cursing a couple of times, she'd noted its mischievous grin and for her it was the only thing to send. After all, hadn't Jace done just that to her, made her trip and fall in love, yeah even in those early days.

Crooking her finger at the gorgeous sight of her young lover. "Tonight... you, me and a very long chat. Then you can have your wish my love. I'll spend the rest of my life in your bed, if that is what you want?" Her eyes gently caressed the honey haired woman with love.

Jace walked over to her and placed her hands round the neck she knew every inch of after last night. "Okay, my place or yours?" Lips captured Catherine's in a searing kiss of lingering desire and possession.

"Yours, most definitely yours!" A breathless Catherine Warriorson responded, with desire threatening to devour her entire being.

The sound of the bell being pushed on her apartment made both women groan.

"Gods, I miss you already." Jace spoke quietly into her black hair, hanging unsecured.

"Tell me about it! I love you Jace, see you later." Placing a soft kiss on her nose, Catherine opened the door and proceeded to walk down to the waiting cab, the drive back having little significance to her.

Paul Strong was greeted by a very enthusiastic but somewhat tired looking Catherine Devonshire. "Did you have a good night?" He asked her as he set a menu in front of her, having been given the table earlier.

Catherine smiled at him wickedly. "You could say that." Picking up the menu she couldn't help the grin covering her face that refused to retreat into its stoic demeanour.

Paul chuckled softly. "Glad someone had some success in their love life."

Catherine raised the formidable eyebrow. "You didn't? Why was that?"

Looking at his menu, he smiled wryly. "James had a party he had to attend, he didn't get home until late and wasn't exactly in a fit state to do anything but sleep it off."

"Sorry to hear that." She smirked in his direction as the waitress arrived to process their order.

"I guess food might be high on your list of things about now?" Paul slyly intoned.

Winking at him from across the table. "Sure, what's your excuse?"

They both laughed as he ordered the largest platter of food he could.

He liked this Catherine Devonshire, this was the woman that you got glimpses of from time to time, but it was certainly out in force this morning; long may it last!

Chapter Thirty-Five

Jace watched Peter walk into her office space and look at her with a mixture of interest and a spark of jealousy.

"You look as if all your dreams have come true in one night?" He asked her quietly, not wanting Hudson to hear as the door to her office was open.

"Maybe they did." Jace quietly answered him back but her smile gave him an answer he was not sure he wanted.

"I'm pleased for you, is it someone I know?" Peter tried not to sound jealous.

"Yes." She said emphatically.

Peter looked at her speculatively, and then glanced at the door to Hudson's office. "Got to go, catch up with you later and you can tell me all about it."

"Oh, I don't think your going to get all the details, but if you buy lunch, maybe some of them!" Jace smiled at his retreating back, he was her friend, and she knew he would be happy for her.

"You're on." With that he entered the other office and closed the door behind him.

Jace dreamily gazed about her as her mind wandered to the glorious night she'd shared with Catherine and what it meant to the rest of her life, simply the beginning of a beautiful reunion of souls.

Snuggling into Catherine's shoulder she felt the heat of the damp skin and the heartbeat that was crazily thumping loudly, oh their lovemaking had been more than she could have hoped for. Everything had been natural, the tenderness Catherine had given her, and she had responded in kind.

Their first throws of passion had been erratic and erotic, both women wanting to satisfy a need that had been burning between them, and they had been consumed with the fire of desire.

Afterwards they gazed in wonder into each other's eyes like starry-eyed lovers, who had gained a knowledge that had stripped them bear, of any other feeling than to be loved and cherished.

"I love you Catherine, you are the love of my life forever and ever!"

Catherine's eyes held the green orbs with a steadfast stare that search for any untruth in the statement and she found none. Lying breast to breast with this woman was her home, she had finally found the piece of the puzzle in her life that made everything she had done recently make sense. Throwing away her old life to take tentative steps onto an unknown path that she wasn't even sure Jace would be following with her. Yet, here she was in her arms warm, sexy and remarkably hers.

"I love you Jace, more than you will ever know. More than I can probably ever tell you in words."

Jace smiled as she bent her head and captured Catherine's lips, sucking her lower lip into her mouth before she raised herself slightly to answer her.

"I'll take action, my love, over words any day of the week."

This time Catherine captured Jace's mouth, as they devoured each other once more in ferocious passion, which each other could only assuage?

The very thought of the love they shared made Jace wish she could call in sick and see Catherine now!

Jace looked at the closed door and waited impatiently for the VIP visitors; she still didn't know who they were. A black Land Rover appeared into view from her window and she watched in fascination as a man came into line of vision, how ever, she was not in a position to see the other party with him, she looked closer.

'Why that's Paul Strong, James' friend! What's he doing here? Doesn't he work for some large corporation or something? Hell, he must be the important visitor, she didn't realise he had that much authority.' Trying to get a closer look at his companion, she craned her neck but to no avail, the person had walked outside her range and view totally. *'Well, this isn't too bad then, she liked Paul Strong.'* Walking over to the coffee machine she started it up and waited for them to enter the building.

Paul Strong came into the office area first, the other person had the door held open for him and he walked casually but confidently into the room. He looked like any middle aged executive with a definite style to his wardrobe, which was expensive but quietly and impressively, so. The other party walked into the area seconds later just as Jace turned back to the machine to make sure she hadn't over filled it.

Catherine Devonshire saw the young woman and smiled briefly, her mind creating images she could certainly do without at this moment, and then she put back on her stoic persona. Hudson didn't need any advantage in this battle.

Jace turned and came face to face with the woman who had indeed made all her dreams come true in one night. The tension beginning all over again as Jace looked her lover over in frank admiration and shock at her appearance in the office. *'She never mentioned coming here today? You never gave her the chance!'* Jace answered herself.

Catherine was dressed in an expensive pinstriped navy blue skirt suit the skirt came to a stop at the top of her shapely knees, which were encased in what she surmised to be silk stockings. Her blouse was a stark white, very plain but obviously in silk. She looked the epitome of a professional businessperson and her stance showing that she exuded power out of every pore. Her hair hanging loose around her broad shoulders giving her a very primitive yet controlled image to the onlooker.

"Catherine?" Jace managed to say as she finished her observation, her mind lost in thoughts of undressing the woman before her.

Paul took the opportunity to state their business. "Nice to see you Ms. Bardley, we have an appointment with Ms. Hudson, would you inform her that we are here." His voice clipped out in a totally businesslike way.

Jace smiled warmly at him, but her eyes never left Catherine's who had been looking at her with a sparkle of laughter in them. "Who shall I say is calling?" Jace asked sheepishly, knowing they would think it strange that she didn't know the visitor's names.

Paul raised his own eyebrows at the question, but duly answered. "Tell her Ms. Devonshire and Mr Strong are here from Xianthos." He looked at the woman next to him and smiled briefly.

"What!" Jace shouted at him, her mind not taking in the answer. *'No, no this is NOT happening, she's not her, and it can't be her!'* Jace's mind was shrieking at the unexpected discovery.

Catherine noticed that Jace had paled, but now was not the time to let her personal affairs get in the way, she had to be focused; Hudson was always difficult at the best of times.

The door to Hudson's office opened as Jace sat heavily down in her chair. "Ah, Catherine at last! Paul, good to see you; please come in, come in! Jace get the coffee will you?" She said sweetly.

Catherine, without a backward glance, followed her into the office and Paul, looking at the younger woman slumped into the seat, gave her a compassionate glance. *'Catherine had obviously forgotten to point that little detail out to Jace, I wonder if she forgets just how powerful that name is in some circles?'*

Jace heard the introductions around the room and the door closed with a definite click. Her head was whirling; she didn't know what to do. What could she do? Hadn't she come face to face with the enemy? *'Oh god, why didn't I listen to her, why?'* Tears threatened to fall as she gathered up some coffee cups and placed them on a tray, all the actions on automatic, and her mind too full of questions.

Slowly she dragged her mind to the task and opened the door to the office and her worst nightmare. Walking on autopilot inside, Peter Adamson got up from his seat and took the tray from Jace. He'd noticed the pale face and her attempts to stem tears. He knew the reason why.

Looking at the person who had caused the pain, however innocently, he noticed she was a little pale herself and was watching the younger woman in earnest, concern plainly etched in what would otherwise be a very cool and composed expression.

Jace was in shock as the realisation of the events sank in.

Hudson, looked at her emotionally distressed PA and also the closed expression on her very important visitor. "Jace, I want you to meet Paul Strong, he's the President of Xianthos and of course you know Catherine Devonshire." Her smile was sickly sweet, knowing the hurt she was inflicting.

Jace looked at Paul and smiled a weak smile. "Paul, good to see you again."

Hudson looked a little put out at Jace's familiarity with the man, but not for long, taking the advantage. "But of course you don't know Catherine by that name do you? She's none other than your reclusive friend C X Warriorson. Small world, wouldn't you say?" She maliciously intoned.

Catherine smiled at Jace, but it soon died as she saw a cold expression come over the usually animated and happy visage that she so loved.

"I need to leave if that's no problem for you Ms. Hudson?" Not waiting for Hudson to answer, she rushed out of the office.

"Oh Jace, shame on you; no words of welcome for your friend?" Hudson smirked at the retreating back.

The two men in the room watched the differing expressions on the three women and each had their own opinions on what was transpiring.

Catherine followed Jace out the door. "Be right back." She stated absently as she pulled the door shut behind her.

"Jace!" Catherine drew her immediate attention with her authoritative voice.

Looking like a bird about to fly out of a cage, she turned to look at Catherine. "What's the problem Ms. Devonshire, the coffee not to your taste?" Her voice carrying the cold front Catherine had seen on her face moments earlier.

"I thought you would be at least pleased to see me?" Catherine softly asked the woman she loved. Catherine watched the emotions wash over Jace's face; they went from surprise, anguish, hurt and finally anger.

"How could you....how could you lie to me?" Jace accused her lover.

Catherine shook her head in surprise, what the hell was wrong here? "I'm sorry, but I don't understand? I've never lied to you!" Was her quiet response.

"You never told me you were...are the Devonshire behind Xianthos?" Jace's tone angry and bitter.

Catherine looked perplexed. *'Why the hell would that particular fact matter?'* "Does it matter? Hell, I don't even go by that name anymore. Most of that part of my life is dead to me now!" Catherine emphatically replied.

"Yes it matters! It matters to me! I hate Xianthos and I hate the person who owns it!" Jace replied with passion, her anger nearly manifesting physically.

The words came like a body blow to Catherine; she recoiled from the venom spat out in words. "Why?" Catherine whispered, her world suddenly starting to crack open around her.

Jace looked at the pain etched into the beautiful face before her, it took all her will power not to reach out and touch it in comfort, but her hatred of all things Xianthos stopped her. "My father had a publishing business in Santa Barbara. You! Bought it out, but you disregarded him as irrelevant. He fought you, you called in all his debts, and he's never been the same. Nor have I!"

"Are you telling me this is about a business deal?" Catherine couldn't believe what she was hearing, she slowly put a hand over her eyes to try and clear the fog that had apparently descended on her relationship with Jace.

"Yes, no...yes it was our family business, our lives!" Jace was completely overcome with her bitter emotions, her ability to make coherent sentences losing the battle.

Catherine tried to make sense of the situation; it hadn't any grounding for such a response from Jace, not to her anyway. "I told you Jace, you wouldn't like some of the things I've done in the past. You told me it didn't matter, did you lie to me?" Catherine asked calmly, yet her guts had reason to want to jettison her breakfast.

"No, no I never lied to you! This is different." Jace looked at her with pain filled green eyes.

"How so? It's okay for my past to affect others, you could ignore that, but because it happened to you, it's different?" Catherine advised her logically.

"Yes." She whispered, knowing she was being totally unfair.

Catherine passed another hand over her eyes in what could only have been a gesture of defeat. Squaring her shoulders she looked at the other woman, who refused to acknowledge her stare? "Then I guess I'm going to have to live with you hating me Jace. Because sure as hell, I can't change what happened in the past." Her voice cracked as she looked over the blonde's shoulder to a picture hung on the wall, unable for the moment to move away.

Jace turned to her and saw the stoic expression settle on the face of the woman that she had loved, in every possible way. "I loved you Catherine Warriorson!" Jace said in a voice devoid of emotion, her heart screaming at her to retract her words.

Catherine quirked her eyebrow at the expression and considered the words. *'Loved? How fitting.'* Catherine turned towards the inner door preparing to depart, changing her mind she closed the gap between them.

Placing her hands around the tearstained face. "No Jace, you loved the dream of a woman I'm obviously not! Funny really, because this woman here before you loves you an awful lot, even now." Catherine spoke in a quiet resigned voice. Her will, the only thing stopping her own torrent of tears threatening to fall.

Bending her head she placed a tender kiss on Jace's lips and left her, swiftly re-entering Hudson's office.

Jace's lips tingled from the contact and tears cursed down her cheeks as she picked up her purse and car keys. The turmoil she felt in her life at the moment was incredible; Jace didn't know what to think, where to turn too, what to do! *'I'll go home, it's the only place left. Maybe everything will make more sense.'*

She left the building.

Catherine re-entered the room and saw everyone glance up in her direction. She gave them a cold stare, except Paul; he knew his boss well.

Hudson wasn't fooled. *'Interesting body language. So there is something going on with those two. I knew it! Oh I'm going to enjoy this even more now.'*

Catherine had years of experience of not showing her feelings in public, even if her heart had been ripped out of her chest and lay bleeding to death at the foot of Jace's desk. Somehow she always rallied round it was instinct. "Okay Hudson, what do you want?" Catherine asked brusquely, no longer interested in the meeting.

Hudson knew that the preliminaries were over, even before they had started, not a bad call. Smiling smugly she pointed at the men in the room. "Maybe they should leave?"

Paul looked at Catherine for guidance, this wasn't a business meeting at all, something was going on that had personal undercurrents.

Peter took the opportunity to leave, not saying a word.

"Well, he can go and take care of Jace, she obviously has some sort of problem today." Hudson said nonchalantly.

Catherine grimaced and moved around in her chair, wanting to physically hit the woman at the desk. "Paul stays, get on with it!"

Paul stifled a chuckle as he recognised the old Devonshire style.

Hudson looked taken aback but recovered quickly. "Fine with me, if you want all your dirty laundry aired in public, that's up to you."

"Believe me the way I feel at the moment, I don't give a damn what you do to me!" Catherine smiled briefly at Paul; he might as well know all the facts.

"I want your sixty percent holding in UCP transferred to me, and a guarantee that you will support with financial aid UCP for the next twenty years." Hudson drummed her fingers on the table as she looked at the woman she desperately wanted, regardless of her feelings for someone else.

Paul got up from his seat and was ready to punch the obnoxious woman himself. Catherine watched his movements and responded to the threat. "Sit down Paul, let her finish. I assume you have something else to say?" Paul reluctantly did so.

Hudson looked at them both and lost a little of her composure, she noticed Catherine didn't seem to care one-way or the other.

"And?" Catherine asked calmly. She was too calm Hudson knew that.

"I want you!" Hudson leered blatantly at her to exaggerate her point.

A sharp laugh was the answer from Catherine as she continued to stare out of the window for a few minutes. Catherine rose from her seat and walked past Paul squeezing his shoulder in reassurance as she headed for the window. "You mean you want my body?" Catherine purred, her primitive instincts now getting a chance to voice themselves.

"Yes." Hudson's voice became hesitant, she hadn't expected this reaction, what the hell was going on in that sharp mind, it was almost as if she was planning to spring traps, like a hunter.

"Right! So if I say no, what are you going to do about it?" Catherine appeared nonchalant about the whole situation.

"If I told you now, Paul would know and it's no longer a secret." Hudson said petulantly.

"Get on with it Hudson." Catherine's sneered her stance at the window clearly angry and frustrated, she needed this like a hole in the head right now.

"Your father told me about your troubles, the drugs, alcohol, the prison in particular. What you did inside to get by, shall we say." Hudson said maliciously.

Catherine said nothing from her position at the window, Paul looked on in embarrassment.

"Your drug dealing, your sex for drugs, your violence in prison! Do you want me to go on?" Hudson thought she had Catherine now, hell, no one wanted this sort of thing public, not in her position surely.

"You made your point, in your usual tainted way Hudson." A very bored voice declared.

"If it gets out your business is going to nose dive. Your precious domestic life will be ruined. I'm sure the authorities in New Zealand will be interested, you have children under your care now; hardly think you're a fit parent. Then there's your love life, it would be a real turn off wouldn't it?" Hudson laughed enjoying the pallor from Paul and the rigid back from Catherine.

Paul got up from his chair and walked over to his boss. "Is it all true?" He knew some of the story; he had been part of it, but not it all.

Catherine smiled wryly at him. "Yes, I'm afraid so. It was a long time ago, seems like another lifetime now."

Paul looked at the calm profile of his boss and then returned back to the agitated Hudson. "Yeah, it was a long time ago and you're not that woman now." He smiled and put a hand on her shoulder.

"Thanks Paul." She continued her observations outside of the window. *'Jace hates me now! Wonder what she will think about me when she finds out about all Hudson's so called facts?'*

"Oh cut the sentiment please, what are you going to do?" Hudson was frustrated it really wasn't going the way she planned.

"Do your damnedest Hudson; only remember once your through, it's my turn." Catherine gave her a chilling look, her ice blue eyes working overtime.

"You think that when all this gets out your going to be in a position to try anything? I'm scared!" She laughed maniacally at the thought.

"Believe me, you should be!" Catherine replied quietly but with a definite edgy menace.

Paul turned to Hudson. "You just made a mistake lady, she's very dangerous when cornered, very like a lioness with her cubs, think on it?"

"You think wrong. It's more like a rat, edging back to the sewer she just crawled from." Hudson retaliated.

"Funny, I would have used that expression for you! In fact, don't be surprised if it's not a premonition of events about to unfold. Oh, to you I mean." Paul gave her a dazzling smile.

"Get out of here, you're nothing but her resident arse kisser." Exasperated Hudson threw her pen at the door.

"Been called worse in my time." He left the room, giving his boss a reassuring glance.

Catherine walked over to Hudson and gave her a stony glance that would have frightened most people. Hudson just didn't give a damn. "Thank you for the offer Hudson, but you pale considerably in comparison to what I know is right for me. Maybe you should think about settling down yourself, with a nest of rats, more to your taste I suspect." Catherine drawled.

"Ha! Don't get clever with me Catherine; I know Jace hates your guts, now she knows whom you really are! Not much you can do about that is there?" Hudson snarled at her.

Opening the door to the office to let herself out, turning briefly she spoke. "I might not be able to do much about that, that's about the only thing you have said that might be factual today. It's ironic really the whole situation, we both came off losers in the name of love."

Hudson looked at the woman with a startled expression and shouted. "I DON'T LOVE YOU!"

Catherine silently walked back over to Hudson and stroked one slim finger down her right cheek, watching the desire fire in the other woman's eyes. "No, you're right, you don't love me, because you can't love Hudson. At least, I found out I can!"

She left the other woman in a rage. Hudson dragged out her file. *'You asked for it, your going to get it! If you won't have me Catherine Devonshire, then believe me no one else will ever hold you! If you thought you were a recluse before, then when I'm finished with you, Howard Hughes will look like the ultimate party animal.'*

Chapter Thirty-Six

"Are you going to see her?" Paul asked Catherine finally, as they sat at the bar in the hotel, each nursing a scotch and water.

Catherine looked up from her drink and gave him a wry smile. "No! It's over." She went back to studying her drink.

"How can you say that? You need to explain things to her. She deserves that! You deserve that!" Paul almost deafened her with his rather explosively spoken words.

"Funny, I tried to explain just that last night. She chose seduction over the truth. Guess we're both going to pay for that delay. She has to live with the fact she seduced a woman she hates, and I have to live with the memory of how much I love her and how it felt to hold her." Catherine gradually let the tears fall. It didn't really matter anymore if anyone saw her this way. What more was there to lose?

"Will you go home?" Paul asked her gently, seeing the tears but making no obvious gesture that would make her self-conscious.

"Can I go home once all this comes out? The authorities in New Zealand are going to want some answers and maybe I haven't got them!" Catherine dejectedly looked into the depths of her drink, which she had hardly touched.

"What about Grace, Destiny and the children?" It wasn't like her to give up.

"I'm going to call Grace with the sordid facts when I go to my room, she deserves to know before the media throw it in her face, then she might want to leave also!"

"She won't leave you!" Paul said adamantly.

Catherine looked in his direction and put her drink down after taking a long drink of it. "You sound so sure, why?" Her left eyebrow rose in question.

"Because if she hasn't in the last five years, no way will she desert you in your hour of need." He smiled at her.

"That sounds so melodramatic, just the sort of thing Grace would say." For the first time since they'd arrived at UCP, she gave him a genuine smile.

"Maybe. Grace loves you as a very good friend and you need one right now." Paul stated the facts as he saw them about her friend.

"What about you? Are you still going to be a good friend and stick around, when this mess goes public?" Her ice blue eyes pierced him with a serious glance.

"Yes, I'm here for the duration, come what may. Might even help our share prices." He tried to bring some levity to the serious conversation.

"You know you might just be right about that." Catherine put a hand on his and held it in a warm hold. "Thank you Paul Strong, for everything."

He patted her hand in sympathy as they decided on the next move.

Jace arrived at her family home and pulled the car into the drive; her father wouldn't be home and Lucy would be at her part time job in the mall.

Taking a deep breath she went towards the back of the house and saw her mother tending the garden, walking slowly over to her she crouched down next to her mother and simply put her arms round the rounder figure, her tears flowing unchecked.

Alison Bardley was at first shocked by the presence of her daughter and then upset on her behalf at the obvious distressed state she was in. *'What the heck had gone on now?'*

Gently cradling her daughter in her arms, she waited for the sobbing form to still a little and gradually guided them both into the house. Sitting her down in one of the kitchen chairs she put on the coffee pot and sat next to her eldest daughter and took Jace's cold hands in her own and gently chaffed them to try and warm them up. "Do you want me to call your father Jace?" Alison had never been Jace's favorite parent to talk her troubles over with, not that she hadn't wanted to; it was something that Jace had always done with her father. Lucy, her younger daughter was totally different.

"No! There's nothing he can do." Jace said tearfully.

Alison looked thoughtfully at her daughter. Jason had explained Jace's problematic love life to her later the evening Jace had gone back to her apartment. Somehow it hadn't surprised her, her daughter had never really taken any interest in any man; mind you, she hadn't in a woman either, until she had spoken to her father. "You need to let it all go Jace, don't bottle it up inside. We're here to help you, you've always known that, we love you." What more was there to say to her heart broken child?

Looking into her mother's warm green eyes, she smiled briefly and gulped back a sob. "I fell in love Mom; nothing big huh?"

Alison smiled. "Well, it's kind of a big thing to us dear. Who is the lucky person?"

Jace gave her a guilty look. "Catherine, Catherine Warriorson."

Nodding her head in understanding, Alison put a hand round her shoulders and hugged her close. "Has something happened to her?"

Jace started to cry again and her mother wondered if something tragic had happened to Catherine Warriorson. "In a way Mom yes, Catherine is also known as Devonshire, Catherine Devonshire, the owner of Xianthos."

Looking perplexed Alison gave her daughter a quizzical look. "What exactly does that mean?"

Jace gave her mother a tired half smile, her father would have understood. "Xianthos took the business from us, remember?"

"Ah, that Xianthos. Aren't we good enough for her, is that why you're upset?" Alison was surprised her daughter would even know the woman, never mind fall in love with her; surely they didn't frequent the same circles.

Jace smiled weakly at her mother. "No Mom, I told her basically she wasn't good enough for me! I told her nothing she had done in the past mattered and when I found out, I just flipped and all my old stored up hatred spilled out."

Her mother looked at her in shock, this wasn't their gentle understanding daughter here, this sounded more like a woman with hate in her heart, and it didn't make sense. "You said what, exactly?"

"She arrived at the studio. I didn't know she was Xianthos. It was a shock. I didn't let her explain. I just looked at her with prejudiced eyes. Mom, I wasn't thinking straight, it happened so fast." Her daughter whispered into her shoulder.

"That isn't like you Jace, you've never judged anyone before without full and complete facts, what was so different with her, especially if you loved her?" Alison felt sorry for the other woman.

"I know Mom, but it was so overwhelming and especially after we had such a wonderful night together. I'm so lost and I don't know what to do?" Jace looked at her mother with a heartbroken pleading look in the green eyes, similar to her own.

"Why not try calling her and apologizing, then see where it goes from there?" Alison looked at the fragility of her eldest child and was surprised at what she would have seen as a lover's spat, hurt her child so much and wondered if there was more to this than a simple identity misdemeanour.

Jace suddenly looked up and her tears stopped for a moment as she looked at her mother with hope. "Do you think she'll talk to me?"

"Does she love you?" Foolish question really, she was sure that the woman who had captured Jace's heart, would have equally lost her heart to this usually kind and compassionate woman in her arms.

"She said she did, even when I...I said things that were hurtful to her. She wasn't easy to get to know Mom. I could have blown away my chances with her with some stupid words!" Jace's sobs increased.

"Words are often greater weapons than actions Jace, with your background surely you know that?" Stroking the blonde head, she tried easing the tension in her child.

"I know, I know. I just want so much to take it all back and say it's okay. Everything she was makes up the person she is today and that's the person I love and need!" Jace turned her head further into her mother's embrace and was held there protectively, which reminded her of Catherine and how she had cradled her that morning, fresh tears started again.

"Then she will understand Jace, believe me she will understand." Her mother gently crooned to her daughter.

Catherine wearily sat at the edge of the bed and looked at the time, it was 1 p.m. She was waiting for Paul to confirm that the Xianthos private jet would take her to South America.

They had agreed, that until the sensationalism of the news became old news she would go and help in the training of the new vice president.

She was virtually unknown on that continent and only Garcia and himself would know her true identity out there, she would take a pseudonym for a month or two, change her hair color, stay low.

Her cell had been cut off, her communications link on her laptop had been changed, and she no longer had the same e-mail address; there was nothing to trace her to her next destination, until she wanted to be found. Grace would be given her new cell number and e-mail address, but it wasn't to be revealed to any one else, unless she authorised it and that wasn't likely under the circumstances.

Looking morosely around the room, she picked up her cell wanting nothing more than to just hear Jace's voice and explain it all away. Hadn't she always said this relationship was impossible! Hell, she had been proved right in a way she hadn't even considered. In a fit of frustration and acute anger she threw the cell at the hotel wall, watching it bounce off and land with a muted thud on the carpeted floor, the casing cracking along one side, rendering the instrument inoperable. Staring at it, she quietly muttered to the empty room. "Guess you just did that to my heart Jace Bardley."

No recriminations, just a resignation of her fate. Previously unshed tears cascaded down her cheeks, she closed her eyes to ward them off, but they continued anyway. Laying her head on the pillow she tried to shut out the thoughts of the woman who had made her feel love in such a profound way, it was a struggle to consider living without her. *'What am I going to do without you in my life Jace! You are the reason for my life!'*

The hotel phone rang. Catherine answered it and smiled, Paul said the jet was ready when she was. Getting up from the bed, she picked up her bags and left the room, as the elevator doors shut behind her, the phone rang again, only this time it rang into an empty room.

Catherine Devonshire-Warriorson had gone!

Chapter Thirty-Seven

Jason Bardley wasn't sure if his eldest daughter would be capable of taking the revelations in the newspapers, but she would need to know sooner, rather than later.

Her distraught appearance when he'd finally arrived home yesterday evening was enough for him to gather that her life wasn't exactly under control. Rather than bring up the story again, he waited impatiently for his wife to give him the edited highlights when Jace had gone to bed.

Jace had refused to eat. She would sit by the phone and will it to ring. He wasn't to know until later that she had tried to contact Catherine Warriorson and had been given the message that the woman had left town without a forwarding address.

Lucy unsuccessfully tried to engage her sister in a discussion on her recent college venue. Jace merely muttered a few muffled words. Eventually the family could take no more of her miserable demeanour and Jason persuaded his daughter to try and rest, that tomorrow would be a much better day all round.

Jason always had that extra soft spot for his eldest child. Most people had thought he encouraged Jace in the family business because he didn't have a son to leave it to. Not so! Jace had a mind of her own even at an early age, and she had hounded her father to take her everywhere he could; he had obliged willingly. Jace was so endearing and would charm the most grizzly of his contemporaries when she went into the office.

Now, here he was a proud father of a child who was experiencing so much pain, and he couldn't do a damn thing to prevent it!

His glance slid over the headlines and the contents of the article and he snorted in disgust. *'Old news, it's all old news, goddamn it was over ten years ago.'* His compassionate nature, a sure sign as to where Jace had picked up that particular character trait. Placing the newspaper under his left arm and a coffee in his right he headed for Jace's room, no time like the present to have all the revelations in the open.

Knocking softly on the door, he heard a muffled enter. Walking in slowly he smiled gently at Jace, who looked like she hadn't slept a wink. "Good morning darling, you okay?" His eyes caught hers in a sympathetic look.

"Hi Daddy, could be better." Jace gave him a weak smile her eyes rimmed red from her tears and sleepless night.

"I know Jace." He put the coffee down by the bedside table and looked at the paper in his hands and finally offered it to her. "You'd better read this Jace."

Jace looked at her father in silent question and then asked. "You look worried?"

"I love you Jace, just remember that and when you're ready to do what you have to do, we'll be there for you okay?" He didn't wait for a reply he left the room.

Jace turned the paper over and with trepidation glanced at the headlines.

'C X Devonshire, Multi-Millionaire owner of the Xianthos Publishing Corporation, revealed as a Drug Taking, Drug Dealing, Alcohol Addicted, Ex-Con. Hiding away from her past in New Zealand!'

Jace flinched as she saw the headline and wanted nothing more than to throw the paper into the nearest garbage disposal. *'So this is what you wanted to tell me and I wouldn't let you? God what a fool I was!'* Picking up her coffee she sipped it slowly wanting a caffeine injection more than anything to get her over this hurdle of lurid scandal or supposed anyway to some. Her eyes strayed to the article and she began the task of reading things about her lover that might actually be true.

C X Devonshire, the daughter of the late Stewart Devonshire the man who created one of the largest publishing empires in the world, has been revealed as heavily involved with drugs and alcohol resulting in a seedy prison term. Devonshire now reclusive in New Zealand has refused to deny any of the following.

In her early twenties, she was frequently under the influence of hard-core drugs and alcohol, resulting in her dealing in drugs to ensure she never ran out. Eventually, this resulted in her being sentenced to a prison term in Germany for drug trafficking. Sources say that she maintained her addiction in the prison by indulging in affairs with both inmates and prison officials to pay for her addiction.

Sources also revealed that while in the prison, she was involved in a violent altercation with two inmates, one of which died as a result. Although she was involved in the incident, it is believed her father was instrumental in influencing the prison board into leniency.

Jace was crying for the young woman, who had suffered the cruelties of drug addiction and still managed to crawl out of the sewer she had tragically fallen into. The person being depicted here wasn't the woman she knew! *'Oh god what are you feeling now Catherine? Who is there to hold your hand? Why did I have to be so naive and stupid?'*

Her eyes scanned the next passage.

Catherine Devonshire 'used' people to help in boardroom take-overs; sources say she would take anyone to her bed if it helped improve her acquisition potential of any business. Many believe that she used drugs in making people think her way was the only way.

Her abandoning of her late husband the critically acclaimed author Adam Warriorson and her young son to become the power hungry, sexually aggressive owner of Xianthos after her father's death was instrumental in both their deaths three years later.

After the deaths of her family, she deceived the authorities in New Zealand into giving her permission to reside in the country eventually taking on the guardianship of two orphans.

The fact that Devonshire refused to deny any of the accusations must concern the New Zealand authorities and the shareholders of Xianthos. Have they got a decent citizen in control of their money and their children, or some drug taking, volatile, enigma, and a time bomb just waiting to explode?

Jace screwed up the paper and threw it at her bedroom wall, hitting a picture and sending it crashing to the floor; the coffee mug following shortly after, making a brown stain on the paintwork of the wall and dripping incriminatingly onto the beige carpet.

The door to her room opened and her father walked in, taking a quick look around the room he immediately sat on the bed and engulfed his daughter in a comforting hug.

"She's not like that Daddy! Catherine, may be many things, but she's not the woman they are portraying. I know that! I'm going to find her and tell her so." Jace whispered fiercely into her father's shoulder.

"Well, with you in her corner Jace, something tells me she might just come out of this intact." He knew what determination Jace had and now she was resolved to help her friend that's exactly what she would do!

If she only got the chance!

Grace had often wondered about the past of her employer and friend. Hell, she was a walking time bomb, which was about the only thing that the newspaper had right.

When Catherine called she'd said the chat she had planned for her return was going to have to take place there and then. It was a surprise and when she'd finished, it had been difficult to think straight.

Catherine's admission of taking drugs at fourteen, anything from cannabis to finally heroin in her early twenties, was a little hard to believe, but the quiet insistence in her friend's voice had made the information both poignant and starkly factual.

Catherine gave no reasons for her fall into disgrace and had little remorse either. It was for her a long time ago and one she deeply regretted but had to live with, her mistakes, her problems!

The drug trafficking had been a little hard for Grace to take, having her roots firmly entrenched in the law abiding ways of her once chosen profession and her parents' staunch up-bringing.

"I never sold to minors Grace, only people in the same position as me, more money than sense. It was a transaction, a way of making money after my father cut me off from my allowance." Her need to make Grace understand this point had taken the other woman by surprise.

The prison term had been difficult! She had a drug problem; it was duly exploited in the prison. Catherine did what others did, no big deal. Her body the only asset, she had to continue her craving for the drugs that would probably one day kill her. The violent episode was entirely a problem of a different nature.

Catherine had quietly explained the situation.

"I was a target for some of the more, shall we say forceful breed that frequent prisons. Having a body abused by drugs yet still holding some form of beauty became distinctly appealing to some of these women and that included the guards, too! Let's just say I have marks on my body that need explaining away from time to time, especially if I take a lover." Catherine had laughed hollowly at the remark, her mind straying to a gentle voice, intrigued at a scar six inches long on her back and several others on each of her breasts, although faded. At close range they were visible and Jace Bardley at been at very close range. Catherine had managed to kiss away the question and used her hands to demonstrate that the time was for touching not talking. "I met someone who would eventually teach me to at least stay alive. The only problem was she died instead of me!" Grace had gasped at the last comment.

"Hey, Catherine do you really need me to know this? I know situations occurred; if it's too much, please my friend, don't push it."

Grace didn't need her friend to explain her life, she was happy to have her alive and not dead as the situation in her early life could quite possibly have dealt to her.

Catherine smiled at the phone in her hand and could almost see the concern on her friend's face; it was something to reach out for. She wasn't finished with this life yet! Not in a big way! Maybe love would never figure in it again but too many other people still needed her to be around. Catherine would do it for them; it no longer mattered what she wanted anymore. Her dreams were over.

"I said I was going to tell you all of it, you get it all." Catherine mock warned her friend.

"Fine, well carry on then. Those kids of ours will want a story soon." Grace tried to ease the tension a little.

"Maria, taught me basic self defense she also helped me to start the treatment to kick the drugs. I wasn't pleasant and when the tension got to be too much she taught me to use music to ease it. The workouts I do at home are a product of Maria's influence; she was a great athlete. I loved her in a way that brought me a measure of peace after the first six months of my prison term. Then a bitch called Katria decided that I was the new game in town and Maria shouldn't have all the spoils. It was quite a normal situation in prison, but this time it turned out the bitch was going to go all the way. She cornered us in the gym area and punched me around a little until she almost knocked me senseless and slashed at me in the back with her knife, when I wouldn't co-operate. Then Maria attacked her. I was watching but it was like living in a slow motion movie, the knife came out of nowhere and Katria ripped her throat open. I moved then, in a haze, and started to choke the living daylights out of the bitch; the strength coming from some place deep down that I didn't realise I had. The guards stopped the fight before I killed her, because sure as hell Grace, I would have relished it at that point. I was in the prison hospital for a short period and spent the rest of my stay in solitary. I'm not sure how but I was released shortly afterwards. I know they're saying it was my father who influenced that decision. I'll probably never know for sure." A silence descended as the two women each mulled over their own feelings to the story.

"Adam Warriorson came to my rescue when my only brother died a month after my release from prison. He saved my life, by offering me security and his love. I took it! Then I broke his heart, and my son's, by going off to be my father's daughter! Ironic when I hadn't even set eyes on my father in over ten years. I was the power hungry executive that always won. I did things to get results, like slept with the odd chairman of the board; but I think it was more enjoyable for them than me! I stopped the drugs back in the prison and Adam made sure I c☐mpleted the treatment. I've been clean ever since I was twenty-three. Alcohol took a little longer as you know, but I was never dependant on it anyway just another way of getting over life's troubles in general. I will never forgive myself for the deaths of Adam or my son, but I have to live with it in the only way I know how." Catherine sounded relieved to have spoken out over her life's disasters. Her heart ached with the image that Jace would read all the so-called facts from a news-sheet, rather than Catherine giving her the personal details as she had narrated to Grace.

"Are you coming home Catherine?" It was the only question Grace wanted an answer to.

"Would you want me to come home?" Catherine asked the tentative question.

"Yes! Never doubt that Catherine Warriorson, never ever doubt it!" Grace passionately insisted in response.

"I have to attend to a business education problem in South America, and if the authorities don't cancel my residential status; yes, I'm coming home!" It was a heartfelt comment.

"You think they might cancel it?" Grace was shocked at the thought.

"Maybe, depends on how the public takes Hudson's little titbits on my life." Catherine answered her matter-of-gactly.

"Have you discussed this with Jace?" Grace heard a sharp in-drawn breath.

"No." Catherine replied shortly.

"Why?" Grace whispered in surprise.

"Ms. Bardley kind of didn't like my alter ego, Devonshire. We had an argument of sorts. Guess she will see all the gory details in the paper tomorrow." Catherine sighed at the thought and her sadness was palpable, even over the phone line.

"You need her Catherine, never more so than now!" Grace pointed out.

"I know, I know I do Grace but try telling Jace that!" Catherine sighed heavily at her end of the line.

"Perhaps I will." Grace answered slowly her mind going over the possibilities.

"No! You will not tell Jace anything! Her decision was made and she chose where she wanted to be! Unfortunately for me it wasn't at my side. I saw the hate in her face when she spoke about my company and me in particular. This might just put the final nail in the coffin. I need to trust you on this Grace. Withhold all the information regarding my whereabouts and any other details that could possibly interest Jace, okay?"

Grace bit her lip as she tried to think of a way to let Jace know without letting Catherine down. There was no way; her choice had already been made. "Fine, Jace Bardley is dead to you."

Catherine digested that last sentence. "Not dead Grace. She will never be dead to me. Make no mistake, she holds my heart and soul."

Grace had talked to Colin, she hoped that he would understand, if not approve. It was conceivable that some of the men, Colin included, might want to quit the ranch. Well so be it!

He had taken the revelations of Catherine's past in stride and told her not to worry. Her main criterion was making sure the scandal mongering didn't harm the children and the bigoted people that she was sure to come across. That had been Catherine's final comment as she ended the call and said she would phone again in a week or so.

The children wouldn't suffer and that would be Grace's task in all of this, that and Catherine's peace of mind.

Chapter Thirty-Eight

Jace finally arrived back at her apartment; it hadn't been easy! When she entered her mind went back to a week ago and the woman who had shared her bed that night. Since that time her life had crashed to pieces before her, and it had all been her fault.

It had been impossible to track down Catherine after she'd left the hotel; numerous calls to Xianthos in New York had been either viewed as crank calls or further invasion of Ms. Devonshire's privacy. The company had closed ranks and no one was talking!

She'd cried copious tears as her calls to Destiny were ignored or as her final one indicated no information pertaining the Mrs. Warriorson's whereabouts would be divulged. Grace hadn't even returned her calls and that had hurt her too. She obviously had no friends from Destiny to help her in her quest to regain Catherine back in her life, what had she done!

Jace had even tried to contact Paul Strong but his PA had thwarted that, eventually breaking down in tears, which the PA although sympathetic still refused to disclose any pertinent details about Ms. Devonshire to her.

Her father had used some of his old contacts in the publishing world to retrieve any possible information about Catherine. The steel barricades had come down heavily on the media and anyone else for that matter who wanted information, it was as if Devonshire had unbelievably gained more respect from her character deficiencies. Not many in the industry believed the garbage of her using drugs to tempt people, she hadn't needed to do that; her intelligence and charisma had always proved adequate enough, not to mention her beauty.

Jace had to see Hudson the next day; going back to her apartment had been the only solution. Now scanning the room she had called home it was now nothing but an empty shell. She went over to her computer and switched it on; at least clearing up her inbox would keep her mind occupied for a little while.

Waiting for the machine to boot up, she made coffee and regarded the wilting flowers all over the apartment. Flowers, which had once been fresh and alive, like her love for Catherine, now dead and dying, the fading blossoms visibly represented her destruction of that love.

Sitting in front of the screen, Jace saw numerous messages, many from selected site digests and several from Peter, then she saw an unusual addy and almost deleted it, but was intrigued by the title.

'A lyric tells it all!'

Opening the mail she gasped at the author!

Jace,

I'm not actually sure if this message will be welcome. You may not even bother to read it. I will understand.

Apologizing was never a strong skill of mine, but I guess I owe you one for not explaining sooner that I was also the 'Notorious Catherine Devonshire'. I'm sure by now my name will be somewhat scandalized.

As I said to you in the office of UCP, I can't change the past and if I'm honest, I wouldn't want to. I might never have met you if my life had changed in any way, which isn't an option that I want to contemplate. You brought love into my life that can never be measured, and I now know what it feels like to put that love ahead of anything else in my life, even my own selfish desires. So, you actually did us both a favor Jace by hating my other life. Now you can't be tarnished by the dark clouds of my past.

Well, I guess by now you know I use lyrics to speak for me and this one is exactly how I feel about you.

Alone

There are words written which speak of love, tokens given that carry the flame.

But never will I look upon a face that illustrates it quite like your face does for me.

Lost and alone, the bleakness blending into your soul, I know I make you cry, I know you hate me.

Friendship is the key, love is the lock, and please let me unlock your love with my key.

It was written in the stars, etched into my heart, I have only silent words for what I feel for you, the truth being, I love you!

Lost and Alone, the bleakness blending into your soul, I know I made you cry, I know you hate me.

I thought that I was over you, but your scent invades me, your body haunts me, your words evoke me, but can you still love me?

Do I beg you to stay, I will, I will just say.

Give me a chance, I'll make it right, nothing can prevent the light of your love has shown me.

Lost and alone, the bleakness blending into your soul, I know I made you cry, I know you hate me.

If you ever hear the song by Infinity, I hope you can think of me a little more favorably.

Goodbye Jace Bardley, and thank you.

Catherine Devonshire-Warriorson

Anyone passing Jace Bardley's apartment that evening would have been struck by the racking sobs of the young woman.

Clarissa Hudson paced her office like a caged animal.

What the hell was wrong with people today? Now she was being sued by Xianthos Holdings for her disparaging comments about their chairwoman's tactics on the acquisition trail.

Paul Strong had spoken to the lawyers immediately after the newspapers had released the story. Hudson thought she was immune from any repercussions, leaving her name out of the article. *'Her father would be turning in his grave, if he knew what Catherine had done, by bringing an action against me! It was the truth anyway!'*

Hudson continued to pace the floor, Jace Bardley was due back in the office anytime and that would be an interesting conversation. 'The bitch hadn't been back in the office for a week and had called in sick! Sick, what a pathetic excuse! Couldn't she stomach the truth either?'

Paul Strong had been adamant that Xianthos would not back down from this case; he would personally see it through. After all Ms. Devonshire had no ties to the company except to get her profit revenues when due.

Hearing the door to the other office open, Hudson stopped her pacing and heard the scrape of Jace's chair on the tiled floor. Waiting for all of two minutes, she rushed through her door.

"I THOUGHT I SAID I WANTED TO SEE YOU!" Clarissa shouted at the pale face of Jace Bardley.

"You did, I was just opening up my desk and then going to let you know I was here." Jace replied calmly, there was nothing this woman could do to her that she hadn't done to herself already.

"Get in here then!" Clarissa barked back at her.

"Okay." Jace stood up and followed the angry producer into her office, closing the door behind her.

"The bitch is suing me, did you know that?" Hudson bitterly stated.

"No." Jace stood in front of the desk and looked at her dispassionately.

"I thought you might know what the bitch was doing. Weren't you sharing her bed?" Hudson sneered at her.

"Catherine didn't discuss business with me." Jace refused to be baited.

"So, you did share her bed; was she any good?" Hudson looked at Jace with frank interest.

"My personal life is my affair, not yours; and whatever she's good at that's surely for you to find out." Jace wasn't going to let this woman have the upper hand.

"Once you found out who she was you abandoned her, am I right?" Noticing the pale cheeks of the woman before her at the comment. "I was right about you Jace, you can't hack it. Life isn't all rosy you know; you must have known she had a history?" Hudson uncharacteristically sounded apologetic.

"Perhaps." Jace replied quietly.

"So, what are you doing here anyway? Thought you would have left now that you're aware that Xianthos owns more of the studio than I do?" Hudson eyed her with interest; she was really quite a presentable looking woman, if you liked the small ones.

"Good point. Actually I am giving you notice Hudson, EFFECTIVE IMMEDIATELY! Good luck with your lawsuit." Jace turned her back on Hudson and heard a sharp gasp.

"You can't do that! You owe me!" Huds□n's mind turned off her speculation of Jace's body and spat venomously at her instead with words.

Turning back to face the woman, she noticed the spots of red in Hudson's cheeks, spots of anger. "I can! I will! I have! I owe you nothing."

This time she had her hand on the handle of the door before Hudson responded. "I'll see that you never work in this town again Jace!"

Jace wanted to ignore the comment but something inside her tempted out the devil inside. "Go ahead. It must be the only thing you're good at, maligning people's character! Give it your best shot because you will only get one chance."

Jace slammed the door in Hudson's face.

Hudson didn't like that one bit. She stormed out of her office as Jace collected her belongings and stood directly in her path to the exit.

"Not so fast little girl. I'm going to enjoy taking you down just like I've taken your 'friend' down. Only you will be begging me to take you back here when I've finished with you."

Jace realised that Hudson was mad. She was so convinced about her power over people that she lost sight of the reality of life. "You didn't break Catherine, so no way are you going to break me."

"If I tell the world about your affair with the wonderful Catherine, wouldn't that be peachy?" Clarissa smiled seductively at Jace.

"You wouldn't?" Jace sent her a pleading look, immediately realising she had made a big mistake allowing her feelings to show.

"Well... you could always let me take her place in your bed, until I tire of you that is. Then maybe you could convince me to keep quiet, what do you say?" Hudson saw the fear in Jace's expression.

Jace's expression took on a look of absolute shock and horror at the thought. "NO!" She finally managed to shout at Hudson.

Clarissa Hudson put a hand out and stroked a well-manicured finger down one of Jace's cheeks and noticed the flush appear - a mirror of what Catherine had done to her the week before; paybacks are such a bitch. "Pity, we could have had a good time. Catherine won't come back to you, you left her, remember?"

Laughing she moved to let Jace go, her body making contact as Jace tried unsuccessfully to manoeuvre around her to prevent further contact with her ex-boss. Cringing, Jace made it to her car, immediately her body reacted to the threat and sleazy comments from Hudson. She couldn't keep her breakfast down and was sick in the car park area.

'I know I left her that's the hardest thing to live with.' Her mind constantly reminded her, Hudson's words reflecting her own.

Grace watched Colin from the porch as he gently coaxed Lisa into a run around the paddock on the pony. The child wasn't the best horsewoman, but she wanted to go on the rides with Catherine and

Jake, when Catherine came back from her travels. Grace sighed and noticed that Jake was walking over to her, he was turning out to be a very interesting and caring boy. He had taken over reading to Lisa now that Catherine wasn't around and Grace had been busy.

"Hi Jake, finished your lesson already?"

"Yes, Colin wants to spend a little longer with Lisa. So, I thought I would come and see if you needed any help?"

"That was thoughtful Jake, but everything is done for the moment here, how about we go inside and have a drink and a cookie?" Knowing the child enjoyed her baking skills.

He beamed at her and nodded his head.

Taking his normal seat at the kitchen table, he looked over at the space opposite him. "When will Catherine come back?"

"Oh, well she has business to attend to and then she's coming home."

"They say she's not coming back." He said quietly.

Looking at him she saw him frown and bite his lower lip. "Now who would 'they' be Jake?" taking a pointer from Jace's book on dealing with the child.

"The kids at school and some of the teachers have asked me if she's home yet." He endeavoured to explain.

"I see. Well, I talked to Catherine recently and she is coming home Jake, trust me." Grace smiled warmly at the boy.

"We won't have to go back to the orphanage will we Grace?" He watched her put down the cups she held and turned to face him.

"No! Jake, Catherine wants you to answer her question when she gets home and if you don't want to go back to the orphanage then you won't, we will both see to that!' Grace got closer to the boy and suddenly pulled him into a hug. "Jake, she loves you and Lisa, and right now the both of you are the most important people in her life."

"Is she in trouble Grace?" He suffered the hug.

"Yes. I won't lie to you Jake, various people are saying nasty things about her and some are true, others aren't. What you have to tell yourself is do you like her enough to still be here for her when she comes home regardless of what other people think of her?"

Jake looked into the serious face of the woman who shared the duties of looking after them and he smiled ruefully. "I don't just like her Grace, Lisa and I will still be here for her when she comes home."

"You know what kid, I don't know what she ever did to get you in her life, but it must have been pretty awesome." Smiling she captured some cookies and set them in front of him, collecting a coffee for herself and handing him a milkshake.

"That goes for you too Grace." He picked up a cookie and settled down to devour as many as Grace would allow him.

Grace actually blushed at the comment and put more cookies in front of him. *'Wonder when this kid had taken charm lessons?'*

Catherine sat in her one room apartment in the centre of Rio de Janeiro and contemplated her future.

'Well, I've got Grace, Jake, Lisa and Colin to go home too for starters. Then there's Paul who will take care of the company for me and probably do a better job than I ever have. Maybe I can get the Reverend to put in a good word for me with the authorities, now that they want to discuss my visa?' Mulling over the only people who cared about her now, she smiled at the gathering darkness.

'Perhaps coming here was the answer to most of my problems, except I miss my home and my family.' The consistent ache in her gut when she thought of the ranch and the coming season change. Winter would be getting a hold now and she had wanted to see the kids in the snow and take them to see some of the spectacular scenery around when the snow covered everything, particularly the glaciers.

Moving out of the small room she entered the bedroom and sat down heavily on the edge of the bed. Her dreams or should she say nightmares had flared to unbelievable proportions and now they had Jace in them to, her angry face as Catherine had last seen her the final element of the dreamscape.

'Funny if you were here with me now Jace, my nightmares would disappear like magic. You could always soothe whatever beast resides inside me, and I would be happy to let you do that. Would you consider being my friend again I wonder? I can't let you into my heart again Jace Bardley it hurt too much when you walked away; but I would give everything I possess to see your smile and have it turned on me again.' Her shoulders shrugging, she went into the small bathroom, realising the futility of her thoughts, they had no conceivable expectation of reality.

None at all!

Chapter Thirty-Nine

Grace had often wondered what it must be like to own a property as large as Destiny with its constant changes with the seasons, and the comings and goings of personnel; not to mention the needs of the numerous smallholders affiliated with the property. She had her wish!

Three months after Catherine had left, not only did she have her housekeeping tasks, but also was the only 'care-taking parent' in residence and she had her hands more than full!

Thank god Colin had taken over the running of everything associated with the ranch that Catherine had looked after. He had taken it onboard without a word and didn't complain when he spent hours in the evening going over bills and forms, which kept turning up for processing. Fortunately for them, money wasn't an issue, and even if Paul Strong hadn't made deposits every month into a ranch account with her and Colin as coassignees, the ranch finances were viable in their own right.

Grace knew Colin watched her in the evening with the children as they settled down to read or watch TV in a companionable atmosphere. He would have a secret smile that she was sure he only ever used when he watched her with Lisa tucked into her lap in the evening. He hadn't asked her on a date since she arrived back after her father's death and she had felt relieved but disappointed also; it didn't always make sense to her these days, life in general wasn't making much sense.

Catherine called twice a week. During the working week she talked with Grace and Colin but on a Sunday evening she would call and the intercom system in the study would be used so that the children could participate in the chat sessions. The children knew she had to be away but they sorely missed her, and the chat sessions she had been persuaded to participate in after a particularly long session with Grace had cheered them all up. Now, it was a weekly ritual and Catherine had never, ever let them down. At precisely seven p.m. she would call and they would all be seated with a hot drink and cookies. It was as if Catherine was in the room with them instead of her small lonely apartment in Rio several thousand miles away.

Grace watched the weather front changing, spring was about to come their way; she was pleased about that at least. Maybe Catherine could come home soon; she was certainly missed.

A pity the New Zealand authorities had been zealous over taking her visa away. One of the things Grace admired about her country was its open-minded approach. Catherine had been doing the diplomatic backslapping for the last three months and was getting close to having her visa returned in some form or other. Fortunately the children had been left well alone; she and the Reverend had worked on that particular problem together. That had been the easy part, no one wanted to lose the sort of financial backing Lucas's trust fund provided and Grace had threatened that in a formidable fashion. Catherine had lost enough her prized privacy had been invaded; Grace doubted that Catherine would ever live a life now without the odd camera or two trailing after her.

Looking at the clock in the kitchen and quickly collecting her tray of goodies for their get together. Smiling at the thought of Catherine so far away and wondered if she had a mug of tea in hand at this very minute. It was something she was going to ask her friend when they spoke it would give them a sense of togetherness and family, even if only for the length of the phone call.

The children would be watching a cartoon, waiting patiently for the hour to flick to seven.

Catherine walked the two-mile stretch that she'd know in her sleep. In fact it helped her sleep, miracle of all miracles. Except tonight she went out earlier than usual, it was Sunday and the family phone call was only an hour away. She loved that feeling of contact with her 'adopted' family. Hopefully she would gain her visa back from the New Zealand authorities next week, although it would only have temporary status.

There was a mix of rich and poor in the area she walked, typical of Rio in many ways truth be told she didn't particularly like the place, because of it's poverty traps but she had few choices at the moment.

She walked in the poorer area, not exactly slum accommodation, but in a few years it would turn into that situation and probably worse. Catherine had run-ins with the local punks in those first few days she'd walked this route, allocating a few busted noses and a couple of broken arms in her wake had stopped that harassment. The punks gave her a wide berth.

She smelled the burning of wood before it came into her line of vision. A small two story house, although to her eyes it looked nothing more than a shack, virtually all wood, burning in the twilight of the evening. If it hadn't been so tragic, it would have been a glorious sight of colours against the backdrop of the early evening skies. People were milling around, no one seemed to be interested in the screams she heard echo from within the burning building.

Running closer to the scene, she caught hold of the arm of an onlooker.

"What the hell is going on here? Have you called the fire department? How many are still inside the building?" Catherine bit out in a staccato voice, bellowing the last comment into his ear.

The man looked at her with little interest or was it with understanding? Yeah, the guy probably couldn't speak English. Damn!

Catherine gave the scene one more cursory glance, and galvanized her body into action. "Is this my destiny?" The unconscious thought drifted through her mind, her voice lost in the smoky night air as she propelled herself into the burning building.

If someone had mentioned that this particular event would be unfolding and she would be in the thick of it, she would have laughed out loud and called them ridiculous. Yet! Here she was, her eyes stinging from the smoke and choking on its intensity, could that be plastic burning? Acrid smoke filling her lungs at every breath she managed to take.

"Hello? Anyone here? Come on, give me a shout?" Coughing into her sweatshirt sleeve, she finally caught a muted cry for help. That was universal in any language, at least.

Entering the room to her left, she saw flames panning to her right and a figure huddled in shock to her left. A woman sat against a grimy paint-peeling wall, cradling a bundle to her chest. "Okay, I'm here." Catherine managed to say noticing the speed at which the flames were engulfing the room she had to be quick. Knocking over any furniture in her way she made a path towards the woman, kneeling down she touched the woman on her shoulder, and saw agonised brown eyes looking at her in trust. Seemed to happen to her a lot, that expression; must be something to do with the eyes. A smile slowly crept across her lips and she pulled the woman up gently to stand beside her. The woman clutched at her hand as the flames suddenly shot out in their direction.

"Easy there, you're going to get out okay." Catherine glanced across to the bundle held tightly to the woman's chest, it wasn't moving, nor did it appear to be breathing, but it was difficult to tell

331

with all the smoke. Now wasn't the time to ponder that particular question. It would have to wait; they needed to get out fast!

Dragging the woman in her wake, Catherine propelled her out of the room, managing to skirt the fireball quickly devouring the room. The external door was open and she pushed the woman out into the open, relishing the opportunity of breathing air not polluted by the smoke from the fire.

Sirens were getting closer. *'Good!'*

Then as she managed a gasp of fresh air; that is, if you could call any air in Rio fresh. A child's scream pierced the night, chilling in its intensity and fear. Catherine looked to the other woman in question, who was being enclosed in a blanket and the bundle being tenderly extracted from her shocked hands by a neighbour.

The young woman she had saved looked at her beseechingly "Carlos," came the strangled response as the woman fainted from her ordeal.

Time was running out!

Catherine ran back into the building as if the furies themselves were chasing her. She noticed the hall had become almost black in the thickness of the smoke and by the clouds hanging in the air on the next level the stairs looked pretty risky.

In for a penny in for a pound!

'Hell what's a little risk between friends?' Her mind supplied as she fought the laboured breathing. Taking the stairs two at a time, she pushed open the first door she came to. Nothing! Well, except for a wall of fire that she was damn sure had singed her eyebrows off. *'Damn!'*

Then the next room came into view, as much view as she could manage with the smoke progressing at an alarming rate through the house her own body producing tears to clear her eyes naturally. She pulled the door open, a little more cautiously this time.

The boy sat in a corner of the room close to the window, although it was closed. He couldn't have been more than five years old, clutching a blanket that had seen better days.

"Hi Carlos?" She gave him a dazzling smile, hoping he could see it through the streaks of dirt and smoke she knew covered her face. "I need you to trust me Carlos, we need to get out fast, okay?" Not sure if he understood her she picked him up in one swift movement and held him against her shoulder.

As if on cue, an explosion rocked the floor of the room and reverberated around the building as one of the walls collapsed, engulfing the room in black smoke the flames that had otherwise been kept out of the room, now trailed dangerously close to them cutting off the door. *'Well, that way's out of the question, only one exit left.'* Opening the window, she shouted at one of the newly arrived firemen, her voice hoarse from the smoke.

"Get the boy!" Glancing at him and smiling she asked. "How do you feel about flying Carlos?" With that she threw the child out of the window and crossed whatever you crossed in this situation.

Continuing to look out of the window and wondering who or what in this living hell would catch her. She didn't notice that a wooden beam from the roof had cracked through the thin ceiling and, as if in slow motion, headed towards her. Catherine's senses picked up something being horribly wrong just as the beam hit her on the left side, cracking her head and shoulder, the fire catching her hair and clothes. Finally, the momentum of the object was propelling her out of the window.

Her last thought as the pain engulfed her and darkness beckoned. *'Why Jace? Why did you marry him?'*

It was suddenly mercifully dark.

Three months had seen changes in Jace Bardley's lifestyle that wouldn't have been expected. To all intents and purposes she was now a happily married woman.

Peter Adamson, rescuing her at the eleventh hour had thwarted Hudson's threats. He had been as good as his word and had married her the following day to defeat the malicious machinations of Hudson.

Her mind in turmoil and distress, Jace had agreed to his suggestion and married him. All avenues to Catherine had been closed to her. Peter was a perceived lifeline; Jace caught it and made one of the biggest mistakes in her life.

Her family hadn't understood the reason for her marriage in haste, not when she'd been so adamant about her feelings for Catherine Warriorson. This wasn't the daughter they had watched grow from a baby into a mature adult, the woman saying her vows to this virtual stranger was an enigma to them. Consequently, Jace had not been home since the wedding.

The wedding was a sham at first; Peter was her friend and doing her a favor. Although eventually after six weeks and too much alcohol at a party they had been to, she finally allowed him into her bed. It was the beginning of the end.

Her independent mind finally reasserting itself after being locked up for weeks in a living hell Jace knew she had permitted to happen. Now they spent whatever times together in a sense of impending disaster, neither wanting to broach the subject that would finish their marriage.

James Thompson had invited them to a party that evening and both wanted to go. Peter would be going to Europe to film a documentary in a week's time. They had argued frequently over Jace's refusal to go with him.

"I have a career of my own Peter. I can't just up and leave it for a year to watch you film." Jace was adamant.

"You're my wife Jace, surely you want to be with me? I'm going to be gone for a year, maybe more if the backers want to do a series." He pleaded with her.

"I can't." Her voice almost broke.

"You can't or you won't?" His voice held a hint of sarcasm.

"Does it matter?" Jace's voice had grown tired of this particular conversation.

"Yes!" Peter angrily spat the word out.

"Then I won't!" She gave him a weary look.

"Is it because of her?" Peter was pushing into territory they had agreed never to discuss.

Jace eyed him with a sad lost look.

"Yes! She might come back one day."

Her admission was breaking Peter's heart. "For god's sake Jace, you left her, remember? She's not coming back! Hudson did the works on her; Devonshire's never going to show her pretty face in this town again, maybe not even the country!" Peter spoke to Jace as if reprimanding a child for taking a cookie out of the jar before supper.

Jace knew deep down what he said was probably correct; she knew that she hurt him deeply by her continued obsession with Catherine. The feeling never went away and she knew that it never ever would. When she'd told Catherine she had waited forever, well that was right and forever was still along way off! "Peter?" He looked at her strengthening gaze.

"Yeah?" He saw her green eyes reflect seriously back at him.

"I think we need to discuss our future." Jace had finally made up her mind to end this charade.

"No!" His voice sounded like he was suffering acute pain.

Jace watched the sadness take over as he finally continued in anguish.

"I love you Jace! If staying here is what you need to do then you go ahead and do it! But I don't want you to leave me!" He had tears settling in the corner of his eyes.

Her heart broke for the man in front of her, he had done nothing in her eyes except give her his love, and here she was throwing it back in his face. Compassionately she held his head to her shoulder. "Okay Peter we'll try to work it out." She whispered her own tears falling silently down her cheeks. *'Though only the gods know how?'* Her mind slipped in for good measure.

The party was in full swing when they finally arrived at the house. James was without doubt an accomplished host. The parties he threw were usually large affairs with lots of people milling in and out all evening, tonight was no different.

Some colleagues had tackled Peter over his new project and he was talking to them intently.

Jace was leaning against a far wall watching a tall-distinguished man talking politely to a young girl dressed in knee high boots, a skirt that just about reached the top of her thighs and a ribbed purple blouse, leaving little to the imagination.

"You know he doesn't bite. Well, girls anyway." James chuckled as he handed her a glass of white wine.

"I know, but to be honest, I haven't seen him since...." she trailed off, her face clearly expressing the hurt behind the memory of that last encounter.

"Yep, I know," giving her a long look. "Come on let's rescue him."

"Oh, I don't think so James, I hardly think I'm on his list of favorite guests. He's Catherine's friend." Jace tugged against the firm hold of her friend's hand.

"Don't chicken out on this Jace, he might have news!" Jace knew that would be her un-doing, any news however insignificant would be welcome to her starved soul.

Walking over, James tapped his partner's shoulder; who then turned to see who wanted him. Paul Strong gave James a smile of pleasure, replacing the polite boredom in his eyes. Then his eyes strayed to Jace who was fidgeting nervously at James' side. They took on a quizzical look.

"Hello Jace." Paul said quietly, James skilfully steered his partner towards the younger woman who was more appreciative of his presence than the individuals he had been conversing previously.

"Hello Paul, how are you?" Not knowing what else to say to him.

"I'm very well. And you?" He looked directly at her with a pointed glance.

"Pretty good." They both lapsed into silence for several seconds.

"I see marriage appears to agree with you?"

Jace winced at the comment. "Peter is good to me. What more can I say?" Her eyes sought out a reaction, but what reaction?

"Nothing more I guess. I heard from James that you left UCP, we're sorry to have lost you," Paul sounded genuine in his platitude.

"Yeah, I went back to my first love, publishing. Ironic wouldn't you say?" She laughed hollowly.

"If that's what you find suits your talents where's the irony in that?" He continued to keenly appraise her.

"I have a post proof-reading for a small publisher in Santa Monica." Jace for the first time since he'd seen her arrive actually looked interested in something. He had noticed her quiet observation of him from her position at the far end of the room.

"Sounds like you enjoy it?" He saw now why his boss had been captivated; her eyes alone snared you in when they became animated.

"I do! I also get a chance to work on my writing. I kind of stopped for a while, now I'm ready to start again." Jace timidly explained.

"I hope you succeed. If you ever need work please call me." He said sincerely.

"Thanks. Are you saying that for my professionalism or because of my ex-relationship with Catherine?" There she had succumbed to her desire she'd mentioned Catherine by name, it tasted so good on her lips to say the name openly again.

Paul looked seriously at her and smiled. "Your professionalism of course. Catherine no longer runs any of the Xianthos operations, she has no direct influence on any decisions made by the company."

"Thank you!" She needed to know. "How is she?" A whispered plea came from her lips.

"Last time I saw her she was tired but okay." He finally responded after a long drink from his beer.

"When was that?" Her heart rate tripled in anticipation of his answer.

"The last day you saw her in LA." He saw her look of confusion.

"I guess I should have known, you're not going to tell me anything! I hurt her I know, and believe me if I could take it all back I would." Her voice choked out.

"I told you the truth Jace, the last time I saw her was the same day you did." Was he going to answer her question? Sure he was. "You hurt her that day sure, but your marriage hurt her more." It wasn't an accusation just a statement.

"She knows?" Jace looked startled.

"Yes." He said quietly.

"I...I didn't do that to hurt her! It was other circumstances." Jace tried to find the words.

"She got the message anyway." He enigmatically replied.

"That would be?" Jace needed to know how much more damage she had inflicted on the woman she loved.

"You don't love her." Paul offered quietly.

"Oh god Paul." With that Peter sauntered across and put an arm about his wife.

"Strong, nice to see you again." His tone belied the sentiment in the words.

"Adamson." He nodded his head. James took the opportunity at that moment to interrupt saying Paul had an urgent call. He left them with a polite nod of his head.

James and Peter began a conversation that partially excluded her.

'She thinks I don't love her? Hades, that couldn't be farther from the truth!' She watched Paul Strong take his call and noticed a shocked expression pass over his face, which he masked quickly as he scanned the room for James. Putting down the receiver he quickly went over to his partner and spoke a few quiet words to him and then quickly disappeared up the stairs.

Something was wrong, very wrong.

"James, are you okay?" She asked in concern.

He looked at her with an almost vacant expression his mind obviously elsewhere. "Jace...yeah I'm fine. Someone we know has had an accident, Paul has to leave. Jace maybe..." He trailed off as he noticed his lover emerge from a room and descend the stairs.

Jace watched looks pass between the two men and Paul looked in her direction briefly, she could have sworn that he was about to say something, when Peter hauled her off to talk to some friends.

When she turned again, Paul Strong had departed and James was engaged in being the genial party host.

Chapter Forty

A mist was clearing and Catherine felt that the fog that had clouded her brain was finally lifting and she would see again.

What would she see?

What did she want to see? That was easy from the first moment she had seen a blonde-haired woman with the most startlingly innocent green eyes, she had wanted to wake up everyday and see that face.

Now she could couldn't she? Jace was the woman who captured her imagination, her dreams, her heart and her soul. When the mist that still hovered was gone, her green-eyed blonde Californian would be standing in the light waiting for her.

A figure was there, she was sure of it.

Taking a tentative step forward she saw her waiting patiently beside a tree, it was covered in apple blossom but the trunk instead of being brown was as white as snow. Jace was waiting, as she knew she would be, hadn't she always over time.

Another step forward and she saw the eyes smiling at her in welcome, however it was too far yet to see the color. Oh yes, Jace was here to welcome her home again; it was as it should be.

As her steps gathered pace she felt as if she was gliding towards her destination, had she died and gone to heaven? It was so quiet here, Jace, the tree and herself. No problems no interfering people who didn't have a life of their own, just the two of them. How it should be, how it was going to be for the rest of their lives it was their destiny to be together always.

As she approached the tree, 'Jace' turned to her. Catherine was astonished to find that it wasn't green but brown eyes that blinked warmly at her. Oh no that couldn't be right, it had to be green eyes, it had to be!

Puzzled she felt drawn to the woman and knew she was vaguely familiar, but she wasn't Jace!

The mystery women held out her hand for Catherine to take, as she did so Catherine shook her head vigorously.

No!

A voice recognizable in the recesses of her memory spoke to her. "It's time Princess."

Turning her head from side to side, she wasn't going to go. Not yet, not now, not until she knew for sure that Jace was going to be at her side. No way was she going to die yet; she had so much left to live for, so very much.

"No it isn't, not yet, not until she loves me again and I know she will, I know it in my heart."

The pale-featured mystery woman gave her a half smile; eyes once filled with warmth now emitted compassion and understanding.

"So be it Princess, we love you too we can wait." That same voice from her memory spoke softly and then the mystery woman disappeared as the mist swirled around her, the fog she thought had gone now reclaimed her in it's embrace.

"Doctor you've got her back!" The nurse, who had been monitoring the resuscitation of the badly injured foreigner and apparent heroine of the hour, said with relief.

Enricho Garcia paced the floor of the hospital critical area. He had been called three hours after Catherine had been in surgery. It had taken the police that long to trace her apartment and find out a contact. Once he'd been informed he contacted Paul Strong, his boss, he needed to know what was happening; now three hours later, he was still waiting for news of her condition.

He'd eventually found out that she was some kind of heroine; her bravery in going into a blazing house not once but twice for people she didn't know in this city was unheard of, especially by a European woman too!

The mother and the young boy had only superficial burns and smoke inhalation, the baby had died from the smoke inhalation in his mother's arms before Catherine had turned up. Garcia felt proud of Catherine as if she was a relative.

He'd invited Catherine to his home on several occasions in the past three months some she accepted, many she hadn't. His wife Angelica was always happy to see her, they had a small daughter who was just learning to walk and the tall stranger was a great climbing frame. He felt that Catherine had some peace on those days that she never appeared to have at any other times. He had read the press about her but, she wasn't the person that was depicted in those tabloids, no she was stronger than the weak person they portrayed to him, she was quite simply incredible!

Paul Strong was on his way and would arrive in approximately four hours hopefully he would have good news for his boss. He knew that Catherine and Paul were friends and it would be a shock to him if anything happened to her. But God didn't do that to Heroes, did he?

It was a question he constantly asked himself for the next three hours waiting alone in a white walled room with little to occupy him but his own mixed up thoughts.

The door opened as the early morning light seeped through the windows of the waiting room. Stirring from the chair stiffly, he was motioned to sit again by the doctor who sat opposite him.

"Are you a relative?" The doctor asked in a quiet voice.

"No, no she doesn't have any relatives in Rio, in fact I don't think she has any living relatives, I work for her." Garcia hurriedly tried to explain.

"I see." He pondered the facts.

"Her friend Paul Strong is due here anytime. He's a business colleague but also a close friend, will that help?" Enricho suggested.

"It is of no consequence. Her injuries are, as you know, severe. She has multiple burns to the body particularly on her head. She has a broken shoulder and her head suffered a trauma that cracked her skull in two places. We will wait to see if she regains consciousness before we can evaluate that correctly." The doctor patiently explained.

"What? If she regains consciousness, what does that mean? Is she in danger?" He asked shocked.

"Well, her injuries are severe, as I told you. The shock alone when she wakes will determine if she can overcome the burns. Then we have to know what the head injury has caused, she is very lucky to be alive. When she wakes she may not want to live, that is always the threat with this kind of trauma. She's a mess. She was a beautiful woman." He stated clinically.

"No! No, she's still a beautiful woman she will fight it, she will live!" He spoke positively.

"You sound so sure?" The doctor looked surprised but pleasantly so.

"She's beaten worse in her life, this episode will not defeat her." He smiled weakly at the doctor.

"Good. She will need constant care for many months, is she in a position to fund that kind of care?"

Garcia snorted. "Oh my, yes!"

"Excellent, when her friend arrives I will talk to you both in detail about her injuries, in the mean time you may see her if you wish." He got up to leave.

Garcia walked with the doctor to the private emergency room and Catherine Devonshire's very still form; nothing to do but wait.

Paul arrived at the hospital at nine a.m., three hours later than he had expected, weather turbulence attributed to the delay of the flight for over two hours. Walking into the reception area he waited impatiently for the receptionist to complete her phone call and talk to him. Drumming his fingers on the desktop, he finally caught her eye.

Smiling falsely at him she asked him whom he needed to see.

"Catherine Devon... no Catherine Smithson, which room is she in?" He asked shortly, the plane journey taking its toll along with the worry over his boss.

"Smithson, no Smithson, ah wait a moment. Smithson yes, she's in room two hundred, the critical wing." With that he headed for the elevator without even saying thank you. He would apologise later.

The time seemed to go slowly in the elevator as he thought about Catherine and what state she was in, if she indeed she had managed to survive! *I almost told her Catherine. I nearly broke my promise to you and told Jace you were hurt. You know I wanted to, but maybe it really is too late for you two after all.'* His mind ceased those thoughts as the door opened to the critical wing and he headed for room two hundred.

Walking into the room he saw Garcia slumped in the chair, he had obviously been here for hours, the man was another devotee of the Devonshire charm that was for sure. He'd heard from other VP's that Garcia extolled the virtues of the owner of Xianthos. Some thought him pathetic, others viewed it as hero worship, but Paul saw it as a genuine friendship in the making. Even Catherine had been charmed to some extent by the man who offered her hospitality, without any catches, particularly after all the media attention around her. Not wanting to disturb him he looked at the person in the hospital bed.

Wires were hooked up everywhere or so it appeared to him, he noticed that her head was swathed in bandages and her nose looked broken. What did he know? Traction equipment was stationed close to the bed as the body was elevated slightly due to some other injury, he couldn't quite perceive was it a broken arm? All you could really see amidst the bandages were the eyelids and they looked swollen and her eyebrows, those formidable eyebrows were gone. He walked slowly over to the bed and wanting to take one of her hands, noticed that the left side of her body was encased in bandages but her right side was relatively unscathed. Reaching for her right hand he sat down next to the bed and just held it, waiting for Garcia to wake, and in about twelve hours Grace would be here too.

He'd rung Grace as he waited for his flight, which had been a difficult call to make.

The phone ringing in the study at seven thirty had all the interested parties finally smiling; they had been worried. Grace picked up the line and turned on the intercom.

"Grace?" The voice of a man at first Grace didn't recognise.

"Guess it's not Catherine then?" Grace said flippantly.

"No, no Catherine is.... she's been. Hey Grace are we on intercom?" Paul decided it wouldn't be good to have witnesses to what he had to say, which would be up to Grace to decide who at the ranch would get to know about Catherine's condition.

"Yeah, the kids and I are waiting for Catherine's usual call to us, she's late." Grace smiled at having to tell Catherine that Paul might be the one keeping her waiting for a free line.

"Can I speak to you for a few minutes, without the intercom?" He asked her gently.

Grace wasn't stupid, she could hear the change in timbre of his voice, something was very wrong! "Hey kids, why don't you go and see what's on TV for a little while, and I'll be with you soon okay?"

"But Grace, Catherine might call?" Lisa said plaintively.

"Hey sweetheart it's okay, Catherine will ring back, and you know that!" Grace smiled at her.

"Okay, but don't be too long." The child said petulantly.

Jake stood up not saying a word and took Lisa's hand they shut the door behind them.

"Okay Paul, it's just you and me, what's she done now?" Grace said in an exasperated way.

"She's in the hospital in Rio." He finally said.

The silence stretched, Paul didn't know if she was still there. Grace was upset; he'd heard the sob in her voice. "What's happened?" Grace finally whispered.

"Not sure. Garcia said she was some kind of heroine, he didn't say much. She's in the operating room now. I have a flight in about half an hour, will get there in about three hours time. Do you want to wait until I find out the score, or are you going to get a flight out?"

"I'm on the next flight out of here. She might never know but I want to be there if.... I want to be there!" She finally said brokenly.

"You know her Grace, she never lets go." He tried to sound confident but failed miserably.

"Yeah. See you in about a day Paul. Give her a kiss from us okay." With that she put the phone down and called Colin.

Now looking at the almost obscured face of his friend, how did he do that, kiss her and not hurt her. He picked up her right hand and gently kissed each knuckle. *'For all of us Catherine, we're here waiting for you, don't forget that!'*

The doctor had been kind, in his own way. Garcia had returned home and back to business, it wasn't the time to tell anyone about this yet. It may never be the time.

Paul had cancelled the rest of the week's schedule, explaining he had a virus and he wasn't capable of traveling, he was the man in charge after all.

Grace had arrived and wouldn't move from Catherine's bedside.

Now, three days after the event, Catherine was finally stirring from her unconscious state. Grace was smiling, Paul still looked pensive, the doctor looked on in interest.

"Come on Catherine, how about you show us those ice blues. Some time soon, well like right now!" Grace said gently, stroking the uninjured right hand slowly.

Gradually one lid opened briefly but slid shut as fast as it opened. A few minutes later after much coaxing, her right eyelid opened and the ice blue of her eyes looked ahead.

Grace looked at the doctor as she noticed that Catherine didn't seem to be responding to the light, there was no stimulation at all.

The doctor used a penlight to flash in the eye and it didn't move he sighed heavily. "Catherine, how about you open the left eye, just for me?"

Catherine tried to move and was prevented by traction equipment on

e tried to move and was prevented by traction equipment on her abused body. "Who the hell are you?" Her voice cracked with its enforced disuse although her tone, clearly the Catherine they all knew.

Paul couldn't help the smile that crossed his face and Grace snorted and laughed softly.

"Guess your vocal cords are going to be okay at least." The doctor stated un-necessarily. "I'm your doctor, Doctor Assanti."

Her left eye opened reluctantly. "It hurts like hell to open this one!" She exclaimed.

The doctor gave it the same examination and he reluctantly nodded his head in resignation.

344

"Haven't you paid the bills around here, why are all the lights off in this place?" Catherine finally asked the question the others had dreaded, after seeing the doctor's expression.

The doctor looked at the other people in the room. Paul looked to Grace and she reluctantly looked at the doctor and he gave her a reassuring look.

"Have you all gone deaf too? Grace?" It was tentative and held for the first time a hint of fear.

"No, no Catherine I'm here. It appears that the blow to your head has caused some problem with your vision." Grace pointed out as tactfully as possible in the circumstances.

Catherine turned her head in the direction of the voice of her friend. "Grace, are you telling me I'm blind?"

Grace pursed her lips in thought. "Yeah, in a nutshell, that's exactly right, teach you to be a hero won't it." Grace tried a touch of levity.

Catherine knew that Grace being funny at this point meant that it wasn't good. So what the hell else was wrong? "Okay, give me the bottom line and a drink too?"

"Doctor?" Grace passed the problem over to him, he knew all the facts, although she snagged a paper cup of water and gently administered a few drops to her friend.

Clearing his voice Doctor Assanti explained the injuries. "Well, it appears that you have suffered blindness that could be temporary, we will have to run tests. You will need months of therapy for your shoulder; it was broken in several places. You will also need skin grafts on your face and left side of your body. That will take maybe the best part of a year to complete. Your hair will eventually grow again as will your eyebrows." He clinically stated.

"Oh, so effectively I look a bloody mess?" She eventually said in a tone that bordered on indifference.

"Yes, but it could all be normal in about a year." The doctor finished.

"Perhaps but the eyes might never recover, right?" Catherine dogmatically continued.

"I cannot say at this point, we need to run tests." He smiled at the others in the room.

"Well, you better get a bloody move on then and sort out those tests, do you think I'm going to stay here forever?" Catherine muttered, her voice gaining strength.

The doctor laughed out loud at the European woman who had indeed more strength of character than he had seen in many years; her injuries without the blindness would have finished many off. This woman was beautiful. But her beauty also transcended the flesh; she had a strength within that no one could deflate. Her other friend had been right, she would fight, and she wasn't finished yet!

"Right away, how does this afternoon sound for the first one?" He asked her, noticing she was tiring.

"Good." She gradually closed both her eyes and mumbled. "Are the children okay Grace? You haven't left them to fend for themselves have you?" Grace heard the old sarcastic humour return in her friend's comment.

"Would I do a thing like that Catherine?" She replied innocently.

"Mmmmm, smart thinking Grace, or you might be looking for another position in life." Her hand clutched at Grace's as a spasm of pain went through her left temple.

Smiling at her friend's unexpected banter, she pressed the hand back in comfort. "Paul is here." Grace said softly.

Paul moved away from the wall he'd been leaning against. Moving close to the bed he spoke softly. "Hi Catherine."

"Hi Paul, so what's with you taking time off to see this wreck?" Paul had to wince at the statement, for how right she was at this moment in time.

"Oh, you know me; always was a little nosy." He laughed softly.

"Glad to hear it. How's James?" She asked sleepily.

"He's fine, sends his love." Paul grinned at her attitude; it had been difficult to gauge how she would react when she woke for the first time after the accident.

"Well, I guess one day I will get to meet him, but maybe we will take a rain check for the moment okay?" Catherine frowned as if she tried to recall a memory and it refused to appear.

"Sure, whenever you want. Jace is fine also." He couldn't help it; if she had changed her mind he would do something about it and quickly.

"You've seen her recently?" It was a whisper. Grace looked at Paul and smiled, she had been thinking the same thing herself. Jace should be here. What the hell did it matter if the woman was married, she needed to know; she needed to be here to help Catherine through the trauma.

"Yeah, the night of the accident. We had a party, she asked about you, how you were." He waited.

"How I am?" Catherine's lips curled in a wry smile. *'Appropriate.'* Closing her eyes briefly she finally opened the sightless orbs and spoke again. "Was she with her...husband?" Catherine asked quietly.

"Yeah, Adamson was there. Jace wants to see you Catherine!" He said quickly.

"No!" Her voice gained extra strength from some unknown region in her battered body.

"Because of your present condition?" Grace asked in interest.

"No. She's married, that should say it all!" A tear slid from Catherine's right eye there was nothing she could do to prevent it.

"She loves you Catherine." Paul said finally.

"No you're wrong, she loved me. Let's have the sentiment correctly interpreted here, not love, loved! She proved that by marrying Adamson. I need to get some sleep." Discussion closed.

Paul looked at Grace and they both had a sad look on their faces, they noticed the even breathing of their mutual friend. "What about coffee?"

"Love one, she'll come round Paul, trust me. Looks like I'm going to get months to work on her." Grace placed her arm on his elbow and they went towards the vending machine.

"I hope so, they both look lost without each other. It's as if they are both searching for something out of reach." He shook his head at the thought.

"They are. I think it's called a soulmate and they are each other's." Grace said simply.

Chapter Forty-One

(Six months later)

Grace smiled as she watched the children canter about the paddock, they had been busy for the past nine months becoming proficient on the back of a horse, or in the case of Lisa the back of her beloved pony Diamond. She wouldn't change him for any of the horses that Colin had offered her recently.

Jake had been given Ruby as a present for his eleventh birthday. Catherine hadn't been on the ranch at the time, but she made up for it when she'd arrived home, four months ago.

She was still struggling to move her left arm, but it was slowly responding and the therapist who came six days a week, said it would eventually be normal. The skin grafts had taken surprisingly well, her own bodies healing mechanism amazing her doctors. She had smiled at their faces on more than one occasion. Catherine was amazing for her recuperative powers, which no one could dispute.

The blindness unfortunately hadn't responded to treatment as well as they had all wanted. Her right eye had eventually cleared a little and she could see images and colours but nothing distinct, mere shadows. Her left eye where the main impact of the blow had occurred was totally useless. For anyone but Catherine she suspected the toll of the injuries would have certainly sent them into depression at the very least. Not Catherine Warriorson!

She had conceded the need for a dog to guide her around the ranch, especially if she left the confines of the house. Fortunately the dog ended up as much a part of the family as it did Catherine's lifeline to the outside world.

Turning to observe the porch Grace saw Catherine sitting patiently with the dog at her feet, she was stroking its ears. Grace could never work out if she did that to ease tension or because the dog liked it, either way it was endearing to watch. There was a serene expression on Catherine's face when she did this particular exercise with the dog.

Venturing out on the porch Catherine glanced towards the sound and her right eye tried to focus on the figure coming towards her. "Grace?" A strong vibrant voice asked.

"Yeah, wondered if you wanted tea before you set off with the urchins?" Her smile one of thankfulness Catherine was alive nothing else was important!

"No, thanks anyway, think I'll have one when we get back. I'm taking them to Cutter's Ridge today, thought it was time they met Lucas and Adam." Her voice quietly explained.

"Good idea, time they met the rest of the family." Grace often wondered what went on in this woman's head, Catherine had never truly opened up to her even in the months of agonising pain she'd suffered. Her solitary bearing of the pain and the emotional turmoil it must have created was heart breaking to observe. There was nothing she could do but be there for Catherine and that she did most willingly.

"Thought so myself, it's Lucas's birthday today."

That surprised Grace; she had never volunteered the information before.

"How are you getting to Cutter's?" Grace asked.

"Colin is taking us to the plateau and then, we will walk. He'll come back about two hours later, unless the weather takes a turn for the worse. He's not going to leave us on the Ridge, that's somethino I would do." She had a sad smile on her face, a bittersweet memory obviously taking over her thoughts.

"Good Colin needs to take a look over at some of the fences." Grace had seen the sad expression; she also knew the memory that Catherine had invoked.

"Have you decided what to do about Colin?" Catherine asked her unexpectedly.

Grace moved towards the railing on the porch and sighed. "Not really."

"What do you want to do?" Catherine continued to stroke the dog's ears and listened intently for the answer.

"If you had asked me that six months or more ago I would have told you that Colin didn't picture in any frame I had available. Now, well he kind of pops up in them all. Strange really." Grace said slowly, almost savouring the words.

"Not strange, only love." Catherine supplied.

"You would know all about that." Grace looked at the tall woman who stood up at the comment, her black hair had grown to the nape of her neck, grey pronounced at the temples these days, and it gave her a rakish ambience. The burn marks travelling down the left side of her face now fading with the grafts. She was certainly a woman you didn't ever forget meeting. Then again, she had always been a force to be reckoned with!

"Yes I would, I just left it a little late to find out." Catherine quietly reflected.

"Its never too late Catherine." Grace said softly.

"Ah, how I wish you were right on that one Grace, how I wish." She sighed heavily and moved closer to the other woman at the railing.

"You know what's wrong with you Catherine?"

"What?" Catherine turned her sightless eyes on her friend, the ice blue gaze unable to focus.

"You're a hero and you refuse to believe it! There are people alive today who can vouch for that, kids close by that have a happy home and people who love them because of you. There are also numerous other kids who will benefit from the gift of the trust fund you set up in your son's name and they will never know that!" Grace challenged her friend.

"Hero?" Catherine snorted. "Get out of here Grace, whatever I am it certainly isn't that! I'm more like the old crock you put out to pasture because its useful days are over." Catherine snorted at the suggestion.

"Okay, have it your way but one day you're going to see it for yourself, bank on it." Grace said confidently.

"How about you're my hero Grace?" Catherine said quietly

"Ah, how you wish Catherine." Grace laughingly placed her hand on the other woman's shoulder.

"I might wish for something more maybe?" A wistful note clearly telling Grace it wasn't her Catherine was thinking about.

"In your dreams Catherine, alas I'm not your type. But I do wonder who is?" Grace watched the expressions flit across the battle scarred face.

"At the moment, I don't have a who." She stated blandly, knowing full well the lie she told.

"I think you still hurt too much at the moment to have a realistic look at what you need or want. But seriously, I didn't have you down as anything other than straight until Jace came along and blew that out of the window. Latency becomes you I might add." Grace chuckled at the thought.

Catherine wasn't sure if she should reply or not, when she did it surprised both women. "The only time I ever felt emotionally involved with another woman was with Maria in the prison, but we never took it to the physical plane, I doubt we ever would have. The other times I'd been with women were in a drugged haze they never counted. That was until Jace, it was different, oh so different." Catherine's voice held an awed quality about it as she spoke.

"Do you want to talk about it?" Grace offered her a shoulder to cry on if she needed it.

"No, not yet anyway, perhaps one day when it doesn't hurt quite so much." Catherine gave her a weak smile.

"Okay I can go with that. May I ask you one question?"

"Sure go ahead, you will anyway." Catherine smiled, her scar tissue tightening on the left side of her face, inwardly making her flinch at the feeling it caused.

"How do you feel about Jace? Now I mean?" Grace knew her words would hit raw spots in Catherine.

Catherine mulled over the question and Grace sighed thinking she wasn't going to get any answer today. "Lyrics tell a story Grace, mine for Jace would be 'Forsaking Forever', you know the one by Infinity?"

"Oh, so you listen to the lyrics too? I often wondered. Now that paints it's own story. Pretty apt for your current situation." Grace laughed softly there was hope yet!

"Modern poetry to music Grace, perhaps I should buy a music studio? Would go with my scandalised image now wouldn't it, the drugs and drink, what do you think?" She laughed depreciatingly.

"I'll go with the modern poetry to music, but no, leave the music studios to the other's. Lady the only drugs you take now are for medicinal purposes and eventually that will stop." She closed her hand over the larger one resting on the rail; the lesson would be over soon.

Jace had been invited for coffee by James Thompson they hadn't seen each other since the party over six months previously, although they had talked on the phone a few times. It was going to be good to see him again.

Now, she watched the LA shopper's downtown at Starbucks, it was her favorite coffee shop in town. Her friend waving furiously at her from the window opposite caught her eye. She smiled widely at him in welcome.

Making his way over she noticed he wasn't alone, following closely behind but stopping to place their order was Paul Strong; her heart leapt when she saw him. He was her only fragile thread to Catherine.

"Hey Jace, how's life treating you?" James beamed at her and bent over to kiss her cheek.

"Good, I can't complain. What about you?" She smiled directly at him, pleasure evident in her eyes at his presence.

"Great, things have been very good, especially now that Paul is based in LA, he glanced over at his partner.

"I didn't realise Paul was going to be with you today?" She stated quietly.

"Sorry Jace, spur of the moment decision by him not me, I might add. When he knew I was meeting you, he got mysterious on me, and wanted to come along, so he was allowed. That, and I want to know what the deal is." He chuckled as Paul made his way over with three coffees of varying choices.

"Hello Paul." Jace held her hand out politely. He looked at it and smiled wryly.

"Guess I don't warrant the kiss on the cheek huh?" He laughed softly.

Jace looked surprised and blushed a little, having no answer for the man now seated opposite her.

"James tells me that your divorce came through last month, sorry to hear it didn't work out." Paul said, although his eyes didn't mirror the sentiment of the words.

Once again the blush spread over her cheeks, it was becoming quite annoying. "Yes. Peter and I split up six months ago; he was going to Europe for a year, so I guess it was a good a time as any to finish it. A clean break was needed. Well, as clean as it gets with this little complication." She patted her belly, which showed the evidence of a pregnancy in the later months.

Paul and James looked at her; she looked like any young mother to be, healthy and presumably happy. The only reason to suspect any different was the semi-permanent sadness that looked out at the world from her green expressive eyes.

"Does he know about the baby?" This time James added to the conversation.

Sipping from her cappuccino, she smiled and nodded her head. "We decided that if I needed anything he would be there for me."

"But you don't need him right?" James supplied cautiously.

"No! I don't need him; the baby and I will be fine. The position I have pays well and I can work from home initially. I have a very understanding boss." Jace smiled at her friend.

"He must be!" Paul said in surprise.

"Actually he's a she, and yes she is!" Jace laughed her eyes sparkling.

"How well do you kno□ her?" Paul asked a little shortly, he hadn't liked the fact that someone else could be involved with Jace.

Jace and James looked at him in surprise. Paul noted their expressions and shamefacedly looked out of the window in embarrassment.

"If I didn't know better Paul, I would think you're looking out for my interests here, when did you take up being my protector?" Jace asked her interest piqued.

Silence stretched out for several minutes; eventually James broke it. "The lady asked you a question Paul?" This was totally unlike his partner.

"From the day Catherine couldn't." He finally replied and looked Jace in the eyes with a piercing stare.

Catching her breath, she almost choked over her coffee. "What? What do you mean?" She responded breathlessly. *'Catherine couldn't? What did that mean?'*

"Jace from the moment you left Catherine, she has always known what you were doing. When you married, where you live, when you went to the gym. It was her way of being in your life but not, s□ to speak. Her prime motive was to see that you were always taken care of; she wanted your happiness above all else even at the expense of her own! She did it so well too, I bet you never knew she had a private detective around those first three months?" He explained mechanically.

"She had me followed? That's an invasion of my privacy!" Jace gasped out, angry with Catherine's tactics. Once again her mind taking a negative stance against her ex-lover instead of being happy she'd cared enough to do that. Her heart became heavy, she immediately wished she hadn't made the statement.

"She thought it for the best, she had to leave the country for a while and couldn't do it herself, not with any degree of success anyway. Don't be angry with her Jace, she loved you at the time."

His final remark brought tears to her eyes. "You said Catherine isn't able or words to that effect, is she ill?" Jace answered him after gulping down more coffee.

James decided that the conversation although interesting could do with a coffee refill for all of them. He held up his cup quizzically, and quickly went to the counter for the refills.

"She's not technically ill. She...how do I put this?" Paul frowned; he didn't want to sound melodramatic.

"Why not try the facts?" Jace gave him her full attention.

"The facts? Yeah, I could do that, how many months are you?" He eyed her swollen belly cautiously.

"Six months and don't worry this baby is staying put." Jace stroked her belly absently.

"Was it conceived on the night of the party?" He looked at her with interest.

Jace stared at him; he had hit the nail on the head. It had also been the night she had finally admitted the marriage wasn't going to work. Her thoughts as they made love had been on Catherine, it had been as if her mind was replacing her husband with Catherine's image. "Yes." She said in a subdued voice.

"I wondered. She was in an accident, a fire that night Jace. We thought we had lost her; she was a mess. To be frank, she still is in many ways." Paul punched out the details in a staccato voice.

"She was injured and possibly dying that night and you never told me? Why?" Came the strangled response, tears now clearly making their way down her cheeks, they were uncontrollable. It would have been useless for her to try and stop them.

"She gave explicit instructions not to disclose where she was or anything about her. We carried out those instructions to the letter, especially once you were married and theoretically it didn't matter what happened to her." Paul shrugged, seeing the pain etched in the face opposite him.

"Where is she now? I assume you're visit here today is to tell me that? Not taunt me more." Jace choked out.

"Catherine has maintained her expressed wish that you are not to be informed of her condition or her whereabouts." He said slowly.

"Right, so what good is telling me all this if her wishes are sacrosanct with you?" Jace gave him an angry look.

"Because I don't agree with her now! Maybe while you were married, she was right to keep things from you. Now...well now you need her as much as she needs you, maybe you might need her even more?" He smiled genuinely at her.

Taking his hand that was resting on the table. "Thank you." Her heart was surely going to burst with happiness.

"Hey don't thank me yet! You've got to get through to our stoic friend, who won't be easy." He winked at her, as she looked perplexed. "You have a couple of things in your favor though. Notably I have a visit planned in a few days to see her and a certain friend called Grace, who says 'hi' by the way, who my dear Jace will get you the opening." He laughed at her tearstained face suddenly having the expression of a Cheshire cat.

"Grace? How is Grace? Is she married yet?" Jace spluttered out.

"Grace is fine, or was when I talked to her yesterday. No, she isn't married yet. She sends her love and says 'don't drown me in those tears you're so famous for'." He laughed at her blush.

"She hasn't changed any then?" Jace gave him a tearstained glance.

"Guess not." He saw James making his way over with the second coffees.

"Good man James. Now Jace, we need to arrange for you to get time off work and make the trip with me; if that's what you want of course?" It never occurred to him that she might not want to go.

"Oh Paul, if I have to give up my job to go and see her I will. Not going isn't even a thought for consideration." It was something she wouldn't do for her ex-husband, but he hadn't been Catherine.

James smiled at the change in the stances of both parties. Great! Everything was going to be just fine, well wasn't it always in Tinsel Town!

Catherine found the trail down to the graves of her husband and son, easily enough, even if she couldn't see it properly.

Colin had pointed certain natural landmarks to the children, just in case he'd explained, as Catherine had snorted at her possible inability to steer them to the right spot.

She could feel that they were close by; she had always felt at peace when she came here, as if Adam and Lucas were willing it from their resting-place.

"Catherine there's a small fenced area behind this outcrop, is that what we're looking for?" Jake asked quietly, he had Catherine's large right hand in his left and Lisa's in his right hand. Catherine's guide dog Rio was in the weaker left hand, it was her way of trying to strengthen the annoying limb.

"Yes, that's it Jake. Do you want to go ahead and open the gate for us to go through?" She turned her sightless eyes on the boy at her side.

"Sure. Here Lisa, take Catherine's hand." He bounced off towards the gate.

"Will this make you unhappy again Catherine?" Lisa asked her in a small voice.

"No Lisa, it's time to let the past go. That's why I want you both to know about my family, you would have all got on marvellously I'm sure of it." She responded softly.

Walking slowly towards the fenced area, they went through the gate, the grass under foot springy and long she could feel it trail over her boots at the ankle. "Needs to be cut here, I think."

"Can we do it for you?" Jake asked her eagerly.

"Why that's nice of you Jake, once a month, okay with you both?" She turned her head to the girl at her side, sometimes it was uncanny that either he or she would speak for them both and they never ever were wrong. *'Some kind of connection here!'*

Silence descended as they shared the beauty of the small valley that held the family the children would never meet.

Jake was the first one to break the silence, which was not melancholy, just thoughtful. "Your husband was old, Catherine!" The boy exclaimed.

Catherine for the first time in months laughed heartily at the arrogance of youth. "He wasn't that old! What must you think of me?" She was still chuckling as she answered him and he leaned forward so she could put her hand through his hair; it was a gesture she had often done when she had been restricted to her bed and they had the story hour together. That had reminded her painfully of the last months of her mother's illness as she had read to her mother and brother. Jake and Lisa now took turns in the reading session, now that she was no longer capable of the task or at least, what she was prepared to admit she wasn't capable of.

"You're not old? Are you?" This time Lisa asked the question.

"I'm older than you both, that is going to have to be your answer to that one." She smirked at them, her face tightening on the left side. The children had never commented or seemed afraid of her condition when she had finally come home four months ago, but the descriptions she had received from the nurses had left her in little doubt that her profile on the left side was scary to most people. Now, it was healing through skin grafts but it still had a way to go.

Rio the dog had been let off her harness so that she could explore in the close vicinity to her mistress. Lisa in particular loved to run around with the dog, it was a wonderful image to conjure up when the darkness threatened to overwhelm her.

"What did Lucas look like?" Lisa's curiosity overcame her promise to Grace not to pry.

"He looked, a little like Jake, dark hair but he had my blue eyes and his fathers smile, Adam had a very engaging smile, a little like seeing Santa Claus on Christmas day." Catherine was awash with memories of her son and husband and they were good memories, from the early days of her marriage.

"That doesn't make sense Catherine, how can a smile look like Santa on Christmas day?" Jake said disparagingly. *'Adults, did they know anything!'*

Laughing again Catherine turned in the direction of the boy's voice and saw his dim outline. "Ah, well Jake it's all a question of imagination, and what do you think about when you imagine Santa smiling on Christmas day?"

"He looks all red and happy and makes people laugh." Lisa said chuckling at the thought.

"Exactly! Jake what about you?" Catherine tilted her head in his direction.

"He has a jolly face, all glowing and happy." He muttered.

"Well, that's how I think of Adam's smile." Catherine said quietly.

The time moved all too fast as they made their way back to the top of Cutter's Ridge, where a ranch foreman was pacing up and down. Catherine smiled as she heard the pacing, one thing for being all but blind was the increase in some of her other senses. She smiled as she approached her friend.

"Been waiting long Colin?" She smirked, knowing that he was probably turning red at the moment.

"No, no Catherine, quite the opposite in fact." He said lamely.

Walking up to him she placed her hand on his shoulder and whispered into his ear. "Liar, but thank you for caring." She walked towards the vehicle she could just make out a hundred yards in front of her.

He was certainly blushing now as Lisa commented on his red cheeks, Catherine had to put her right hand over her mouth to stop the laughter, she was sure her ranch foreman wouldn't appreciate it.

They all clambered into the vehicle and took off back towards the house.

Chapter Forty-Two

Grace was excited, very excited.

Jace was coming; she would arrive at any time now with Paul Strong. They had both agreed, now that Jace wasn't married, it was no longer necessary to keep the truth from her. Catherine hadn't been in a condition to check up on Jace for months and when she had finally asked, they had been honest but not exactly factually in everything that had happened to Jace in the past few months. They had said she was well, which she was most definitely; pregnancy gave her a glow according to Paul anyway. They had omitted her divorce and well, the baby that was going to be up to Jace; as a matter of fact everything from here on in was entirely up to Jace.

This was all to do with love and what could only be described as the uniting of two old souls no matter what Catherine thought.

A vehicle was approaching from the West gate; it had to be them. Going onto the porch she waited with baited breath for the visitors to alight from their vehicle. Paul Strong was the first; he quickly went round to help the rather pregnant Jace Bardley from the car.

Jace saw her friend and a smile that simply made most lighthouses dim in comparison fix itself on her face. *'Yep, Paul had been right she was certainly glowing.'*

Walking quicker than Grace expected Jace was suddenly flying up the stairs and into the older woman's arms. "Oh Grace, how I've missed you!" Came Jace's heartfelt words.

"Well, let me look at you Jace?" Grace finally extracted herself from the hug she had received from the younger woman. Turning Jace to face her, she noted the pink cheeks and the sparkling eyes and obviously the protruding belly that gave her very much the pregnant look.

Jace was a little embarrassed at the scrutiny and her cheeks coloured up at her friend's intense look. "You don't look so bad yourself?" Jace countered.

"Yeah, keeping up with those kids and not to mention Catherine, who I swear has decided she wants another crack at being an adolescent, keeps me going." She laughed.

Oh, how Jace had missed this simple pleasure of friendship with this woman. She had lost so much by being bitter and plain stupid.

Paul decided to make his presence know at this moment. "Well, ladies I know you have lots to talk about but just as a point of interest, where is our esteemed leader?"

Grace smiled at him. "Hi Paul, good to see you again. She's showing the kids, a special place in her heart." She hugged the man as Jace gave her a puzzled look at the statement. Grace had never missed much in her entire life, well, at least it never got boring she always thought to herself. "She has taken them to Cutter's Ridge and the family plot."

"Ah." Was all Jace could muster.

"Right! Let's have some refreshments and get a plan into action; we haven't much time." Grace walked into the kitchen from the porch.

Her visitors followed closely behind her.

Sitting at the familiar kitchen table the young pregnant honey-haired woman reminisced; the place brought so many memories to her mind that tears began to fall before she even realised it.

Grace turned from her ministrations over making coffee and laughed happily. "That's my Jace, never could stop that river flowing could you?" Grace turned to Paul and saw him give the younger woman an indulgent smile. "Told you she would cry all over you Paul, was I right?"

"Yeah." He admitted as Jace wiped her tears and gave them a watery smile.

"What did I do in life to deserve you both thwarting Catherine?" Jace had wanted to ask this question for some time now.

Grace finally decided to answer. "You did what only you could do Jace, you loved Catherine wholeheartedly. She has never been the same since and it has helped her stay alive strange as it seems. Especially when you left her." Seeing the startled look in Jace's face, she gently touched her cheek in understanding. "She forgave you Jace, you helped her achieve something she thought she'd never experience, Love! For those of us who care about her, what's happening now goes beyond what Catherine wants, or what you want, it is just a matter of what the fates decide is our destiny, it's often difficult to define, if indeed we ever can. You just have to accept it and take what happiness it allows."

Jace considered what Grace had said and knew she had no tangible answer. "So what can I expect when I see her, not verbally but physically?" Paul had not divulged Catherine's state of health to

Jace; he had hoped Grace would be better at that than he ever could be.

"Glad you asked, she's not the woman you met a year ago!" Grace looked at Jace shrewdly.

"Oh, I know that Grace, but come on has she grown two heads or something as drastic?" Jace returned Grace's gaze with a strong one of her own.

"You know something Bardley, you can be real impatient at times." Grace laughed at her friend.

"Yeah, well when it involves the woman I love, give me some slack okay?" Jace laughed at the teasing from her friend.

"Good call." Grace laughed and placed a comforting hand on her shoulder.

"Catherine suffered severe burns to her head and left side of her body, skin grafts are working, but like everything it takes time. You can see the ravages of that battle on her left profile. Her shoulder was broken in several places and some sort of motor problem has occurred to her left arm, the therapist is working on that, it gets a little better everyday."

Jace had kept her face blank of any expression it must have been horrific at the time of the fire, what she must have gone through.

"I guess I can cope with that, is there anything else?"

"Yes." Grace turned a serious face to Jace's and pulled her unexpectedly into an embrace that made her shudder at the shear intensity of the emotion Grace was emitting.

"That would be?" Jace kept her eyes glued to her friend's.

"Catherine is blind. Well, to all intents and purposes she's blind!" Grace softly explained the final injury.

Jace hadn't heard that! No, she hadn't heard Grace say Catherine was blind. Not to have the light of recognition shine from those ice blue eyes; they were so much a part of Catherine! "It's not fair!"

"Few things in life are ever fair Jace, but she's alive and I for one will thank God for that miracle everyday of my life." Grace said emphatically.

Jace looked at Grace and their glances locked in a shared emotion. "You say she's blind to all intents and purposes, exactly what does that mean?"

"Catherine can make shadows out with her right eye, but her left is totally blind." Grace gave her the facts.

Nothing was said in the room for several minutes, each had their own thoughts and all had a certain Catherine Devonshire-Warriorson as the main subject.

"Do you want to leave?" Paul finally said.

"Leave?" It was a whisper from Jace. *'Did they think that Catherine being blind would change her mind? What kind of love was it that would shrink from a disability? No! This was her heart reaching out, it didn't matter if Catherine was blind, deaf and dumb, she was here for the duration, and her soul demanded it!'*

"Yes leave, before she knows you have been here?" Paul asked her again.

"I don't want to leave! I want to hold her in my arms and thank god, whichever one that might be! That she's still alive for me to even have the opportunity to be in her presence, to embrace her, eyesight or no eye sight!" Jace responded her voice gaining in strength at each word.

"You know you say the nicest things Jace." Grace finally rejoined the conversation smiling.

"Must be the Californian genes." Jace flippantly replied.

"Good to hear, you must tell Catherine that one, maybe she won't be so anti-Californians in the future, can't be good for a steady relationship." Grace chuckled.

Walking towards the window of the kitchen, she saw a vehicle approach, time to put on that tea. "Well Jace, I hope you're up to this, she's about to get home."

Jace watched as Colin got out of the Land Rover, with Jake getting out of the front passenger side; Lisa falling out of the large vehicle making Jace laugh softly, the girl was exactly as she remembered.

Her eyes saw the door of the rear passenger side open and a dog jumped out of the vehicle, then waited patiently by the door, it's very demeanour indicating that it was waiting for someone important. Then long legs encased in jeans slid out gracefully, a tall form appearing from the vehicle with ease. Jace watched, as the person she had resigned herself to never seeing again was now, so close; so very close. Jace noticed the stiffness to the walk; the reaching for the harness of the dog was obviously an effort. Jace's heart started beating faster, and she winced as she saw pain etched in the beloved face of the raven-haired woman. Yet there was a confidence about the woman that belied her afflictions, she walked towards the house without a care, Lisa taking her right hand and skipping along constantly chatting to her tall companion. Jake had fallen into step beside Colin as they strolled off towards the stables.

Catherine was getting closer and closer.

Grace came over and placed a comforting arm over Jace's shoulders and smiled at her. "Sit Jace, she will go to her study now."

"How do you know that?" Jace asked puzzled.

"Ah well, let's just say she always does and our Catherine is a creature of habit these days."

Catherine ambled into the main house along with Lisa, who was the only one to enter the kitchen, she looked around and her eyes met Paul's and she smiled shyly at him. Then, she saw Jace for the first time; the child gave a whoop of joy and hurled herself at the body before her.

"Hey, be careful Lisa, Jace is having a baby." Grace admonished the child, but smiled to take the sting out of the words.

"Jace, Jace you came back to us?" The child was starry eyed and she was crying. Gently cradling her smaller form close to her, Jace placed a tender kiss on top of the small head.

"Did you do what I said Lisa?" Jace asked the child with tears of her own now appearing.

Grace just swallowed rapidly at the words and the emotions.

"Yes Jace, every time she was sad I held her hand. But she needs to have a hug from time to time too." The child said innocently.

"Glad to hear that Lisa. Thank you for loving Catherine for me while I've been gone." Jace spoke into the little girl's ear.

"That's okay Jace, I love Catherine too." Lisa whispered into Jace's ear.

Grace made tea and got Catherine's mug ready. "Your turn to serve the boss I think Jace, you up for it?"

"Oh, yes I'm certainly up for that and more." Jace replied happily.

"Great, don't forget to put it on her right side or she will know it's not me immediately."

"Thanks Grace." She hugged the other woman and took the mug of tea, and smiled at Lisa and Paul as she left the room.

Lisa turned to Grace. "Will Jace be staying forever now Grace?"

Grace smiled at the child and glanced briefly at Paul, who shrugged his shoulders. "It's hard to say Lisa, Catherine and Jace had a disagreement and they need to work through it, just like you do with Jake."

Lisa turned to Grace in all seriousness and a twinkle entered her eyes. "Oh well Grace, she will be staying then, because Jake and I always make up."

"Well, it's not always that easy Lisa." Grace tried to explain that adults didn't always act logically.

Getting up from her chair Lisa went over to the kitchen door. "Yes it is Grace, because they love each other, like we all do." With that comment floating in the silent kitchen, she skipped out of the door towards the stables; she wanted to be the first to inform Jake of Jace's return.

Grace looked at Paul who was grinning broadly. "Guess she got that one right!"

Catherine stood at the window of the study, something she did frequently. The fact that she could not see out of it; never deterred her; it just fueled the need to be there more often. One day.

She never turned when the door opened and 'Grace' entered. Hearing the mug placed gently on the table, she sighed heavily and pondered her recent visit to Adam and Lucas's graves with the children; it hadn't gone to badly. Her mind pre-occupied with other thoughts, she never heard the loading of the CD player in the room, it was only the faint strains of a record she vaguely recalled filtering into her consciousness that alerted her to the fact that maybe it wasn't Grace.

"Grace?" The commanding voice that Jace loved spoke into the room.

Jace looked at the older woman as she'd entered the room and had to stop herself running over to her and apologising on bended knee, the months had not been kind to either of them in any way.

Jace after placing the mug on the right hand side of Catherine, walked over to the CD player in the room, pleased things hadn't changed.

Placing the CD she had brought with her in the player, she pressed the play button and waited for a reaction, it came swiftly.

"No." Jace answered and then saw the shift of the body away from the window and gaze sightlessly into the interior of the study. Jace saw the expression of disbelief; hope and sadness appear on the marred features of Catherine's still very beautiful face. This woman had captured her heart and only she had the key to allow it to feel happiness again.

Walking over to the other side of the desk, she approached Catherine as the music played the intro to 'I'm Here'," by Infinity.

Jace placed a gentle finger on Catherine's lips as she tried to say something. "Please listen." Jace softly entreated her as she placed her smaller hand in Catherine's larger one.

You came into my life, not expecting anything, not wanting anything.

From the first day you challenged me, you offered me a world I never dreamed of.

At a distance your words pierced my heart, I feel your eyes protecting my soul.

You never cease to amaze, you are the life that I crave I'll always be here.

Never questioning the darkness I live, you tell me of the happier things.

As I task the demons to fight, will you fill my lonely soul with light?

There will never be enough words to describe this feeling inside,

When you whisper my name and leave doubt in the shade.

I'm here waiting for you until you want me too.

You never cease to amaze, you are the life that I crave I'll always be here.

With my heart in your hands, please keep it steadfast and safe.

I will let you teach me about love, if you let me follow my heart and that heart will forever be beside you.

Love will always touch my soul if you're there to follow me whole.

Be my light in the dark, let me be your love that makes you spark.

I'm here waiting for you; please accept it as true.

You never cease to amaze, you are the life that I crave I'll always be here.

The words of the song pounded deep in Catherine's heart. She flinched.

The song ended and Jace managed to stop Catherine from dropping her hand.

"Why did you come back? I haven't changed." Catherine said bleakly.

"No you haven't, but I have." Jace said in earnest.

"I can't be what you want Jace, there are too many obstacles, especially now!" Catherine's face showing annoyance and frustration.

"Do you have any idea of exactly what I want from you?" Tears spilled down Jace's face, her eyes taking in the almost vacant ice blue eyes and the tense expression she saw on Catherine's face.

"Love, happiness, stability, no bad dreams. How's the husband?" Catherine responded gently, but her tone turned harsh as she mentioned Peter Adamson.

"Peter and I are divorced. It wasn't working." Jace admitted ruefully.

"I'm sorry, he seemed a nice guy." Catherine feigned solicitude.

"Oh Catherine, now I know you're lying to me! Hades, you never talked to him except in anger. He helped me out of a situation I thought I couldn't handle, I should have had more faith." Jace simply said.

"What situation would be so bad you married a man you didn't love?" It was something she had wanted to know from the day she found out about the marriage; she was helpless to stop herself from asking.

"Hudson. She threatened to expose me as your lover."

Catherine expelled a sharp breath. "Obviously you wouldn't be happy with that situation and the circumstances knowing who and what I was?" Catherine finally said quietly. Her heart dropping at the thought that Jace had been ashamed of their relationship and association.

"No you don't understand! I just couldn't find you, all the avenues had been closed to me, what did it matter what I did with my life if you weren't in it! I used Peter to try to appease some of the pain, the pain I caused myself. I couldn't find you to tell you it didn't matter; none of it mattered, except my love for you. I'm sorry I hurt him and I'm sorry I hurt you Catherine!" Jace's voice was completely full of the pain and anguish she'd caused.

Catherine visibly paled at the comment. "I shut all the doors."

"You sure did." Jace let a tiny smile curve her lips; perhaps she had reached through to her.

"Where do we go from here?" Catherine asked; her eyes staring in her direction but for the most part unfocused.

"How about we start with friendship and see where we go from there?" Jace proposed tentatively.

"Is it going to be a long distance friendship?" Catherine wasn't sure she wanted the answer.

"Guess I should tell you one more thing before I answer that." Jace said slowly, her heart pumping hard.

"What is it?" Catherine cocked her head to the side and listened intently, her stance becoming anxious.

"You once asked me to consider helping you bring up two children if I recall?" Jace looked carefully at Catherine for any sign that her words were unwelcome.

"Yes, that's right." Catherine drawled.

"Well, how would you feel about it being three children?" She placed the right hand she held over her bulging stomach.

Catherine didn't know what to say, what to think, or what to feel. Her hand was resting on the belly of her ex-lover, who was heavy with child, in fact it was moving under her hand. Her smile came unconsciously, the face taking on the expression of one being given a gift.

"What about Adamson, surely he will want some say in bringing up his child? Might be a little put out if he knew I would be influencing his son or daughter?" Her voice sounded harsh, particularly to her own sensitive hearing.

"Catherine, Peter knows I would take every opportunity to find you. He's too busy with his movies to be bothered with a child now anyway." Jace gently explained.

"What about later, will he want to see the child?" She wasn't convinced this was a good idea.

"I won't stop him if he does want to see the child, will that be a problem?" Jace held her breath.

Catherine pondered the question for a few seconds. "Guess not. I can always be away from home if he shows up."

Jace gazed directly at the woman she loved, knowing Catherine would perhaps never experience the gift of sight again, or probably never see clearly the child Jace would bring into the world, never see those beautiful eyes look at 'their' child in love and laughter. *'Catherine, one day I'm going to tell you how this child was conceived, because it's as much your child as it is mine, even Peter knows that!'*

"So, is it a yes?" Jace finally responded.

"I guess one more mouth to feed won't kill the bank balance." Catherine finally managed to say, her throat suddenly becoming very dry.

"Well, in that case to answer your earlier question. No! No, not this time Catherine, no more long-distance friendship for us. Let's face it my love; you get into too much trouble without me. I thought maybe I could get a job close by, any ideas?"

Catherine laughed heartily at the comment. "It's possible I know of a position which might suit you." A smile played around the lips of the woman's gaunt features, she had certainly aged. Jace now noticed the grey at the temples in her hair that hadn't been there the last time they had seen each other.

"Then you want us to try again?" Jace said hopefully.

Catherine considered the question, her hand delicately balanced on the swollen abdomen of her friend; Jace nearly panicked when Catherine took longer than anticipated over the answer.

Catherine relinquished her tentative contact with Jace and turned back towards the window.

Suddenly the left hand that was scarred from the fire, reached out and gently with little strength behind it, took Jace's hand in hers. Putting the hand to her lips, she kissed the knuckles reverently and a smile radiated from her face and a glowing light to the ice blue eyes as they looked at the smaller woman, not really seeing. "The X stands for Xianthos."

Jace chuckled, it had taken a year to find that out and what a year!

'Wonder what would have happened if she had learned that from the first day?' Catherine had said she would never reveal it unless she trusted someone implicitly. Hadn't that been one of the first conversations they had ever had?

Now to make the woman at her side realise it wasn't just friendship she needed, but her love too! Jace had her work cut out on that front, but hadn't Catherine offered her trust again? That was certainly a bridge worth crossing; it was a journey she was more than willing to take. Something to strive for and they had lots of time to do so. Hadn't she once said the one word to encompass her feelings, *'Forever'*.

Her soul, now firmly locked in place with the one at her side, she had finally defined her destiny and come home.

The End

Author Bio:

JM Dragon:

A forty something happily married English woman who enjoys writing net stories as a stress reliever; and with it, the opportunity to meet lots and lots of people from all over the world via the net.

A professional procurement and logistics manager for some years, she is currently embarking on another adventure, migrating to New Zealand from the United Kingdom in the autumn of 2002.

A keen supporter of her local community she is a trustee of a charity providing medical equipment to the local hospitals and community health issues.

Along with the passion for writing she loves dogs, gardening and travel.

Order These Great Books Directly From Limitless Dare 2 Dream Publishing

Title	Price	
The Amazon Queen by L M Townsend	20.00	
Define Destiny by J M Dragon	20.00	
Desert Hawk by Archangel	15.00	
Golden Gate by Erin Jennifer Mar	18.00	
Love's Melody Lost, 2ndEd. by Radclyffe	18.00	
Paradise Found by Cruise and Stoley	20.00	
Spirit Harvest by Trish Shields	15.00	
Storm Surge by KatLyn	20.00	
Up The River-out of print **...While supplies last...** by Sam Ruskin	15.00	
Fatal Impressions by Jeanne Foguth	20.00	
	Total	

South Carolina residents add 5% sales tax.

Watch for these titles:

Guardian of My Heart by Charlsie Todd
Deadly Rumors by Jeanne Foguth
Mysti: Mistress of Dreams by Sam Ruskin
Encounters I and II by Anne Azel
Up The River, Revised Second Edition by Sam Ruskin
Amazon Nation by Carla Osborne
Omega's Folly by Carla Osborne

Please mail your orders with a check or money order to:
Limitless Dare 2 Dream Publications
100 Pin Oak Ct.
Lexington, SC 29073

Visit our website at: **www.limitlessd2d.net**